FROM HEAVEN TO EARTH THEY CAME

BOOK 2

MAKER FROM THE LOST PLANET

A Sci-Fi Adventure of Gods and Aliens

BY NEAL ROBERTS

CHAPTER 1

THE MOMENT DAVID was safely inside Inanna's pyramidion and the hatch slid shut behind him, he could feel the spacecraft rising gently from the ancient platform at Baalbek like a well-balanced elevator in a brand-new building.

There'd been no strapping in of passengers, no rumbling of rockets, no erupting off the pad. To the contrary, after the clamorous farewell David had received outside on the platform, this compartment seemed the hushed entryway to an ancient temple deeply embedded in solid rock. The cool, moist air had a barely detectable odor of lime, and the lighting was comfortably low.

The walls were nothing like he'd expected. Though straight as wallboard, their surface was far from smooth, closely resembling the rough mineral finish on the handheld transmitter discovered in the luggage lent him by Doctor Zia, survivor of the Great Flood.

David wasn't surprised that Inanna and General Shulgi had disappeared around a corner the moment he set foot inside the spacecraft, but he *was* surprised that the small crowd entering behind him had dispersed just as quickly. He'd expected that some subordinate would be assigned to him, at least to get him to his quarters. Without such guidance, not only had he no idea where to go, but he was still holding in his hands the few things he'd brought aboard. In one hand he held a laptop and the portfolio containing his commission and, in the other, Elijah's mantle, which seemed to have become dormant since its self-willed bout of wriggling.

Somewhere nearby, General Shulgi shouted, "Well, then, who the devil fired it?"

In a moment, the general rounded the corner with a subordinate in tow, a Middle-Eastern-looking young man in a military skirt called a *shendyt*; he was a few inches taller than David—rather short for an Anunnaki.

The sight of David standing alone, still holding his things, stopped Shulgi in his tracks and appeared to drive from his mind whatever he'd been shouting about. "What are you doing here?" he asked David.

David shrugged. "Where should I be?"

"Do you mean to say *nobody's* shown you to your quarters?"

"Correct, general."

"I regret the lapse," said Shulgi, turning to his subordinate. "Must I do everything around here? What do you people do after I return to my own ship? *Nothing?*" Shulgi pointed to David. "The ambassador should have been installed in his quarters immediately."

David changed the subject. "General, I apologize for meddling in matters beyond my concern, but did I overhear you saying that a shot has been fired?"

Shulgi snorted. "Yes," he replied. "Someone on your planet has fired a missile at this spacecraft. We're maintaining safe distance for now. Do you have any idea who would fire on us?"

"No, sir," said David. "Indeed, there are few nations on Earth with missiles capable of reaching space. *Which* such nation would be foolhardy enough to fire on an Anunnaki craft without provocation is beyond me—indeed, it's almost beyond comprehension. Would you care to enlist the assistance of the United States in this matter?"

Shulgi's eyebrow rose in bemusement. "Would the United States be willing to provide assistance?"

"Absolutely, general," said David. "It's my country's intention to reach a peaceful accommodation with the Anunnaki."

Shulgi nodded skeptically. "Whether that's possible remains to be seen," he muttered, "but I shall bear it in mind." He turned to his subordinate. "Kassam, take the ambassador's things to his quarters."

David handed Kassam the laptop, portfolio, and mantle.

"Ambassador," said Shulgi, "if you will please accompany me to the conn."

David was stunned.

Shulgi noticed his befuddlement. "What's wrong?"

David shrugged. "I'm humbled by your trust in inviting me onto the bridge."

Shulgi smirked. "Who knows? Perhaps you can help identify the aggressor nation."

David bowed courteously. "I'll do my best, general."

"But I have one request."

David braced himself. "What's that?"

"Please don't repeat your threat to splatter my brains all over the pavement."

David gritted his teeth, abashed at the coarseness of his own recent outburst. "Very well," he said, "if the general promises not to call me *mayfly*."

The general nodded.

"You do realize," said David, "that I would never have said that if you hadn't tracked me to the ends of the Earth … and cornered me?"

"It wasn't *I* who did that," came the cryptic reply. The general turned on his heel and escorted David to the elevator. To David's surprise, the elevator greeted each of them by name and sought a reply before moving.

WHEN GENERAL SHULGI and David stepped off the elevator onto the dimly lit bridge, five or six other officers were already seated there on well-upholstered chairs designed to protect their occupants from considerable shock.

Moving images were everywhere, though none seemed to be projected onto a screen; in fact, there appeared to be no projectors and no screens at all. Images seemed rather to appear out of thin air—*in* thin air. In front of each officer was an image evidently dedicated to his or her function, small and mostly monochromatic; at the base of each such image was a constantly refreshing spreadsheet, above which appeared a curve or a polygon whose contours changed as it was replotted every few milliseconds to reflect new data pouring in.

There were several images at the front of the bridge, which were brighter, comparatively large, and colorful, evidently there to be seen by all.

Front and center was a large hologram of an oncoming missile. Although it appeared to be moving at a constant rate of speed, David couldn't be sure whether that reflected the actual state of affairs or, alternatively, the tracking mechanism had been programmed to keep the image steady.

"Is that the offending missile?" asked David quietly.

Shulgi nodded. "Can you tell me whose it is?"

David studied the image. Though at this distance it was difficult to be sure, there appeared to be some identifying marks on the nose cone. "What's its range?" he asked.

Shulgi consulted a monochromatic chart that suddenly floated before him. "About a thousand kilometers."

"Is it moving at a constant velocity?"

Shulgi consulted his floating chart once again. "Direction and speed are constant. It's moving at about twice the speed of our ship. It's difficult to see how it could accelerate much, as it was likely launched from the surface of the Earth and, given earthlings' limited technology, must have used nearly all of its fuel in escaping Earth's gravitational pull."

David wondered how much information he should be sharing with Shulgi. "True—unless it's a *multistage* missile. Is an orbital camera sending us this video?"

Shulgi nodded.

"Can you move it in for a closer look at the nosecone?" asked David. The irony did not escape him that mere weeks earlier he was asked by a U.S. submarine captain to identify certain spacecraft, one of which he now inhabited.

Shulgi spoke his order aloud, evidently to no one in particular. "Nosecone. Maximum magnification."

A hologram of the nosecone, which bore three repeats of an emblem that seemed familiar to David, filled the front of the bridge. David pointed at it. "If this is what it looks like, the repeated insignia represents the five tenets of the religion of Islam," said David. "The center vertical line represents a sword."

"Where do you know it from?" asked Shulgi.

"It resembles the emblem on the flag of Iran," said David, "but I hasten to add that it's not identical to the Iranian emblem." He looked at Shulgi thoughtfully. "We should bear in mind that this *could* be a false-flag provocation. Do we know where the missile was launched from?"

"None of our craft caught sight of the launch," said Shulgi, "but it's unlikely it was launched from the eastern hemisphere."

"Because of your disabling ray?"

Shulgi smiled. "Yes … which you managed to disable, however briefly."

David shook his head. "That was weeks ago. I doubt that such occasion had anything to do with the launch of this missile," said David.

"Presumably, it was launched much more recently."

"Correct," said Shulgi, indicating the image on the screen. "This missile was launched within the past few hours. We learned of it while we were on the landing platform. That's one of the reasons we cut the ceremony short. Incidentally, what do you mean by a *multistage* missile?"

David was surprised by the question. "I take it the Anunnaki have not used such missiles for a long time. As you recognize, Earth's missiles are still powered by fossil fuels. Each stage of a multistage missile contains its own fuel. The first stage, known as the *booster*, feeds the big rockets at the bottom end of the missile. Its fuel is consumed in achieving and maintaining escape velocity. Once its fuel has been exhausted, in order to minimize subsequent fuel use and maximize the acceleration of later stages, the booster is jettisoned, decreasing the mass of the remaining vehicle. That's why I suggested that a multistage missile *can* accelerate once in orbit or in space."

"Is the one chasing us a multistage missile?" asked Shulgi with concern.

David shrugged. "I expect so, although you can see that the booster's still attached." He turned to Shulgi with concern. "The missile may be holding onto the booster to lull us into feeling safe. If that's their plan, they would jettison the booster only at the point when, realizing our peril, we would nonetheless be unable to escape impact." Assaying the possible intentions of those who launched the missile, he suddenly became alarmed. "Is Queen Inanna still aboard?" he asked.

Shulgi nodded anxiously.

David was exasperated. "Then why haven't you shot down the missile?"

"This pyramidion doesn't carry weapons of aggression," said Shulgi, clearly chagrined.

"Well," said David impatiently, "this would rather be a *defensive* use of weapons, don't you think?"

"Perhaps. But we're not *certain* of its intention."

David was mystified by the Anunnaki. Though he'd benefitted by their self-restraint, their code of ethics nonetheless escaped his grasp.

"Have you tried to establish communications with the missile?" he asked.

"Yes, but no one answers. We think it's unmanned."

"Well, if it's hostile, as we must presume it to be," said David, "how long till it's too close for us to escape impact?"

Shulgi thought for a moment. "I suppose it depends upon how quickly it accelerates once it jettisons the booster."

"General," said David excitedly, "you can't *wait* for it to drop its booster. If it's hostile, that may be too late for you to escape."

One of the seated officers spoke aloud. "General," he said, "we are receiving a request from the Dagon craft to establish communications."

"*Aaach.* The frog people," muttered Shulgi, rolling his eyes.

"General," said David, abashed, "if you're going to establish a video link with the Dagon, I don't think I should be seen on your bridge. I'm a *diplomatic* officer, after all."

"It will not be a problem, ambassador," said Shulgi quietly. "If a question arises, I'll make it clear that you're here solely to observe." Raising his voice, he said, "Permission granted to send and receive audiovisual with the Dagon. Put them on the front holograph."

A large hologram of a hideous green figure with a long face appeared before them. David wondered whether this was Brosa, the Dagon who'd helped him disable the Anunnaki's ray.

"General Shulgi," said the Dagon, "I am Captain Brack. It is good to see you again. *Glick.*"

Shulgi sighed loudly. "Brack, please make this short. We're being dogged by a missile."

Brack nodded. "We wished to let you know where the missile was launched from, General Shulgi, in case it helps you."

"Thank you, Brack. Was it launched from the vicinity of Baalbek?"

"No," said Brack. "It emerged from the Beaufort Sea in northern Canada at the moment your pyramidion first touched down on the platform."

"Thank you, Brack," said the general. "We'll get back to you." The green figure nodded politely. "End transmission."

The Dagon's image vanished, and was replaced by that of the incoming missile just as it violently jettisoned its booster, and the second-stage fuel ignited. In a moment, the second stage had blasted clear of the satellite's view.

"It's coming on fast," said David.

Shulgi hit a virtual button, sounding a loud shipwide alarm.

CHAPTER 2

IT WAS FULL dark at Baalbek, and the U.S. motorcade was beginning to move out.

Not only had every limo been reinforced to repel an attack, but, once under way, it would be protected on one side by a heavily reinforced troop transport. The U.S. communications trailer, a full-size, retrofitted moving van, had just decoupled its power from the landline when the first inkling of bad news trickled in from NORAD.

Agent Victor Wilson was wearing the headphones at the time. His eyes went wide. He turned and shouted to the driver. "Vasquez, *hold up!*"

Camilla Vasquez glowered back at Wilson from the driver's seat. "I can't wait, Vic. We've got orders from the anti-terrorism guys to bring up the rear, and the mission statement says, *Nothin' stops the motorcade.* The locals don't exactly love Americans, and without us covering the rear, there's just a coupla old Fords back there."

"I'm not screwin' around, Vasquez," said Wilson impatiently. "We're gettin' a report of a rocket fired at the spacecraft, so don't just do something. Stand there."

"The rocket was fired at *which* spacecraft?" she demanded loudly.

Wilson angrily whipped the phones off his head and turned to Vasquez. "Waddya *mean*, which spacecraft? The one that just took off from here."

"With Canarsie on it?"

Wilson rolled his eyes and pressed the left headphone to his ear. He held a finger to his lips to shut Vasquez the hell up.

"Shit," Vasquez muttered under her breath. She waited a second for Wilson to jot a few notes on a steno pad, and then asked, "What are you using to communicate? A laptop?"

Wilson looked at the device before him. "Uh, yeah."

"You don't need a freakin' *land line* to power that," she said. "Un-less you're tellin' me we'll lose comms if I move, I'm movin'." She fired up the engine, well aware that the van's onboard antenna ran off a heavy-duty battery that wouldn't be charged unless the van's wheels started moving and *kept* moving.

Wilson put the phones back on his head. "Excuse me a sec," he said into the mic. He turned to Vasquez. "You got a secure line to POTUS's limo up there?"

"Yeah."

"Then let's move to the back of the motorcade," said Wilson, "but give POTUS a heads up and tell him to expect my call. Heavy news comin' in. He's gonna want to hear it right away."

Vasquez chunked the van into gear and they began wobbling over lumpy terrain. She pressed the accelerator to catch up with the Fords.

THE LIMO IN the middle of the motorcade carried the President, Admiral Simmons, and his adjutant, Lieutenant Commander Catharine Weldon.

"So, lieutenant commander," said the President, "how long have you known Professor Schubert?"

"Only about a month, Mister President."

The President smiled. "Admiral Simmons tells me you've grown quite fond of him. I take it you've been through some rough patches and come through together."

The dashboard buzzed in the driver's compartment.

Catharine forced a smile. "Yes, sir. Comrades in arms, so to speak."

"So, you expect to continue seeing him?"

Before Catharine could answer, the driver rolled down his partition.

"Mister President," said the driver, "it's Camilla Vasquez, who's driving the communications van. She says they've got some news you're going to want to hear right away."

Catharine gritted her teeth. She'd already been worried that some-thing bad might happen to David while aboard the Anunnaki craft and prayed that it hadn't. It couldn't have. Not so soon.

The President frowned and asked the driver, "Good or bad?"

"She didn't say, sir," said the driver, "but she didn't sound happy. Either way, I expect you'll know in a matter of seconds."

The dashboard buzzed again, and the driver picked it up. He spoke with the caller for a moment and turned to the President.

"Sir, it's the comms van again. Agent Wilson this time. You want to take this on the squawk box? I'm assuming everybody back there has clearance."

"They do," said the President. "Close the partition and put it on speaker, please."

"Mister President, this is Victor Wilson, NSA," said the voice. "I'm in the communications van at the tail end of your motorcade. We just got a secure call from NORAD. They have high confidence that a multistage missile was fired at the Anunnaki craft … the one with Canarsie aboard."

All eyes darted toward—then away from—Catharine, who maintained an impassive expression.

"When was it fired?" asked the President.

"NORAD says it was fired while the target craft was still on the ground, while everyone was watching the Queen."

"Is it about to hit the craft?"

"Not immediately, sir. NORAD says it's got a ways to go."

The President's dismay was palpable. He rubbed his eyes with his fingers. "Has NORAD narrowed down the launch point?"

"Not precisely, sir, but they think the launch was underwater, and came from the far north of Canada. They said they'll have better data once they've collated the images from several satellites, but that'll take some time."

The admiral hit the Mute button and said, "If the launch was underwater, that puts a pretty strict limit on the number of possibilities. We're probably looking at a submarine with ICBM launch capabilities. That's, maybe, five navies in the whole world—*max*. The only one that can do those launches with total reliability is … us. And this launch would have been in our zone of influence." He took his finger off the Mute button.

"Damn!" muttered the President as he shifted anxiously in his seat. "That'll put us right into the suspect's chair." He turned back to the speaker. "What's NORAD's best guess right now?"

"Hold, sir. They're workin' on the numbers, but I'll ask for a wild-ass guess." There was a brief pause before Wilson came back on. "They said it looks like the launch point was in the Arctic Ocean—the Beaufort Sea—close to land. They're gonna transmit some maps. I'd like to send them on to you in real time, sir, but you don't have display capability in that limo, and it would be a breach to send them to your phone unencrypted."

The President looked frustrated until he came up with an idea.

"Got any extra seats in the van, Victor?"

There was a moment's hesitation. "We've got a few vacant seats for the next showing, sir. How many behinds you got up there?"

"We got three up here, Vic."

"Sir," said Victor, "if you'll protect me from the wrath of the Secret Service, I'll invite y'all back here. But I'd appreciate your not mentioning my name. They don't take kindly to stoppin' a presidential motorcade in hostile territory."

"I'll explain it to them, Victor. Be there in a few minutes. Keep your eye out for those charts."

The President phoned the head of the Secret Service detail and suggested that the occupants of the presidential limo needed to move back to the communications van. To his surprise, his suggestion was greeted with good cheer; evidently, it's good practice to put the POTUS someplace unexpected. The Secret Service improvised a plan to execute the shift under cover of a copse of trees only two miles ahead.

Inside ten minutes, the move was executed and the three were seated next to Victor looking at four large video screens, two of which were occupied by various maps of Canada, some political, some topographic—one even a roadmap.

As Victor raised his hand to indicate points of interest, the van went over a particularly rough patch of road.

Victor shouted. "Hey, Vasquez! Precious cargo here. We got breakables."

"I didn't build these damn roads," she responded with irritation, then muttered, "I'd like to find the sumbitch who did."

"As I was about to say, Mister President," said Victor, "the precise location of the launch appears to have been right over here in the Beaufort Sea."

"Looks like it's just off a river delta," said the President. "What river is that?"

The admiral said, "It's the Mackenzie River, Mister President, flows from south to north, like the Nile. It's the second longest river system in North America."

"Longer than all but the Mississippi?" observed the President.

"That's right, sir," said the admiral.

"What's the source of the Mackenzie?" asked the President.

The admiral searched his memory, but came up empty.

Catharine supplied the answer. "Great Slave Lake, sir."

"*What?*" said the President.

"Great Slave Lake," repeated Catharine. "It's an unfortunate name that's got nothing to do with slavery. *Slavey* is the language of certain indigenous peoples up there."

"Great Slave Lake," intoned the admiral. "I've actually heard those words—and *recently*, too. Can't remember the context."

"Does anybody live that far north?" asked the President.

"Well," said the admiral, "there's Yellowknife, the capital of the territory. It's on the lake's northern shore." He turned away as though straining his brain. "Oh, what was it I heard about that lake? Something ... something of ours went missing." He turned to see all eyes on him. "*What?*"

The President said, "We're waiting to hear from you what went missing."

The admiral clapped his hands. "Yeah, that's it. An exploratory sub went missing a couple days ago right in that area."

"It sank?" asked the President.

"No," replied the admiral.

"How can you be sure it didn't sink?"

"Like some other U.S. submarines, it has a passive sensor that transmits a unique signal if it gets flooded or breaks apart. No such signal has come."

"How many aboard?" asked Catharine.

The admiral shrugged. "Small crew. Maybe ... *five*? All sciency types."

"No distress signal? No flotsam spotted?" asked Catharine.

"Nope," replied the admiral. "Why?"

The President shook his head gravely. "Given what we now suspect, they may have seen something they shouldn't have."

"Precisely what I was thinking," muttered Catharine.

"Whom should we send to check it out?" asked the President.

"If I may interrupt, sir," said Catharine. "What's the sub's power source?"

The admiral clearly didn't like where this discussion was headed. "Diesel-electric," he admitted reluctantly.

"*I'll* go," said Catharine. "I'm certified to pilot the sub. I'll find out what happened and, if it's still recoverable, I'll recover it."

The admiral regarded her skeptically. "Perhaps you haven't spent enough time lately being pursued by aliens? Or ... perhaps you're in need of yuletide plans?"

She smiled. "Alien invasions have a way of spoiling Christmas plans. Come on, admiral. You said it yourself: We're gonna be blamed for this launch ... and we're not guilty. Maybe the disappearance of the sub from the lake had something to do with the underwater launch at the other end of the river."

The President looked at the admiral as though the admiral's recommendation might well affect his opinion of the man.

The admiral asked, "What's the nearest population center to the launch point?"

"Let's see," said Victor. "That's gotta be at least two thousand miles downstream from the lake." He used the mouse to zoom north to the mouth of the Mackenzie River. The print on the map was small and the language strange. He squinted. "It looks like alphabet soup. Tuktoyaktuk," he sounded out carefully, "formerly Port Brabant."

Victor brought a Wikipedia article to the screen. "There's fewer than a thousand people up there. Not surprising, considering the air temp this time of year is a balmy twenty below zero." He turned to the admiral. "It's on the DEW Line, sir."

The President turned to the admiral. "The DEW Line?"

The admiral said, "*The Distant Early Warning Line*, sir. You probably know it by its more recent name, the *Northern Warning System*, but intelligence types like Victor here have never caught up with the name change. The DEW Line was the line of radar stations set up during the Cold War to notify NORAD in the event the Soviets were to launch an attack over the polar route. It's relevant for present purposes only 'cause it means we may have people up there with signals intelligence capability."

The admiral sat back and looked at Catharine with misgiving. "Fine," he said, relenting, "but I want you to do an overflight of the launch area in a fighter, just to see what's there. Also, you can do a separate overflight of the lake to see if you can spot the sub—and the crew, if they've been separated. But use a chopper on that one. If there are any marines up there, we'll see if we can get you a nice safe Super Huey. And there'll have to be some Royal Canadian Mounted Police in the chopper."

Catharine said, "But—"

"Not negotiable," said the admiral, cutting her off.

"Admiral," she said anyway, "I believe the Canadian Forces have jurisdiction there now."

"Well," said the admiral turning to the President, "after the President has a heart-to-heart with the Prime Minister, I'm sure the RCMP will be sending along a few of their finest Mounties."

The President bowed to the inexorable. "Okay. But the Prime Minister will ask me, so I'll ask you *first: Why Mounties?*"

"Because, in spite of the best laid plans," said the admiral pointing to Catharine, "there's a good chance this chopper detail is going to end up in the Arctic woods, and the RCMP are *her* best shot at survival." He turned to Catharine and shrugged. "'Course, if you end up splashing the fighter in the Arctic Ocean, it's a moot point; in that case, you won't be needing the chopper *or* the Mounties."

Catharine gulped.

The van slowed to a halt. Agent Vasquez applied the parking brake and announced, "We're arrived at the airstrip, Mister President. What the—?" She peered through the windshield out into the darkness, where lights were flashing red. "We're bein' waved aside," she said. "Somethin's goin' on." She drew her sidearm and turned around to Agent Wilson. "I'm lockin' this door on the way out. You don't open up for anybody else but me. Got it, Wilson?"

"Got it," said Wilson absentmindedly, without taking his eyes off his video screens.

Vasquez clucked and said impatiently, "And *goddam it*, take out your sidearm and make sure it's loaded!"

"Check," said Wilson.

Vasquez got out talking to herself and slammed the door.

Evidently alerted by the earnest click of the doorlock, Wilson reached for his holster, and realized he wasn't wearing it. He smiled apologetically at his passengers and searched through his top drawer for his pistol. He found it, cracked it open, realized it was unloaded, and searched again for a clip, which he found and smacked it into the grip. He smiled with chagrin. "Sorry," he said.

"No sweat," said Catharine as she picked up an Uzi and lay it across her lap.

The President and admiral looked at her with surprise.

She shrugged. "I borrowed it from one of the agents when the motorcade stopped to move us back here."

There was a pounding on the back of the van. The welcome voice of Agent Vasquez came through the door. "It's me. Don't shoot!" The rear doors swung open and agents helped them down. Though the sun had gone down some time ago, the heat still rose in waves off the tarmac.

The senior agent walked over to the President. "We had a little debate about whether to show you this or just tell you about it, Mister President. The show-me crowd prevailed. Please follow me to Air Force One, paying especial attention to your limo as we pass."

Sticking out of the limo were two javelins that had apparently been launched mechanically from the same point of attack. The javelin points had penetrated the outer metal on the rear door about a foot apart, but had gotten no further in.

The President shook his head wearily. "It's like you said, admiral. If the only weapons people have are pointy sticks, they'll kill each other with pointy sticks."

The three stood there, wondering not so much whether the Anunnaki would deem mankind worthy of saving, but whether it *was* worth saving.

"Come with us on Air Force One to Heathrow, Catharine," said the admiral. "From the plane, we'll arrange your connection to Yellowknife."

"Thank you, sir," she replied. "Meantime, I hope we'll be monitoring that missile."

The President, eyes still peeled on the javelin shafts sticking out of his limo, said, "Count on it."

CHAPTER 3

THOUGH HENDRICK WAS usually comforted by the company of his trusty AK-47 and a double shot of Mexican tequila, this afternoon he missed having someone to play cards with. The barkeep was asleep (or, as Gary would say, "passed out drunk") and Festus was off on a supply run, which left Hendrick morbidly preoccupied with the hair on the back of his forearms.

When, a few weeks earlier, Hendrick had been told to destroy a handheld transmitter from another world, he'd taped a stick of dynamite to it and driven it in his Jeep to a big pit where the Germans used to dump slag from a nearby mine. The moment Hendrick tossed the transmitter into the pit, he'd raced back to his Jeep and sped away. The dynamite had soon exploded, safely disposing of the transmitter.

But the dynamite had also breached the unearthly battery, which exploded with a fury equal to a fission bomb.

As best Hendrick could calculate, by that moment he'd put roughly a quarter mile between himself and the explosion. Feeling the concussion behind him, he'd kept the pedal to the metal until arriving at Gary's airstrip ten miles away, where he showered vigorously for an hour. Finding fresh clothes in an open locker, he'd dressed and headed to the instrument room, where he used a Geiger counter to test his whole body for radioactivity. Though he'd found none, he doubted that he'd been fortunate enough to escape with no ill effect, and so waited anxiously for some telltale sign of radiation poisoning to appear, such as nausea or light-headedness.

After feeling fine for a couple of days, the rational part of Hendrick's brain realized he was out of danger (and had probably never been in it).

Yet, in the back of his mind, horrifying images lingered of Harry Daghlian and Louis Slotin, the two engineers who'd lost their lives in the early days of nuclear weaponry while "tickling the dragon's tail." Both engineers had died from near-criticality accidents. But Hendrick's brush with doom, if that's what it was, consisted of being exposed to an uncontrolled nuclear explosion, which seemed rather *more* hazardous than near-criticality, so he took no comfort from the difference.

For the past two weeks, he'd carried Gary's portable Geiger counter with him everywhere, and remained obsessed with the prospect of losing body hair, which would be a sure sign that he'd received a major dose of radiation. For the zillionth time, he reassured himself by brushing the hair on the back of his left forearm with the barrel of the Geiger counter. No hair fell out, and the counter reading remained well within tolerance.

He was startled by a loud ringing that made his heart pound, until he realized it was his phone.

"Hendrick here," he said as nonchalantly as he could.

The connection was thin. "Hendrick, y'all sound tense. You okay?" The west Texas drawl unmistakably belonged to his boss Gary, who was last seen flying his cargo plane over the nuclear explosion on his way to London.

"Dude!" said Hendrick. "I was beginning to think your plane broke apart. You were supposed to be back three days ago. What happened?"

There was a high-pitched whine on the line, followed by Gary's voice doing a reverse-fade. "Long story, chief. We got boarded in Casablanca on the way back. Fortunately, we were empty, so the charges fell apart. Is everything okay there?"

"Yeah, man. Everything's fine here. A little boring."

"Is that, *er, fire* still burning?"

"I'm in the *Paso*, boss. Let me step outside and I'll tell you for sure." The little bells on the door rang as he stepped outside and peered into the distance. "Yeah. Black soot's still spewin' into the clouds. Looks like it just happened yesterday."

"Yeah," said Gary, "that's what I expected. Hey, listen, chief. We'll be takin' off in a couple hours from Casablanca, so you won't be seein' us till tomorrow night sometime. But we needed some help from the U.S. State Department to get ourselves free, so we ... uh ... *I* decided we had to give 'em some information they were lookin' for ... and they're on their way to talk to you right now. They'll be arrivin' soon."

"Oh, man!" exclaimed Hendrick with dismay. "You gotta have con-traband all over this place. They're liable to take me in just for bein' in *charge*."

"No, no, no," said Gary in his most reassuring voice. "There's nothin' there." Obviously concerned that someone might be listening, he added, "Not that there ever was, but we went over the place with a fine-tooth comb before we left. Place is clean. Besides, they're not goin' there to investigate us ... or you. They just want to know about that transmitter."

"They wanna know how to blow one up?" laughed Hendrick. "*That* I can tell them over the phone."

"No, chief. They're tryin' to figure out what it was made of."

Hendrick went back inside, shaking his head. "You saw as much of it as I did, boss. Why don't *you* tell 'em?"

"Because I can't remember *shit* right now. We tied one on at the Gonçalves' family estate in Cadiz. Had a couple gallons of Andalusian wine to myself, and it took me two days to sleep it off. All I can remember about that gizmo is that it was the size of a hefty jackknife. They want to talk to somebody who saw it for more than a couple seconds. Seriously, Hendrick. I wouldn't put you in harm's way."

"Why do they want to know what it was made of?"

"They wouldn't tell me. But, well ... you remember that guy who stood up to the aliens in London a couple weeks ago?"

Hendrick strained to remember. "Yeah, I remember: 'The Guy from Parnassus.'"

He must have said something funny, because Gary laughed aloud.

"The Kid from Canarsie," said Gary, correcting him.

"Yeah? What about him?"

"Well, you remember the guy who was with me and Gonçalves when we flew over your explosion?"

"*My* explosion?" Hendrick threw his free hand in the air. "Please don't call it that, boss. It wasn't my fault."

"I *know* it wasn't," said Gary. "Stick with me. I'm just tryin' to draw a connection here, man. Now, you remember that guy, right? He arrived with a beautiful blonde? That guy *is* the Kid from Canarsie."

Hendrick tried to remember everything he could about the guy, which wasn't much. On second thought, there was *something* he could remember. "That's the guy who left the transmitter here."

"Right."

"So why don't they just ask *him* about it?" demanded Hendrick. "He had it longer than I did."

There was an exasperated silence on Gary's end. Finally, he spoke.

"You gotta start keepin' up with current events, Hendrick. At least turn on the TV once in a while! They *can't* ask that guy 'cause he took off in a spaceship last night while he was bein' watched by about eight billion people. I take it you were *not* one of 'em."

Hendrick shook his head. "No, it sounded like a big fake to me. A *goddess* come down to Earth? Ridiculous."

Gary laughed. "You gotta see the pictures, chief. She's all that and a bag o' chips!" He was called away from the phone for a second, but came back on right away. "Gotta go, Hendrick. Make me proud. And if you can do anything useful for 'em, make your best deal. There'll still be a place for you when you get back. Besides, you're not leavin' the place unmanned."

"Well," said Hendrick, "Festus is on a supply run, so there's really nobody to put in charge."

"Waddya mean?" asked Gary. "Wierzbowski's there, isn't he?"

Hendrick sighed and glowered at the unconscious figure sprawled face-down across the bar.

"Well, his *body's* here," said Hendrick, "but, boss, he's not even in charge of *himself.*"

"Better not let *him* hear you say that," said Gary. "He can be very sensitive."

"Well, at the moment, he's totally numb."

"Lights out?"

"Like a drowned lantern."

"He'll just have to watch the place. Gotta go. Best o' luck."

Click.

Hendrick turned to the bartender's immobile form. "Wierzbowski," he said in conversational tone. No reason to startle a man known to wake up swinging his fists.

No sign of movement.

"Wierzbowski," he said a little louder. "Come on, man. Time to rejoin the living. You may be in charge soon."

Still no sign.

Wondering what he did in another life to be stuck in this desolate ruin, Hendrick mimicked Wierzbowski's speaking voice. "Oh, Hendrick," he said to himself. "Thank you for waking me from my drunken stupor for the millionth time. You're not such a bad guy after all."

Hendrick resumed his own voice in reply. "Nor are you, Wierzbowski. You have a great personality. Like a sponge."

Resolved to do something to wake up the bartender, Hendrick put his hand on his shoulder and shook him mildly. "Thomas," he said, congratulating himself for not only knowing that the man had a given name, but for knowing what it was. "Thomas, the boss needs you to do something for him."

It became clear there'd be no reply for some hours, if not days.

Exasperated, Hendrick firmly grasped the drunk's shoulder and pulled him up straight on the barstool.

To Hendrick's amazement, Wierzbowski didn't stop moving when he was erect on the stool, but instead continued straight back into a shelf full of liquor bottles that went flying off in every direction and shattered on the floor. The drunk flopped off the stool onto the floor, his body lodging awkwardly in the narrow space between the bar and the few unbroken bottles.

The place was a mess, but the thing that really shook up Hendrick was the glimpse he'd caught of Wierzbowski's flaccid facial expression, which could best be described as ... *dead*. Both eyes had momentarily opened, but one was rolled up in his head while the other aimed straight ahead, unseeing. Much as Hendrick wanted to, he couldn't just leave the guy there.

The biggest problem with having a health emergency in the *El Paso* was that the nearest hospital was at least an hour away, so whatever first aid Wierzbowski was going to get would have to come from Hendrick himself, who knew almost nothing about first aid.

Cursing his fate, Hendrick put a hand under each of Wierzbowski's shoulders and dragged him around to the front of the bar, kicking a few barstools out of the way and leaning the drunk's back against the bar. Carting a body around was hard work, and Hendrick was out of breath and sweating profusely.

At that moment, the bells on the door jingled and a white guy walked in wearing a suit and tie, carrying a briefcase and looking like he'd sweated through clothes he hadn't changed in a week. The man put down the briefcase, looked impassively at Hendrick, then at the drunk.

"Should I come back?" the man asked with no hint of irony. "Is this a bad time?"

Hendrick felt sure he was about to be arrested. The scene was an invitation to misinterpretation, so if this new guy was racist this would not end well.

"Are you a cop?" he asked the newcomer.

"Not ... here. Not now," said the man with a smirk. "Didn't my friend Gary tell you I was comin'?"

Hendrick regarded the man uncertainly. "He told me *somebody* was coming to talk to me, but—"

"I'm Agent Duffy, FBI, and—don't worry—I know you didn't roll this guy."

"How could you know that?" asked Hendrick.

"Because you'd be the first *hombre* ever to roll a bartender without touchin' the till, and while leavin' an AK-47 in plain view outside his own reach." Duffy pointed to the rifle sitting on a tabletop. "*I* could get to it before you—and I'm overweight and dyin' from this frickin' heat." He shook his head. "You'd make a lousy thief."

Hendrick snorted derisively. "That's because I'm *not* a thief." He nodded toward the unconscious bartender. "Can you help this guy? I think he might be dead."

Duffy squatted next to Hendrick and looked closely at the drunk. "Well, if he's dead … then, *no*, I can't help him. For that you'd need a priest." He placed two fingers on the drunk's neck and shook his head curtly. "This guy's not dead." Then he equivocated. "He's well on his way out," said Duffy, "but he ain't dead yet."

"How can you tell?" asked Hendrick.

"Well, he's got a pulse … but a thready one." Duffy pointed to a small blood trail that started behind the bar and led to Wierzbowski's butt, as though it had been scratched by a shard of broken glass. "Besides that, he's bleedin' a little, which means his heart is pumpin', such as it is. Does he always drink like this?"

"Pretty much, yeah."

"How old is this guy?" asked Duffy.

"I don't know. Maybe fifty?"

Duffy turned to Hendrick. "And how old are *you*, if you don't mind my askin'?"

"I'll be thirty in a few weeks."

Duffy frowned. "Young guy like you shouldn't be hangin' with an old drunk like this. I don't know what got him drinkin' like this, but this guy's beyond hopeless. You don't wanna end up like him, and it's awful easy to do when you hang around with drunks. You married?"

"Yes. You?"

"Same," replied Duffy. "Well, there's hope for you because you got responsibilities to other people." He pointed with his chin at Wierzbowski's insensate form. "You could call the hospital, I suppose," he said, "but I doubt he'd want you to. My guess is he'd be embarrassed being rolled in on a gurney and he'd refuse whatever treatment or advice they offer 'im. The guys I've known like this are usually ready to accept whatever fate the gods throw at 'em, y'know? But it's up to you."

"I don't know," said Hendrick, at a loss.

Duffy, who obviously found squatting uncomfortable, pulled out a chair from one of the tables and sat down. "I came in a rented car. If you're sure you want to get this guy to a hospital, you and I could drive 'im there. That'd prolly knock a solid hour off his arrival time."

Hendrick equivocated a moment and shook his head. "Let's leave him as is. I'll just make sure he can breathe, and let him wake up like he always does."

"Wise move, kid," said Duffy, picking up his briefcase and putting it on the table. "Besides, that'll make it easier for us to talk about what I came here for."

Hendrick stooped over, put his fingers under Wierzbowski's nose, and took some comfort from feeling his breath. He got up and washed his face with soap and water at the sink in the wet bar. "You?" he said, inviting Duffy to wash up.

"No, thanks. I'm gonna need a swimmin' pool when I'm done here, anyway. I think I'll hold off." On second thought, he added, "But I could sure use a glass o' cold water."

Hendrick took a couple of ice cubes from the minifridge, tossed them in a glass with some water, put it in front of Duffy, and sat across the table from him.

"So," said Hendrick, "how can I help you?"

Duffy took out a ballpoint pen and a yellow legal pad with questions written on it. "You remember taping some TNT to a transmitter and throwing it into a pit a couple weeks ago?"

Hendrick nodded. "Yes. It's not the kind of thing I'm asked to do usually, so … I remember."

Duffy made a notation on the yellow pad. "You wouldn't happen to know whether the fire's still burning there, wouldja?"

"Let me show you something," said Hendrick and walked toward the door.

Duffy tried to beckon him back. "If it's all the same to you, I'd prefer not to leave this lovely tavern for the time being."

"You don't have to leave. Just come onto the porch, so I can point out something to you."

Duffy got up and followed him onto the porch.

Hendrick pointed to a spot on the horizon where a column of soot rose high into the sky. "That's where the hole is," he said.

Duffy whistled softly. "Geez, will ya lookit that? You musta thrown that transmitter in, what, *three weeks* ago? And it's still burnin' like a sumbitch." He looked worriedly at Hendrick. "Is that … nuclear?"

Hendrick hesitated. Regardless how long he'd fretted about his condition, he'd never actually gone out there with a Geiger counter. "I don't think so, but I'm not sure."

"Well," said Duffy, "how about you? I saw you had a Geiger counter next to your weapon. You musta tested *yourself*, no?"

"Curiously, I've never had any sign of radiation poisoning—or even more than ambient radiation."

Duffy was apparently stuck on the definition of ambient radiation, but was too proud to ask. "So … that's *good*, right?"

Hendrick sighed. It felt good to hear his judgment ratified, even by this guy who evidently knew nothing about the topic. He held the door open for Duffy and they went back inside to the table. Wierzbowski hadn't moved a muscle.

"Now," began Duffy, "you got a good look at the transmitter—the housing, not the electronics, right?"

Hendrick nodded. "Right. I didn't see the insides at all."

Duffy smiled crookedly. "Good thing you didn't try to open it. Or you and this fine establishment woulda been no more." He glanced around the tawdry *El Paso*, stopping momentarily on Wierzbowski, and shrugged at his own description. "Was there any writing on the transmitter?"

Hendrick closed his eyes and concentrated.

"Yes," he said, "there was."

Duffy sat up in surprise. "There was? What did it look like? What did it say?"

"The lettering was in red. I don't know what it said because it was not in an alphabet I can read. It looked like… Israeli lettering."

"I don't suppose you could draw out the letters on a piece of paper?" suggested Duffy.

Hendrick shook his head. "No. I couldn't, I'm afraid."

"Were there any numbers?"

"I don't think so."

"You don't remember?"

"Well," Hendrick explained, "there are many ways to write numbers, but there were no Arabic numerals. No Roman numerals."

Duffy wrote some notes on his legal pad. "And what did the housing look like?"

"Hard to describe. It certainly didn't look like something you'd see in a store today … on Earth. But, after all, it was from another planet, wasn't it?"

Duffy nodded. "Did you watch Inanna's landing last night?"

"I didn't. I expected it was fake."

Duffy shook his head. "It wasn't. I was there. She was real. Anyway, the only reason I mentioned her is that the transmitter came from her planet."

"I'm not surprised," said Hendrick. "If such a handheld object were manufactured on Earth today it would probably be housed in a hard resin case, like a hair dryer. This was not resinous. It looked and felt like a mineral of some kind, or a combination of minerals. Several colors were streaked through it, some lighter, some darker. It looked very much like it was cut from natural stone."

"What did it *feel* like when you held it?"

"The surface was sanded smooth, but not flat. There was no pitting, no jagged edges. It was like you were running your hand over a composite rock that had been carefully shaped with a sander, perhaps polished. There was enough unevenness to make it easy to grip. It wouldn't slip from your hand."

Duffy removed from his briefcase a few small teardrop-shaped metallic ingots, some stones, and some flaky minerals. He set them out on the table. "Okay, I'm gonna show you some … specimens, and you tell me if the transmitter's housing looked like the specimen. Okay?"

Hendrick nodded.

Duffy picked up a small ingot of silver and looked at Hendrick.

Hendrick shook his head. "That's silver. It didn't resemble silver."

Duffy picked up another small ingot and showed it to him.

Hendrick asked, "Have you ever held a U.S. penny in your hand, Mister Duffy?"

"Of course."

"I have, too. Didn't it look just like what you're holding in your hand? That's copper. If the housing had been copper, I would have recognized it immediately."

"How about this one?"

"That's aluminium," said Hendrick, giving it the British pronunciation. "Obviously, no. Same answer."

"This?" asked Duffy, showing him another.

"No. That's molybdenum."

"This?"

Hendrick rolled his eyes. "Magnesium. No. Look, if it had resembled a single element, I would have told you. I'm familiar with nearly all of them, both in their pure forms and in most naturally occurring forms."

Duffy picked up an ingot that vaguely resembled aluminum, but was a bit shinier.

"No," said Hendrick. "I believe that's chromium and you shouldn't be handling it with bare hands. It's highly toxic."

Duffy put the ingot back in his briefcase, and showed Hendrick another that looked similar but was shinier still.

Hendrick believed he recognized it, and said with some alarm, "Put that down and don't pick it up again without proper gear."

As a show of defiance, Duffy continued to hold it up.

"Mister Duffy, you're hurting yourself."

"I'll be the judge of that," Duffy said adamantly, then wavered, "but, just out of curiosity, *how* am I hurting myself?"

Hendrick shook his head. "You're almost certainly burning your hand."

Duffy took out his copy of the periodic table of the elements and ran his finger down it. "No, Mister Smartguy. Its atomic number is lower than uranium, so how's it gonna burn my hand?"

"Unless I'm sorely mistaken," said Hendrick, "that's technetium. Of the elements whose isotopes are *all* radioactive, it has the lowest atomic number. It's much lower down than uranium. There's perhaps a five-in-six chance that the one you're holding is radioactive. Foolish odds for you to be playing, no? Put it down."

Duffy pointed his chin at the Geiger counter. "Show me."

Hendrick shook his head. "I will, but only if you put it down right now. Otherwise, you'll just have to remain in suspense … until your hand falls off."

"Okay, you win," said Duffy and deposited the ingot on the table, withdrawing his hand.

"Mister Duffy, you'll wish to keep your hands away from your face for the time being." Hendrick flicked on the Geiger counter switch, pulled the barrel out of its perch, and waved it over the ingot. It crackled wildly.

Duffy's eyes went wide and he stared at his hand.

Hendrick shook his head mournfully. "Now go scrub your hands thoroughly with soap and water at the wet bar. Don't spare soap, water, or effort."

Duffy hopped out of his chair and ran to the sink, where he scrubbed his hands in earnest. When he nervously returned to his seat, Hendrick waved the barrel over his hand. It crackled, but only slightly.

"Not too bad," said Hendrick.

"How do you know all this?" asked Duffy. "What are you, some kind of geologist?"

Hendrick smiled. "Yes. I'm some kind of geologist."

"Really?" asked Duffy.

"I have a degree in geology from Addis Ababa University in Ethiopia."

Duffy was compulsively rubbing his hands together. "Then why are you a triggerman for Gary?"

"I'm not a triggerman," said Hendrick, showing some irritation. "I'm no killer. There are marauding bands all over this area. Gary needs his property protected."

"Sorry. I misspoke. Why are you carryin' water for 'im?"

"As you pointed out earlier, I have people to take care of. When the Germans gave up on the local mines, I was out of work." He shrugged. "Gary didn't need a geologist, but he was paying well."

A sudden snort escaped from Wierzbowski and his head jerked.

"Sleeping beauty awakes," said Duffy sarcastically, then returned to business. "I got an uncle who pays more than Uncle Gary. You got a problem workin' for Uncle Sam?"

Hendrick shook his head. "Not on principle, no."

"You got a criminal record?"

Hendrick shook his head.

"You got any history as a communist or subversive?"

"Nope."

"Uncle Sam'll pay you twice what Uncle Gary's payin' ya."

Hendrick held up four fingers.

"Why do you need four times what Gary's payin' ya?"

"I'll have to be away from my wife, won't I?"

Duffy nodded.

"She hates that."

"But what's in it for Uncle Sam that he should pay that much?"

Hendrick sighed. "I'm the only geologist in the world who saw this thing. I'll work on the problem until you know precisely what it was made of. I guarantee it." Hendrick knew perfectly well there could be no guarantee, but he'd learned a bit from Gary about bluffing, and about deciding how much exaggeration one could get away with. *Make your best deal*, he'd said.

"Okay," said Duffy. "Get your shit and let's go."

"Okay," said Hendrick, "but if you're going to take those samples with you, we have to pack them properly. There's some stuff in the hangar I can use. Let's go."

CHAPTER 4

On the bridge of Inanna's pyramidion, General Shulgi pressed the alarm button, which started crew members running to their battle stations. In a moment, he muted the alarm on the bridge, though it could still be heard coming from some distance down the hallway.

To no one in particular, he said, "Connect me to the commander of Lord Enki's spacecraft."

In a moment there appeared a giant hologram of another general's face. "Yes, General Shulgi?" it said. "I take it this has something to do with the weapon about to destroy Queen Inanna's pyramidion in—" he referred to a floating screen of his own "—two minutes."

"Yes, General Ningishzidda," replied Shulgi. "We most humbly request the assistance of Lord Enki in neutralizing the weapon."

Ningishzidda half-smiled. "May I ask why Inanna the Great does not rather call upon her esteemed grandfather, King Enlil, for this purpose?"

Shulgi was mildly irritated by the question. "General," he said, "as you know, King Enlil is too far away to intervene in time."

"How unfortunate!" said Ningishzidda. "Are you aware, general, of the origin of the missile?"

"Not precisely, although the Dagon have—unprompted provided information about its likely launch point." Shulgi's anxiety was growing to the point where it had begun to show—which was no doubt Ningishzidda's object. "Permit me to point out that in another minute, our request will be moot and Queen Inanna will walk with her Creator. It's unlikely Lord Enki would greet such news with equanimity."

"Please don't speculate about Lord Enki's feelings, General Shulgi. It's most unbecoming." Ningishzidda pressed a button. "Oh, look at that!" he said. "We had more than thirty seconds to spare! Well, you need no longer be concerned about the missile. The turnabout command has been sent."

David, whose eyes had been riveted to the oncoming missile, expected a *turnabout* command to turn the missile about and send it on its way. But that's not what happened. Instead of turning away, the pursuing missile maintained its oncoming orientation. But its small guidance rockets flamed out, flipped into reverse position, and reignited, so that the missile rapidly began receding from view. In perhaps a half-minute, it had disappeared entirely. David couldn't help but wonder whether Enki had learned to make time run backwards.

"Turnabout?" said Shulgi. "I would have presumed a shootdown would be most efficient." He pressed a virtual button, and the local alarm went silent.

Ningishzidda arched an eyebrow. "And *I* would have presumed General Shulgi would wish to know who fired upon his queen."

"Well, there is *some* advantage to that, I suppose," Shulgi admitted.

Ningishzidda nodded indulgently. "We should have that information in no more than a few days. As you know, it can take some time for a missile to retrace its steps, especially when they're written on nothing but air and space." His face grew in size, as though he were trying to get a closer look at the bridge. "Is that Professor *Schubert*? Why, it is! So good to see the two of you getting along. Well, please don't hesitate to contact me again whenever the next person tries to kill my dear cousin." His smiling face disappeared.

Shulgi was quietly mortified at the rough handling he'd received from a member of the royal family—and in front of a complete stranger, no less. He turned to David with chagrin.

"I present to you the Nibirune royal family."

David nodded his head. "You can really feel the closeness," he said sardonically.

"Heartwarming, isn't it?" said Shulgi.

"I notice that Ningishzidda made reference to King Enlil. Has the king's father Anu passed, then?"

Shulgi nodded. "And he is sorely missed."

"My sincere condolences. When did His Majesty pass?"

"Just recently, during this Shar," said Shulgi somberly, then remembered whom he was talking to. "Perhaps a thousand Earth years ago."

Outwardly, David nodded sympathetically. Inwardly, his mind was boggled by the reminder that there were living beings who could characterize as *recent* an event that occurred a thousand years ago.

AFTER THE BOOSTER was jettisoned, the computer aboard the second stage of the missile operated smoothly until being hit with Ningishzidda's turnabout signal that knocked out its main program and replaced it with a mirror image. Consistently with its new program, its guidance rockets momentarily shut down, assumed retro orientation, and fired up again, so that in a matter of seconds the missile was moving backward at the speed at which it had formerly advanced.

The most sophisticated routine in its new program was designed to instruct the missile to slowly retrace its own trajectory based upon a number of factors, chiefly, the missile's pre- and post-jettison mass, the quantity of fuel remaining in the booster at the time of jettison, the most advanced position the missile had reached and its velocity at that position, the mass of the nearest planet (in this case Earth), and local conditions, such as atmospheric density and prevailing winds.

Under the control of the turnabout program, the second stage would methodically retrace its steps, assume an altitude one kilometer above its original launch point, broadcast its global position … and detonate its nuclear payload.

David had no way of knowing, but *turnabout* was a merciless weapon of pre-emptive revenge, or *prevenge*, as it was often called.

⟶∘⟷∘⟵

QUEEN INANNA'S MAIDSERVANT Shiduri fetched David from the bridge and escorted him to his quarters, where the door was emblazoned with a ten-inch-high rendition of the Stars and Stripes. As soon as David saw it, he knew there was *something* not quite right about it, but he was too tired at the moment to figure out what it was.

Near the door to his sizable quarters sat a plexiglass conference table and eight chairs. His laptop had been carefully placed on a separate table, evidently to be used as a desk. Next to it, Elijah's neatly folded mantle rested on the folio containing David's ambassadorial commission.

At the end of the room opposite the door were a bed with one thin blanket and a well-stocked bathroom with a toilet, shower, and sink.

In keeping with Inanna's rules for David's diet, Shiduri had brought along a covered bowl containing a dressed salad of fruits and vegetables for him to enjoy in the privacy of his room. She placed it on his desk for later, then pointed out where to find towels and supplies, how to lock his door, and how to call if he were in distress. She even told him where to go if he got hungry in the middle of the night. He thanked her sincerely.

She bowed, and he reciprocated.

"Her Majesty is fast asleep," said Shiduri as she prepared to leave. "Do you want a woman?"

The breathtaking juxtaposition of those two thoughts sent David's mind reeling. Did Shiduri mean to suggest that Inanna would be sleeping with *him* if she weren't already asleep? Or that, as she's presently asleep, she'd be unaware of his sleeping with *another* woman? Or that, as she's presently unavailable, she'd have *no objection* to his sleeping with another woman? (This last he included for completeness only; as far as he could tell, no woman would ever consider saying such a thing.)

But those questions were subsidiary to the overarching one: *Which self-respecting servant offers to procure a woman for her mistress's guest?* Then he remembered that certain cultures had been known to impress women into sexual slavery during wartime.

"Shiduri," he said graciously, "this is no longer done on Earth. It is considered a violation of a woman's right to choose her own partner … or no partner at all."

"What about a *man's* right to choose?"

He smirked. "It's a man's plight to earn a woman's love and persuade her several times a day that he *has* earned it. It's not a perfect system, but it works in most cases."

She gave him a patronizing smile. "But you are the famous Piddle Panossi. I am sure I would have no trouble finding a most willing volunteer."

"That's very flattering," he said, "but, no, not for me. Thank you. And you must never repeat the offer to me, please."

Shiduri shrugged as if to say now she's seen it *all*, and hesitated before turning to go. David swore he could read the next question in her mind, which would have been, *Do you prefer boys?* Fortunately, she'd apparently thought better of it, for she remained silent, closing the door behind her.

This conversation left him with two abiding thoughts: First was that there were evidently innumerable ways to mangle the phrase *The Kid from Canarsie*, which, although it began as a mere newspaper headline, would surely someday serve as his epitaph. Second was how much he already missed Catharine. He resolved to send her a necessarily bland email.

As he hadn't eaten in several hours, he uncovered the salad bowl that Shiduri left him. Its presentation was quite appetizing, full of color and sweet, earthy scents. It took him a moment to realize that he'd never seen any of these fruits or vegetables before. As farming had long ago been introduced to earthlings by Enlil, however, it seemed likely that the plants in his bowl were Nibirune progenitors of plants he ate every day on Earth. He pushed some of the strangest-looking items aside and concentrated on those that appeared to have an earthly counterpart. The dressing was tasty. Concentrating on the *probably* lettuce, *possibly* tomatoes, and *not-quite* peaches, he ate his fill.

Once he finished, he put the bowl aside and powered up his laptop, mindful (as he'd been warned by the State Department) that everything passing over the computer would be recorded, read, and analyzed by his hosts. He loaded a browser and logged onto his personal email account.

"Dear Catharine," he wrote, "The quarters here are nice and clean and everyone is being very nice to me. (What a *nice* email, he remarked to himself, rolling his eyes.) It's been uneventful so far, though there was a slight glitch at the very beginning. But it's all been resolved now. Not to worry. I already miss you a great deal. How are you faring? Perhaps we can manage a video call? Let me know soonest—Not Trevor." He clicked on the Send button and exited the browser, preparing to retire for the night.

It didn't occur to him that Catharine might be headed across the Arctic Ocean to track down and capture (or kill) whoever had taken a shot at him.

⟶∘⟪⟫∘⟵

UNFORTUNATELY, THERE APPEARED to be no way of getting from London to Yellowknife on a U.S. Navy jet without stopping at Vancouver first.

While Catharine was still on Air Force One to Heathrow, the admiral (with a little help from the President) arranged for Catharine's flight to Yellowknife. More importantly, he'd also located a TOPGUN U.S. Navy fighter pilot named Buck Buchanan, who happened to be on leave in London, and arranged for him to accompany Catharine on the flight from Heathrow to Vancouver and then serve as her pilot on the overflight.

⟶∘⟪⟫∘⟵

THE FIRST LEG of the trip from London to Yellowknife was a daytime flight over much of the Arctic Circle, including a long patch over Greenland; the flight was referred to as "daytime" because it would include a few hours' interruption of the long Arctic night. As the cabin was nearly empty and the flight attendant immediately supplied her with a blackout mask, Catharine fell asleep before Buck boarded. Neither Catharine nor Buck was in uniform.

Crossing over Baffin Island into the Territory of Nunavut, Catharine awoke and pulled up her mask. There was dim Arctic sunlight in the cabin. According to experience, that meant it was no earlier than late morning and no later than mid-afternoon.

In the seat next to her sat Buck, the hotshot pilot the admiral had dug up for her. He was sound asleep, regardless that he wore no blackout mask, and his mouth hung open.

He must have sensed Catharine watching, because he woke up, which she could tell only because one of his eyes opened a slit before closing again. He muttered almost inaudibly, "Too goddam bright in this cabin."

"We're over Greenland in December," she said. "If you don't like daylight, just wait a few minutes. It'll be gone."

No reply. On the tray in front of her traveling companion lay two empty shotglasses, a half dozen squeezed-out lemon slices, and a half-empty shaker of salt. She decided to test just how burnt out he was.

"You've had the breakfast of champions, I see," she observed.

With both eyes still closed, he smirked groggily and said, "No, ma'am. That's Wheaties. What *I* had was"—He worked his mouth into a moue of disgust—"tequila."

"No Wheaties?"

He smirked again. "Well, I *had* some, but I … tossed 'em up."

"That's disgusting," she said.

"Why, thank you, ma'am. That's what I was goin' for."

"You didn't really throw up your Wheaties, did you?"

"No, ma'am. I'm a steely-eyed F-35 and F-18 pilot and a U.S. Navy lieutenant." He said with supreme confidence, "I can hold *my* Wheaties."

She smiled despite herself. "I sure hope you sober up before you get to Vancouver, lieutenant," she said.

"Ain't goin' to Vancouver," he mumbled.

"Well," she said, "if you'd open your eyes all the way, you'd see we're halfway there."

"Ain't goin' to Vancouver," he repeated sleepily, trying to moisten his dry mouth.

"Well," she said, "that's what our *tickets* say."

He opened the same eye again, this time leaving it open.

"'Scuse me? You *navy*, ma'am?"

"Yeah, I'm navy. How do you plan on getting to Yellowknife without stopping in Vancouver?"

"Well, if you take a good look at an aerial map, ma'am, you will find that Yellowknife is *on the way* to Vancouver. If we were to fly to Vancouver first, we'd be goin' about three thousand miles out of our way."

"I noticed that, lieutenant, but that's the flight plan."

He sat up, earnestly moved his mouth close to her ear (yes, definitely tequila) and whispered to her, "I know the pilot." He winked conspiratorially. "When we land in Yellowknife on the way, you and I will save almost a full day each. Besides, you and I were the only reason this bucket was goin' to Yellowknife in the first place. Did you know that? It's true. So, I figure we're savin' Uncle Sam about forty grand in the process."

She couldn't help but smile at his audacity. Besides, it would be good to arrive early for a change. She looked around the rest of the cabin, which was sparsely populated by a few sleeping people. "You suppose the other passengers won't object to an unscheduled stop at Yellowknife?"

He turned his head slowly for a bleary survey of the rest of the passengers.

"All *six* of 'em?" he asked. "They don't look like a rowdy bunch to me. I doubt they'll even notice. Besides, it'll add no more than an hour to their trip. Considering what they're payin' for airfare—which is *nothin'*—they'll still count themselves lucky."

She nodded with amusement. "What are you planning on doing with the extra time in Yellowknife?"

He opened his eyes all the way at last. "What's your rank, if I may be so bold?"

"Lieutenant commander," she said with a wry smile. She outranked him, if barely.

He looked at her skeptically. "*You're* a lieutenant commander?"

She nodded.

He steadied his gaze, looked at her face in a manner that was admiring but not provocative, and sighed dreamily. "They should make 'em *all* look like you."

"I'll ignore that. And just in case your plans for your extra time in Yellowknife included me, you can forget those, too. What *I* want is for you not to touch another drop of spirits until you and I safely part ways."

The flight attendant saw them conversing and came over with a glass of water each. Buchanan downed his in one gulp and said, "Thank you kindly."

"Can I get you anything else?" asked the attendant.

"I'd like some frosted flakes," said Catharine, "and my friend here would like some Wheaties."

The attendant raised her eyebrows at the flyboy.

Buck smiled wanly at the attendant, pointed to his upper arm and said, "You can't see 'em now, but I've got two broad stripes." He pointed to Catharine's upper arm. "*She's* got two broad stripes, too, *and* a skinny li'l one in between." He held in a belch. "I'll have the Wheaties."

Catharine suppressed a laugh. The flight attendant went to get their orders.

"Mind if I ask you something, Buck?" said Catharine.

"Nope, so long as the answer won't get me court-martialed."

"They say some men drink to remember, and others to forget."

He turned to her skeptically. "Ya can't fool *me*. That's not a question."

"I figure," she said, "the way you drink, you must have some kinda story."

He nodded his head dispassionately. "The way I drink"—he shrugged—"I suppose I *must*."

"So, what's your story?"

He thought long and hard, and said, "I can't remember."

She laughed aloud, and he joined in.

She said, "You know why I want you sober?"

"So's I can fly?"

"Yeah, but … did the admiral tell you the mission parameters?"

"Oh, sure," he boasted. "The admiral 'n me? We go *way* back."

"So you know that, when we do the overflight, there's a possibility they could take a shot at us?"

He sloughed it off. "All in a day's work," he replied.

"And," she whispered, "they have nukes."

His eyes opened wider.

She added in a whisper, "And they could be from another planet."

His jaw slowly dropped. "Are you *shittin'* me right now?"

She frowned at him. "You said the admiral filled you *in*."

"I lied," he confessed. "I just wanted to look cool."

She smirked. "Didn't work. Listen up. We should go over this once before we land."

WHEN CATHARINE AND Buck got off the plane at Yellowknife Airport in their navy-issue parkas, the sky was full dark, it was snowing lightly, and the thermometer was plunging to fifteen below.

No one came to meet them. No surprise there, since they were eight hours early. They crossed through the terminal to hail a cab to Joint Task Force North Headquarters. The cabbie got out to put their bags in the trunk, and Buck opened the rear door to let Catharine in first. As she slid to the far end of the seat, something outside caught her eye.

Under a nearby streetlamp stood a group of serious-looking young men in warmup suits and parkas, with what she deemed a conspiratorial attitude. All of them had the same style beard: long, and squared off at the bottom like the galoots who'd loitered outside the clothier's in Paris. Two resembled the loiterers so closely that she instinctively glanced at their hands, half-expecting to see one of them carrying her purloined laptop.

Probably just a bunch of lumberjacks, she told herself on second thought. There *had* to be lumberjacks all over the Northwest Territories, *didn't there*? There were so many trees.

But these young men were not burly and coarse. Neither were they drinking, laughing, or acting intoxicated. From their demeanor, it was clear they were not telling dirty jokes, as young men are wont to do. In fact, they weren't even talking. So what the hell were they meeting about outdoors with the temperature dipping so far below zero? She drove the thoughts away like so many phantoms in the night.

But there was no denying the tingle up her spine.

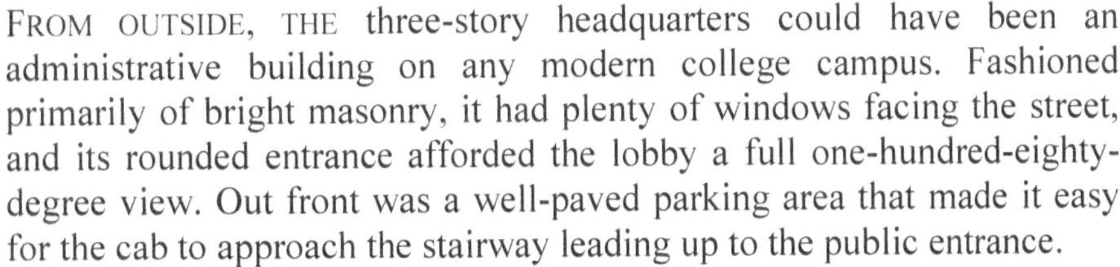

FROM OUTSIDE, THE three-story headquarters could have been an administrative building on any modern college campus. Fashioned primarily of bright masonry, it had plenty of windows facing the street, and its rounded entrance afforded the lobby a full one-hundred-eighty-degree view. Out front was a well-paved parking area that made it easy for the cab to approach the stairway leading up to the public entrance.

At the front desk, Catharine introduced herself and Buck as U.S. Navy. The clerk looked them up and down, and asked whether they weren't early. Obviously, the admiral had called ahead. Catharine acknowledged that they were indeed early and offered to check in at one of the hotels in town and return at the appointed hour. The clerk seemed as though she wasn't quite sure whom to call, but ended up calling a young female lieutenant, who met them at the desk.

They handed their U.S. Navy IDs to the lieutenant, who put them on a scanner and punched a few keys. In a matter of seconds, the IDs were authenticated and she'd received an order to escort the guests to the base commander.

"Commander's on the third floor," she chirped, handing back their identification. "Elevator or stairs?"

"Which do *you* prefer?" asked Catharine.

"Oh, I'm a stairs person," said the lieutenant as she began walking. "Canada takes pride in having everybody in uniform keep fit and trim and, with all the snow and ice, it's kinda hard to get exercise much of the year, except in an indoor gym. Anyway, I like the stairs."

"Stairs it is," said Catharine.

As they began their climb, Catharine asked whether it was the fashion in town for local lumberjacks to wear square beards and warmup suits.

The lieutenant smiled and said, "No, ma'am, just the Martians. Where'd you spot them?"

Catharine was nonplussed. "We saw some guys like that at the airport. Did you say … Martians?"

"Yeah, they started showin' up here a few months ago. Some kind of loggers, I guess. You can see 'em movin' all around the lake, mostly at night. 'Course, up here it's night most of the time, especially *this* time of year. Some of the locals at Fort Providence say they've seen 'em shuttling small craft on the Mackenzie River all the way to Tuk and back, and that they like to set up camp on the ice floes in the lake."

"Isn't that dangerous?" asked Catharine. "Can't the ice crack and drown them all?"

"Not up here, ma'am. Not this time of year. There are even ice roads in these parts. You know what those are?"

"Tell me," said Catharine.

"They're ice floes so thick that you can reliably drive a loaded semi-tractor-trailer over them with no danger of falling through."

"No dirt beneath them?" asked Buck.

"None at all," said the lieutenant.

Catharine smiled vacantly. "So, why do you call 'em Martians?"

The lieutenant laughed. "Oh, y'know. They look like they're in one of those cults where you have to see different members before you realize they're dressin' alike on purpose. Then, you figure, that's probably the way *everybody* dresses wherever they come from. But no matter how hard you try, with some of 'em, you can't figure out *where* people would dress like that, so we just say they're from Mars and call 'em Martians."

Buck chimed in. "Anybody check 'em out? Make sure they're not up to no good?"

The lieutenant replied, "We usually leave that kind of thing up to local law enforcement." She laughed. "Besides, what *could* they be gettin' up to around here? Stealin' timber? Robbin' the Bank of Montreal? I'm just kiddin'. Actually, we *have* a branch of the bank up here but, as far as anyone can tell, all they have there is computers. Honestly, I don't know *what* that branch does." She shrugged. "Maybe they write mortgages for the few houses in town. Here we are," she said, stopping before an important-looking door, "commander's office."

⸻ ◦◦◦ ⸻

"So, you'll need a B or D model of the F-18, correct?" asked the commander, a spit-and-polish type with a pencil mustache and a nearly pure English accent that marked him as being from an old-line Canadian family, probably here since before the American War of Independence.

"That's correct, sir," said Buck.

"Who's the VIP who'll fill the second seat?"

"That would be me, sir," said Catharine. "The admiral wants me personally to take a look."

"Give us a couple hours to refuel and de-ice," said the commander, "and then you can go up as soon as you like. I suppose there's no chance you'll tell *me* what you're looking for."

"Sir," said Catharine, "that would be impossible, as neither of us has any *idea* what we're looking for. I suppose you could say we're looking for the unexpected."

"Back in the day," said the commander, "my flight instructor warned us against superfluous overflights. 'If you don't know what you're looking for,' he'd say, 'you're looking for trouble.'"

Catharine leaned forward. "That choice has been taken out of our hands, sir. When we come back, will you have a Super Huey and a few Mounties ready for a thorough overflight over the lake? We'll need thermal imaging, sir. The best you've got."

"They're on call for next light. I thought you'd want to go up during daylight hours. Around here, that's by appointment only."

Catharine nodded. "Actually, sir, we'd prefer that we take the F-18 up so we arrive up at the Arctic Ocean at first light. But for the *lake* overflight, I'm most interested in the two hours immediately *after* sunset. We should be back by then. If you could arrange it so we go boots-in-the-air during the last half-hour of sunlight, that would be perfect."

She didn't say why, but the technical manual for the missing minisub indicated that the exterior paint on the minisub's bridge was heat-absorptive and would light up an infrared scope for a couple of hours after sundown. She kept her fingers crossed that the sub was on the surface, and that the feeble sunlight in these polar climes would be strong enough to trigger the glow.

She had her doubts.

"Weather permitting," said the commander, "we'll try to accommodate you. Meanwhile, why don't you two get some sleep in the resident quarters in back? You've got a fair wait time. Might as well be fresh."

BASED UPON ALL relevant data, the Anunnaki turnabout program concluded that the place where its host missile was launched was the Beaufort Sea near Tuktoyaktuk, Northwest Territories, and that the missile would reach its point of launch, broadcast its location, and detonate its nuclear payload in approximately twelve hours.

CHAPTER 5

MAYBE IT WAS the excitement of the ceremony at Baalbek, or a lingering adrenaline rush from being chased by a nuclear missile, but David's sleep was uneasy. The small light coming through the window had evidently been enough to wake him. He sat up in bed and watched the innumerable stars of the Milky Way drift slowly by.

He flipped on the table lamp by his bed, and his eyes wandered to various items in the room. Not that interior design was a particular interest of his, but he recognized the lighting fixtures as Art Deco. There were no wall-hangings except clocks, all of which were set to New York time. The walls themselves were composed of the same substance as those in the hallways and on the bridge, a rough stone smoothed to a pleasant finish.

He faulted himself for failing to bring along a paperback or two, but shrugged it off, as he expected he wouldn't be reading much for pleasure anyway. Something was bothering him, and it had to do with Catharine. He looked over at his laptop, which was powered down just as he'd left it. *But why leave the laptop off?* No one had cautioned him to be frugal with energy, which the Anunnaki seemed to regard as abundant.

As David thought more of his situation, he realized that the laptop was his only point of direct contact with Earth. If Catharine was going to respond (or not) to his email, the laptop would be the only place where he'd find out. He shoved his thin blanket aside and got up to switch it on.

As he waited through the startup process, his attention shifted to Elijah's mantle lying next to the laptop, and considered whether to put it on. There *was* a sudden chill in the air, and it *did* seem inconsiderate for his hosts to have relegated him to a single, thin blanket. Nearly moved to put the mantle over his shoulders … he hesitated.

Though the mantle seemed to lie there lifeless, in David's mind it contained a strange and living magic. To don a mantle of such historical and religious significance could never be a mundane gesture. In the right hands, it had parted the waters of the Jordan River and played a part in countless other miracles. *Had Elijah worn this mantle when he brought the widow's son back from the dead? When the fire of the Lord that he'd called down on the animal sacrifice consumed the wood, and the stones, and the dust, and soaked up the water from the trench?*

Lighten up; it's just a cloak, cajoled a lighthearted voice. *Put it on.* Though the voice seemed a little like Shawn's, David recognized that as a trick, for if Shawn were actually here, he would have grabbed the mantle and put it on himself first, in case something bad would come of it.

It's not Elijah's cloak, the voice assured him. *Yahweh would never suffer his cloak to be handled by false gods such as the Anunnaki Marduk, whose defeat at the hands of Yahweh was prophesied by Jeremiah.* David recognized that the crafty internal voice couldn't be his own, as its mastery of the Bible exceeded his. He shivered to think it might belong to Yahweh's great adversary.

His hesitation arose not from fear for his physical safety, but doubts about his worthiness to don a garment having a direct connection to Yahweh. Realizing that he could engage in this internal debate all night without reaching a conclusion, he shook off the spell that had come over him, and reminded himself that he had *not* gotten up to contemplate the cloak at all, but to check for emails from Catharine.

He loaded his browser and an email program. There were the usual ads, a few *attaboy* messages from students who'd just completed the course he'd been teaching when his whole life was turned upside down by interplanetary intrigue.

But nothing from Catharine.

Where is she? What is she doing? Would she ever reply? It's inordinately difficult to tell from the back of a woman's head whether she harbors any interest in a future with you. His hopes fell further as he realized the obvious. If Catharine had meant him to feel hopeful, she wouldn't have *shown* him the back of her head in the first place.

Okay, if Catharine wasn't going to respond, he'd email the admiral and keep it businesslike. He composed a quick status report to the admiral and added at the end that he'd emailed Catharine but heard nothing back from her, hoping his addendum would seem like an afterthought.

Unsatisfied with the draft, he copied and pasted it into a word processor, rewriting it a half-dozen times to make it look as though it had been dashed off with little thought. At the end of this twenty-minute exercise, he reread it silently.

It read as though it had been rewritten a half-dozen times to make it look as though it had been dashed off with little thought. He copied and pasted the text back into the email program, and hit Send. The admiral knew precisely how he felt about Catharine and couldn't be fooled, anyway.

The room was deathly quiet. His eyelids grew heavy and, as he'd done many times on Earth, he fell asleep in front of his laptop and drifted into a silent dream.

His deceased wife Sharon was here in his room, wearing a midnight blue nightgown, looking as comely as she ever had in life. She smiled, as though to say, "It's me, not the goddess." Indeed, he felt at peace with this mute assurance, and sensed no intrusion by Inanna, who was probably sleeping soundly only a few hundred feet away.

Sharon sat down next to him at the laptop, opened the wallet she'd lifted from his nightstand, and began to leaf through the photos. To prevent hurt feelings, David reached out gently to discourage her from doing so, for mixed in with his wallet photos of Sharon were a few of Catharine. Sharon was nobody's fool, and she'd obviously recognize that his carrying photos of Catharine in his wallet meant that he was moving on with his life. He felt like an unfaithful heel. Maybe Catharine was wrong about him. Maybe he was a Trevor after all.

But, to his surprise, Sharon smiled at him as though laughing off his concern. She wanted him to know that she knew about Catharine and approved of his moving on. Although that should have provided him with some comfort, it had precisely the opposite effect, making him feel far worse. He touched her face to assure her that he still loved her, but she seemed unconcerned.

Sharon then pulled out his two wallet photos of Catharine and showed him first a candid of him and Catharine taken as they entered Hyde Park a couple of weeks earlier. That was a happy day that he and Catharine had spent entirely together. David's eyes welled up and his throat tightened. Sharon smiled sadly at him, but he knew it was because it pained her that he felt so guilty about moving on.

Then she looked at the other photo, the one that Catharine had given him. It was a wallet-size copy of a professional headshot of Catharine in uniform taken upon her promotion to lieutenant commander. Somehow on that day, years before David met her, Catharine had managed a professional-looking smile that allowed both her intelligence and good-natured irreverence to shine through.

Sharon looked at the photo apprehensively, as though worried that something bad was about to befall the officer in the photo. She rose and pointed behind him at the window looking out into space. When he turned his desk chair, he found that the window no longer looked out on the Milky Way, but rather at Earth; North America, in particular.

Sharon extended her hand to indicate a point in the Arctic Ocean just north of the Canadian land mass. When he could discern nothing of interest there, he turned to her questioningly, but her eyes were pinned to that spot and she continued pointing to it.

Suddenly, a pinpoint of light appeared at that place on the Earth, so intense that it seemed that Earth's image was nothing more than a two-dimensional painting between him and the sun, and that it had been pierced by a pin, letting through the sun's agonizingly bright blaze. After David watched for a few seconds, the light blossomed into a mushroom cloud that grew and grew. He felt as though he were hurtling toward it. Closer and closer it came. At the moment when he thought he must be consumed by the nuclear furnace, he spotted a small fighter aircraft even closer to the blast, struggling to remain airborne.

Waking with a start, his head jerked backward so hard that his chair nearly overturned. He threw his arms forward as a counterbalance and unintentionally smacked one hand into the laptop screen. Fortunately, he neither fell over nor knocked over the computer.

The images from his dream remained before his eyes as if he'd just seen them in waking life. He was sure that the woman was Sharon. The *real* Sharon, whatever that might mean. And she was telling him that Catharine is in danger.

His email app chimed, and he called up the header of the newest email. It was from A.H. Zia, M.D., Ph.D., addressed to *His Excellency Professor David Schubert, Ambassador of the United States of America.* He clicked on it and read the text: *Doctor A.H. Zia, Ambassador of Lord Enki, requests the honor of calling upon Your Excellency for an inaugural visit at the earliest possible time at your chambers aboard the Pyramidion of Her Majesty, Queen Inanna, Beloved of Anu. Doctor Zia will be docking at said pyramidion in a half-hour and would be pleased to attend at an hour most convenient to Your Excellency.*

David typed his reply immediately: *Ambassador Professor Schubert would be most pleased to receive an inaugural visit by Ambassador Doctor Zia as soon as Doctor Zia can attend at Professor Schubert's chambers aboard the Pyramidion of Her Majesty, Queen Inanna,*

Beloved of Anu. He hit Send.

David had a half hour to clean up, which he intended to put to good use. As he rose, he was surprised to see a jacket fall from his shoulders and caught it before it hit the floor. It was Elijah's mantle. With no recollection of putting it on, he folded it neatly, kissed it as he would a holy relic, such as the Torah or a skullcap, and placed it carefully back on his portfolio.

He turned to face the window where, once more, the only thing visible was the Milky Way.

⎯⎯⎯⎯⎯⎯⎯⎯⎯⎯⎯⎯⎯⎯⎯

THERE WAS A knock at the door. It was Inanna's maidservant Shiduri.

"Come in," said David, stepping out of the bathroom, having just donned his obligatory Sumerian gown.

Shiduri entered and bowed. "I trust Your Excellency slept well?"

"I did, Shiduri. Thank you. And you?"

She smirked at his egalitarian attitude, apparently unaccustomed to being asked about such personal matters as the quality of her sleep. "I slept well. Thank you, Excellency."

"And," he said, "I trust Her Majesty slept well despite the excitement of last evening."

Shiduri bowed. "Her Majesty is well. She never concerns herself with military matters."

Considering that Inanna's very life lay in the balance of last night's *military matter*, David found that a bit surprising. Shiduri pointed toward the door. "Doctor Zia is waiting in the hall. He wishes to pay his respects."

"Oh," replied David. "Has he arrived already? By all means, show him in."

Shiduri let Doctor Zia in, and left.

Zia was dressed impeccably as ever, in what appeared to be a ten-month version of the heavy navy-blue suit he seemed always to wear. He bowed courteously and pointed back toward the door. "Have you noticed, professor, that the American flag on your door has one more stripe than it should?"

David was surprised that Zia would notice. "I knew there was *something* wrong with it, but wasn't sure what it was."

"Yes," mused Zia, "the bottom stripe on this version is white, not red, as it ought to be."

"Perhaps to commemorate the fourteenth of the original thirteen colonies?" asked David jocularly. "I'll be sure to ask Shiduri to have it corrected."

"Well, now that that's out of the way," said Zia, "allow me to tell you that it's heartening to see how rapidly you've come up in the world, Professor Schubert."

"Why, thank you, Doctor Zia," David replied.

"It's indeed a pleasure to see you again," said Zia, "especially under such auspicious circumstances. Permit me to pass along Lord Enki's highest regards." Zia looked about the room, then tapped his jacket pocket with a questioning look.

"Oh, certainly!' said David. "I'm surprised that you smoke."

Doctor Zia laughed silently and mouthed the words, "I don't smoke." From the indicated pocket he removed a device that looked similar, though not identical, to the location transmitter that had been concealed in Zia's luggage. He pressed a button on the device and placed it on the conference table. A warm, undulating sound filled the room. He silently invited David to sit by him at the table.

David selected a seat perpendicular to Zia's and pointed to the device. "What's this?" he asked softly. "And why is it housed in the same stone that lines the walls of this pyramidion?"

Doctor Zia spoke at a normal volume. "Now that this device is operating, we can speak with a reasonable expectation of not being overheard. As for the device's case, it's made of a naturally occurring composite—naturally occurring on *Nibiru*, of course. It's called *Nibirode*, and it's of some familiarity and comfort to the Anunnaki, as the deepest caverns on Nibiru are largely comprised of it." He picked up the device and openly admired its appearance. "Although no two pieces of Nibirode are identical, every piece consists of the same variety of minerals, albeit in somewhat different proportions."

"Interesting," said David as he examined the device on the table. "So, you think this place is bugged?"

"Every place in Queen Inanna's control is *bugged*," Zia declared. "I assume that this chamber is no exception, notwithstanding that (since it is now an embassy) bugging it would violate diplomatic law. Incidentally, you may find her disappointed that you admitted me so early in your visit."

"I'll bear that in mind." David shrugged. "But that's part of our arrangement. I can speak with any Anunnaki representative who'll talk to me." He leaned into Doctor Zia and whispered. "Incidentally, do you recall the bags you lent us so we would resemble tourists?"

"Yes," said Zia.

"There was a location transmitter sewn into one of the seams."

Zia was shocked. "What did it look like?"

David pointed to the anti-eavesdropping device sitting on the table before him. "Much like this."

"What's become of it?" asked Zia. Before David could reply, Zia winced and asked, "Is that what caused the explosion in southern Africa?"

David nodded. "We're fortunate no one was killed or seriously injured."

"Well," Zia said defensively, "I expect that, if Inanna gave it any thought, she wouldn't have expected anyone to breach the battery. On your planet, don't you simply toss everything away?"

David was surprised. "Wouldn't it have exploded if it had been burned with the trash?"

Zia looked at him askance. "If it had simply been thrown away, it would not have exploded. The heat of a trash fire wouldn't have breached the battery. For the battery to explode, it would have to be physically *breached*—and at a time when it still contained considerable energy. How *did* you dispose of it?"

David shrugged. "I believe it was taped to a stick of dynamite and thrown into a pit."

"What is the explosive ingredient in dynamite?"

"Nitroglycerine."

Zia smirked. "That'll do it."

Zia searched his memory for a long time.

"What are you thinking of?" asked David.

"I'm trying to remember how long I had that bag, so I can assess what Inanna may have learned from the transmitter." He relaxed. "Never mind for now. Permit me to ask: Is there anything I can do for you?"

"Well," said David hesitantly, "I've been waiting to ask you this, so you should expect quite a request."

Zia nodded sagely, as though he already knew. "You want to meet Lord Enki."

David was shocked. "How did you know?"

"Every creature wants to meet its maker. Remember Frankenstein's monster?"

David was impressed by Zia's awareness of English Romantic literature. "Of course. But unlike Frankenstein's monster, I hold no ill will toward Lord Enki."

"Ah, yes," said Zia thoughtfully, and recited from memory a line spoken by the monster to his creator, "I ought to be thy Adam, but I am rather thy fallen angel.'"

David silently considered the parallels between the plot of that story and his current predicament. "Incidentally, when you say *every* creature wants to meet its maker, do you include the Anunnaki in the class of 'creatures'?"

Zia smiled fondly. "Ah, the Great Questions. I think I'll leave those to be addressed by Lord Enki."

"When can I meet him?" asked David, his heart pounding in anticipation.

"Let me find out," said Zia, taking out his phone. He texted off a few lines and put it back in his pocket. "They'll be back to me in a few minutes. Meanwhile, if I may ask, where is the blonde beauty who accompanied you to Africa?"

David sighed. "I'm embarrassed and saddened to admit that I don't know. She was on the platform yesterday for my inaugural kiss by Queen Inanna."

Zia grimaced. "Oh, my. Yes, I hadn't thought of that. How did she react?"

"Pretty much as you'd expect. She stormed off the platform before I even boarded this craft."

"Have you tried to contact her since?"

"Yes, but she hasn't gotten back to me. I even contacted her boss, but he hasn't gotten back to me yet, either."

Zia shrugged. "She may be busy on other matters."

Zia's phone buzzed. He took it out to look at it. "You're in luck," he said. "If you accompany me back to Lord Enki's pyramidion, he will see you. But it has to be a short meeting, as the Council will soon be meeting to try to identify the person or persons who launched that missile yesterday." He said hesitantly, "I'm not sure the Queen would want you going to Lord Enki's pyramidion before she does."

"I don't work for the Queen, Doctor Zia. How long is the trip to Lord Enki's craft?"

"Not long," said Zia, "perhaps a half hour. I'll see if we can get some food for the shuttle."

"Great idea, but I'm not permitted to eat any animal products," David mentioned.

"Nor am I," said Zia. "It's not healthy for the sons of Adam."

"May I bring my computer?" asked David.

"Certainly. There are a few things I really should tell you before you're admitted to see Lord Enki," said Zia.

"Shall I wear Elijah's mantle?" asked David.

"I don't see the harm in it, as it was Lord Enki who ensured it would be given to you." Zia looked at David uncertainly. "You should know that Lord Enki does not look precisely … as we do."

"You mean to say he is more Queen Inanna's size?"

"Well, no. I mean, he *is* larger than we are, but—the men in the Anunnaki royal family … *change* as they reach extreme age."

"How?"

"Well, their voices deepen and they begin to feel the burden of their longevity—"

"So far, they sound like *us* when we age."

Zia shook his head. "*No*—well—you'll see quite soon."

CHAPTER 6

JUST AS LORD Enki's pyramidion came into view in the shuttle's forward window, David and Doctor Zia finished their meals and Zia's valet Enkidu began clearing away the debris.

From a distance, Enki's pyramidion had seemed the same size as Inanna's, but as the shuttlecraft approached it became clear that Enki's was at least twice the height and width. Enkidu skillfully docked the craft, and it took only about thirty seconds for the air pressure in the cabin to equalize.

As the doors opened to the pyramidion proper, they entered a nibirode-lined hallway where Zia was greeted by Yasmin, Lord Enki's principal housekeeper. As she was clothed in simple Sumerian dress, she might have been mistaken for one of Enki's more mundane servants, so a few measures had been taken to distinguish her appearance. Her shapely face was beautifully made up and she sported a sturdy gold chain from which hung a golden caduceus bejeweled in rubies, yellow sapphires, emeralds, and lapis lazuli. The overall effect was stunning, and David wondered whether Inanna would resent Yasmin on such grounds.

"Yasmin," said Zia, "is Lord Enki in the presence chamber?"

"He is, Doctor Zia," she replied and turned to David with a comely smile. "Is this Professor Schubert, about whom we have heard so much?"

David bowed courteously. "At your service," he said.

Yasmin tittered. "Hardly, professor. It is I who am at *your* service." Turning back to Zia, she asked, "Shall I escort the professor to Lord Enki?"

Zia shook his head. "That won't be necessary. I'll escort him."

David and Zia took an elevator up a few flights. As on Inanna's pyramidion, the elevator greeted each of them by name and moved only when they began to speak. When the doors opened on Enki's floor, David's breath was stolen by what greeted him. This level of the pyramidion was about twice the height of the level from which they'd just come. Some twenty feet from floor to ceiling, it exhibited a kind of capaciousness never seen in spacecraft made on Earth.

Immediately outside the elevator began a wide, dimly lit hallway. At its opposite end stood two imposing doors, fourteen feet in height, fashioned of darkly stained, polished wood resembling mahogany. Emblazoned above the entire width of the double doors was a glowing inscription in Hebrew lettering spangled in precious gems of many colors. Although David had learned as a child how to sound out Hebrew words, this inscription, like the Torah, bore no vowels to guide him. And he'd never acquired much of a Hebrew vocabulary.

With Zia right behind him, David approached the doors and stood in awe of the inscription. "What does it say?" he asked.

Zia took a big breath, as though he'd been asked this most consequential of questions many, many times. "The nearest I've come to an English translation is: *No Malice But What You Bring.*"

David nodded slowly, hesitant to take another step, his breathing restricted by the weight of the moment.

Zia shuffled and said, "Your spoken reply to the inscription is awaited. I'm forbidden to help you compose it."

For a moment David felt helpless, but then realized that the required reply was obvious. He said aloud, "I bear no malice."

The words had barely left his mouth when the lock clicked open and one of the doors opened an inch. He turned with trepidation to Zia, who looked on staunchly.

"Prepare yourself," Zia urged.

David sighed. "I think I might stand here until I die of old age, and yet never be prepared … for this."

He put his hand on the door that was already ajar and shoved it gently inward, surprised at how easily it moved. Before even stepping inside alone, he was struck by the twin scents of limestone and clean moisture.

Though the large, dim hall was beautifully finished and bore no sign of rough stone, still it felt like a chamber in a cavern far underground. No light entered the room from outside and there were, as far as David could see, no internal lights either, save for a few along the floor that phosphoresced like runway guides. David was awestruck, for the source of nearly all light in the chamber was Enki's own person.

On a throne across the room sat Enki, a muscular blond Anunnaki whose height David guessed to be nearly eight feet. From his eyes shone golden beams that made it impossible to look into his eyes or even study his face. On his torso he wore a simple white robe much as depicted in ancient Sumerian reliefs, and from his waist hung a traditional *shendyt.*

"Come forward, *adam*," said Enki. The voice, though effortless, was the loudest and deepest David had ever heard, the words echoing sonorously off the stone walls before dying away.

David moved forward hesitantly until he was perhaps ten feet from the glowing figure. He bowed respectfully. "Good morning, Lord Enki," said David, his voice sounding thin and dull by comparison, like that of a mouse addressing a man.

"Ziusudra tells me you wish to meet your maker," said Lord Enki. "When first I found your kind, you ate only plants and drank out of puddles with the lower animals. There was much promise in you then, much willingness to help one another. Together with my half-sister Ninharsag, I fashioned you into what you have become. And now you are as numerous as the stars in heaven." He sighed. "But, as nature would have it, we inadvertently made you more like ourselves in temperament than I care to admit. That failing—and your uncontrollable drive to procreate—have nearly destroyed you."

David was humbled by this assessment from one who'd been there from the Beginning.

Enki resumed. "As for seeking your ultimate Maker, I regret to tell you that you and I are on the same quest. Just as you are a creature, so am I. Just as you seek the Ultimate Cause of all things, so do I. Your search for the Ultimate Cause must continue past this day and this place. While I regret your disappointment, I cannot profess to have created the universe. Nor does King Enlil, nor did King Anu, our father before us."

David hung his head low. "It is I who am sorry to have disappointed you, Lord Enki. For thousands of years, the best among us have striven to improve our conduct and the conditions endured by all mankind, succeeding only in part and only occasionally. Despite the best efforts of many, we have suffered frequent setbacks of which we ourselves have been the principal authors."

Enki nodded in understanding. "As have we. Even now, we suspect that those who fired the missile at Inanna's craft are of our own kind, some fully, others perhaps only partially. But they all bear the mark of the Anunnaki."

"I expect," said David, "that the armed forces of my country are even now investigating the launch point of the missile."

Lord Enki turned his head askew. "Do you mean that they are traveling to the launch point even now?"

"I expect so."

Enki pressed a button on the arm of his throne. "Ningishzidda, are you there?"

"I am, my lord," came the reply.

"Ningishzidda," said Enki, "did you order a shootdown of the missile fired at Queen Inanna's craft?"

"I rather ordered a *turnabout*, my lord."

"Why?" Enki shot back. "You know we never turn a missile about to detonate in any area unless we know it to be populated solely by combatants responsible for the launch."

What's this? thought David with alarm. *A turnabout sends the missile back to explode at the launch point?* He broke out in a sweat.

"It's the Arctic Ocean, Lord Enki," said Ningishzidda. "I thought it reasonable to expect there to be no more than a handful of non-combatants."

"We do not slaughter *any* non-combatants, Ningishzidda, unless there is no choice," said Lord Enki in his booming voice.

David was reminded that the Lord allowed Abraham to dissuade him from destroying Sodom and Gomorrah though there be no more than ten righteous inhabitants. Evidently, this was Anunnaki custom of long standing.

Enki snarled, "Countermand the turnabout order at once!"

"It's too late, my lord," Ningishzidda entreated. "The turnabout missile is in its final orbit and will no longer accept a self-destruction order."

"How much time is there before it reaches its detonation point?"

"Let me check, my lord." Ningishzidda paused. "Just less than one Earth hour."

David raised his hands to his head in dismay. *So, that's what Sharon was telling me: Catharine has been sent to the launch point and a nuclear explosion!* "Lord Enki," he said, "please excuse me. I need to contact my government."

⟞➤∘⟤⟚∘⟝

"SURE WOULD BE nice to know what we're lookin' for," said Buck over the intercom of an F-18D Hornet darting out of a clear southern sky with just a hint of daylight behind it. The air was frigid, the sky cloudless, and there was a clear view of the snowy ground.

"Just keep your eyes open, Buck," said Catharine from the rear of the cockpit. "If there's nothin', there's nothin'. But, as far as we know, there's no way to launch a missile undersea without some kind of submarine platform."

"If it was a sub," said Buck, "then they're mobile. What are the odds they'd still be hangin' around, waitin' for us to find 'em?"

"If they're still around, chances are it's to take a shot at us." She laughed. "Be especially careful if they've got square beards and warmup suits."

Buck laughed. "You really *hate* those guys, don't you?"

She thought of their flight up here. "Remember that metallic reflection I saw when we flew over the shore at Great Slave Lake?"

He laughed. "Don't tell me you could see those guys down there. *Nobody's* got eyes that good."

"No," she said, "but I just *know* that was them crawling around down there."

"They give you the heebie-jeebies, huh?"

"I hold a grudge," she said. "If it's the same guys, those bastards already took a couple shots at me on the ground in Paris. Let's see how courageous they are when they're starin' up the business end of a twenty-five-millimeter cannon. How many river craft did we see comin' up here on the Mackenzie River?"

"Two, as far as I could tell," he replied.

"What're the odds they were being piloted by those guys?" she said. "Wouldn't you like to stick one up their ass?"

He laughed. "This is a reconnaissance flyover, lieutenant commander. We don't even have a *primary* target, let alone targets of opportunity. You *know* there's only one way we can take a shot at them."

She visually scanned the icy ground below and muttered, "They have to take a shot at us first."

"Couple of minutes we'll be feet wet," said Buck, meaning that they'd be over water. The jet banked to starboard. "Take heart. We'll soon be at maximum exposure to a shot from a submarine."

<hr>

"LORD ENKI," SAID David, repressing panic, "I expect that someone I know is heading for the launch point. I need to notify them to stay clear of the area, or they will surely perish."

Enki thought quietly for a moment, and David could imagine what was going through his mind. *I have let this ambassador know vital military information. I could forcibly detain him until the information becomes useless. But what would that gain us? Innocent people would be killed, and we would have given the earthlings grounds to condemn us as heartless butchers.*

There was a knock at the big double entrance doors.

"Come," said Lord Enki.

Doctor Zia entered. "You have need of me, my lord?"

David had been watching closely, and was certain Enki had done nothing to summon Doctor Zia. Zia had just … shown up.

"Evidently," said Enki, "the ambassador knows someone who will be killed by the turnabout missile, which will detonate in less than an hour. Please escort him to the communications room and provide him with every possible assistance." He turned his unnerving eyes toward David. "Do what you can, ambassador. If you have no luck, come back to me."

Before leaving, Zia said to Lord Enki, "Only four members of the Council have come in person, my lord. As you instructed, I've had them escorted to the Council chamber upstairs. King Enlil is prepared to participate holographically."

Enki did nothing to conceal his disappointment. "Only four?"

"Yes, my lord."

"Well," said Enki with a shrug, "I suppose over these distances it can't be helped. But, as you know, when my father sat on the throne, if we were within reach, we bent the laws of physics to attend in person. Now, go help the ambassador save his friend."

⟶○⟣⟨⟨⟨○⟵

THE MAIN WINDOW of the Council chamber looked out on Earth's western hemisphere from the Way of Enlil, so that its viewpoint corresponded with the Tropic of Cancer. In present sight was the very north of the United States and the totality of its vast northern neighbor, known as Canada.

At the center of the chamber stood the historic Council table built ages earlier at the instruction of their numinous ancestor An, to accommodate the Twelve Great Ones. Carved from dense, dark wood ripped from trees of ancient Nibiru (some now believed to be extinct), the table bore the scoring, dents, and scratches of millennia of furious argument.

Though the composition of the pantheon itself would necessarily change with the death or disability of its members, the number of the Twelve Great Ones would remain forever constant.

Ningishzidda was already in attendance, as he'd already been aboard and had had no need to travel. He rose respectfully to welcome the agèd Shamash and Sin, cupping the hand of Shamash in his own.

"Tell me," said Shamash, "will we see the courageous Ninurta at our meeting?"

Ningishzidda embraced Shamash, who'd been retired from active life for many years, and said, "That is very unlikely."

"No," said the old man with evident disappointment, as though he was hearing it for the first time. "Why not? He is such a powerful ally."

"Do you not remember the time Ninurta used the forbidden weapons against Marduk in the Sinai Desert"—he nodded toward Sin—"a desert named for our cousin Sin—and then the poison cloud destroyed Sumeria and took the life of Ninurta's own wife Bau?"

"That's terrible," said the old man upon hearing the ancient news as though it were a current event. "Is Bau dead, then?"

Ningishzidda nodded his head respectfully, though this must have been the thousandth time he'd reminded the old man of these events of so long ago. "Oh, yes, dear Shamash. Bau died, and Ninurta has never really recovered." He led the doddering old fellow slowly to his seat, and said, "May I fetch some tea for you? Or perhaps for you, Sin?"

Both declined, preoccupied with thoughts of bygone days.

The door opened, and Queen Inanna entered the Council chamber accompanied by her maidservant Shiduri. The three male Anunnaki already in attendance rose respectfully and lowered their gaze as Inanna was escorted to her seat at the table.

Shamash smiled. "Young woman, you are so beautiful! You remind me of my twin sister Inanna."

Ningishzidda looked at Inanna as though begging her to forbear from her usual snappishness, but to no avail.

"I *am* your twin, old man," said Inanna. "Have you forgotten your own sister?"

Shamash drew a noisy breath. "Inanna! That cannot be. How do you stay so beautiful? So young?"

She dismissed the question with a wave and a retort. "I eat right," she replied.

The lights suddenly dimmed.

"Ah, the Lord Enki comes," said Inanna.

Everyone rose. The door opened, and Enki entered with Doctor Zia at his side.

"Good morning, my lord," said Inanna, catching sight of Zia, "but must you bring *him* here?"

"You're quite right, my lady," said Enki in his deep voice. "No one may remain at Council other than family. Alas, that means that the lovely

Shiduri must go, as well." He signaled Zia to return to helping David.

Zia held the door for Shiduri on their way out.

Enki took a seat at the center of the table and pushed a button. "Please admit King Enlil whenever he's ready to join us."

In a couple of minutes, a colorful glow slowly appeared in the chair directly across from Enki and resolved into a man-sized moving hologram of King Enlil that glowed nearly as brightly as Lord Enki himself.

Everyone bowed to the king's image.

"Welcome, brother," said Enki and paused more than two minutes for his greeting to reach the king millions of miles away, and for the king's reply to return over the same distance.

"Thank you, Brother Enki, and welcome, cousins," said Enlil. "Please resume as you were. I am most relieved to see the lovely Queen Inanna unharmed. I understand there was a serious incident a few hours ago. Please proceed with your meeting."

Enki folded his hands and spoke to the image. "There was indeed a serious incident, Your Majesty. I've convened this meeting of the Council to discuss what measures should be taken in this regard."

Shamash spoke out of turn. "*What* happened a few hours ago?" he asked, notwithstanding that he'd already been told.

"Shamash," said Enki, "someone on Earth fired a missile at Queen Inanna's pyramidion."

Shamash's eyes went wide. "Who fired it?"

"That's a very important question," said Enki indulgently. "Does anyone have a suspect they'd care to take up with the Council?"

"Why, it must have been an earthling!" said Shamash. "Someone who doesn't wish to see us return."

Enki shook his head. "I doubt that to be the case. For one thing, our disarming ray was in operation in the entire Arctic region at the time of the launch. As far as we can tell, the earthlings are as yet incapable of overcoming our advanced defenses to any extent. Evidently, they've taken to throwing sharpened sticks at one another. Unfortunately, we haven't come up with a ray that disables sharp sticks." He turned to the image of Enlil. "I fear the culprits are persons—*not* earthlings—nursing a lasting grudge against the Anunnaki. Perhaps these persons have begun to colonize the Earth themselves and wish to discourage Anunnaki from doing the same, but we have yet to determine who that might be."

"There's always Zu," said Inanna quietly. "Perhaps under the banner of Anzû, the fire-breathing dragon. Of course, it was Ninurta who ultimately defeated Anzû and retrieved the Tablets of Destiny but, alas, Ninurta is absent."

Enki reminded Shamash, "Ninurta has not been seen by any of us for many years. He is still mourning the death of his departed wife."

Inanna turned to Enki. "Ninurta was not allowed to finish his task, for when he dragged Anzû before Lord Enki for judgment, Lord Enki—against all advice—decreed his banishment, rather than death, thus assuring that Anzû would live on to vex us. To put the mortals at ease, the execution of Anzû was publicly 'reenacted' year after year, but in fact the execution never took place."

Enki turned on Inanna. "What was Anzû's crime, again? Oh, that's right. He *stole* the Tablets of Destinies from Enlil, without which no one could land on Earth or leave it."

"You subtly imply that *I* stole crafts and wisdom from *you*," Inanna said with irritation. "May I remind my cousin Enki that you *gave* them to me freely?"

"That was when I thought of you as my own daughter," said Enki, "a mistake I shall never repeat. I assumed that you would show me the *fealty* of a daughter, and that, should I require your return, you would come back. Instead, you refused my several clear demands for your return. In fact, you refused to return despite my minister Isimud following you to the ends of the Earth a half-dozen times and commanding you in my name to return."

Inanna looked at Enki darkly. "How could I believe Isimud, when he told me that Enki had demanded something that Enki *himself* had personally assured me he would *never* demand? I could not countenance the dog's insolence in calling his lord a liar. Even now, I can barely believe that you wished to take back from me all you had given."

"Ingrate," said Enki with a sneer.

"Seducer," replied Inanna.

"*Seductress*," Enki shot back.

Ningishzidda interrupted this family spat. "This is a waste of the king's time. Do you think we might get on with items of current business instead of revisiting ancient history?"

When the simmering cousins settled down at last, Ningishzidda said to Enki, "Father, do you really believe that no one other than an earthling or Anzû could possibly bear a grudge against the Anunnaki? Have we behaved so admirably as that?"

"There are many who've held grudges against us," replied Enki, "mainly for refusing their demands for immortality. Foremost among them we must count Gilgamesh. Later, many pharaohs also felt cheated by our refusal to confer immortality upon them. By definition, however, all those men are long dead."

"Some may have living descendants," observed Inanna.

"What about the frog people?" asked Ningishzidda.

Enki shook his head emphatically. "We have known the Dagon for thousands of Sars. Never have they made a single aggressive move against us, although I will grant you it's unnerving to be the object of unremitting scrutiny."

"They could have put *others* up to it," said Ningishzidda. "Could they not?"

"To what end?" asked Enki. "What do they need?"

Ningishzidda smirked. "Another swamp to breed in?"

Enki interrupted. "Ningishzidda," he admonished, "it is difficult enough for the king to manage the foreign affairs of Nibiru without your insulting regimes that have consistently supported us."

Inanna said, "But the Dagon *did* fire a weapon that neutralized our disabling ray long enough to necessitate Shulgi's withdrawal from the field at Westminster."

Enki said, "Let us await the king's view," and they sat quietly waiting for Enlil's delayed response.

Enlil shook his head impatiently at Inanna. "Beloved of Anu," said Enlil forbearingly, "at Westminster the weapon was not fired at us, nor did its discharge neutralize our disabling ray. It was our overhasty *response* that did that. Besides," he continued, "what was at stake at that pointless confrontation? Inanna, how many casualties were suffered by Shulgi's forces?"

Inanna bowed contritely in her seat. "None, my liege."

The Council awaited Enlil's reply.

At last, Enlil continued. "And the Dagon warned us that a missile had been fired at your pyramidion, and also informed us of its probable launch point. Enki, my brother, I think we have insufficient information to determine who our adversary is. Until we have more information on that question, it is impossible to develop a strategy, except to remain on alert at all times, and expect the unexpected. I leave you to that task; I have other matters before me at the moment. The southerners on Nibiru have presented a whole new set of demands for me to address. I will discuss them with you later, Lord Enki. Now, if there are no objections, I will leave this Council meeting for now, and remain available on call. Go in peace, my subjects," said Enlil's image, and the others bowed as it faded out.

Enki glanced around the room. "Thank you all for coming. I remain open to suggestions. Conference adjourned."

As everyone rose to leave, there was a frantic series of knocks at the door. Enki pressed the Release button, and in rushed David and Doctor Zia.

"Lord Enki," said Zia excitedly. "We have spoken with the American authorities. They confirm that the ambassador's friend is performing an overflight of the launch area, but their base's communications have been knocked out by a blizzard and they are unable to communicate with the craft."

THE FIGHTER HAD just reached the launch site and was doing its high-altitude overflight. The plan was to do a lower overflight on the way home. Though daylight had dimmed, a little remained.

"You catchin' that metallic glint down there?" asked Catharine.

"I see it," replied Buck.

"Is that on land or in the water?" she asked.

"Looks like maybe … an ice floe?"

"So what's made of metal?" asked Catharine.

"Have no idea. Didn't look like much. Definitely not a launch."

The fighter's alarm sounded.

"Shit!" said Buck. "Musta been radar, 'cause it's lightin' us up. Strap in tight!"

"What do we do now?" asked Catharine, completely out of her element.

"Now?" said Buck, suddenly adopting that professionally calm fly-boy attitude Catharine had grown to respect. "Now we flip over, dump a load of Grade-A Reynolds aluminum foil chaff, and head for the ground."

"Why the *ground?*" she asked as the blood suddenly rushed to her head, disorienting her. She couldn't believe Buck was laughing aloud, like he was having fun.

"'Cause if those are radar-guided missiles, they can see only what the guy who fired 'em can see, so we're gonna put as much crap between him and us as we can. If *he* can't see us, the *missiles* can't, either."

"What if they're *not* radar guided?" she asked.

"Then I'm doin' this all wrong, and we're gonna have to hit Reset."

"Great. What can we put between him and us?" she asked.

"Name it. Hills, buildings, trees—"

"*Trees?*" she shouted. "How low can you go in this thing?"

"Let's find out," he said, beginning a power dive that left Catharine's stomach about two miles above her head. "When we get down to the treetops, I'll say go. You stick your arm out and grab an orange."

"Hilarious," she said, hanging on for dear life.

"Sorry," he said, "it's a lot funnier when you're over Florida. No orange trees up here, I guess, but I couldn't think of what anybody'd want from these snowy trees. A snowball, maybe."

Now they *were* flying just above the treetops.

"Coming up on the bad-guy SAM installation," said Buck. "Looks like only one shooter. Damn! It *is* on an ice floe!"

Two missiles appeared up ahead, moving away from them.

"The missiles are already confused. Look, they're going by on your right, so give 'em the finger. Comin' up on the SAM site now. You want me to tear up those square-bearded bastards for ya?"

"Frickin *'eh!* Make a bunch o' holes in their goddam warmup suits."

But, just as Buck was taking aim at the SAM site, a godlike voice came to them from above.

⟶◦⟫◦⟵

"AMBASSADOR," SAID ENKI, "Is the overflight in orbit or in the atmosphere?"

David answered glumly. "In the atmosphere, my lord, but I have no way of letting them know they're in peril."

"I'll talk to them," he assured David.

Could it be? David wondered. *Is it possible?*

"How?" he asked.

"Never mind that now," said Enki. "But they won't be expecting to hear from me, so we must convince them. Where do you want them to go?"

"Yellowknife," David replied. "That's the base they left from."

"And what can I tell them," asked Enki, "so they'll believe that the message originated with you?"

David's mind raced, and his mind lighted on a bit of intimacy only he and Catharine would know. "Say the message is from *Not Trevor.*"

Enki looked at him skeptically, shrugged, then turned to his son. "Ningishzidda, what were the launch coordinates?"

Ningishzidda called the coordinates up on a virtual screen that float-ed above the Council table.

Enki examined the coordinates, raised his mighty arm, and pointed his finger at that location on the Earth's surface, visible through the great window.

"I, Lord Enki of Nibiru," his voice rang out, "beseech you, on behalf of *Not Trevor* to return immediately to Yellowknife base. Know that you are under immediate threat of nuclear annihilation if you remain where you are. Go now, as fast as you can!"

IT TOOK A moment for Catharine to regain her senses. "Buck, did you hear that?"

"What do you mean, did I *hear* it?" said Buck. "I think it knocked my fillings out. It's burned onto my brain! Who the hell is *Enki*? Who's *Not Trevor*?"

"*Not Trevor* is the Kid from Canarsie," she replied, "and only he and I know that. Make a sharp left immediately and go south with all the speed you can muster! Forget about the squarebeards. Let 'em fry in their own juices!"

The jet banked to port and the afterburners shoved Buck and Cath-arine back in their seats.

Buck glanced at his dials. "Uh oh," he said.

"What?" she demanded.

"We've got company," he said, "dropping from orbit. Could be the nuke. It's only about ten miles back."

"Buck, go faster or we're toast!"

"I will, but I've gotta get a little altitude, or the concussion could smash us into the ground!" The nose climbed steadily.

About thirty seconds later, Buck said, "If I run wet like this for too long we won't have enough fuel to reach Yellowknife. And there are no happy landings for this aircraft between here and there."

"What do you mean, *run wet*?" asked Catharine.

"*Wet* means with afterburners. Those babies go through fuel like a fire hose sucks water. Dry means *without* afterbu—"

A mechanical female voice came on the radio and interrupted him. "Turnabout destination attained," she intoned. Then, in infuriatingly calm tones, she rattled off a set of coordinates (sounding too close for comfort), and ended with a single word:

"Detonating."

In a few seconds the cockpit flashed with a white light such as nothing Catharine had ever imagined. The explosion she'd overflown in Namibia was in no way comparable to this. The Namibia explosion had been perhaps a kiloton in strength and may not even have been a fission bomb.

By comparison, the bomb behind the plane right now left no doubt it was a far more powerful *fusion* bomb whose explosive strength would be measurable in *megatons*.

Five seconds later, the jet was hit with a shock wave that rattled its bones and forced it down about a thousand feet. Thanks to Buck's foresight, that still left them at an altitude of about a thousand feet.

But they'd flown into a blizzard, and Buck pulled them back up to normal cruising altitude to get above it.

"My butt's hot," said Buck with a smirk. "How about yours, lieutenant commander?"

"I just hope we don't die of radiation poisoning," said Catharine, ignoring his inappropriate remark.

"Nah," said Buck. "We had to be thirty miles from Ground Zero at detonation, and movin' away like a bat out of hell. We'll be okay." He glanced at a video screen that looked backward from the cockpit. The explosion had sprouted into the upper levels of the atmosphere and was spreading out into the classic mushroom-shaped cloud. Although the sun had left the sky, it was still brighter than day. "Well, one thing's certain," he said with a dry mouth. "That SAM site is no more." He relaxed a little. "Glad *that's* over with."

Catharine gritted her teeth. "It's not over with until we've kicked some squarebeard butt of our own."

"Let's not get ahead of ourselves," he said. "We've got another tough task to accomplish first."

"What's that?" she asked.

"Landing this jet in a blizzard."

"Isn't it equipped with an arresting hook?" she asked.

Buck rolled his eyes. "Yes, it is, ma'am," he said patronizingly. "And a U.S. aircraft carrier is equipped with an arresting *cable*. Now, if you could just direct me to the nearest U.S. aircraft carrier on Great Slave Lake, we'll be all set."

"There are no carriers on the lake," she mumbled.

"Exactly," he replied. "Fortunately, there *are* some airstrips on land that have an arresting cable, usually only one apiece—and just for emergencies. Let's hope Yellowknife is one of them, and that the cable's not frozen. I'll call it in."

But his call garnered no reply from Yellowknife base. Buck checked his radio frequency and tried again. There was definitely someone *trying* to reply, but they were out of range.

"What does that mean?" asked Catharine.

"I think Yellowknife power's out," he said, "and their emergency power isn't strong enough to reach us here. I'll try again in a half hour."

Chapter 7

The President and Admiral Simmons sat across from each other in the Oval Office. After a final, futile attempt to get through to the F-18, the President hung up the phone.

"Sorry, Bob," said the President morosely. "I'm fresh out of ideas. Even the satellite can't get a message through to the F-18 or Yellowknife. Must be a *killer* blizzard up there. Atmospheric conditions are hostile, and the base's main power is down."

"It's an *air base*," said the admiral, refusing to give up. "Air bases have backup power, don't they?"

"*Ours* do," said the President. "The Canadians'?" He shrugged. "I suppose they do, but they probably just protect emergency systems: medical equipment, local heat, refrigeration, and so forth. I would have bet their communications would be up; but even if they have full power, comms can be degraded by weather conditions if they're bad enough. I'm sorry, Bob. I know how much you care for Catharine."

The admiral stared at his shoes for a while, unwilling to take the next step. "Well," he said, "I'll have to call the ambassador with the bad news. Maybe there's something they can do from up there." He brushed some lint from his jacket. "Besides, Buck and Catharine could have been grounded by the weather before even taking off from Yellowknife."

The President nodded encouragingly. "Or they could already have finished with the overflight and cleared the area. We just don't know."

The admiral put his hand on the phone. "Can I call from here?"

The President nodded, and the admiral picked up the phone.

"Hello, David?" said the admiral. "We've pulled every rabbit out of the hat. Nothin' doin'." *Pause.* "*Nah*, we tried that. Even the satellite. But, hey, did you try everything *they* can do from up in orbit? They gotta have superpowers, those people." *Pause.* "Well, you go ahead and try that. If the guy could make you and me out of monkeys, he can do anything." *Pause.* "Yes, of course. Go ask him right now. I'll let you know if we hear anything."

Click.

The President needed a cup of coffee. He picked up the intercom.

"Holly?" he said.

"Coffee's on its way up, sir," said Holly. "I'll knock when it's here."

"Okay, thanks," said the President.

The admiral shook his head. "Sooner or later, I'm going to have to call Catharine's father. He's U.K. Coast Guard."

"Does he know about the mission?"

The admiral shook his head. "No."

"Then don't call him until you know for sure. You'll just worry him."

"If we can't get a message to her," said the admiral, "I won't be able to wait indefinitely. Her father's entitled to know. This waiting is killin' me."

"It'd be worse for *him*," said the President.

There was a knock at the door, and coffee service was wheeled in. The phone rang and the admiral picked it up.

"Mm-hmm. Mm-hmm."

The President watched from behind his desk, and was pleased to see the admiral's face suddenly light up and fill with wonder. "From his *hand*?" *Pause.* "*Not* Trevor? What the hell? Oh, *Trevor*! He was that haughty upper-class twit in the U.K. Clever choice on your part. She hates his guts." *Pause.* "Is there any way she can confirm she got the message?" *Pause.* "I don't know. Through his *other* hand? Okay, let me know as soon as you learn. I'll do the same."

Click.

The admiral looked at the President with mixed emotions, but one of them was hope. "Enki—that's the head guy up there—sent an evacuation order to the lieutenant commander *by hand*."

"He sent a messenger?" asked the President dubiously.

The admiral shook his head. "He raised his *hand*, pointed to the original launch coordinates through the spaceship window, and spoke the message aloud. David's convinced she'll receive it, but there's no way to know until they report in and Yellowknife's communications are restored."

"I take it the aliens don't know who fired the nuke at them?" said the President.

"Evidently not," replied the admiral. "But David seems to have gained their confidence already, and they seem not to suspect *us*."

"Well," said the President, "that's something, especially since we have no way of defending or retaliating if they were to take action against us. My question is, who fired the missile? Because whoever did it obviously overcame the Anunnaki's disabling ray. We're already at the mercy of the Anunnaki. But this means we're also at the mercy of whoever figured out how to disable their ray."

"By the way," said the admiral, "how's that project going? Any of our geniuses figure out what materials will block the ray?"

"Not yet," replied the President. The intercom buzzed, and the President picked up. "Who is it, Holly?"

"I've got two calls with lots of generals on the phone, sir. They called at the same time. Do you want NORAD or the War Room at the Pentagon?"

"Patch them together and tell them to wait," the President said and hung up. "Geez," said the President sardonically, "I wonder if there's been a nuclear explosion near the North Pole."

The admiral pointed to the phone with his chin. "You better talk to the brass now, or they're liable to do something you wouldn't like on the pretext that they couldn't get hold of you. Want me to wait outside?"

The President's eyebrows shot up. "Not on your life. In fact, you answer the call. Put 'em on the squawk box."

The admiral pressed the button. "Oval Office. Admiral Bob Simmons here. The President is here, but signing some papers. Can I help you?"

Several voices spoke at once.

"Now hold on, everyone," said the admiral. "Who's the ranking officer?"

After a moment's delay, the Secretary of Defense came on the line. "Depends what you mean by *officer*, admiral. This is SecDef."

"Well, that sounds about right to me, Mister Secretary. What shall I tell the President this call is about?"

"Admiral," said the secretary, "we've received an unprompted voice message from way up in the Arctic Circle, which was immediately followed by detonation of a hydrogen bomb at the same coordinates." Frustration was evident in the secretary's voice. "Admiral, would you please put the President on now? This is pretty urgent."

"He's listening, SecDef. I promise you."

"Okay, well, the voice message—a female voice, but it sounded mechanical—announced its coordinates and said it was detonating."

"Strange," said the admiral. "In which language did it make the announcement?"

"English, admiral."

"How big was the explosion?"

"Far as we can tell? Thirty megatons."

The admiral whistled softly. "Wow! They must have been going for some big fish. What's up north that would warrant such a huge payload?"

"That's what's got us all scratching our heads, admiral. There's nothing up there but a few Eskimos—Inuits—indigenous people."

"How far was the detonation from the nearest population center?" asked the admiral.

"Gotta be seventy miles."

"Seventy miles?" said the admiral. "Any submarines up there?"

"Not that we know of, admiral. And definitely not one of ours. I thought of that immediately, since these are virtually the same coordinates where that renegade launch took place recently." There was the sound of papers being shuffled. "Admiral, I'm not sure I've mentioned this yet, but the nuke appeared to drop in from orbit. Also, I just received a message that, a few minutes prior to detonation, a surface-to-air missile was launched nearby. We don't know if there was some connection."

The President and the admiral locked eyes. The President spoke for the first time on the call. "Did the SAM hit anything, SecDef?"

"Oh, hello, Mister President. Not as far as we can tell, but we've got computer guys all over the data from that few minutes. We'll let you know if it turns out the SAM hit anything."

"Give that top priority," said the President. "We had some important people in the area, and we need to know."

"Yes, sir."

"Before you get preoccupied with identifying who fired the nuke," said the President, "our ambassador to the Anunnaki just told us that the Anunnaki didn't shoot down the missile that was fired at them, but rather turned it back to detonate at its launch point—"

The Secretary of Defense interrupted. "We've had battlefield weapons for years that do the same thing—"

"I'm aware, SecDef," said the President. "The nuke that detonated was probably the one that was originally launched against the Anunnaki. While I expect you'll check the accuracy of that intelligence against your fissile data, at the moment we don't regard the nuke as having been fired upon the USA or Canada either by the Anunnaki or a hostile terrestrial power. Please feel free to share that assessment with Canadian intelligence. If we can keep this whole thing within the intelligence community, that would be great. If we can't, I'll address the nation and put everyone's mind at ease as well as I can."

"Okay, Mister President, but I strongly doubt we're going to be able to keep it quiet. Thirty megatons of TNT shakes a lot of dirt and releases a lot of fallout into the atmosphere, and with all the seismic and sniffing equipment around the world—"

"Do the best you can," said the President. "Thanks. Gotta go."

"YELLOWKNIFE," BUCK SAID into the mic for the fifth time, "this is Yankee F-18, coming from the north. We've got a pilot and one VIP aboard. Request clearance for landing. Over."

The last four calls had resulted in what sounded like the beginning of a crackly transmission, but no voice had followed.

At last, a recognizable voice came on, interrupted by intermittent static.

"Yankee F-18, this is Yellowknife. We read you, and we see you on air traffic control. Do you read us? Over."

"Yes!" said Buck with great relief. "We got our tailfeathers singed up north and we're a little low on fuel, so if we could do this on the first pass, that would be great. Over."

"We're moving tons of snow every minute trying to accommodate you." The voice snickered. "Now, what'll you do for your northern neighbors if we can manage that? Over."

Buck glanced at Catharine with a wink, and replied. "I'd say that would get our northern neighbors a hearty round of Molson's the kind you *can't* get in the States—and three verses of the Canadian national anthem. Over."

"Nobody down here knows a third verse, Yankee, so we'll be interested to hear what you sing. Over."

"Hell, Yellowknife, we'll *compose* a third verse if you don't have one, but right now we've got to get this bad boy on the pavement in one piece. You got a runway long enough? Over."

"Oh, we've got plenty of runways over a mile long, but I doubt we can get that whole length cleared of snow by the time you get here. Over."

"You got an arresting cable?" asked Buck, clenching his teeth. "Over."

"We were hopin' you'd ask, Yankee. Yeah, we got one, and should be able to clear the snow off, *oh*, eight hundred feet of runway before you reach it. How's that? Over."

"Yellowknife, you are the True North, strong and free," said Buck. "But could we prevail on you to clear the same distance *past* the cable? Over."

"We don't have much additional clearance after the cable, but you'll be stopped cold before that point, won't you? Over."

"How much clearance you got after the cable?" asked Buck. "Over."

"About two hundred feet. At the end of that is a big pile of sandbags to stop you from overshootin' into the supply hut. Over."

"Could you clear those two hundred feet? Over."

"Don't trust the cable? Over."

"Well … I know some old guys who were on the *Eisenhower* when one of the damned things snapped," said Buck. "Over."

"Gotta be one in a billion," said the radioman. "But we'll clear the snow right up to the barrier. Let me know when you're a couple miles out. Your runway will be the only one lit. Don't be nervous when the firemen shove their Geiger counters in your faces. Over."

"So … you know about the *event* up north?" asked Buck. "Over."

The radioman scoffed. "Kind of hard to miss, Yankee. For a minute there, we thought the sun had come up again. Needless to say, we're glad to see *you*. Over."

Buck smirked. "Not nearly as glad as we are to see you, Yellowknife. Over."

"Nothin' to it, Yank. Over."

For the next few minutes, Buck brought them slowly down, and it seemed the further they dropped, the heavier the weather got. Heavy, wet snow splattered big drops against the canopy.

"Any particular reason you're concerned about the cable?" asked Catharine.

Buck sighed. "Never landed with a cable in Arctic conditions. Cable's rubber, I guess. I don't know if it can get brittle or even freeze. Sure would be nice to have enough runway ahead to abort and make another pass, like on a carrier. But, what can I say? Beggars can't be choosers." Buck checked his gauges and resumed chatting with Yellowknife. "Two miles out," he said. "Over."

"Puttin' the lights on for ya," said the radioman. "Over."

The runway lights switched on.

On approach, they could see that the snow had been cleared as well as it could be while snow was still coming down. No white spots that could throw them off at an angle.

"Comin' in," said Buck, landing the fighter. "Over."

When they touched down, the slush that had collected around the landing gear slowed them down quicker than expected. By the time they reached the cable, they must have been going no more than thirty miles per hour.

The hook grabbed the cable. They slowed down further until the cable restrained them with a comforting firmness.

Suddenly, the cable snapped, releasing them to continue their slide toward a wall of sandbags only two hundred feet ahead.

"Shit," said Buck under his breath. "We're goin' slow, commander. Only about twenty miles per hour. But stay strapped in, and prepare for impact."

Instinctively, Catharine clenched her teeth, turned her head to the right and pressed her left shoulder against restraints that pushed back at her hard.

The jet came to a halt just short of the sandbags.

"Whew!" said Buck, and started whooping. "Those squarebearded bastards can't get *us*! Not with a SAM, not with a frickin' *nuke*, not with a Grade-A Arctic blizzard." He turned to Catharine. "How you doin' there, lieutenant commander?"

She rubbed her shoulder. "*Ow!*"

"Whatsamatter?" said Buck.

Two firemen knocked on the bubble and Buck popped it open. Wind and snow blew in, and two firemen reached Geiger counters into the cockpit and waved the barrels up and down Buck and Catharine.

"These Yanks are clean! No glow at all!" shouted a fire fighter to the other groundcrew members. "Welcome back, sir," he said quietly to Buck.

But Buck was looking at Catharine with concern. "Looks like the lieutenant commander got a little bound up in her gear. Handle with care." He leaned into Catharine. "Sorry, ma'am. I owe you one."

"Will do, sir," said the groundcrewman. "Harris! Williams! Help the lieutenant commander out. Handle with great respect and care!"

Catharine was feeling more than a bit woozy.

"I'm Williams, ma'am," said the groundcrewman. "Where does it hurt?" He unbuckled her restraints.

"Left shoulder," she said. "Just feels like a pulled muscle. I'll be all right. Just lift me up and put me on the tarmac."

Four strong arms firmly picked her up out of the cockpit without so much as touching her left shoulder and lowered her to the snowy tarmac, where she winced in pain and rubbed her shoulder.

Buck walked up to her.

"C'mon, commander. It's bad form to occupy a runway once we've landed—especially when they've gotta work so hard to keep it clear o' snow and ice. May I walk you over to the nice warm visitors' room inside the building?"

She looked at him askance. "You may *not*. Have you forgotten we're going out on the lake?"

He was taken aback. "Look around you, ma'am. The base commander is not gonna muster a bunch o' Mounties to conduct a search under these conditions. I checked with the ground crew. They say it's fifteen below, goin' down another ten!"

She rubbed her shoulder, and said, "Let's go see the base commander."

He was tempted to throw his helmet to the tarmac.

"Are you *serious*?" he demanded.

She looked at him deadeye. "Damn *right* I'm serious. And if he won't muster the Mounties, I'll steal a heated John Deere Gator and go out myself."

"Ma'am," said Buck, becalming himself, "let's step into the building and figure out how we're gonna do this."

She perked up. "So, you're going with me?"

"Yeah," he said listlessly. "I told ya. I owe ya one. Didn't expect to have to pay it out so soon, but I'll be damned if I'm gonna be the one who's gotta explain to the President and the admiral why their blonde girl never came back."

"I like your spirit," she said. "But I have a better idea. I'll go back to my room and get some pictures of a few missing Americans I'd like you to see. We'll discuss them in the conference room. Then we'll visit the commander together."

He shrugged. "*You're* the one directin' this funeral, ma'am."

⸺◦◦⟨⟩◦◦⸺

BECAUSE THE WEATHER was so bad and communications were down, they had their choice of conference rooms.

Catharine had brought her briefcase. As soon as Buck sat down, she handed him a photograph of a pretty young blonde in a black wetsuit. "This is Kathy Wilson, fish biologist from Provo, Utah, wife, and mother of two (three and five years)."

She put the photo back in the briefcase and handed Buck a photo of a youngish black fellow beaming at the camera. "Here's Malcolm White, Augusta, Georgia, expert in geology specializing in river and lakebeds. He researches worldwide layers of ash laid down when the Earth was bombarded by asteroids. Husband, father of three (seven, eleven, and thirteen)."

Buck threw his hands up. "Enough show-and-tell," he said. "How many more are there?"

"Two more scientists."

"And what do they have in common?" he asked.

"They—with their U.S. Navy research minisub—disappeared somewhere on Great Slave Lake a few days ago."

He frowned at her. "Their sub probably went down with them aboard."

"One might think so, but this particular sub had an alarm system that would transmit an SOS if it was breached or sunk. No such transmission was received."

"And you think you spotted the sub on the surface this morning?" Buck asked skeptically.

"Yes," she said. "You see, I'm no flyboy like you. I'm a submariner, Perisher-certified in diesel-electric submarines like theirs. I've been on that model sub more than once. I can operate it, but not alone. I need a minimum of two more hands, preferably four."

He looked dismayed. "I have two hands, although being out on a lake in the dark when it's twenty below does not bode well for keepin' them. Also, I don't know the first thing about submarines."

"I'll tell you what to do," she said. "But first, we have to board it. There's a possibility that these fine Americans are being held prisoner or that they're already dead. If they're dead aboard the sub, it will take us five minutes to confirm that. If they're being held prisoner aboard the sub, there'll be a firefight. But we'll have the advantage of surprise and a complement of flash-bang grenades to give us the edge."

Buck raised his hand like a reluctant pupil. "I'm not … real good … with firearms … except for aerial gunnery."

"Hence my wish for some Mounties. Those guys are all tough, but *some* are experts at close-in fighting."

"You know what neither you nor I are particularly well trained for?" he said.

She raised her chin. "What?"

"Arctic survival," he said shaking his head. "If we go out there, we're likely to end up dead from the elements."

"Again," she said, "Mounties are great for that."

"Let's go see the commander," he said, rising.

⟶∘⟨⟩∘⟵

THE BASE COMMANDER glowered at Catharine. "You want me to pull a half-dozen Mounties out of their homes on a filthy night like this, and you can't even tell me what you're looking for?"

"I can only tell you if we find it, sir," said Catharine.

"Well, that's not good enough, is it? Just how did you plan on getting … wherever you're going?"

"As we mentioned earlier, sir," said Catharine, "a Super Huey … if you've got one, with thermal imaging capabilities."

"Oh, I've got one, but conditions are such—"

"You *promised*, commander," said Buck. Catharine was quietly delighted that Buck had come to her aid.

"Flying in this weather—especially over water—is out of the question," said the commander.

"We understand, sir," said Catharine. "Then how about a Gator? That is, unless you've still got an operational Caterpillar half-track."

The commander fingered his thin mustache with his right thumb and forefinger. "The Cats we have would be far too heavy. If you went anywhere near the lake—which you'd end up doing, as you don't know the terrain—it would be swamped immediately. I could send you and a couple of Mounties. You'd require two Gators, as they can't hold four. But you'd have to promise to keep the equipment off the lake surface. I know how tempting it can be to drive over the lake, but it's too early in the season for it to be reliably frozen at any point, and much of this lake is *two thousand* feet deep. You'd surely drown."

Catharine glanced at Buck and replied to the commander. "Stands to reason. If we have the Mounties to guide us, we'll keep the Gators off the lake for sure. We give you our solemn word."

"I have two men in mind," said the base commander. "They're both single, so I think they won't feel any great loss for having to leave home tonight. They're among the best trackers we have around here and they were brought up on the lake. One of them is descended from French trappers; the other of Slavey … First People, as we call them."

"They'd fit the bill perfectly," said Catharine. "When can they be here?"

"I'll have them waiting for you with the two Gators in front of the building in an hour. That's assuming they can make it. Of course, there's not much else to do in this weather but drink and sleep."

Catharine rose and saluted. "Thank you, sir."

The commander regarded her askance. "I thought U.S. Navy doesn't salute indoors."

"You're not U.S. Navy, sir, and this is a special occasion. Thank you so much. I'll be sure to commend your extraordinary assistance to the admiral."

The commander shook his head. "Just wear the heaviest clothing you can find, and make sure every square inch of your skin is covered the whole time you're out there. Don't make me sorry I indulged you on this nameless errand."

CHAPTER 8

After transmitting the message to Catharine's fighter in northern Canada, Enki dropped his arm to his side and turned to David.

"I expect your friend has received your message," said Enki.

"Thank you, my lord," said David. "I thank you more than words can say."

Inanna, who'd waited impatiently, spoke up at last.

"Who's *Trevor*?" she demanded.

David turned to her. "I've never met Trevor, Your Majesty."

"Then why does his name figure so prominently in your message to your ... friend? In your *signature*, no less."

David bowed. "In confidence, my friend once told me of an untrustworthy man named Trevor, so I sometimes refer to myself as *Not* Trevor to distinguish myself from him."

She turned away, looking ... hurt? "You're a born diplomat, professor." She turned back to David, who felt immobilized in the beam of her gaze. "Let me be plain in my question. Your friend is a *woman*. Correct?"

"Correct, Majesty."

With evident consternation, Enki said, "Professor, please go now and, if you would, commend to your superiors the Anunnaki efforts to save your friend."

David bowed to Enki. "Thank you again, my lord," he said, bowed separately to Inanna, and departed with Doctor Zia.

Alone with Inanna, Enki turned to her with as much forbearance as he could muster. "It's a mystery to me why, of all the males in the universe, you have chosen once again to concentrate your efforts on an earthling. He obviously feels that an intimate alliance with you would be inappropriate, given his planetary loyalty and ... his other entanglements."

Inanna pouted. "In affairs of the heart, my lord, I feel less than impelled to accept your lordship's guidance. David is descended of Joseph.

Because of the inbreeding of his tribe, his genetic composition is, except in irrelevant detail, that of Joseph himself. How can you counsel me against rekindling an affair of the heart where my belovèd was lost to death?"

Enki shook his head impatiently. "Put aside whether his genes are identical to Joseph's. David, as you call him, is *not* Joseph. He was born into a different world than Joseph, a different time, and thinks of himself—and the world—differently than Joseph did. Besides, Ziusudra has informed me that David is well-versed in the tale of Gilgamesh, which memorialized in stone the miserable fate of many of your male conquests, dear cousin. Perhaps David wishes to avoid being chased down and trampled by the Bull of Heaven."

Inanna turned on him angrily. "And I'm sure your sycophant Ziusudra said nothing to dispel Gilgamesh's slanders against me!"

"To the contrary, Ziusudra informed David what kind of despicable man Gilgamesh was. If more work needs to be done in clearing your name, however, *you* will have to do it, dear cousin. But let me point out that you have a greater concern at this moment."

Enki pointed through the window at the Arctic launch point. A pinpoint of light flared up there, as though to punctuate his meaning. *"That,"* said Enki, "was meant for you! Perhaps that will help you focus on the matter at hand."

Inanna looked on with trepidation at the fusion explosion mushrooming in Earth's Arctic. "Very well," she said. "But, if you feel the need to negotiate an arrangement whereby David's *friend* comes to visit the Anunnaki, make sure that her staying as a guest on my pyramidion forms no part of the deal."

"And where shall *David* stay?" demanded Enki.

"Why, on *my* pyramidion, of course," said Inanna. "That is already part of the deal." She smiled wryly. "And I have it in writing."

⋙∘⟨⟩∘⋘

THE TWO GATORS pushed through the dark blizzard, north along Yellowknife Road, keeping Great Slave Lake to their left. There was reputed to be a two-lane blacktop under the sleet, but in a storm of this magnitude it had been effectively reduced to a single lane, its center marked by a double yellow line that intermittently disappeared under windswept snow.

Both Gators were heated and running on a full charge, their wipers thrumming rhythmically. The only difference between them was that one was fully enclosed while the other sported an open-air pick-up over the rear wheels large enough to transport any lost scientists they might recover. At the base commander's insistence, each Gator was driven by a Mountie.

Since Catharine was the one who'd said she spotted a surfaced mini-sub when the sun was up, it was she who now occupied the passenger's seat of the foremost Gator.

She squinted to peer out over the lake, but the Gator's headlights projected a glare so garish it hindered her vision.

"Can you dim the lights a bit so I can see the lake?" she asked the driver, a Mountie who went by the single name of Clarence.

"Yes, ma'am, I can," said Clarence, "but didn't you say that the metal you spotted looked like it was moored at a little peninsula that jutted out into the lake about fifteen miles southeast of a land-bridge that crossed the lake goin' west?"

Catharine was pleased to see how carefully Clarence remembered her description of the location. In fact, Clarence's description was even more concise than hers had been. "Yes, Clarence, but—"

He interrupted. "And you said it looked like the peninsula was connected to a couple of smaller ones juttin' further west out into the lake?"

"Yes, but what does that have to do with the headlights?" she asked.

"There's only one place that fits that description, ma'am, and we won't approach it for another twelve miles or so." He turned to her with a smile that was pleasant enough, but could have used a little dental attention.

"So, you'll know when to slow down?" she asked.

"Yes, ma'am." Clarence turned the headlights down slightly anyway. "You want us to leave these Gators a half-mile away, and approach on foot?"

Catharine deferred to Clarence's greater expertise. "I suppose so," she said. "If that's the sub, I have no idea whether it'll be guarded."

Clarence laughed. "To decide on a plan, ma'am, you gotta ask yourself whether you're *certain* there'll be no bad guys there. And certainty's hard to come by."

"I have no idea whether there'll be bad guys there, and I don't want to stumble carelessly onboard because, if they've got hostages, they could kill them before we even see them."

"That's why you brought the stun grenades, *eh*?" asked the Mountie. "Flash-bang 'em up good, and board the vessel with sidearms?"

"Yeah," she said, "but considering how noisy this blizzard is, I think maybe I could creep aboard and sneak down there."

Clarence kept his eyes on the road, but cocked his head. "Dat's some risky bidness dere, lady." He glanced at her form. "How much you weigh, if you don't mind my askin'?"

She shrugged. "Maybe a hundred twenty pounds."

His laugh started on a keening note that dropped quickly and ended in a chesty guffaw.

She smiled. "What's funny?"

He pointed toward his feet. "Ya see da boot I'm wearin' right down dere?"

"Which one?"

"The one I got on de accelerator."

"I see it," she said. "What about it?"

"Dat boot weighs more dan you," he said. "You got a good chance of goin' unnoticed for a while, but if dey catch onto ya, dey'll kill ya real easy. Da quarters is too small." He looked at her form again. "You got a bulletproof vest?"

"I'm wearin' it," she said indignantly.

"How 'bout a helmet?"

"Got one in the back."

Clarence shook his head silently. "Gotta think you're better off goin' with the flashbang. Disable 'em, then go in and clean up."

"But if they're elsewhere in the vicinity," she observed, "they'll hear the bang and come running."

"Us three'll be out there waitin' for 'em," he said. "We'll take 'em out quick."

She considered his suggestion, which had undeniable merit, but she preferred to avoid a firefight entirely, if possible. "We'll sneak up on 'em and see what it looks like when we get there."

"Sounds good," he said, picking up the microphone. "Hey, Trapper. You there?"

"Where else would I be, Einstein?" came the humorous reply.

Clarence cycled through his keening laugh again. "We got ten more minutes, then a go-slow. Tell Mister Buck to get his weapons ready. When I pull over, you pull over right behind me, and kill the lights and the engine right away. Commander says we take the last half-mile on foot."

"Roger, Clarence."

THE BLIZZARD LET up just as they pulled over, which could be seen as a good sign, but could just as easily render them more visible to the enemy, which would be bad indeed. Either way, it was still agonizingly cold, and the thought that a misstep could result in a fall into a bottomless frozen lake was enough to keep everyone alert.

As they tramped northward along the waterline, Catharine couldn't stop thinking how humiliated she'd be if the metallic object was still there but turned out to be something mundane, like an aluminum rowboat or a dumpster.

Clarence dropped back to talk to her. "Check out the horizon across the lake."

She looked where he was pointing and was surprised to see a break in the overcast developing just above the western horizon, the clouds rimmed in cold silver. "Yeah?" she said.

"Dat's gonna make it a lot more likely we'll be seen. Also, the wind's let up a lot. So, if there's bad guys in dere, dey're a lot more likely to hear us comin'." He peered ahead, and brought up the night-vision goggles affixed to a strap around his neck. "Dere it is, about five hundred feet ahead. Looks like a trash can stickin' up over da dock with a ladder stickin' out of it. Stop here a minute. Take a look through your goggles." He waved to Buck and Trapper to stop and get down.

As Catharine brought the binoculars up to her eyes, she hoped that Clarence's description would prove accurate, because his description was exactly what the minisub would look like, moored to a dock.

And there it was, a trashcan with a ladder sticking out of it. Hardly the harshest description of a sub she'd ever heard. Submariners habitually referred to their own subs as sewer pipes.

She strained to see whether the lid of the trashcan was open or shut. As far as she could tell, it was shut, but that didn't mean anything. In these freezing temperatures, any occupants would have to keep it shut just to avoid freezing to death. The real question was whether the hatch was dogged shut from inside. If it was, they couldn't sneak in, and would have to go to Plan B. And at the moment they had no Plan B.

Buck and Trapper crept up behind.

"Permission for me to go in first?" asked Buck gravely.

"Why?" asked Catharine.

"Because I'm expendable," he said with a grim smile.

She almost laughed in his face. She whispered, "You know what it'd cost the Navy to replace your sorry ass, Buck? About fourteen million bucks, and years of training. Permission denied."

"*I'll* do it," Clarence said, "unless you want me to follow you. But I gotta tell ya, lieutenant commander, the first one into a confined space like that is takin' his life in his hands big time."

"I know, Clarence, but I've been aboard this model sub a few times, and I know where everything is, and where everybody could be hiding. I'll do it myself. Besides, I brought sneakers."

"Better keep doze suckers dry," said Clarence. "You get 'em wet, dey'll turn to ice, and you're liable to lose a foot or two."

"Duly noted," she said. "Except for the minisub, this dock looks vacant. Buck and Trapper, prepare your night vision rifles and take positions on that ridge overlooking the dock. It's got a clear view of the hatch. Please don't shoot me. If I come up and give you guys a double flash, that's the all-clear and your signal to come aboard." She turned to Clarence. "Clarence, come with me to the dock. If you hear gunfire, don't just run in blindly like the cavalry, okay? Use your head."

"You're not gonna use a stun grenade?" asked Clarence.

She shook her head. "No, those things can actually kill our own people. C'mon, let's go."

She put her gear down at the end of the dock, exchanged her boots for sneakers, pulled out her trusty Glock, and began creeping up to the hatch with Clarence right behind. When they were fifty feet away, he tapped her on the shoulder.

"What?" she whispered.

"Remember," whispered Clarence, "de air inside is warm, but the outside air is twenty below. When you open dat hatch, the cold air will drop down like a rock, and dey'll know right away dat de hatch has been opened."

Good point. She turned to him. "So what should I do?"

"Open the hatch and step down in a single motion, 'cause once it's open a crack, you're committed. But if you hear a commotion down there *before* you step down, it means they're comin' up at ya. In that case, step back on the dock and prepare for a firefight. One more thing."

"What?"

"Take my machine pistol with you," he said, offering it to her.

"No, thanks," she said. "There's not enough room down there for more than a few people. I'd rather go with my semi-automatic Glock. Besides, I've got to hit on every shot; otherwise, I could pierce the instrumentation, in which case we'd lose the sub and the whole trip would go for nought."

"Suit yourself," said Clarence. "I'm right here."

With the Glock in one hand, she crept up to the sub. When she tugged at the hatch, it opened easily and she was hit with a blast of warm air. There was a dim light down there, but no apparent noise or activity. As she stepped down the ladder, she heard what sounded like a whimper that became louder the further she descended.

As she stepped down off the ladder and turned toward the cabin, the sub looked deserted. *So, who's whimpering?*

Catharine stepped around to all likely hiding places and found no one, but as she entered the dorm area, there was a blindfolded young woman in a submarine coverall cowering on the floor by one of the bunks. Her hands and legs were bound together with white tape and secured to a vertical pole. Most cruelly, a thick piece of the same white tape covered her eyes.

Catharine knelt before the woman and removed the tape from her eyes, which must have hurt badly.

The woman winced and gasped. When she recovered from the immediate shock, she looked at Catharine in sheer terror—with just a hint of hope. Evidently, she'd been expecting someone much worse. The woman had the strong features of a Native American, although of which tribe (or even which region) Catharine couldn't hazard a guess. Her eyebrows were sharp and dark, and her eyes nearly black.

"I'm U.S. Navy," whispered Catharine. "Is anyone else aboard right now?"

The woman, obviously relieved by the prospect of rescue, shook her head emphatically.

"Do you expect them back straightaway?" asked Catharine.

The woman shook her head again.

"I'm going to remove your gag, but please keep your voice down and don't say anything but your first name. Okay?"

The woman nodded. She couldn't have been much older than twenty-five. Catharine removed the gag.

"I'm Lorraine," said the woman.

"Hello, Lorraine. I'm Catharine. I'm going to bring aboard the others in my unit. We'll cut you loose as soon as we return. Okay?"

"Better than okay," whispered Lorraine. Now that Catharine had a full view of Lorraine's whole face, it was obvious she'd been beaten. There were bruises and lacerations all over her face, especially around the eye sockets. Some sick bastard really went to town on her.

Catharine climbed halfway out the exterior hatch and double-clicked her flashlight toward the others. She went back down, but made sure she could hear the men's approaching footsteps before stepping off the ladder.

Buck was last to enter through the hatch. Catharine called up to him. "Dog the hatch, Buck. We don't want anybody following us down here."

"How do I ... dog the hatch?" asked Buck with a tenuous expression that made it all too clear he didn't know what a hatch was, or what it meant to dog one.

Sometimes Catharine wondered whether navy personnel weren't a little too specialized. She simplified the instruction. "Pull the door firmly shut and turn the wheel clockwise until it won't turn any more. Then shove it hard to make sure it's secure."

"I'm on it," he said.

She turned to the Mounties waiting at the base of the ladder.

"We've got an American aboard. Name is Lorraine. I found her bound and gagged. I've removed both."

The Mounties turned to go to the woman, but Catharine hadn't finished advising them. "Before you go back there," she said, "know this: It's clear somebody beat the crap out of her. So, she's gonna be nervous."

"She may have resisted," said Clarence. "God bless her."

"Amen dat," said Trapper.

"Clarence, go to her, identify yourself, and *gently* remove all her restraints. Ask her to await my arrival before she begins talking."

"Where are *you* goin'?" asked Trapper.

Catharine glanced about. "You'll notice we've got light and heat in here. I'm going to check on our power sources to make sure we don't run low. I'll be right there."

As expected, the minisub was diesel-electric, right in Catharine's wheelhouse, so to speak. To run submerged, the sub needed electrical power from the battery. Running on the battery, such a sub was at its stealthiest; it was invisible from the surface, and made less noise than any non-nuclear weapons platform on the planet. But the battery's charge would last only so long and, since a sub couldn't depend on having a power landline at the ready, it was equipped with an alternative power source, namely, a diesel engine.

The diesel had two uses. First, it could directly power the sub while on the surface. But that was noisy and would generally be done only in case of battery failure or when the sub was temporarily out of service.

The diesel engine's *preferred* service was to drive a generator that recharged the battery.

The main limitation of a sub with diesel-electric propulsion was that it could not remain submerged once its battery charge ran low. In a battle situation, that drawback could prove deadly, as it made the sub vulnerable to a "hold down," a maneuver forcing a sub's crew to choose whether to surface or asphyxiate. To increase the battery's charge, the crew would have to run the noisy diesel engine, which required surface air. In case the sub found itself in a setting where its battery ran low but it couldn't surface to run the diesel engine, it would need to "snorkel," that is, raise a snorkel mast above the surface and run the diesel until the battery was recharged, after which the sub could lower the snorkel mast and once again submerge and run silently.

Catharine checked the battery first, which was down to about one-fourth charge. Judging by the charge remaining, Catharine surmised that the prisoner had probably been here alone about thirty-six hours.

Catharine then checked the diesel tank, which was nearly full; that was good. She would have liked to start recharging the battery immediately, but first she had to move the sub someplace where it could safely make noise without alerting the bad guys.

BUCK, CATHARINE, AND the two Mounties sat in a semicircle facing Lorraine, who looked absolutely exhausted. She needed a bathroom break pretty badly.

When Lorraine returned from the latrine, Catharine did the questioning. "Lorraine," she said, "do you know where the others are?"

Lorraine choked on her words. "*They* have them."

"At the time you were separated, no one had been killed or badly injured?"

"Not yet."

"Who are the bad guys?"

"I don't know," Lorraine said fearfully. "They never said a word, just pointed guns at us and signaled us to move."

"How many of you good guys are there?"

"Five, including me."

"How many bad guys?"

"I think I counted five, but it's hard to say. They have those stupid square beards and brown hair, so they all look alike."

"If there were only five of them, and there were five of you, they must have gotten the drop on you."

"They did. They came here lookin' like a bunch of lumberjacks on a pole-guided raft, smiling and waving at us."

"How did you five respond?"

"Stupidly, as it turned out. We all went up on deck, smiled and waved back. And why not? It's not like we were here on some kind of secret mission. And then the bastards took out their … tommy guns and made us get on the raft."

"Did they bring you all to the same place?

"They took us to an ice floe where they had this aluminum shed and shoved us all in. It wasn't much of a shed, but it kept *us* in, and most of the wind and snow out."

"How did you get separated from the others?"

"One of us was pregnant. Paula. She's a geologist from Stanford, pregnant with her first. I didn't like the way they were handling her. Roughly, y'know. I stood up to them." She looked up with her bruised face and said, "So they treated *me* even worse."

"They beat you while you were in the shed?"

Lorraine nodded vacantly.

"Did they bind you up while you were still on the ice floe?"

She nodded again. "Two of them taped up my arms and legs, then stuck me back on the raft and poled me back here. When we got here, they literally dropped me down the hatch. May have broken a rib or two. Then one of them came down, taped me to that pole, blindfolded and gagged me, and left."

"Do you have any weapons aboard?" asked Catharine.

"Not guns like you guys, but we have some underwater stuff."

"Such as?"

"This minisub has a loadout of ten spring-loaded spear guns." Lorraine pointed with her chin toward an armory cabinet.

Catharine looked to Clarence. "Check 'em out."

Clarence opened the cabinet and removed one of the spear guns. The brass spearhead was massive. He whistled softly. "Freakin' *harpoons*," he said.

Lorraine nodded. "The minisub's previous deployment was to the Caribbean, where there are monstrous sharks. I guess they didn't bother to change the weapons loadout for north-temperate deployment." She winced at Clarence's handling of the spear gun. "Careful with those, chief," she said with an apologetic smile. "They pack quite a wallop."

"Whom do you work for, Lorraine?" asked Catharine.

"NOAA," she replied. "National Oceanic and Atmospheric Administration."

"Oh," said Catharine, "the global warming crowd?"

Lorraine nodded.

"How long were you taped to that pole?" asked Catharine.

"I don't know," Lorraine replied. "There's no daylight in here, and I was blindfolded. Maybe a day. Day and a half."

"Now for the big question," said Catharine. "Can you lead us back to the ice floe?"

"Yes," said Lorraine confidently. "Honestly, when they first brought us there, I was too overwhelmed to keep track of our progress, but when they rafted me back here, I studied every inlet. I'll get you there … 'specially if you give me one of those harpoons, as your Mountie calls them."

Catharine wondered if Lorraine might turn out to be a loose cannon. "We're going there to get your friends, not kill people. Understand?"

"I understand," Lorraine said ingenuously.

"How far to the ice floe?"

"About ten miles."

Catherine looked up at the men, who all seemed ready to go.

"Where are the sub's charts?" said Catharine. "I want to get away from this dock, dive as soon as possible, then move somewhere we can safely run the diesels till we have a full charge. We're down to a quarter charge."

"You're in luck," said Lorraine. "I'm the navigator." She got up and winced, favoring her left side.

⟶∘⟨⟨⟩∘⟵

THE MINISUB CAST off and moved south toward the lake proper on battery power, with the intention of remaining on the surface until such time as Lorraine could tell them it was safe to dive.

Catharine said, "I'd like to check on the power plant once more before we dive. Can I leave you up here alone to get us to the dive point?"

"Sure thing," replied Lorraine. "It'll be maybe three-quarters of an hour."

Catharine left the conn. Passing the three men, she tapped Buck on the shoulder. Buck broke off his conversation, followed Catharine into the power plant, and closed the door behind him as though he was the one who'd requested the meeting.

"She's lying to you, y'know," he said dispassionately, more a declaration than a question.

Catharine raised her eyebrows without much surprise. "What makes you say that?"

"Science dweebs don't use words like *deployment* and *weapons loadout*."

"I noticed that," said Catharine.

"And how would *she* know about the sub's previous deployment?"

"She could have been *on* it," suggested Catharine.

"I suppose, but would she call the current deployment *north-temperate*?" said Buck. "Hell, I don't think *I* knew that word before flying for the Navy. And, by the way, she used the *right* word. This lake is not Arctic. It's *northern temperate*, just like she said."

"Those are all valid grounds for suspicion, I suppose," said Catharine.

"Science dweebs don't warn professional weapons handlers to be careful with weapons, either. And here's the capper. Clarence told me that those harpoons, as he called 'em, are explosive-*tipped*. And, if you hold one in your hand, you can *feel* it's capable of sinking into sheet metal. There are no sheet-metal sharks—not even in the Caribbean."

Catharine furrowed her brow. "Who'd put a weapon aboard a research sub that could sink the ship?"

"And she *knew* it could," said Buck. "That's why she warned Clarence."

"Well," said Catharine, "if she's lying to us … then who's she really working for?"

"And what was this sub's real mission?" said Buck.

"Her fellow crew members might not even know."

"In fact, I'd say it's *likely* they don't know," said Buck. "But *she* sure as hell knows."

"Leave it to me," said Catharine.

"What are you gonna do?" demanded Buck.

"Talk to her."

"Even though she's lied to you?"

Catharine shook her head. "There's one thing she's not faking. *Somebody* beat the daylights out of her. Those bruises are real. More important, her *fury* is real. She wants revenge, and not against us. I don't want to threaten her if we can avoid it. We may need her. Hell, we *already* need her. I want her at the wheel when we have to make our escape."

"She'll *really* be in a position to screw us over once we're completely dependent on her," said Buck, evidently unsatisfied.

"Like I said," said Catharine, "leave it to me."

"By the way," said Buck, "what did you bring me here to talk about?"

She smirked. "This."

⟶⟶○◁▨▷○◁⟵

THEY DOVE THE sub. Catharine and Lorraine ran a series of tests confirming hull integrity, and ran some diagnostics confirming the operational status of all sensors and instruments. They ran the sonar feed through two pairs of headphones at the conn so they could listen at the same time. After establishing that everything was in good order, they put at least fifteen miles and a half-dozen peninsulas between them and the ice floe where Lorraine's crewmates were being held, and ran the diesel until the battery was fully recharged.

"How long till daylight?" asked Catharine.

"At least eight hours," replied Lorraine. "It's not an issue. One thing *might* be an issue, though. The sky has cleared out, and there's a gibbous moon."

Catharine fretted. "You've been on the ice floe. Will they see us coming?"

Lorraine nodded. "Yeah, unless they happen to be lookin' the other way. The floe's not near the shore. It's surrounded by deep water, which is pretty calm."

"Ready to go?" asked Catharine.

"Ready when you are."

"Okay, bring down the snorkel mast, and let's dive," said Catharine. "Then I'll ask you to pilot us to a point a quarter mile from the ice floe. What does your sonar see in the water?"

"There's nothin' movin' around anywhere near us."

Catharine gathered the men and said, "Okay, gentlemen, here are my concerns. First, I'd rather avoid a standup fight, but if we're going to have one, I want to take them at unawares."

"How do we do that?" asked Trapper.

"We're going to scope out the thickness of the ice floe. If it's no more than a few feet thick at the point closest to the shed, we're going to ram it."

Clarence's eyebrows popped up about as high as they could go. "Ram it? You mean smash into it?"

Catharine nodded. "From below."

"Won't dat destroy da sub?"

"The bridge of this minisub is heavily reinforced, just in case it ever gets stuck under ice and absolutely has to surface. It's like a goat's head, built to deliver—and absorb—a major impact."

"What weapons are we gonna carry?" asked Clarence.

"That's my next concern. Of course, we still have the machine pistols and automatics, but if that's *all* we have, then we could be screwed. I'm afraid they might not work."

"Why wouldn't they work?" asked Trapper.

Clarence rolled his eyes. "Dude, don't you watch the news? The aliens are sendin' down a ray that disables all weapons—"

"Even guns?" asked Trapper.

"Even guns," said Catharine. "Not in all places at all times. However, since we're not going to know for sure whether the ray is effective out here on the lake, I want you all to fully load your guns and carry them on a strap, keeping your hands free to handle your main weapons."

"Da *harpoons*," said Clarence with a knowing smile.

"Right. *Two* harpoons apiece. They're scary when they're pointed at you. They'll fire even if the ray is on, since they're springloaded—"

"The ray doesn't work on springs?" asked Trapper.

"Nope," Catharine said. "Springs are mechanical, not chemical or nuclear—and the harpoons'll punch a hole in a target, regardless whether the tip explodes."

"Let's do it," said Clarence. He opened the armory cabinet and handed out the spear guns. "Don't springload 'em till we're ready to go out the hatch. What's the rules of engagement, commander?"

Catharine handed out eight-by-ten headshot photos of each of the hostages. "Lorraine gave me these. Memorize these faces. They're the hostages. They're what this mission is about." She took a deep breath and exhaled. "Okay," she said, "here's the mission. There are four good Americans on that ice floe. One is pregnant, and all the others are married with children. By any known rules of war, they're non-combatants and should never have been beaten or held captive as they have been. The mission is for us to get them *all* into this sub in good condition, dive, and get the hell outta Dodge. If we can do that without firing a shot, great. But the mission requires us to get *all* our people out. *Nobody* stays with the bad guys. If, in order to get all the hostages, we have to waste some of the bad guys—or *all* of them—the mission's still a success. Any questions?"

"What if Big Mama shows up during the operation?" asked Buck.

Catharine knitted her brow. "Big Mama, meaning—?"

"Meaning their cavalry. An outside contingent."

Catharine looked Buck straight in the eye. "Then waste Big Mama, too. Just be careful with your weapons. Don't kill *our* people."

She grabbed a harpoon and walked back toward the conn.

The three guys waited for her to step out of view.

"Dat's one *cold* blonde!" whispered Trapper admiringly, exchanging silent high-fives with Clarence. "Never woulda guessed it. Thought dis was gonna be some Kumbaya shit. 'No way,' she says. '*Ice* 'em.'"

Buck shook his head. "She said only if we *have* to. Remember that part, too."

"WE SHOULD BE about a quarter-mile from the floe about now," said Lorraine rubbing her left side. "You want to take a peek?"

"This 'peek' may trigger hostilities. Put us somewhere so, if they look out, the moon's not right behind us," said Catharine. "And bring us to a full stop. I don't want them eyeballin' a feather from the scope. By the way, what's periscope depth in this craft?"

"Fifteen meters, ma'am," said Lorraine, then hesitantly added, "That's fifty feet."

Catharine shot her a dirty look, as though to say, *no kidding*?

"Sorry if I seem pedantic, ma'am," said Lorraine. "I know you're navy, but there's all *kinds* of navy: Death from above, death from the surface, and death from below."

"And you're from NOAA," Catharine said sarcastically. "I'm Perisher-qualified in diesel-electric, kid."

Lorraine let go a soft whistle. "Yes, ma'am. Okay, we're at periscope depth at full stop. Our heading (if we were to move) is due north. No surface or submerged craft anywhere around. Target's dead ahead. Moon is at nine o'clock; thirty degrees above the horizon. My guess, based upon conditions when we dove (which is more than an hour ago now), is that there's a cloudless sky."

Catharine grabbed the talker. "All hands to the conn, right now. Weapons in hand."

In thirty seconds, Buck led the other two to Catharine, all bristling with weaponry. "All present, ma'am," said Buck nervously.

"We're about to put up the periscope. I want everyone to stand by for two contingencies. Stand by for a possible quick dive, in case they look too ready for us. *But*—the more likely alternative is as follows: If they see us and they start scrambling to get ready, or if I think they're not wise to our presence at all, we're going to ram the ice floe at speed. There's gonna be a helluva jolt, so hang on. Then you three're gonna follow me up and out of the hatch. First thing is, we have to sort out the hostages from the bad guys, so I hope you studied those photos. Next, we do the necessary to take back the hostages." She looked at Buck. "If Big Mama shows up before we're away, waste her and all her little friends. Ready?"

"Ready, ma'am," said all hands.

"First mate," said Catharine with her heart in her mouth. "Up periscope."

Lorraine brought the periscope up, and Catharine peered through.

For some unknown reason, everybody on the ice floe was outdoors in the moonlight. She counted nine people, all in heavy parkas. She'd been afraid they'd be masked, which would have made it difficult to distinguish heroes from villains, but the four faces on the left were showing. They were probably the hostages, lacking facemasks because they'd been abducted during good weather and had no opportunity to bring heavy weather gear. The faces on the right were partly shielded from the cold by half-masks; they all had square beards and carried weapons.

Catharine's mind raced. *Why are they all out here? Are the hostages about to be shot?* Maybe.

With the element of surprise, conditions were nearly ideal for a direct assault. While things would have been even more ideal if the enemy had posted a sentry who'd fallen asleep, Catharine guessed that only happened in the movies.

"Down periscope," she ordered, and Lorraine pulled it down. "We're going in. They're all outdoors by the near edge of the ice floe. The hostages have no face coverings and no weapons. They're on the left at the moment. The bad guys have square beards, partial face coverings, and weapons. They're on the right, at least for the moment. Ready?"

Buck scratched his head and said, "Why are they all outdoors? It's twenty below."

"What difference does it make?" said Trapper. "They're lined up."

Catharine turned to Buck. "You're right. It might make a lot of difference in the end. But for this decision, it's a go. XO, dive the ship, put us under the floe, and surface into the ice."

"Yes, ma'am," said Lorraine, strapping on an impact helmet and buckling herself to her station. "Hang on, all hands. Grab something, and watch those harpoon tips!"

Everybody else crouched down and grabbed onto something—anything vertical that looked like it was fastened to the hull.

"Thirty seconds," announced Lorraine. "Brace for impact."

Chapter 9

For Catharine, awaiting the impact was agony. A firefight in the middle of one of the largest and deepest lakes in the world was now imminent—not a possibility, but a certainty.

And it was my choice, she told the court-martial panel in her mind. *It was the right tactical decision based on all available knowledge.* But deep down she knew that, in hindsight, any reasoned decision could be made to look improvident—even reckless. But that would happen only if the mission failed. Screw it. They can bill me. *Just don't fail.*

"Prepare for collision," said Lorraine.

The words were barely out of her mouth when the hull smashed upward into the ice and crashed through.

"XO," shouted Catharine, "put on the bridge searchlight and keep this sub steady until further notice!" She ran up the stairs, opened the hatch, and stepped onto the bridge. The three men followed close behind.

As from a balcony, Catharine stood on the bridge looking down at the brightly lit hostages and their captors, whose situations had remained almost precisely as they'd been a full minute ago … almost as though they were *waiting* for something. *Why the hell are they all out here in the freeze?*

"Nobody frickin' move," Catharine shouted at the squarebeards, realizing there was a good possibility that, although they wouldn't understand the words, they'd understand the implied threat. Nobody moved. So far so good.

"*Drop your weapons and raise your hands!*" she shouted. Nothing happened. She mimed the dropping of weapons and, to her amazement, all but one dropped their weapons and raised their hands.

But there was that one holdout, the one nearest the hostages. He still held a machine pistol. He wasn't pointing it at anybody and he wasn't close enough to a hostage to grab one, but he was obviously considering it, something Catharine *really* wanted to discourage. She decided to act as though he was just too stupid to know he'd already been defeated.

"Mister Buchanan," shouted Catharine over the din of cracking ice, "escort those hostages aboard."

"Yes, ma'am," shouted Buck, uneasy in the knowledge that there was a non-compliant gunman only a few feet away.

As Buck stepped down from the sub onto the remains of the ice floe, he glanced downward to assure his footing. To his amazement, at some indeterminate depth below the ice floe a small object glowed a bright yellow. At first, he thought it was a reflection of the sub's searchlight. Then he realized it couldn't be that, because it was slowly getting brighter … and bigger.

"Commander," said Buck.

But Catharine was adamant with the tension of command. "Not now, Mister Buchanan. Bring me those hostages, two at a time. *Then* we'll talk."

Buck stepped forward and took the hands of two of the hostages. They gratefully accepted his help, and quickly accompanied him to the sub. He assisted them up onto the bridge and Trapper escorted them down the hatch.

"Mister Buchanan," she said, "please escort the other two hostages aboard."

But Buck knew enough about standoffs to know that Catharine needed to be informed about the impending danger. The yellow glow deep in the lake was now clearly round, and getting brighter and bigger. Now it added both red and blue to its spectrum, bringing to Buck's mind an illustration on the cover of an old ELO album featuring a flying saucer.

"Commander, this can't wait!" he announced.

She glared at him, jut-jawed.

He pointed straight down. "Big Mama's comin'," he said.

She wanted to smack her head for failing to realize it. *That's what they're out here for. To be transported into space.*

Catharine now realized she was about to lose her tenuous control of the situation. She turned and shouted down the hatch, "Clarence, Trapper! All weapons to the bridge! NOW! NOW! NOW!"

She turned to see Buck escort one more hostage to the sub and help her up to the bridge. The hostage was noticeably pregnant. She mouthed *thank you* to Catharine as she passed and carefully climbed down the ladder into the sub.

Catharine's mind raced. *Three out of four is a failure. And failure is not an option.* At first she wondered why Buck brought only one hostage this time, but then realized that the pregnant one had spontaneously made a run for it and reached Buck before she could be stopped. That left one more hostage, an African-American man about thirty years old.

An enormous flying saucer breached the lake's surface a few yards to the left of the ice floe and suspended itself twenty feet above the surface. Ice water from the lake flowed off its edges, spraying both the ice floe and the sub. Catharine blinked her eyes to convince herself that what she was seeing was truly there.

Far larger than the minisub, the saucer glowed in primary colors and emitted a low hum. On its bottom were several colorful rings that rotated at different rates around a motionless, ivory-colored hub, on which appeared three repeats of what looked like a hand-drawn Islamic calligraphy of a red dragon rampant, with a small crown on its head.

From the minisub's bridge, Catharine could see that Buck was as mesmerized by this colossal disc as she was. That was a bad sign. It meant that both of them had taken their eyes off the ball at the same moment.

A loud hum came from the saucer, and two parallel cracks of bright white light appeared on the saucer's bottom extending from its inner ring to its periphery. A moment later it became clear that the cracks were the edges of a ramp being lowered toward the ice floe.

Catharine turned back to the non-compliant gunman, who was taking a step toward the remaining hostage.

"Drop it!" she shouted.

But the gunman ignored her and took another step toward the hostage, evidently intending to salvage some small part of his mission.

But before he could take another step, Catharine fired her harpoon at the base of his beard. It struck its target dead on, and the gunman's torso exploded like a stick of dynamite, spraying dark fluid all over the ice, spattering the surrendering gunmen and remaining hostage alike.

A six-inch swatch of the foolhardy gunman's warmup suit wafted down onto Catharine's parka. She grabbed it and put it in her pocket.

Clarence and Trapper emerged from the hatch and hopped down from the bridge onto the ice floe just in time to see the end of the ramp touch down onto the ice. Instantly, the four surviving squarebeards ran up the ramp and disappeared into the belly of the beast.

Clarence took up a position at the base of the ramp. Pointing up into the ship, he shouted, "Dey're massing. Dey're coming down to da ramp."

"DIRECT ALL FIRE TO THE TOP OF THE RAMP!" Catharine nearly screamed. "GIVE 'EM EVERYTHING YOU'VE GOT!"

The other two men flanked Clarence, and together they hit their mark with six harpoons fired in rapid succession and a couple of hand grenades. Explosions thundered inside the spacecraft and red flame spewed down out the opening. Catharine couldn't imagine anything in a closed space surviving such withering fire.

Suddenly, the top of the ramp erupted like a magnesium flare into white-hot light and, with the mournful sound of contorting metal, the whole ramp sagged to one side. From that point, no one on the saucer could possibly have used the ramp. It was simply out of commission.

"Withdraw to the sub!" shouted Catharine. "Maintain suppressive fire on the same spot!"

The fire from their weapons was having such dramatic effect, the men hesitated to withdraw.

"Get up here, dammit!" she shouted. "*Move it!*"

As the three were running low on ammo anyway, they grabbed the remaining hostage and raced to the spot where Buck had first stepped down from the bridge. One at a time, they leapt back onto it and ran up to Catharine, where they joined her and turned to gaze at the burning ramp.

"Anybody got marshmallows?" quipped Trapper.

"Nice work, gentlemen," said Catharine. "Get below … smartly."

As soon as the last of them stepped off the ladder, she shouted down the hatch. "XO! All back full!" She squatted down and gripped the railing in front of her. The sub lurched backwards like a race car leaving the gate in the wrong direction.

Once confident that the sub had extricated itself from the ice floe and could move freely, Catharine took a lone last glance at the hovering saucer, which seemed to be developing a subtle wobble. In the distance to her left, from the corner of her eye, she caught sight of two more saucers like the one burning in front of her, but the distant ones were undamaged and rising fast. Assuming the saucers were all of the same size, she estimated the nearer one to be about four miles away, and the other about eight. Both loomed high over the huge lake's central basin and continued to rise.

Catharine climbed partway down the ladder, far enough to close the hatch, dogged it, and dropped the rest of the way down.

"XO, turn toward the dock at Yellowknife, dive to fifty meters or as near as you can safely get, and proceed ahead standard."

Buck ran up to Catharine. "Commander, we've got to move faster than that."

Catharine turned to him. "I just saw two more saucers only a few miles away. If we go any faster, we'll make so much noise that they'll find us in a couple minutes and put us on the bottom."

Buck pleaded. "We may not last another couple minutes if we don't get the hell away. Didn't you see the flareup in the saucer we fired on?"

"What do you mean?" she demanded.

"Two things. First, that fire was burning so hot, I think we may have ignited the saucer's fuel supply, whatever it is. Second, that craft is losing its ability to remain aloft."

"How?"

"The entire lower half of its hull was deformed by the fire. The ramp is literally *falling off.*"

"Can't they just jettison the ramp?"

Buck shook his head vigorously. "No, they can't. It's *integral to the airframe.*"

"What does that mean?"

From the conn, Lorraine could be heard shouting. "The ship is submerged, depth fifty meters. Turns are ahead standard. Heading to Yellowknife dock. XO has the conn."

Buck grabbed Catharine by the elbow. "It means the saucer isn't *air*worthy, let alone *space*worthy. It can't fly. It's just gonna hover there until it breaks up or collapses into the water."

"And then?" she asked.

Buck shook his head in disbelief that thus far he'd failed to get his point across. "Maybe the fire goes out," he said with a shrug, then leaned into her and kept his voice down. "But, more likely, it explodes like an incoming meteor and puts out a shock wave big enough to break this sub into pieces."

Catharine nodded, turned to the conn and shouted. "All ahead flank!"

"Permission to cavitate?" came Lorraine's rulebook response.

"Permission granted. Cavitate." Catharine turned to Buck. "I hope you're right, because with all the noise we're making, we could be tracked by a kid with a string and a couple of tin cans."

Buck waved off her concern. "The aliens already *know* how to find us. If they don't destroy us, it's because we're just not important enough."

Catharine smirked. "We just destroyed one of their crews. That would show a certain lack of empathy on their part, wouldn't it?"

"Have you *noticed* much empathy comin' from the squarebeards? Those bastards rough-handled a pregnant woman and beat the crap out of another young woman who'd had the brass to speak up for her."

"Speaking of that brash young woman, I want to find out what the scientists know about her. Bring that Malcolm White guy to the dorm for me, would you?"

"Sure."

<hr>

"Before you get started," said Malcolm White, a little teary-eyed, "I want to thank you and your crew for saving us. In my head, I was already up in space *knowing* I'd never hug my kids again."

"The U.S. Navy is proud to be of service … *Doctor* White?"

He smiled. "*Mister* White, for the time being. I was just awarded my master's degree in environmental science at Emory."

"Congratulations. You must have impressed the hell out of somebody to be chosen for this lake project. Who hired you?"

"My faculty advisor said I'd be perfect for it. I was a little nervous going to the bottom of such a deep lake, but, hey, that's my field of study. What am I gonna say? No?"

"Is your faculty advisor a man or a woman?"

"Man."

"Who contacted *him*?"

"He … didn't say. More like winked."

"Meaning what?"

White equivocated. "I got the feeling it was connected to national security."

Catharine nodded. "Tell me, Mister White, what did you know about Lorraine before you showed up here?"

He shrugged. "Nothing. Never met her. Never even heard of her."

"How about the others? Had you heard of *them*?"

"Not only heard of 'em, I'd read their published papers. Excellent scholars. I was proud to be chosen to work with 'em. Actually, to get back to something you were saying: I didn't just *show up* here. The whole crew got together before flying up."

"Got together *where*?"

"Langley, Virginia."

CIA. Catharine couldn't help but roll her eyes. "Were you given instructions about what exactly you'd be doing?"

"No, just that we'd be working on things we were well versed in."

"Did anybody brief you when you got here?"

He shook his head. "Never got that far. We got shanghaied the first day we came out to the sub."

"Who was supposed to brief you?"

"Lorraine. She was the only one who knew what we'd be doing."

"Has she published?"

He shrugged. "Not in this field, that I know of. I have no idea if she published in some *other* field. To tell you the truth, she didn't seem all that familiar with *any* of our fields."

"The sub was here before you got here?"

"Must have been. We came out to the sub at first light after arriving at Fort Providence."

"Is that where the sub was docked?"

He nodded.

"Never reported in at Yellowknife?"

"Not that I know of. That's a military base, right?"

She smirked. "Yeah. Why'd Lorraine get beat up by the square-beards?"

He looked askance at Catharine. "What'd she tell you?"

"That she stood up for your pregnant colleague."

"That's true. She did."

"So, Lorraine just got *mouthy*?" asked Catharine.

"Is that what *she* said?" he asked skeptically.

"Mister White. *Malcolm*, if I may …"

"Malcolm's fine," he replied.

"Malcolm, don't worry about what Lorraine said. Why'd she get beat up so badly?"

He looked uncomfortable answering. "When we were left alone with just one of the … squarebeards, she smashed him in the face and grabbed his machine gun. She actually had it in her hands, too, but when she tried to fire it, nothing happened. Must have had some kind of user-specific safety or something."

"And they beat her?"

He winced. "Mercilessly. And we all just had to sit there and watch it. She's one tough lady."

"Okay, Malcolm, thanks. That's all I need for now. You can rejoin your friends, but don't tell them what we talked about, okay?"

"Okay," he replied hesitantly. "Did I overhear you telling Lorraine to take us to Yellowknife?"

"Yeah."

"Can we get home from there?"

"Assuming we get there in one piece, yeah. The Canadians have been very accommodating. Why? Did you leave something at Fort Providence?"

"Not a thing."

When Malcolm seemed hesitant to leave, Catharine realized he was working up the courage to ask something.

At last, he said, "We weren't really brought here to study the lake bottom, were we?"

She was pretty sure the answer was *no*, but, given her position, she was unsure how to respond.

Malcolm said, "We were here to provide a cover story if we got caught investigating that flying saucer thing, weren't we?"

Her smile tightened. "Can't discuss it. I'll tell you this: If you're smart—and you sure *seem* to be—you'll never suggest any such thing to another human being as long as you live."

"Not even to the others?" He pointed over his shoulder to indicate his fellow scientists.

"Not even them."

"Not even my wife?"

"*Definitely* not."

Malcolm left the room, and Buck came in right away.

"So, what'd ya learn?" he asked.

Catharine took a deep breath. "Lorraine lied. She's not a scientist, yet she was in charge of the mission. She joined the contingent at Langley, Virginia—"

"Oh, so she's a horse breeder," said Buck drily.

"Shut up. No," said Catharine wearily. The fatigue was really catching up to her. "This sub was already at Fort Providence when they got here."

"Fort *Who*?"

"Fort Providence. It's on the western end of the lake, pretty much at the source of the Mackenzie River. It's a two-horse town in the summer. In the winter, all they got's reindeer. In any event, the crew never touched down in Yellowknife, which explains why the Canadians had no idea about the mission."

"How the hell did the sub get to this lake?" asked Buck. "D'ya think it took the Arctic route and went south up the Mackenzie?"

"That would be like going to China by the Northwest Passage. No way I'd take this tin can under the big ice. And I have more experience than Lorraine."

"C-5?" suggested Buck, referring to America's largest cargo aircraft.

"That's what I'm thinkin'," she said, "but it musta been a long time ago. If it arrived recently, it would have had to land at Yellowknife. But the CO apparently has no knowledge of its arrival." She waved away the question. "The CIA has logistics down pat. They can get *anything* to *any* destination. Honestly," she said with a big yawn, "I'm too tired to care. But there's one thing I'd like to attend to right away."

"What's that?" he asked skeptically.

"I'm gonna tell Lorraine what I think of her. She placed the mission at risk by failing to tell me what we might find under the ice."

"You and I already suspected that."

"But *she* didn't know that!" Catharine was getting hot under the collar. "She's *still* never told me she works for the agency."

"She's not *supposed* to tell anybody."

"I'm a lieutenant commander in the U.S. frickin' Navy." She stood up to begin her march to the conn. "I'm gonna tell her what I think of her."

"Not *now* you're not," said Buck in an insubordinate tone that sounded like an order, which ticked Catharine off all the more.

"What do you mean, I'm not, *lieutenant*?"

"I mean you're not, *lieutenant* commander. We still need her. She's piloting this ship, and it's got five civilian passengers aboard, not just you, me, and the Mounties, but *important* people."

"I don't give a shit. I'm gonna let her have it."

"Never punch down," he said lazily. "Hand me your sidearm."

"Don't be ridiculous," said Catharine. "I'm not gonna *shoot* 'er!"

"*Who knows?* You haven't heard what she has to say yet! I mean, she's had a bad day, too. As you pointed out, somebody beat the crap out of 'er."

That slowed Catharine down a bit. "Oh, yeah," she said. "I forgot to mention that she was beaten so badly because she actually hit a square-beard and took his gun. It wouldn't fire because of some kind of personalized safety."

Buck smirked. "I can see your court martial now:

Question: The agent had risked her life to steal a weapon in aid of a pregnant woman's escape. Correct?

Defendant's Answer: Yes.

Question: It was *after* that when you beat the crap out of the agent. Correct?

Defendant's Answer: Yes.

Question: You'd been in combat that day, had you not?

Defendant's Answer: Briefly.

Question: Had you discharged your weapon?

Defendant's Answer: Only once.

Question: To what effect?

Defendant's Answer: My round struck one of the enemy, who exploded.

Question: So, you *were* a little worked up when you went to speak with the agent, weren't you?

Defendant's Answer: Not really.

Question: How about the day before? Had you seen any action *that* day?

Defendant's Answer: A little.

Question: A little? Didn't you evade a surface-to-air missile, narrowly escape a thermonuclear blast, and crash land an F-18?

Defendant's Answer: Well … *sorta.*"

Buck's humorous colloquy had sucked the wind out of Catharine's sails, and she could barely remember why she'd been so upset.

She began to laugh, and Buck joined in.

That's when Lorraine shouted. "Everybody grab onto something. HERE IT COMES!"

WHEN THE FIRST shock wave hit, the sub lurched forward so fast that anyone standing up would have had to sprint aft in order to avoid a fall. But there was insufficient time and space to run, and no human being could run that fast. Everyone standing collapsed to the deck.

While most were lucky enough to avoid colliding with anything on the way down, a few arms flailed into hard structures, such as the steel struts supporting the seats.

The left side of Buck's face smacked into a bulkhead, though fortunately he avoided leading with his nose. Dazed, he collapsed to the deck in no apparent hurry to get up.

Catharine, who'd just sat down at the head of a lower bunk, was thrown onto the mattress and bounced off with sufficient force to launch her up into the wire mesh supporting the upper bunk, which flung her back down, her head barely missing the steel frame. Clutching the sides of the frame, she buried her face in the pillow.

The second wave, while not as surprising or severe, lasted much longer, and was capped by the repeated, stupefyingly loud banging of metal on metal, such as Catharine had heard only once before, while touring a Boeing sheet metal plant at the admiral's side.

Everything bolted to the deck shivered and rattled until it seemed the sub would break apart from the stress.

But it didn't. When the noise and the rocking began to die down, Catharine opened her eyes with dread, and muttered, "Lorraine," for if Lorraine had lost either consciousness or control of the sub, their chances of survival would be nil.

Catharine ran to the conn, barely noticing the moaning people lying on the floor inspecting themselves for injuries.

At the conn, Lorraine was still standing upright, buckled to her station and wearing an impact helmet.

Catharine could have kissed her. "Damage control?"

"From what I can see on the gauges," said Lorraine, "the hull's fully intact. You might take a quick tour of the engine and battery rooms but, unless you see a bunch of water or hear some spray, we're good to go." Lorraine turned to her. "Good thing you gave the order to evacuate at flank speed."

"Why? How far did we get from the explosion?"

Lorraine did a quick calculation in her head. "At least fifteen miles."

"*Fifteen miles?*" Catharine said in wonderment. "Must have been some explosion. I thought we might have gotten depth-charged. Hey, did you—?"

"No depth charge," said Lorraine, shaking her head.

"How can you be sure?"

"There was no *splash*. The way I was taught, when a depth charge hits the water, there's always a splash. Besides, there's nobody around here to *drop* a depth charge. There are no destroyers on the lake and, as far as I know, no ASW choppers." Anti-Submarine-Warfare choppers were equipped with depth charges.

Lorraine looked in Catharine's general direction. "No, this was a remote, submerged explosion. I heard a seismic rumble a few seconds before the shockwave hit us, which means your flyboy was right. The spacecraft hung up there as long as it could. When it fell into the icy water, the airframe broke up and leaked the main fuel supply, which came into contact with the white-hot flame and … *kaboom!*"

Buck staggered into the conn holding a wet compress against the left side of his face. "We've got another problem," he said through his bruised mouth.

"What's that?"

"Looks like one of the scientists is about to give birth."

Catharine awaited further information. When it wasn't forthcoming, she asked, "Did her water break?"

Buck seemed a little confused by the question. "If it did, there'd be a puddle under her, right?"

The two women looked at each other and rolled their eyes. "Yes, Buck," said Catharine patronizingly. "There'd be a puddle under her, or a very wet mattress."

"I didn't see either of those," he said.

"*I'll* go," said Catharine.

"No, wait," said Lorraine. "I'm a certified midwife."

Catharine, shocked at how versatile this young woman was, nodded. "Okay, I'll take the conn. Anything I need to know?"

Lorraine beckoned Catharine over, swiftly removed her helmet, and buckled it on Catharine. Then she did the same with the restraint harness. "Only that we're still forty-five minutes out of Yellowknife. You should raise Yellowknife on the radio in a few minutes, and—just in case this lady gives birth—tell them to have a MedEvac chopper waiting for us at the Giant Mine dock. Hold on." She turned to Buck. "Anybody else hurt out there?"

Catharine rubbed her shoulder, which hurt a lot more than it should have. Then she remembered that the latest insult to her shoulder came on top of the wrenching it got when the F-18 broke loose on the runway just a few hours ago.

Buck winced as he removed the compress from his face long enough to speak. "Plenty of scrapes and bruises, but nobody unconscious, bleedin' out, or strugglin' for air."

Lorraine nodded and turned back to Catharine. "Tell 'em to send MedEvac for two, and standard choppers for another half dozen."

"Okay," said Catharine, and shouted as Lorraine left, "Captain has the conn."

Buck leaned heavily on the edge of the nearest sink, wrung out his compress, and ran cold water over it. He carefully put the compress back to his face and turned to Catharine. "Lorraine's pretty handy to have around, eh?"

At first Catharine ignored the comment, but she could feel Buck's eyes boring into her. "I suppose," she admitted.

"All that, and a midwife, too," he said through the pain, and took a seat.

After a moment of silence, Catharine turned to him. "You figure on using your spare time to *gloat*?"

He looked up at her innocently and shook his head as though she'd clearly misunderstood his intentions. "No. I thought I'd use this spare few minutes to allow my face to swell up out of all proportion, thank you."

"Sorry," she said. "Go lie down on one of the bunks. I got this."

CHAPTER 10

THREE QUONSET HUTS had been set up on the Cornell campus in upstate New York to house graduate students ostensibly engaged in agricultural geology experiments.

The interior of the hut to which Hendrick was assigned was partitioned into four residential compartments, each having a bed, a desk, a four-by-four table, a coffee maker, and a desktop computer hard-wired to the network. Although each compartment had a door capable of swinging shut, none of the partitions went all the way from floor to ceiling, so any sense of privacy was purely illusory.

When Hendrick entered the Quonset hut he was assigned to, there was no one else around. Walking down the central hall looking for his compartment, he passed one whose door had been left ajar. He stopped and peeked in.

Whoever occupied the compartment was manifestly deficient in housekeeping skills. Directly on the tabletop—without benefit of intervening tablecloth—sat a half-eaten Subway sandwich. Scattered around were breadcrumbs, shreds of lettuce, and a stray dollop of mayonnaise. A Coke Zero can rested on its side, having apparently been knocked over only after its contents had been consumed. Hendrick shrugged. At least this wasn't *his* compartment.

Hendrick identified the compartment assigned to him, tossed his duffel bag onto his bunk, and lay down for a moment to catch his breath. After a brief snooze, he was awakened by a knock at his open door.

"Hi," said a young man with sandy hair, piercing blue eyes, and a few extra pounds around his belly. "I'm Ham Fisher, short for Hamilton. I'm a geology student at Stanford. Are you Hendrick?"

Hendrick rubbed his eyes. "That I am, Mister Fisher."

"Welcome."

"Thanks," said Hendrick. "How long have you been here?"

"About a week and a half. You're from Namibia, right?"

"Well, I came here from Namibia," replied Hendrick, "but I'm originally from Ethiopia."

"Cool," said Ham. "What's it like living in Africa?"

Hendrick stopped himself from rolling his eyes. "Well, it has its ups and downs. It would take more than a moment to describe it."

"Tell me while we get something to eat," said Ham with a beckoning wave. "I'm buying."

"Why are you buying?" asked Hendrick.

"I'm in a good mood, and my family has money."

Hendrick snickered. "Where are we going?"

"Well, there are some good bars in Ithaca but, to tell the truth, I'd like to give the hockey team a wide berth. They can get pretty rambunctious. Let's go to Moosewood downtown. Food's great and they respect your privacy."

"Do we have something private to discuss?" asked Hendrick.

"If you want, we can talk about … the project."

Hendrick was warming up to going, but wasn't done questioning this fellow just yet. "What makes you think the hockey team won't be at Mees—"

"Moosewood. Well, it's vegetarian." He did a comical imitation of a cave man. "Hockey man love meat!"

"I'm up for Moosewood," said Hendrick. "Let's go."

⸻ ⟶∘⟨⟩∘⟵ ⸻

WHILE MOOSEWOOD WAS far more inviting than any restaurant in Omitara, as soon as they walked in Hendrick's feelers went up. As he'd expected, there were many tables of young people, and a few of older back-to-nature types, but one table was occupied by two impassive young men seated across from one another not saying a word. They sported similar-looking square beards and an earpiece in one ear.

The maître d', a young woman about twenty years old, was a lithe, raven-haired beauty with full lips and an aura of mystery. She sidled up to Ham in a manner both familiar and coquettish.

"Good to see you, Mister Fisher," she said. "Would you and your guest like to sit at your usual table?"

Before Ham could answer, Hendrick touched him lightly on the shoulder. "Do you suppose we could sit at a different table?"

Ham looked at him askance. "But you don't even know which table it is."

"Please," said Hendrick pleasantly, "indulge me."

Ham shrugged and said to the maître d', "Well, Elaine, perhaps you could give us a different table this afternoon."

She smiled. "Okay, then." She glanced about the room and pointed to a vacant table. "How about the one next to your usual?"

Ham looked to Hendrick to see if that met with his approval.

"How about that other one over in the corner?" asked Hendrick, silently berating himself. *You're being crazy. Nobody's spying on you.* But the more he considered it, the less crazy it seemed.

The maître d' smiled and sashayed them over to the corner table, where she asked if they'd care to order drinks.

Ham waited for Hendrick to respond.

For some reason, Wierzbowski came to Hendrick's mind. He smiled abashedly, and said, "None for me, please. I've been cutting back."

Ham said, "Hendrick, how would you like to split a big bottle of Pellegrino?"

"Pellegrino? What's that?"

"It's a brand name for sparkling water," said Ham. "No booze."

"That would be great," said Hendrick. "Can we have that with the meal?"

"Of course," the maître d' replied, and walked away with Ham's eyes glued to her hips.

"How long have you been coming here … to this restaurant?" asked Hendrick.

"Since I arrived in Ithaca. Why do you ask?" asked Ham.

Hendrick shrugged. "Probably nothing."

"No, really. Why?"

"Have you come to this restaurant with other people on the project?"

"Sure."

"Did you talk about the project while you were here?"

Ham's eyebrows slowly rose. "Oh." He gave it some thought. "Yes, I guess we did. Why?"

A male waiter came over, described the specials, took their orders, and drifted away.

Hendrick said, "Have you met a love interest since you arrived here who seemed almost too good to be true?"

"That's kind of personal," said Ham, reddening. "Why do you ask?"

"I'll tell you, but don't look away from me, okay?"

"Okay," said Ham, obviously wondering whether the guy he'd invited to lunch was a complete nutjob.

Hendrick said quietly, "Did you see two guys sitting at a table when we came in?"

Ham waited, apparently for a more thorough description.

Hendrick continued. "They both had square beards and wore ear-pieces. And they were *not* talking to each other."

Ham was obviously fighting the impulse to turn and look. "No, I didn't."

"As you've settled on a favorite table at this restaurant, it would have been a simple matter for them to bug your table."

"Seriously?" said Ham incredulously. "Are the guys still here?"

As if on cue, the two squarebeards stood up, paid their check without exchanging niceties with the cashier or so much as glancing around, and left through the front door.

"They just left," said Hendrick.

"So, they probably weren't here to listen in on our conversation, then."

Hendrick scoffed. "*That's* your conclusion?"

"What's funny?" said Ham. "If they were here to listen to our conversation, they wouldn't leave."

"They *would* if we sat at a table that wasn't bugged."

"Has it occurred to you that they might just have finished eating?" asked Ham indignantly. "Why don't we just ask Elaine when they got here?" he said, and began to turn.

"Don't turn around yet," Hendrick admonished.

"Why not?"

"I don't mean to intrude, but … have you begun dating Elaine?"

Ham became sulky. "That's none of your business."

"Okay, then we'll just continue to wonder."

"Wonder *what*?"

"Whether she's in league with them—or been bribed," said Hendrick.

"Don't be ridiculous. Why would you even *think* that?"

"So you *are* dating her?"

Ham was exasperated, but kept his voice down. "Suppose I am. Why would you think she's in league with them? And, permit me to point out that we don't even know that *they're* doing anything wrong."

"That's true, we don't," said Hendrick. "Of course, I *could* check your usual table … for a bug."

Ham resigned himself to whatever game Hendrick was playing. "If you find a bug, that would tend to substantiate your paranoid hypothesis about those two guys. But how would that help you find out whether

Elaine is in on it?"

"*How?* I could also check the table she suggested as an alternative when we decided to change from your usual."

Ham blushed.

Hendrick worked for Gary and had played poker for a long time with many different people. He'd learned long ago how to bluff convincingly, and could see that he'd succeeded in instilling substantial doubt in Ham's mind. "When you found me asleep at the Quonset hut, where were you returning from?"

"Tennis."

"Do you still have your equipment in your backpack?"

Ham nodded.

"Would you mind lending me a tennis ball?" asked Hendrick.

Hendrick could see that Ham's mind was working overtime. *Are those guys really spying on me? Have I been duped by Elaine?* And, finally: *Can I sneak a ball out of my backpack without being seen?* From Hendrick's point of view, the only interesting question was the last, and he'd have to leave the answer to Ham.

Since the backpack was readily accessible, Ham unzipped a small compartment designed for a tennis-ball can, pulled the cap off the can, and removed a ball, which he slipped to Hendrick under the table.

Hendrick began nonchalantly tossing the ball from one hand to the other and speaking animatedly to his companion until the ball escaped his grasp and rolled under Ham's customary table.

With apparent embarrassment, Hendrick rose to fetch the ball. He glanced up at the underside of Ham's customary table and the one next to it. A miniature microphone-transmitter had been taped to the underside of each table.

Hendrick returned to their present table and resumed his seat. The food arrived at that moment, a beautiful array of vegetarian dishes that made his mouth water.

When the waiter walked away, Ham said, "Well?"

"Let's talk about other things while we're enjoying this feast. Where did you attend undergraduate college?"

"Binghamton. It's about fifty miles south of here." And so went the conversation.

Hendrick momentarily glanced only once in Elaine's direction. She was openly glaring at him, but he pretended not to see.

As THEY LEFT the restaurant, Ham said, "Shall we just walk back to the hut? Unfortunately, just about all the Cornell students are on Christmas break, mostly home with mom and dad. So there's not much to do."

Hendrick replied, "First, let's go someplace we can talk, where there are lots of other people."

"Well, I don't know about *lots* of other people, but we could go to the Ivy Room at Willard Straight Hall. There are usually people hanging out there."

In the Ivy Room, Ham sat on an ancient leather couch. Hendrick found a heavy old upholstered chair and dragged it to a spot right next to the couch, so they could speak without raising their voices.

"Okay," said Ham. "Spill. Was the table bugged?"

Hendrick gave himself a moment to adopt the right tone, because he'd be delivering unwelcome news. "Yes. In fact, both tables were bugged, and not very scrupulously, either. I didn't get a chance to check all the other tables, but I'd be surprised if any restaurateur would take the trouble to wire *every* table for sound. To say nothing of the illegality of doing so."

Ham looked as though his dog had just been put down. "Did Elaine know?"

"I believe she did. She not only subtly encouraged you to go to your usual table (which, by itself, proves nothing), but she already had the *adjacent* table in mind, and proposed it when you declined your usual. Also, when I looked up at her during the meal, she was openly angry with me."

"Why would she be angry with *you*?"

"Because she realized I had checked for (and found) a bug. From her perspective, some dope momentarily letting a tennis ball get away would have been no bother. But when the dope examined the bottom of the table, she realized what he was looking for, knew he'd found it, and knew he'd report it to you. She knew her deceit would mean the end of the good thing she had going with you."

Ham rubbed his eyes sadly. "Do you think she's one of *them*?"

"I have no way of knowing, but it seems clear that, at the very least, she'd accepted a bribe to allow someone else to eavesdrop on *your* conversations. How could you trust such a person again?"

Ham was crestfallen. "So, she probably wasn't attracted to me at all, then."

Hendrick shrugged. "I wouldn't draw that conclusion. You said you're from a wealthy family?"

Ham nodded sadly. "Yeah. I'm descended from one of the Founding Fathers of the United States. My branch of the family still has plenty of money and social standing."

Hendrick nodded. "Well, if they're all like you, they deserve it."

That brought a smirk from Ham. "Thanks."

"Did *she* know about your family?"

"No."

"Then she probably *did* find you attractive. I expect she was mostly angry at *herself*. For a few lousy dollars, she blew her chance to be with you. From your point of view, let's face it, you got off easy. Can you imagine being *married* to someone who'd sell you out for a few pieces of silver?"

Ham smiled. "Well, since you put it *that* way …"

Hendrick stood up. "Come on, let's walk some more, so we can talk about the project without worrying about being overheard."

They exited the building and walked to the Arts Quad, with its criss-crossing paths.

The big quad was virtually abandoned during Christmas season. "Tell me," said Hendrick. "How are you going about this business of trying to identify a mineral composition that defeats the ray?"

Ham sighed. "It's been pretty haphazard, really. One of us gets an idea that a particular class of minerals might work, so we order some samples and wait a few days for them to arrive. When we get them, we do chromatography, measurements of purity, and so on. Then, once we've identified a few representative minerals in the class that seem promising, we take them out to a nearby farm where we keep the electromagnetic measuring equipment, and put each composition to the test. If it doesn't block the rays, we enter that result into our database of tried-and-failed compositions, and move on to the next brilliant idea."

Hendrick nodded. "How long does this process take?"

"It depends upon the availability of materials. We've got to track down a producer, provide them with written assurance of our authorization to handle the materials, some of which are pretty volatile or toxic, and then wait for the truck."

"The truck?"

"Yeah," said Ham. "That's how the materials are shipped to us. The whole process can take a couple of weeks to get the materials and classify them. Running the tests takes only a few hours." He laughed darkly. "It doesn't take long to realize a test has failed."

"And how many classes of materials do you have in process at one time?"

Ham shrugged. "One, usually, since one of us thinks he's got the physics worked out before we even start the process, so we're just waiting to prove it works and declare victory."

"How many cycles have you gone through since the project began?" asked Hendrick.

"Two. No wait … three, if you count the one for which we're now …"

"Waiting for the truck?"

"Yeah."

"And how many compounds are there that at least one of the researchers deems promising?"

Ham sighed. "Probably tens of thousands."

"So, even if this trial-and-error process pans out, it could take decades, right?"

"One of the guys did some calculations. At this rate, a brute-force system like ours could take *centuries* to find out that nothing works."

"And you're testing only a few examples in an entire *class* of compositions, so that if one that you haven't sampled *would* work, you'd never know, or you'd find out only by merest chance."

"Yes," said Ham, "although we closely measure every parameter in the hope that even a composition that fails could indicate promise in the other compositions of the class."

"And so far?"

"*Nada.*"

"How many people are working on the project?"

"Eight, though most of those are grad students who are doing this only part time. They're under a lot of pressure to publish … on other topics, of course."

"Are you controlling for isotopes?"

"Not really. We're using commonly available isotopes. Most scarce isotopes are completely unavailable. They'd have to be manufactured, and there's not a lot of available manpower and equipment to create oddball isotopes."

"I see," said Hendrick. "Listen, I'm expecting a call on my mobile phone in ten minutes, and I'd rather not take it back at the hut. I'll meet you there in an hour. And *I'm* buying lunch tomorrow, okay?"

"Okay, see you back at the hut," said Ham with a smile, as he walked off toward the eastern edge of campus.

HENDRICK WAS CONTEMPLATING a statue of the university founder when Agent Duffy called on the encrypted mobile phone.

Hendrick answered. "Hello?"

"Mister Hendrick, I hope you've reached Ithaca in good condition," said Duffy.

"I'm in Ithaca in good condition, thank you," said Hendrick, "but this project is not in good condition. In fact, I'm wondering if I'm just wasting a lot of my time and your money."

"Already? When did you get there?"

"Four or five hours ago."

"What could you have learned in such a short time?"

Hendrick sighed. *Where to begin?* "First of all, project security, to the extent there is any, has already been breached."

"How?"

"One of your geologists arrived ten days ago and adopted a favorite table at a local restaurant. It's been bugged. And a girl who works there, who's been flirting with the geologist, accepted a bribe to allow his table to be bugged."

"Oh," said Duffy, "shit."

"There's also no security at the Quonset huts. I walked into the hut without showing any ID or even talking to anyone. The interior partitions don't go from floor to ceiling, so everyone can hear everyone else. Also, the computer network is accessible through the university server. If the university server has been hacked—as *all* university servers have been, from time to time—then, so has the project. Security for this project has been less than serious."

"How do *you* know so much about security?"

"Seriously? I worked for Gary."

"Gary wouldn't approve?"

Hendrick chuffed. "Gary wouldn't play *solitaire* in a facility that's so badly compromised, let alone conduct business there. As you also know, he doesn't leave his businesses unattended—ever. And neither should you."

Duffy had been thrown back on his heels. "Well, look, we can fix all that."

"Not unless you can turn back time, you can't. At least, not completely. The most you can hope for is to prevent future leaks." He sighed. "What this shows me is that you don't take this project seriously."

"What do you mean?"

"Look, this is as important as the Manhattan Project. You want to learn how to disable the aliens' rays in order to put the USA on equal footing with the aliens, but that's not the most urgent of your problems."

"It's not?"

"No, because if some other country learns how to disable the aliens' rays before the USA does, they've got you over a barrel. The other country can use nuclear blackmail to force concessions from the USA and there's nothing you can do about it. You *must* win this race. But, instead of putting the project somewhere secure, you stick it in the middle of an Ivy League campus where half the students would oppose it merely on grounds that it's under military jurisdiction."

"When you and I were on our way to the States, you said you were curious about the project's methodology," said Agent Duffy. "Are you satisfied with that?"

"Not at all."

"I'll tell you what," said Duffy. "Let me see if I can patch in the admiral, since this is kind of his pet project. Are you someplace secure?"

"I'm on a quad at the university," said Hendrick, "looking at a statue of"—he peered at the corroded plaque—"Ezra Cornell. But I wouldn't go back to the hut to talk, because that's worse."

Duffy sighed again. "Hold on."

The late December sun was already dipping below the westward mountains and a chill breeze rose up the hill making Hendrick shiver.

"Hello, Hendrick?" came the voice of an older man. "This is Admiral Simmons."

"This is Hendrick," he replied. "I'm very pleased to make your acquaintance, admiral."

"Same here, Hendrick. Agent Duffy has explained to me the security problems you've encountered already. We'll have a squad up there tomorrow to reassess security needs and lock the place up tight. But he tells me you've also got some problems with the project's methodology. Can you explain them to me?"

"Well, I'll tell you what little I've learned about their methods in the few hours I've been here. One geologist will propose a promising class of minerals that might block the ray. He then identifies a manufacturer and calls to obtain samples of common forms of the mineral, but not all forms. It can take weeks for the manufacturer to prepare the samples and send them to the project by truck. Only one such class of minerals is examined at each turn. At this rate, to run through even the most promising minerals would take decades. As I was telling Agent Duffy, this project is of highest importance—"

"Duffy said you likened it to the Manhattan Project," said the admiral.

"I did," said Hendrick, "and I stand by that."

"And you're right to do so. What improvements would you suggest?"

"Well, because of career pressures, some of these scientists are preparing papers in unrelated matters. The first thing is: This project should be their *only* job until we've got the answers we need. There must be several teams, with each team processing ten or fifteen mineral groups at a time. (There will have to be a central database, so that no team wastes time duplicating the efforts of another team.) But there's another thing we should be doing at the same time in light of the slow and unpromising nature of this process of elimination."

"What would that be?" asked the admiral.

"Well, admiral. This ray is being imposed on us by people from another planet. I expect that the people utilizing the ray have developed one or more compositions that will stop it from being used against *them*."

"Stands to reason," said the admiral.

"Now, different celestial bodies have different minerals in abundance. The dirt on Mars is different from the dirt on Earth. In addition, different celestial bodies have different isotopic signatures, that is, atoms of the same element on different celestial bodies may have different numbers of neutrons. Conversely, the Earth and its moon have similar isotopic signatures, which is why most scientists believe that Earth and its moon have a common origin. Now, I believe Agent Duffy mentioned that Planet Nibiru originated outside of our solar system."

"Correct," said Agent Duffy.

"Therefore, there's no reason to believe that the composition that will block the ray will readily be found on Earth. Even if we could copy the composition on Earth, the isotopes native to Nibiru and Earth may differ, and the effective isotopes may not be native to Earth. So our copy might not work."

"Where are you going with this?" asked the admiral.

"There may be no composition on Earth that will block the rays. What we need are mineral samples from Nibiru."

"Duffy," said the admiral, "do we have such samples?"

"No, admiral."

"We did, briefly," said Hendrick.

"When?" asked the admiral.

Hendrick shook his head mournfully. "Before I was instructed to blow it up." He shook his head. "I held it in my own hand."

"How do you know it came from Nibiru?"

"That's what I've been told," replied Hendrick. "Besides, it had writing on it that looked like Hebrew."

"Isn't it more likely it came from Israel?" asked the admiral.

"No, on Nibiru they speak a language that's *like* Hebrew, but isn't *precisely* Hebrew. Besides I doubt even the Israelis can create a battery that explodes so forcefully."

"I don't get it," said the admiral. "I thought what you blew up was an electronic device."

"It was, admiral," said Hendrick, "but it was contained in a housing of some composite mineral that I can still see in my mind's eye."

"What did it look like?" asked the admiral.

"A composite stone, like marble, shot through with veins of muted colors."

"Can't visualize it," said the admiral.

"Me neither," said Duffy.

Then Hendrick remembered what the device made him think of the first time he saw it. "You may find the comparison ridiculous, but it bore some slight resemblance to … marble halvah."

"Marble … what?" asked the admiral.

Standing before the statue of Ezra Cornell, Hendrick was glad he was alone, because he blushed from ear to ear. "It's a sesame-based confection from the Middle East—but you can get it in any grocery store."

"In the States?" asked Agent Duffy.

"Yes," said Hendrick, "at least in New York."

"I'll get you some, admiral," said Duffy.

"Why would you get marble halvah?" asked Hendrick. "The resemblance between the confection and the mineral is purely visual."

"Because," said the admiral, "we have an ambassador on one of their spaceships. He can keep an eye out for what you're describing."

"Are you referring to the Kid from Canarsie?" asked Hendrick.

"Yes," said the admiral.

"Isn't he Jewish?" asked Hendrick.

"Yes."

"Then he already knows what marble halvah looks like," said Hendrick. "It's one of the many things Jews and Muslims have in common. I expect he's eaten it many times."

"Sir, I wouldn't talk about it over the equipment he's got up in orbit," warned Agent Duffy.

"No need," said the admiral. "We'll see him soon enough."

CHAPTER 11

AT SEVEN IN the morning, Miriam Azeri awoke in her room at the Grosvenor Hotel in London and checked her phone. There was one voice message. She pressed a button to hear it.

"*Um.* Hi, this is, *um*, Shawn McCauley. I'm a friend of David Schubert, the one who was released the other day at Baalbek in Lebanon. I mean, it was *me* who was released, not David. Anyway (sigh) I was given your number by (reading) U.S. Navy Catharine Weldon. I mean, the *Navy* didn't give me your number. And *she* didn't decide to give me your number, either, meaning Miss Weldon. Or *Ms.* Weldon. It was *David* who asked her to do that. David … *Schubert*, I mean. I'm in London … now. Anyway, *um*, he said *you'd* be in London and that you'd enjoy the breakfast buffet at the Grosvenor Hotel with me. I mean, not with *me*, especially. Even *without* me. He just said you enjoyed it. You don't have to go to a breakfast buffet with me … or at all. It's up to you, whether you want me to go with you … or not (sigh). Anyway, if you'd be interested in this morning's buffet … or me—or *both*, please give me a call at the number I'm calling you from, which should show up on your phone." *Pause.* "You should consider getting one of those services where a caller can listen back to his message and re-record it (sigh). Anyway, this is Shawn McCauley. I look forward to … hoping to … hear from you."

Between the end of Shawn's message and the moment he hung up, there was an inordinately long pause and a final exasperated sigh.

Miriam had seen an image of Shawn on the jumbotron as he was being released at Baalbek. He was a good-looking fellow, tall, with blond hair and blue eyes. And, although he'd seemed quite confident when he was with David, on his own he'd seemed less than certain of himself. And his lack of confidence seemed to have carried forward through his phone message.

She listened to the message twice more; by the end she felt flattered—tickled, even. It was quite charming to have an experienced field agent from the State Department prove so abjectly artless in asking her out on a date.

She called Shawn back.

"Hello?" he said. "Miriam?"

"How did you know?" she asked.

"Well, your name showed up on the screen," he said.

"So, you already have me in your directory?"

"I hope you don't find that presumptuous, but lately if I don't put a name in my directory right away, sometimes I forget."

"Oh? So, *but for* your directory, you would have forgotten about me?" she said, joking coyly.

"I know I'm not too good at interpreting this sort of thing, but … I think you're teasing me," he said.

"Yes," she said without elucidation.

"Yes … you're teasing me?"

"Yes, I'll meet you at the buffet in an hour."

"Oh? *Oh!*" said Shawn. "Shall I get a cab and come pick you up?"

"Well, where are you coming from?" she asked.

"I have a room at the Grosvenor."

"I see," she said with a smile. "So do I. Can you get a cab to pick me up at my room?"

"I … I doubt it."

"Well, in that case, I'll meet you at the buffet in an hour."

"Oh? Great! That's great. I look forward to it."

He sounded excited, a reaction she hadn't gotten from an eligible fellow in all too long. And it felt great.

She knew she couldn't reach David to thank him, since he was off-world. But Catharine was a different story. Miriam had last caught sight of her standing on the American reviewing stand at Baalbek a few days ago.

Catharine had been clear that the most reliable way to reach her, or get a message to her, was to call her personal number. Fortunately, Miriam had entered it into her phone's directory, so all she had to do was press a button.

Catharine's phone rang a few times and her outgoing message came on. Miriam waited through it patiently and left a grateful message.

While it would have been wonderful to have Catharine to speak with at whim, Miriam knew that Catharine was a busy and important woman who'd just completed a major effort in establishing David's embassage (in space!).

Miriam imagined Catharine horizontal, happily basking in the sun in the Bahamas, oiling herself with sunblock and downing her second daiquiri.

In fact, Catharine *was* flat on her back, but under lesser circumstances. She was at a military hospital in the Northwest Territories, being intravenously rehydrated, examined for frostbite, and having an MRI taken of her shoulder in search of soft-tissue tears.

⟶⟶∘⟵⟵⟶∘⟵

CATHARINE DOZED ON the verge of wakefulness, vaguely aware of hospital personnel bustling about the hallway, occasionally shuffling into her room to check a monitor or make a notation. About ten minutes earlier, there'd been a good-natured commotion at the nearby nurses' station. One nurse had said excitedly, "Here? Now? Get Carl right away; he's got the hookup."

A short time later, there was a new set of footsteps. Someone of heft shuffled in wearing paper slippers (so it had to be another patient) and plopped down on a chair next to her bed. At the same time, something heavy on squeaky wheels was being wheeled toward her room from the other end of the hallway. She supposed she'd soon be meeting *Carl* with his *hookup*, whatever that meant.

Reluctantly, Catharine opened her eyes and glanced at the seat next to her bed. It was occupied by Buck, sporting a pair of shiners and a swollen bruise on the outside of his left eye.

"Hello, Sleeping Beauty," he said with a smile.

She looked at him with disappointment. "Are you the best they could do for a Prince Charming? Your face is all … lopsided."

"Well, if you'd learned how to steer one of those sewer pipes, you wouldn't have left one of your passengers in this condition," he said. "Besides," he countered indignantly, "your face is shiny and your hair uncombed. I'm surprised your mommy let you go to school in that condition."

She smirked. "This condition is good enough for you, laddie."

"Ah," said Buck, "but is it good enough for your adoring TV fans?"

Just then a big orderly wheeled in a video station with a widescreen monitor on it. He jockeyed it around a few times until the monitor was just above her lap.

"What's this?" she said.

"I'm Carl, thanks for asking. This device"—he laid one whopper of a hand on top, clacking it with his ring—"was designed back during the COVID-19 epidemic. So many patients had died alone that they came up with this gizmo to give the patient a chance to wave goodbye to loved ones virtually."

Her eyebrows rose. "Has my condition taken a turn for the worse?"

Carl laughed. "Not at all. This gizmo's also useful when the brass wants to speak with a wounded soldier or sailor."

Catharine involuntarily shot up to a sitting position, ignoring the sensors taped to various parts of her body. "Bring me a mirror, some wipes, and a hairbrush!"

Carl looked at his watch. "You've only got two minutes till the call."

She gave him a dirty look. "Then why are you standing there instead of doing what I asked?"

Carl threw his hands up defensively and, in a minute, came back with the wipes and a handheld mirror. A nurse showed up with a comb from the gift shop, still in its wrapping.

While Buck looked on with amusement, Catharine made herself look fresh, if not quite ready for a royal ball.

"How do I look?" she asked Buck.

"It's like I said on the plane," he said with a sigh. "They should make 'em all look like you."

This time she didn't mind the remark.

Carl, who'd stepped out a moment to talk to the duty nurse, came back in. "Are you ready for your closeup?" he asked.

"Surrounded by comedians," remarked Catharine. "Yes, I'm ready."

Carl threw a switch, and a picture appeared on the widescreen. It showed two unoccupied Stickley chairs set up in front of painted wainscoting, above which was an expanse of vertically striped wallpaper. In the top center of the frame was a painted portrait of Thomas Jefferson, which Catharine knew to be an original.

"Wow," she muttered.

"What?" asked Buck.

"That's the real deal. It's the Oval Office," she said humbly. "Those chairs are about six feet from the *Resolute* Desk."

"Been there?"

She nodded. "Once."

The audio picked up a couple of subdued male voices mumbling to each other just outside the frame. A moment later, Admiral Simmons entered the frame, turned toward the camera, and just stared for a few seconds like a worried father.

"Good Lord, Catharine, it's good to see you in one piece."

"Thank you, admiral. It's good to see you, too."

The admiral sat down in one of the Stickley chairs and leaned in toward the camera. "Is that *you*, Buck? You look like shit. How the hell did *that* happen?"

Buck glanced at Catharine. "Well, admiral, look who you paired me up with. She's got one hell of a right cross."

"In that case, it serves you right," said the admiral. "All kidding aside"—he was interrupted by a flurry of activity just outside the frame—"I've brought a friend." He beckoned to someone offscreen.

The President entered the frame and took the seat next to the admiral.

The admiral turned toward the President. "Did you want to say something first, Mister President?"

"No, you go first, admiral," came the reply.

The admiral turned back toward the camera. "Let me address you individually. First you, Buck. That was a helluva flight you had there, buckin' a SAM missile and a thermonuclear blast. Our friends the Canadians told me that, when you landed, you had about enough fuel left to get to the corner drug store."

Buck shrugged. "Well, admiral, I knew they were gonna bill us for the whole tank," said Buck. "Damn! I *knew* I shoulda made another pass."

"I assume you'd fired up the afterburners?" asked the admiral.

"Had to, sir. I had precious cargo I needed to get away from the nuke."

"You did, indeed," said the admiral. "The President has a question for you."

"Buck," said the President. "Have you been awarded the Navy Cross?"

"No, Mister President."

"Let me ask you again, Buck," said the President wryly. "Have you been awarded the Navy Cross?"

Buck glanced at Catharine, who smiled from ear to ear. He cleared his throat and hesitantly proposed a different answer. "*Yes?*"

"Right answer, lieutenant," said the President. "Congratulations. The paperwork's been submitted and signed by me. Give it a couple of weeks. In the meantime, until this crisis with the aliens has been resolved, you're prohibited from disclosing to anyone the action that resulted in the award."

Buck gulped, nodded, and croaked out the words, "Yes, sir. Thank you, sir."

The admiral looked severely at Catharine. "And as for you, lieutenant commander, there is good reason for you *not* to be awarded the Navy Cross."

Uh oh, thought Catharine. Now she'd find out how she screwed up.

The admiral nodded. "And that is because you are an intelligence officer, and I deem it inimical to the interests of the Navy to publicly award you a medal while you're still engaged in the action that resulted in the award. However, you *have* been awarded the Navy Cross and, upon discharge from the service or earlier termination of said action, the medal will be *publicly* awarded." He flashed her a devilish smile. "Congratulations."

Tears formed at the corners of Catharine's eyes as she contemplated prior recipients of the Navy Cross, most of whom had made sacrifices far greater than hers. Many had laid down their lives. She choked up.

But, with all eyes on her, she refused to weep. Still, try though she might, she *couldn't* bring herself to talk.

The President leaned toward the admiral and quipped, "It's a first, Bob."

The admiral said into the camera, "They tell me the weather's cleared—to the extent winter weather *ever* clears in Yellowknife. I've sent up a small team to debrief the two of you and the others involved in the operation. So you sit tight for a couple days. Meanwhile, you can bask in these well-deserved awards." He slapped his thighs. "Okay, our common business is done for today. However, *Catharine's* video session is not done. Buck, I'm going to ask you to go back to your room before I switch Catharine's video feed."

Buck stood, saluted the President and the admiral, and separately saluted Catharine. Still stunned, Catharine wanly returned his salute from her bed. Buck marched out with a spring in his step.

"Catharine," said the admiral, "stay tuned. Somebody special wants to talk to you. While there's encryption on the signal, you'd best regard your conversation as though being broadcast in clear."

Catharine nodded, still unable to talk.

The admiral and the President disappeared, replaced by the image of David Schubert gazing fondly at her, nearly overcome with worry.

That did it. She wept openly.

David waited a bit for her to let it out. "I seem to have this effect on more and more people all the time."

As he'd hoped, she laughed through her tears. She blew her nose.

"So …" he said, "are you okay?"

"Yeah," she said. "I'm fine, if a bit achy."

"And everybody else on the mission?"

She smiled reassuringly. "One of the rescued hostages has given birth to a healthy boy, seven pounds two ounces. On the other hand, my pilot is a little beat up. He was fine all through the attack on our plane by the surface-to-air missile and then, of course, the hydrogen bomb, but he clobbered his head on the floor of the submarine. So … how have the past few days been on *your* end?"

David's mouth hung open. "Well, pretty calm … by comparison. I didn't know you'd gone through most of that stuff, but I'm pretty sure you can't discuss it with me in any detail unless the admiral gives the okay."

"Well, I can say this much," she said. "I found the critters who launched that missile at you, and a whole bunch of them are *really* sorry they did it."

"Oh? Did they apologize?"

"I'm sure they would have," she said meaningfully, "given the chance."

His eyes flashed to let her know he took her meaning. "Well, *Not Trevor* was lookin' out for you and thought he'd failed, but the Big Cheese stepped in and got the message to you."

"How'd the Big Cheese manage that?" she asked.

He shook his head in bewilderment. "I have no idea. And I *watched* him do it. Some kinda mix of technology and magic. At least, that's what it looked like to me."

"And … the girl of your dreams?" she asked.

He looked on Catharine fondly. "That's still *you*. And the other one … she's not a problem. I suppose she got discouraged."

"Don't count on it," said Catharine. "That's a strong urge she's tackling."

"I got a message from Shawn," said David, changing the subject, "thanking me for getting him Miriam's number. Have you heard from Miriam?"

"I haven't checked my phone yet. I expect I'll have a message or two from her." She smiled. "You know how we ladies love to talk."

"I've heard," said David. "You're not going on any more … *expeditions* soon, are you?"

"None on my dance card."

"Good," he said. "I don't want to feel like I may be doing all this for nothing."

Catharine was glad there were still tears in her eyes from earlier, so David wouldn't see how touched she was by his remark. She wasn't even sure he knew the import of what he'd just said, that his achievements would be meaningless if she weren't here for him.

"I was worried you'd never talk to me again," he confessed.

She smoothed her blanket. "That was never the plan," she assured him. "I just lost it when … Her Majesty pasted one on you, and you nearly swooned."

"Yeah," he sighed, "you can put that one on my *greatest hits* reel."

"Don't you worry. I've already spliced it in."

He snickered. "Well, that's a positive sign. Let's talk every couple of days, okay?" David pleaded. "I suppose, with the navy watching, I shouldn't say too much about how I feel about you."

"Don't waste a thought worrying about how the navy thinks you feel about me. Tell *her* how you feel about me."

He nodded dubiously.

"What's the matter?" she said suspiciously. "Not sure you want to?"

He shook his head. "I'm just wondering what it feels like to be jettisoned out into space with no breathing apparatus."

"That would be an act of war on her part."

He rolled his eyes. "That's a great comfort, Catharine. Thanks so much."

⸻ ❧ ⸻

David was reading in his room on Inanna's pyramidion when he received a phone call on his computer from Doctor Zia. David sat in front of the computer and pressed Connect. Zia was beaming his accustomed smile.

"Good morning, Doctor Zia," said David.

"Good morning, David."

"What can I do for you, my old friend?"

"Well," said Zia, "I wished to make myself available to answer any questions you have about our friends the Anunnaki."

"I have many," said David.

"I expected you would," said Zia. "Which are foremost on your mind?"

"Well, at the risk of sounding small, foremost is a personal question that's boggled my mind from the beginning."

"What's that?"

"Why is Queen Inanna interested in me, in particular?"

Zia smirked. "You've now asked me a question for which I can only guess at the answer. As you know, Her Majesty hardly confides in me."

David nodded. "But what is your understanding?"

"I hesitate to convey to you the understanding I've gleaned from Lord Enki, as his mind is sharp and subtle, and he invariably makes reference to historic people and events unfamiliar to me. I'm a relative newcomer, as you know, having arrived on the scene barely thirteen thousand years ago."

Though David was always impressed by Zia's longevity, he was less favorably impressed by this unresponsive flurry of words. David said nothing, but sat as though waiting patiently. (Actually, by nature he was *impatient*, but he'd come to terms with the need for the pretense of patience in diplomatic discourse.)

"Let me tell you what little I understand on this topic," said Zia. "Some months ago, Her Majesty commissioned a genetic analysis of your person."

"Where did she get the necessary material?"

Zia shrugged. "Honestly, I don't know, but it could have been something as simple as a discarded coffee cup."

"But what made her focus on me in the first place?" asked David.

"You were spotted by someone attending a convocation of Sumerologists you also attended at the invitation of a friend. The one who spotted you had known Joseph of the Bible personally, and thought you strikingly similar to Joseph in appearance."

"I had no idea those events were attended by immortals," said David. "In any event, it seems a strange reason to perform a genetic analysis on someone."

"Her Majesty had *also* known Joseph personally, and knew something different from that recorded in the Bible."

"Which was?"

Zia continued. "According to the Bible, the dreams that Joseph interpreted were those of the great Pharaoh. Isn't that what the Bible says?"

David nodded.

"Her Majesty knew that, in fact, they were Joseph's *own* dreams."

"But who would have altered the true story?" asked David.

"Pharaoh. You see, since such time as Enlil granted kingship in Egypt, receiving prophetic dreams from the gods had been the sole prerogative of Pharaoh. But that *particular* Pharaoh was unable to receive such dreams and, when he learned that Joseph *could* receive them, he saw Joseph as savior of his kingship. Take the dream of the seven-year feast followed by the seven-year famine. Seven years after the night of the dream a seven-year famine would have come—with or without Joseph. But *without* Joseph's dream, the people of Egypt would have made no effort over the next seven years to store enough grain to carry them through the ensuing famine, which would have left the people starving to death and the Pharaoh in jeopardy of bloody rebellion on account of his failure of leadership."

"I take it," said David, "that Her Majesty does not receive prophetic dreams."

"Her Majesty can send *erotic* dreams, which is common among royal Anunnaki women. In fact, Inanna *excels* at that. But she can neither send nor receive *prophetic* dreams. Hence, much of your value to her lies in your ability to receive prophecy."

"Who else can send prophetic dreams?"

Zia shifted uncomfortably. "This brings us into the domain of theology. Our departed King Anu was known to have sent such dreams, as are both his sons, Lord Enki and King Enlil."

"Are Enki and Enlil the only remaining Anunnaki who can send prophetic dreams?"

"Apparently not for, on occasion, they've *received* them. Presumably some of those sending them are males. But we're unsure."

"Received them from *whom*?" asked David.

"We're not sure, as I said. But for the Anunnaki king to receive them implies that even *he* serves at the sufferance of an Intelligence greater than his own."

"Do the Anunnaki have faith in the Eternal?"

"You'd have to ask them individually," said Zia, "but it's my guess that Lord Enki does."

David cocked his head. "Is that Intelligence the *Yahweh* who appears in the Bible?"

Zia smiled. "*Yahweh*, which means something like 'whomever,' has a complex history in Earth's affairs, only part of which is understood by the Great Ones. You may wish to ask Lord Enki about his beliefs in such things."

"What will I learn?"

Zia said, "Some of the miracles attributed to Yahweh in the Bible might not have been performed by Him. On the other hand, some *might*. One thing the Anunnaki know, having invited to Nibiru the earthlings who were the most devoted believers in Yahweh: All such guests have retained an unquestioning devotion to Yahweh throughout their sojourn on Nibiru. By the way, two such guests acceded in passing along their mantle to you."

It took a moment for David to realize the implications. "You mean, Elijah and Elisha live still?" His mind boggled.

Zia smiled coyly, which somehow broke the spell. "Have you other questions?"

"Why do you all speak English like Englishmen, with only a slight Middle Eastern accent?"

Zia let go a chesty laugh. "Because we've all been studying and speaking English since before you were born. As you know, I've been on Earth a long time. It was I who told the Anunnaki that, with the rise of the United States after the War Between the States, English was destined to become Earth's undisputed *lingua franca*. That has given us plenty of time to learn spoken English. Of course, English *grammar* is a bit more complex than that of the Romance Languages of French, Italian, and Spanish.

"One big advantage to learning *written* English is its phonetic alphabet; it's far easier to learn that than some of the Far Eastern languages, which are written in a seemingly unlimited number of ideograms. On the other hand, most inexplicably, modern English *spelling* reflects pronunciation of the language as it has not been spoken for the past four hundred years. Very tricky."

"But *why* did you all learn it?" asked David.

"Because we knew we'd soon be approaching Earth again."

"Seems like a lot of work for a visit of a few years' duration," said David.

Zia regarded him askance. "What you really want to know is the Anunnakis' intentions regarding Earth."

David smiled. "Now that you mention it."

"You'll wish to speak to Lord Enki about that," said Zia evasively.

"Very well," said David. "Can you tell me this, however? How many Nibirunes are there?"

Zia hesitated and sat back. "That's another question for Lord Enki."

David scoffed. "It hardly seems a sensitive topic. After all, I'm asking for nothing but the results of your latest census, which I expect are shared with the Nibirune public."

"As I said, that's for Lord Enki."

"Okay, let me ask something even more innocuous," said David. "Do most Nibirunes live on the surface of the planet, or underground?"

"It depends upon Nibiru's distance from the sun at any given time. When the planet is close enough to be gently warmed by the sun, Nibirunes tend to migrate to the surface. When the planet approaches the sun so closely that the surface becomes unbearably bright, however, few remain on the surface. In deep space, on the other hand, they tend to remain below."

"But where do they grow their food?"

"Of necessity, much agriculture and animal husbandry take place underground."

"Fair enough," said David. "I was looking forward to our next chat. Thank you for such answers as you could provide, and for telling me whom I might ask for others. Now, was there something *you* wished to discuss with *me*?"

"Yes," said Zia. "Yes, indeed. We were … hoping for some sort of reconnaissance concerning what happened the other day in the Northwest Territories. Your friend was there, obviously on your country's behalf. But we don't know what happened, either before or after the detonation. Can you share anything with us on that score?"

"I expect so," said David. "Let me make a call to the admiral. He'll probably wish to ensure that anything you hear will come directly from a person in the intelligence service. I'll likely learn it at the same time you do."

⟶○⟨⟩○⟵

DAVID STOOD ALONE at the official entrance to Enki's pyramidion awaiting the arrival of three U.S. intelligence officers.

By comparison to the residential sector where David's quarters were located, this official sector of the craft was businesslike, comprised of a single long hallway, vacant and sterile, extending in either direction from the elevator, all of its walls resembling gray-painted drywall. The hall was lined with doors, each equipped with an automated locking system to ensure privacy. Some rooms were used for large conferences, while smaller ones served as "breakout" rooms for private conferences, much as vacant jury rooms are used in courthouses. All rooms were buffered for sound, and only a few had sidelights on either side of the entry door. At one end of the hallway was a room large enough to hold not only the Council of Twelve but an equal number of visitors. That was the room to which David would ultimately be escorting the intelligence officers today.

The tiny blue point of a fiber optic cable lit up next to the elevator, indicating that docking had commenced. Assuming all went smoothly, David had only another two minutes to wait.

The elevator car dinged a few levels up, followed by a swooshing sound in the elevator shaft and, in seconds, the doors opened wide on three figures.

First off the elevator car, wearing U.S. Space Force service dress blues, was Lieutenant Callow, the young man who, a few weeks earlier, had expressed envy of David's good fortune in being selected by Queen Inanna as a love interest.

Following Callow were two people in U.S. Navy service dress blues. One was a senior male flyer wearing a Navy Cross and a name tag reading *Buchanan*. The left side of his face was a bit swollen and bore the yellow of a recovering bruise.

The smaller of the two Navy people wore a skirt. It was Catharine Weldon, her blonde hair slightly longer than it had been the last time David saw her face to face, her skin a bit more weathered (from her Arctic adventure, no doubt). To David's eyes, she looked as vulnerable and lovable as any woman could. *She* was his Venus. David took her by the hand and—heedless of the two men who accompanied her— embraced and clung to her as though she were life itself. Because of her shoulder injury, she shuddered momentarily in his embrace, then fully reciprocated. While they didn't kiss, they both clearly wanted to.

Buck sighed, looked at Lieutenant Callow with chagrin, and said, "Some guys have all the luck."

Callow stood his portfolio on end between his legs, leaned against the wall, and folded his arms. Looking at the two lovebirds, he wistfully shook his head and said, "An embarrassment of riches."

David returned to the present and, looking a bit embarrassed, took a half-step back from Catharine. "Good morning, lieutenant commander," he said.

"Good morning, Mister Ambassador," she replied, straightening her uniform. "May I introduce these two gentlemen?" She pointed to Buck. "This is Lieutenant Buck Buchanan. He's been helping out as my pilot the past week or so. Never mind the bruise on the left side of his face; the only thing he got fresh with was a submarine bulkhead."

David stepped forward, shook Buck's hand, and pointed to his be- medaled chest. "That's an impressive medal you have up top there, lieutenant. It looks like a Navy Cross. Recent vintage?"

Buck smiled proudly. "Quite recent, sir."

David smiled knowingly. "Congratulations. You've earned it. Please accept my thanks both for bringing home precious cargo, and for my freedom. May I call you Buck?"

Buck smiled. "Well, you sure can after saying *that*, Mister Ambassador."

"David, to you," said David, moving his gaze to Callow. "And who's *this* fine young man, lieutenant commander? He looks vaguely familiar."

"This is Lieutenant Callow, Mister Ambassador. He looks familiar because, as you may recall, he acted as your Greek chorus in an abortive meeting with the admiral."

"Oh, yes," said David, "the one who was so impressed with Queen Inanna's public relations."

"Will Her Majesty be attending today's meeting?" asked Callow.

"You know," said David, "I'm not sure about that. I expect she's been invited, but whether she attends will probably depend upon whether she regards this meeting as being military in nature (in which case, she would profess to have no interest) or diplomatic. In any event, if she's not at the meeting, I may be able to arrange for you to meet her at some later date."

"That would be terrific, sir."

"Meanwhile," said David, "*welcome*, lieutenant."

"Please call me Clifford, Mister Ambassador. I'm really just here to take notes on your style with women."

"Call me David, Clifford." David pointed to Clifford's portfolio. "But I expect you're here to do a lot more than that."

Buck stepped forward. "Any pointers for us, David?" he asked.

David escorted them partway down the hall till he identified the room set aside for his breakout conferences. "We have a few minutes. Let's just step in here a moment."

David closed the door behind them. "First of all, don't rely on any place onboard not being bugged. We're on their turf, after all. The main Anunnaki you'll be talking to are royalty and peers of the Crown. You should bow your head as a show of respect, but do not genuflect or kneel; you represent the United States of America and we don't do that stuff. Besides that, I assume you all know that the King of Nibiru is Enlil. Although he's not physically present on this craft, he may participate holographically."

"Holographically?" said Clifford.

"Yes," said David, "as a three-dimensional image, probably sitting in a chair. If he appears in that form, talk to his holographic image as though he were right there, bearing in mind that there's a nearly three-minute delay before anything you say reaches him, and an equal delay for you to hear his response. That gets cumbersome, so keep any back-and-forth to a strict minimum. He is known as King Enlil, but you should address him as Your Majesty, and refer to him as *His* Majesty.

"Another thing: the *de facto* Anunnaki leader on this ship is Lord Enki. Address him as 'my lord,' and refer to him as 'his lordship.' If there are other lords present and there might be confusion, you may call him 'My Lord Enki.' Be forewarned, Enlil and Enki are ancient beings. Enki and his half-sister created mankind from an early hominid, so show some respect. Also, Enlil and Enki *look* quite different from both us and the other Anunnaki."

"How so?" asked Buck.

"As they age, males in the royal family … change. By now, they're big, they have deep voices, and they … glow."

"*Glow?*" said Buck apprehensively.

"Just be prepared for it," said David. "As for Inanna, if she's here: She's a queen, although of precisely *what* we're not sure. She is *not* King Enlil's wife, but a distant cousin to Enlil and Enki, who are half-brothers to each other. One last thing. Do not lie to them. Enki especially will see through it immediately. He'll take offense and have you removed from the meeting. If there's something you can't tell him, then tell him so, but don't lie to him. Okay?"

"Piece o' cake," said Callow.

Buck gave David a thumbs-up.

Catharine winked at him, which filled him with joy.

CHAPTER 12

Lieutenant Callow placed his notes on a portable lectern resting at the foot of the long table.

David could see that Callow also had a looseleaf binder containing copies of photographs, which David assumed would be needed only if Callow's virtual slide presentation proved incompatible with the Anunnaki monitors mounted on walls all around the room. General Shulgi entered alone, and the Americans all rose and stood at attention with their hands at their sides.

"I shall soon usher in the Council of Twelve or their representatives," said Shulgi. "Please wait for all members to be seated before you take a seat, and rise when you speak or are spoken to; otherwise, you should be seated. If you have any questions of protocol, I will be available to provide advice. Please direct unprompted questions to *me*, unless you are spoken to by a member of the Council."

David rose and said, "Thank you, general."

Since the time of the Sumerians, each member of the Council had been assigned a numerical rank, with sixty being the highest, currently assigned to King Enlil.

First to file in, in reverse order of seniority, were the nine least senior members. All the Council members were substantially larger than ordinary human beings, but appeared to be similarly proportioned to humans. Most looked vaguely Semitic, although some had definite Nordic features and coloring. After filing in, they remained standing, and Shulgi announced Queen Inanna, the third-ranked of the Council, having a numerical rank of forty-five. She entered and stood at her place near the head of the table.

Callow was smitten with Inanna at once. At first he couldn't take his eyes off her, but then remembered his place and, in an act of will, respectfully averted his gaze.

Next to Inanna stood a large chair that could only have been set aside for the member having a seniority value of fifty, namely, Lord Enki.

The lights were dimmed, and Enki entered. The Americans (other than David, who'd met Enki earlier) were visibly taken aback by his lordship's size and glowing presence. They bowed their heads and waited for all the gods to be seated.

Enki said in his low booming voice, "Professor Schubert, perhaps you would do the honor of introducing to us the three people you have brought with you today."

David bowed. "I extend my thanks to you, Lord Enki," he said, "and to all the august Council of Twelve for hearing us today." He decided to introduce his friends in order of rank. "Two of these kind people are officers of the United States Navy."

Indicating Catharine with his outstretched hand, David said, "This is Lieutenant Commander Weldon. She is one of the two very grateful people saved from nuclear holocaust by your lordship's outstretched hand."

"Delighted," said Enki with a fond smile, drawing a disdainful look from Inanna that was probably noticed only by the Americans. David was reminded of Doctor Zia's remark that Catharine, by her coloring, could well be Enki's own daughter.

"This gentleman," continued David, "is Navy Lieutenant Buchanan, who piloted the craft that escaped that awful fate."

Both Catharine and Buck bowed their heads respectfully.

"And this young man is Lieutenant Callow of the United States Space Force, who assists the same gentleman as does Lieutenant Commander Weldon, namely, Navy Admiral Simmons who, although he is not present, sends his respectful compliments and heartfelt thanks to all the Council."

Enki nodded to Shulgi, who said to the Americans, "You may be seated."

Shulgi looked to Enki, who nodded again.

Shulgi turned to the Americans. "Which of you," he asked, "will tell the tale of your tribulations in the icy lands of Canada?"

David signaled Shulgi with his hand. Shulgi gestured for him to rise and speak.

"If the Council would be amenable: Before we share such information, we respectfully request the Council's assurance that any action the Council may take on Earth resulting from such information will be undertaken only in cooperation with the civil authorities of the country in which such action will be taken. Our nation, namely, the United States of America, speaks only on its own behalf, and cannot afford to be seen as inviting, or consenting to, the Council's intervention in earthly affairs in violation of the rights of any other nation."

Enki glanced at each member of the Council. "Seeing no objection by the Council, we freely give you such assurance. In the interest of full disclosure, permit me to inform you, Professor Schubert, that this conversation is either being viewed by King Enlil now or will likely be viewed by him shortly."

"Thank you, my lord," said David. "We thank the absent King Enlil for his kind attention." He resumed his seat.

Callow recounted Catharine and Buck's overflight in some detail, with illustrations shown on the video screens: their evasion of the surface-to-air missile, and the warning they received through Lord Enki that enabled them narrowly to avert disaster.

"But," said Callow, "I expect the portion of the mission that might identify the perpetrators of the attempted mass murder of the Anunnaki took place during recovery of the missing American submarine."

Lord Enki signaled to General Shulgi, who rose and said, "The Council wishes to hear from Weldon on this question, as she evidently led that portion of the mission."

"May it please the Council," said Catharine with a polite bow, "I have received the highest level of training available on Earth for the operation of diesel-electric submarines." She took a deep breath and began the tale. "Late in the day when Her Majesty Queen Inanna landed at Baalbek, we received a warning from American Intelligence that an unidentified missile had been launched toward Her Majesty's pyramidion from a submerged platform in the Beaufort Sea. The admiral had already received information that a small American submarine at Great Slave Lake with several scientists aboard had disappeared without triggering a radio transmission that *would* have been heard if the submarine had been flooded or destroyed.

"The admiral observed that the lake is the source of the Mackenzie River, which empties into the Beaufort Sea near the missile's suspected launch site. I volunteered to investigate the suspected launch site and then attempt to recover the submarine and the missing scientists." She pointed to Buck. "Lieutenant Buchanan served as my pilot. During our overflight, we were fired upon, unprovoked, by an unidentified surface-to-air missile installation."

Shulgi interrupted. "Pardon me, Weldon. Lord Enki would pose a question."

Enki leaned forward thoughtfully. "Did the missile launcher bear any identifying markings?"

"I saw none, my lord. I expect that Lieutenant Buchanan saw none, either." She paused long enough for Buck to indicate his agreement. "Effective defense against such a missile requires the targeted aircraft to drop out of view of the launch site. As Lieutenant Buchanan observed, the missiles themselves are blind. They can see only what the launcher sees."

"And did the missile itself bear any markings?" asked Enki.

"Our aircraft and the missile were traveling in different directions too fast for us to see."

Enki nodded gravely.

"Please continue," said Shulgi.

Catharine took a deep breath. "When we returned to the airfield, we rested briefly and then went to investigate something which, from the air during daylight hours, had looked suspiciously like a small submarine. As it turned out, it *was* the American submarine we were looking for. One of the crew members had been bound up and left aboard. We freed her, and she guided us to the place where the scientists were being held captive. We found them being detained on an ice floe on the lake."

Shulgi asked, "Could you describe whoever was holding them captive?"

"They appeared all to be young men wearing square-looking beards, which is a term I use to mean that their beards were cut straight across about the level of the breastbone. On the ice floe, where it was extremely cold, they were all dressed in heavy parkas and boots. But I believe I'd already seen some of them by the airport in Yellowknife, and those were wearing warm-up suits."

"Before going to Yellowknife," said Shulgi, "had you ever seen a group of men wearing square beards?"

Catharine glanced briefly at David. "A few weeks earlier, I saw a few in Paris. They appeared to be in possession of a laptop computer belonging to me that had been stolen from the admiral's airplane in midflight."

"How could they steal it while the plane was flying?" asked Shulgi.

"The plane was flanked by two long spacecraft that sent some sort of scanning beam through the plane, momentarily blinding our pilot. When the craft left our vicinity, they shut down our airplane's engines, which had to be relit on an emergency basis. The only thing missing when they left was my laptop computer."

"One related question," said Shulgi. "Please tell the Council what a warmup suit is."

"Certainly," replied Catharine with a smirk. "It's a suit for exercise or casual wear consisting of pants and either a jacket or a sweatshirt. Often, it has a single, light-colored vertical stripe up the side of the pants. However, I can enhance my description." She reached into her jacket pocket and drew out a clear polypropylene bag containing the swatch of soiled cloth that had wafted down to her during the firefight.

An audible murmur erupted among the Twelve.

Lord Enki smiled and said, "You have done well to keep this. Is the fabric in the same condition as when you obtained it?"

Catharine replied, "Our navy demanded to examine it, but I refused to turn the whole thing over, to avoid it being altered or contaminated in any way. I expected that the Anunnaki would learn much more by examining it in its original condition. Nevertheless, I was ordered to cut a two-inch-square piece from the swatch and give it to the naval laboratory, which I did, but the swatch in this bag is otherwise in the same condition as when it came to me."

Shulgi regarded her gravely. "Did the navy laboratory tell you what they found?"

"Yes," said Catharine, "but much of it pertained to the chemical composition of the cloth, which is beyond my comprehension. They also explained that certain bodily fluids had dried on it."

"And what did they tell you the cloth was made of?" asked Shulgi.

"They said it appeared to be a textile woven from the fibers of a plant, much the way we use cotton—but it was *not* cotton."

"Did they say which plant it was?" asked Shulgi.

Catharine shook her head. "No, general. They said the plant was unfamiliar to them."

Shulgi turned to Enki and waited.

Enki asked, "What fluids had dried on the cloth?"

"The blood, bile, and … fecal material of an unfamiliar species."

Enki said: "The one who wore the garment from which this swatch came: Was he a handler of beasts?"

It took Catharine a moment to realize that she was being asked whether the fluids were those of the wearer or of another species. "My lord, we saw no sign of any beasts. I think we must assume that the fluids came from the wearer."

"Why would the wearer have such fluids on his person?" asked Shulgi.

"I realize now that I have not recounted my brief encounter with this person. He was one of the hostage-takers. My company had disarmed all other hostage-takers and separated them from the hostages. The person wearing this cloth refused to surrender his weapon and instead lunged for the last remaining hostage. Under the circumstances, I was required to … shoot him with such weapon as I had at hand."

"What type of weapon was that?"

Catharine blushed. "It was an explosive-tipped spear."

A few members of the Council squirmed queasily.

"It struck him in the gut," added Catharine.

Inanna raised her hands to the heavens and clucked her tongue. "*This* is a task for a *woman*?" she demanded, turning angrily to Catharine. "Why don't you just grow a pair of balls?"

Enki turned on Inanna like a bull turning to charge. "How *dare* you insult our allies and guests, Inanna? If this is the way their kind chooses to assign tasks between the sexes, who are we to say nay?"

"I'd think their *men* would have something to say about it," replied Inanna, flashing anger unmistakably at David.

"Please don't blame David, Your Majesty," said Catharine.

David rose. "Majesty, I was not present at the scene. I would much prefer to have performed the necessary act myself, but Weldon was there, and it needed to be done to save the life of at least one hostage, and possibly the whole mission."

Inanna sulked. "She shouldn't have been put in that position."

"*Inanna!*" bellowed Enki, then composed himself. "Silence on this point."

Shulgi moved the discussion along. "Tell the Council, Weldon, how your mission concluded."

"A saucer-shaped aircraft emerged from the icy lake and hovered about seven or eight meters above both the ice floe and the submarine. It lowered a ramp to the ice and several of the hostage-takers escaped up the ramp into the craft. When we saw the enemy massing to descend, my men concentrated their fire at the top of the ramp, where it met the hull of the craft. This caused a major fire on the craft which allowed our submarine to back away from the ice floe, submerge, and escape."

"What happened to the spacecraft?" asked Shulgi.

"We couldn't stay to see, general, but after speeding away from the scene for about twenty minutes, there was a tremendous explosion behind us that nearly sank us. We managed to right ourselves and return to the nearest base. We believe that the craft hovered as long as it could, then exploded when it struck the icy water."

"Why didn't it fly away?" asked Shulgi.

Catharine nodded toward Buck. "If I may defer to Lieutenant Buchanan on that question."

Shulgi nodded to Buck, who rose. "The ramp was an integral part of the craft's airframe, general. When our firearms set aflame the metal joint where the ramp met the remainder of the airframe, the joint quickly began to burn like a magnesium flare. The airframe quickly became deformed and incapable of flight."

"Do you think its occupants were killed, Buchanan?" asked Shulgi.

"We have no way to be sure, general, but I expect their only alternatives would have been either to die on the exploding craft or leap to Earth through a white-hot flame. If they leapt and weren't burned to death, perhaps they reached the ground safely. Their craft was only twenty feet or so in the air, so the jump might have been survivable."

"But it's possible the enemy had no survivors of the incident?" asked Shulgi.

Before Buck could reply, Catharine stood and said, "If I may, general?"

Shulgi nodded.

"From that craft, yes, it is possible there were no survivors. However, just before we escaped in the submarine, I saw two similar saucer-shaped craft that appeared to emerge from the lake a few miles away at the same instant. They rose into the night sky and disappeared. I suspect that the occupants of those craft survived, as they were not involved in the fighting."

Enki asked, "Did anyone fire on your submarine during your escape?"

Catharine knitted her brow. "Strangely, no, yet it would have been a simple matter for them to find us."

"Simple?" asked Enki. "Why simple? Were you not in a submarine boat?"

"Yes, but we were barely submerged, and moving so fast that we made tremendous noise and left a trail of bubbles on the still waters of the lake." She shrugged. "Yet, they seemed to pay no attention to us. I expect they may have tracked us back to the dock, but they never shot at us, or tried to contact us. I must say that their indifference toward our company seemed to me to show an extraordinary lack of empathy on their part for their own squarebearded soldiers."

Enki said, "You should avoid concluding that they've forgotten their vendetta against you. At the very least, they have an incentive to destroy you in order to dissuade others who might be inclined to oppose them."

Catharine bowed in agreement.

Enki asked, "Have you ever seen one of these squarebearded people in the company of a woman?"

Catharine replied, "No. I believe that I've never seen a female of their kind."

Enki smiled. "You're assuming they're male."

Inanna rolled her eyes humorously. "Enki, they wear beards!"

Enki ignored Inanna's comment, turned to Catharine, and asked, "Have you ever seen these squarebearded people speak to one another?"

"No, my lord," said Catharine, "yet they seem capable of acting in concert with one another."

"Has it occurred to you," asked Enki, "that they might communicate with each other telepathically?"

"It has occurred to me, my lord," replied Catharine, "but my information and training are insufficient to support my coming to even a tentative conclusion."

"Were there insignia on any of their equipment?" asked Enki.

Catharine nodded. "Yes, there were insignia on the bottom of their saucer—at least three repeats of a single device."

"What did it look like?" asked Enki.

Catharine struggled to describe the image in her mind's eye. "It looked like a … calligraphy of a red dragon … wearing a small crown."

"Professor," said Enki, "what was the insignia on the enemy missile?"

"I'm not sure it was a representation of anything in particular, my lord," said David, "but I expect your ship's databank has a photograph of it, as I saw it clearly in a holographic image."

"Shulgi," said Enki, "please call up the image."

Shulgi said aloud, "Image of recent enemy missile."

A two-dimensional version of the holographic image David saw while on the ship's bridge appeared on monitors all around the room.

"That's it!" exclaimed Catharine. "That's the same design."

David couldn't suppress his surprise and said to Catharine, "You see a dragon in that?"

She turned to him. "Don't you?"

The other two Americans laughed, but their mirth was not matched by members of the Council.

David's smile disappeared and he bowed apologetically. "I regret the outburst, my lord."

"That's quite alright," said Enki, "and the situation would indeed be humorous, but that we suspect the insignia is being used by our oldest and deadliest adversary."

"Who is that?"

Enki sighed. "He was once Enlil's servant and has gone by many names over the millennia. Although his original name was Animdugud. He has long been known as Anzû. During ancient times, he betrayed Enlil and all the Anunnaki by stealing the Tablets of Destinies."

"The Tablets of Destinies, my lord?" said David.

"It was what you would today call a *database* of the precise positions, velocities, and orbits of all astronomical bodies of significance to either Nibiru or Earth, as those were the important destinations at the time. I had compiled the Tablets over millennia at enormous expense to the Anunnaki. It existed only in tablet form and we'd made no copies, as we very much wished to keep such information to ourselves."

"Are there Tablets of Destinies presently, my lord?"

"There is a digital Tablet of Destinies infinitely more detailed and complete than that stolen by Anzû, and we maintain multiple encrypted backups at remote locations."

"What happened to Anzû?" asked David.

"He was defeated by Ninurta in a great aerial battle. But, when the time came to pronounce sentence upon Anzû, he was exiled rather than executed."

David asked, "And Ninurta—is *he* still alive?"

Enki replied, "We believe so, but he has not been heard from for thousands of years. He has never been able to overcome the death of his wife, who was killed by the deadly wind that emanated from the first nuclear explosions in the Sinai Desert some four thousand years ago. You would call such a wind 'fallout,' I believe. Incidentally, the earthly cities of Sodom and Gomorrah were destroyed in the same series of explosions."

"Does your lordship know why Anzû has reappeared now and, in particular, what he is doing on Earth?" asked David with a nod to Shulgi, as David seemed to be having a one-on-one conversation with Enki, contrary to protocol.

"Since the recent launch of the missile that came perilously close to Queen Inanna's pyramidion," said Enki, "we have begun to suspect that Anzû has been on Earth a long time, wishes to conquer it for himself, and will brook no interference."

"Do you suppose, my lord," said David, "that Anzû believes the

Anunnaki have conflicting designs on Earth?"

General Shulgi rose from his chair and loomed over the table toward David. "How *dare* you impugn the Council's motives?"

Before David could open his mouth, Enki said, "Peace, General Shulgi. The professor asked simply whether we believe that *Anzû* thinks we wish to dominate the Earth. Isn't that your question, professor?"

David, who couldn't take his eyes of Shulgi, replied, "That is precisely my question, my lord, and is nearly the way I phrased it. I must say, I find the general's defensiveness on that score … disturbing, to say the least."

"Your question was understandable," said Enki. "It's often those with the worst intentions, such as Anzû, who project their intentions upon others. Rest assured that the general is simply being protective of the Council, which, of course, has no intention of dominating the Earth. On the other hand, I doubt the United States would like the Council to look the other way while Anzû conquers your planet."

"To the contrary, my lord," said David, relenting, "I expect that the United States would be inclined to seek the Council's assistance in frustrating Anzû's intentions—although I must admit that I have had no discussions on the question with the President, the Secretary of State, or the admiral."

"And I expect," said Enki, "that the Council would be inclined to provide such assistance as it reasonably could in that regard."

"I will inform the President of your lordship's kind suggestion," said David with a bow. "I *can* say now, my lord, that the United States wishes to be able to utilize its weapons to defend itself from other *earthly* powers, which it is currently unable to do because of a ray being emitted by the Anunnaki."

Enki shrugged. "That cannot be helped for the time being, professor. Those measures have been put in place to protect us."

David said, "Apparently, Anzû has found a way around such measures."

Enki raised an eyebrow and nodded. "Let me provide you with this assurance: In the event that your country's sovereignty is challenged by another power, whether earthly or unearthly, please contact me immediately, and we will tailor the rays to enable your country to take such measures as may be reasonably necessary to defend itself."

"I shall so inform the President, my lord."

Enki rose and said, "The Council thanks you for your cooperation and will quickly inform you of its findings concerning the swatch you brought us. For those who are leaving, we wish you a safe and quick return journey to Earth."

"General Shulgi," said Callow, who hadn't been heard from for a while, "may we take photographs while we're here?"

Enki replied, "Only of yourselves, and only in the public area. Nowhere else, and you may not take pictures of any Council member, at least not on this visit. We'll see in the future. It may be that Queen Inanna will consent. She has, after all, the most adored face and form in the long history of Earth." Enki gave a low, respectful bow to Inanna, who received it as though she had it coming.

⟶⟶○⟨⟨⟨⟩○⟨⟶

IN THE HALLWAY outside the elevator, the four Americans smiled and took snapshots of themselves in every conceivable combination.

"Why would General Shulgi have gone out of his way to make sure we only take pictures *here*?" asked Callow.

David shrugged. "I suppose every royal family has such rules."

Catharine, Callow, and Buchanan stood up against a smooth grey wall while David took a snapshot using Catharine's phone. As he viewed the picture he'd just taken, he gave them the thumbs-up but couldn't help thinking with mild regret how much warmer the shot would have looked if they'd been standing up against the smooth sandstone lining the private quarters.

David shook hands with the men and gave Catharine a warm hug that he wished would never end. "I'll see you all soon," he said, mostly to Catharine.

The elevator door closed.

It took everything David had to keep from tearing his hair out. He suddenly felt unbearably miserable and alone.

⟶⟶○⟨⟨⟨⟩○⟨⟶

ALTHOUGH THE AMERICAN shuttlecraft was painted in the colors and design of the U.S. Space Force, it was really a slightly modified F-35B, a vertical-takeoff and -landing (VTOL) version of a standard navy jet that Buck had flown hundreds of times.

As the F-35B was principally an in-atmosphere craft, it had necessarily been modified. For purposes of flight in extremely rarefied atmosphere, the F-35's jet could transform into a rocket, drawing oxygen from tanks welded to the airframe.

The plane would dock with an orbiting craft in two steps. In the first step or "soft dock," the F-35's jet/rocket would turn down and push the cockpit straight up into a docking chamber on the receiving craft. The receiving craft would lower clasps onto hooks integral to the F-35's airframe both fore and aft of the canopy, and grab the F-35 firmly. During the second step or "hard dock," the receiving craft would lower a seamless gasket onto the F-35's airframe and use a suction device to assure an airtight seal. The canopy would then be popped open from inside the cockpit, and pilot and passengers would climb aboard the receiving craft. Another modification made to render the F-35 spaceworthy was the addition of heat shielding to the bottom of the craft.

Buck regarded the F-35 as the most agile and elegant of fighter aircraft. As he deemed it perfect in its original state, naturally he hated these modifications. They threw off the craft's speed, feel, and balance. The addition of the oxygen tanks was bad enough, but the heat shielding made it fly like a brick.

When they boarded the F-35 for their return to Houston, Callow buckled Catharine into the VIP seat, as she had neither much flying skill nor much interest in learning about the plane.

Callow turned to Buck. "I'm sorry I couldn't let you fly us up here, Buck. No offense intended."

"None taken," said Buck, who was itching to fly the craft now.

"Now, before I let you take hold of this baby," said Callow, "remember: Though it looks like a fighter, it's not a fighter any more. To put it in nautical terms: It's not the yacht; it's the dinghy. Gets ya from Earth to orbit, from orbit to Earth, and that's *all*."

"Does it have a cannon?" asked Buck.

"It's got both a standard cannon and a *laser* cannon," replied Callow devilishly.

"Then it's a damned fighter," said Buck. He turned to Callow. "Look, I get it," said Buck. "I'm not here to hotdog it. Let's get goin'."

"Have you ever used a laser cannon before?" asked Callow skeptically, as he closed the canopy and secured it.

"Only in a simulator," said Buck, "but I get the drift. It's got no arc. It's a straight shooter."

Callow smiled. "That's right, you don't have to anticipate the target's motion so much or shoot far ahead. Take the seat of honor, Mister Navy Cross."

"Don't mind if I do," said Buck, as he put on his helmet and buckled himself in. Callow did the same in the seat next to him.

Buck pressed the Release Requested button, and an alarm rang signaling that the shuttle was about to be forced downward by the mechanical ejector. Buck smiled at Callow. "What did that guy say in the movie? 'We're on an express elevator to hell. Goin' *down!*'"

The F-35 dropped like a rock but remained upright. The engine automatically reverted to its horizontal orientation and thrust them forward like a leaf in a tornado.

The control column felt a little stiff to Buck, which he attributed to the extra weight of the heat shield and the drag added by the oxygen tanks. But otherwise it maneuvered much like an unmodified F-35, and, like any F-35, the sensors provided situational awareness better than any fighter in the world. This fighter's computer was looking in every direction at once, and bringing to Buck's attention both what he needed to know and whatever he *asked* to know.

As the F-35 reached cruising speed, a fast-moving blip appeared in the rear-view sensors.

"What the hell is that?" asked Buck.

Callow cast him a dubious look. "I have no idea."

"Well, he's comin' on fast," said Buck, "and he looks hostile to me."

CHAPTER 13

THE BOGEY WAS approaching fast from behind.

"Can we raise him on the radio?" asked Callow.

"I'm not waitin' here to find out," said Buck as he sent the F-35 into a dive and turned to port. "If you can reach the radio from there, be my guest."

"Can you see any insignia on the bogey?" asked Callow. "Otherwise, I have no idea what frequencies to try."

"Try all the common ones," said Buck. "Meanwhile, if this bastard follows me, I'm gettin' behind him. Let *him* worry about *me*."

Callow unbelted himself to reach the control panel to Buck's left. He stood up, fiddled with the frequency dial, and picked up the mic. "Aircraft in this vicinity, identify yourself immediately."

No reply.

Buck checked the visual display. "Looks like a flying saucer," he said. The bogey was doing its best to follow them. "Strap back in, Callow. I'll take care of this."

"In a minute," said Callow.

Suddenly, a laser flashed just in front of the plane.

"Shit!" shouted Buck. "He just took a shot at us!" Buck barrel-rolled and changed direction.

There was another laser blast just ahead. Buck twisted to get out of the way, and this time brought the nose straight up.

"Careful, Buck!" shouted Callow. "You've only got enough oxygen to go rocket with this thing for a couple minutes. Better head down to denser atmosphere."

Buck reversed direction and headed down again, figuring that by now the bogey's head was spinning. Buck's certainly was.

Callow lost his footing and tripped, falling backwards with a nasty-sounding thud.

"Callow!" shouted Buck. "You okay, man?"

Silence.

"Answer me!" said Buck. When there was no reply, he muttered, "Oh, fer chrissakes."

Buck heard a seatbelt snap open behind him. "*Lieutenant Commander Weldon*," he shouted, "secure that seatbelt immediately and don't ever unsnap it again during flight."

She buckled herself back in.

"Can you tell me about Callow?" demanded Buck.

"Yeah," said Catharine, barely able to hold down her breakfast through the jet's sudden, violent maneuvers. "He's out cold. Must have hit his head."

"Do you see blood?" asked Buck.

"No," said Catharine a moment later.

"Thank God for small favors," said Buck and yanked the column, violently changing course again. At least the F-35 was getting down to denser atmosphere, so its engine could burn fuel using ambient air and would no longer need to rely on the limited oxygen supply in the tanks.

He checked his rear scope, and the bogey was still following him, a little sloppily, but that was understandable given that Buck was dancing all over the sky to stay out of his cross-hairs.

Catharine said, "I was gonna try to get Callow back to his seat and strap him in."

Buck shook his head with exaggerated motion, so she'd be sure not to miss it. "Can you reach him without unbuckling?"

"I think so."

"If you can," he said, "drag him by the shoulders and seat him in front of you. If you can sit him up, put one arm around his collarbone and use your other arm to hold his head as still as you can. Now, if you'll pardon me, I'm in a dogfight here."

The altimeter said he was down well into the atmosphere, and the red indicator had shut off, meaning he was free to forget about the oxygen tanks.

"Okay," said Buck, "I think I've dragged this bastard down to our element." He looked at the image through the rear camera, which clearly showed that the craft was a small saucer. He grabbed the column tight. "Let's see if this guy spent his childhood productively, reading dogfight tales from World War I. Hang on to Callow—we're gonna do a loop, which means we'll be inverted at least part of the time."

He pulled up just in time to avoid another laser shot. "Okay, you bastard," he muttered, as though talking to the opposing pilot. "That's the *last* free shot you get."

In a moment they were upside down, and Catharine was hanging onto Callow's limp form which, but for her efforts, would have crashed into the canopy.

"Oh, you *stupid* bastard," said Buck as they passed behind the saucer and took up a position in his rear. "You wasted your childhood eatin' ice cream with the other kids. Well … *EAT THIS!*" He pulled the trigger on the cannon. The tracers showed rounds repeatedly hitting dead center.

In a fiery moment, the saucer was torn to shreds and exploded. "Hang on!" shouted Buck. "We're gonna pass through his wreckage."

When the F-35 righted itself, Catharine caught the full weight of Callow's loose body and had to struggle to hold onto him. She felt something snap in her shoulder and a white-hot pain shot across her back all the way to her jaw, the kind of pain so all-encompassing that it allowed for no sound to escape her—not so much as a gasp.

As they passed through the bogey's wreckage, the cockpit went momentarily black from the smoke. When daylight returned, a brownish-red fluid from the remains of the opposing pilot had spattered all over the forward half of the canopy, smearing upward like rain driven up a car's windshield by a heavy gust.

"Well," said Buck nonchalantly, "ruined *his* day." He checked his instruments and scopes. "Scopes clear. We're alone up here. Now let's get this brick to a runway."

Callow opened his eyes, sat up on the floor, and turned to Catharine, rubbing his forehead. "Whu—What happened?" he asked groggily.

Catharine hadn't yet caught her breath when Buck laughed derisively.

"Hey, space cowboy," said Buck, "keep your hands off the girls. Now, sit down and buckle yourself in so you can help me land this tub."

It WAS ANOTHER overcast, early winter's day in Ithaca. Though Hendrick was usually the first one up and out of the Quonset hut, this morning he hung around the little canteen nursing a second cup of coffee.

"You comin', Hendrick?" shouted Ham Fisher on his way out.

"I gotta make some calls this morning," said Hendrick. "You go on ahead. I'll be there in an hour or so."

The slowness of the group's progress in identifying a composition to block the Anunnaki ray had inevitably led to a great deal of frustration, which seemed to have a different effect on each geologist in the group.

While the lack of progress increased the pressure on them to find something promising, at the same time it made it seem increasingly unlikely that the next hour—or indeed *any* given hour—would make any difference.

There must be another way, thought Hendrick, so he resolved to retrace his steps in this affair. Eight o'clock in the morning in Ithaca was ... two o'clock in the afternoon in Windhoek. He picked up the secure phone given him by Agent Duffy and dialed Gonçalves' cell phone. It was picked up right away, but the voice was Gary's.

"Hey, chief," said Gary's familiar voice. "Wassup? You make a million bucks yet?"

Hendrick smiled. "Not yet, boss. How about you?"

"*You'll* never know, chief. You wanna talk to me?"

"Well, actually, boss, I called Gonçalves' phone 'cause I wanted to talk to—"

Gary laughed. "Gonçalves? Well, he's knee deep in motor oil at the moment, so it might take a while for him to come to the phone. Anything I can help you with in the meantime?"

"Well, probably. I just didn't want to bother you with details. Remember when the guy from Parnassus came to the *El Paso*?"

"Like it was yesterday."

"He left the transmitter with you that ended up starting that slag fire, right?"

"Right," replied Gary, a note of interest in his voice.

"Well, did he have anything else with him that looked like the transmitter?"

There was a long silence. "You know what? I think he did. Hold on. Let me ask Gonçalves." He cupped his hand over the phone and shouted something that Hendrick couldn't make out. The conversation went back and forth for nearly a minute before Gary came back. "Yeah, there *was* somethin'. It was about the same size as the transmitter and had the same kind of ... soapstone feel to the handle."

Hendrick threw his free hand up. "*Soapstone!*" said Hendrick. "I couldn't think of the word."

"Well, it's a descriptive word," said Gary, "but the handle didn't *look* like soapstone at all."

"I know," said Hendrick, "it looked like marble halvah."

Gary laughed. "Yeah, it did. A little. Anyway, the other gizmo they brought with them was a ... waddya call ... a *jammer*. It was actually jamming the data that the transmitter was tryin' to send. Messed up situation." There was a momentary pause. "And now you've gone and made me want some halvah."

"Yeah," snickered Hendrick, "so, uh … where is it, boss?"

"The halvah?"

Hendrick rolled his eyes. "The *jammer*, boss. Where is it?"

"Oh," said Gary, "hold on." There was another shouted back-and-forth, and Gary came back on the line. "Sorry, chief. They took it with 'em."

"Are you sure they didn't leave it in the parts closet?"

"Nah," said Gary. "We did a clean sweep of the place before we left, like I told ya. No way I'd leave contraband … or even curiosities … in the place, with the police visitin' us at least once a month. They'll take anything that's not bolted to the floor."

Hendrick said, "Did they—?"

"Hold on there, chief. I just remembered. Just after we overflew your atomic bomb, I asked the Kid from Canarsie whether he still had the jammer with him, and he said he did. They must have had it with them the whole flight and taken it with them when they got off at Heathrow."

"Can you give me his phone number?" asked Hendrick. At last, he felt he might be getting somewhere.

"He's still up in space, chief, surrounded by aliens. Best not to call him there, if you get what I mean."

"Yeah, I get it," said Hendrick. "What about the lady?"

"Wasn't she *somethin'*?" said Gary dreamily.

"No, I mean, can you give me her number?"

"Chief, I'm surprised at you. I thought you were happily married."

Hendrick rolled his eyes again. "I mean, so I can call her about the jammer."

"Oh!" said Gary. "Well, I can give you an old cell phone number I have for her." He read the number aloud from his phone directory, and Hendrick wrote it down. "But listen, that number's old. If it doesn't work, there's someone who'd have her current number, and your friend Duffy would be able to connect you with him."

"With whom?"

"The admiral," said Gary. "Admiral Simmons."

"I've spoken to the admiral about other things. If I need to, I'll get his number from Duffy. Hey, boss, there's one other thing that's been on my mind."

"Wuzzat?"

"Wierzbowski. How's he—?"

"He's in the hospital, chief," said Gary gravely, "in bad shape. A few days after you left with Duffy, Wierzbowski tied one on again, and we couldn't wake 'im up for nothin'. We drove him to the emergency room, and they took him in and detoxed him, but he hasn't been fully conscious since then. Cirrhosis. They're feedin' him through a tube, but his liver's failin'. He's on his last legs, the docs say."

"Oh," said Hendrick morosely, "sad to hear."

"It is—but, hey, you don't know what he was like *before*. Interesting guy. Someday when you get back, I'll fill you in. He saw some real hard times. But some really good times, too."

They said their goodbyes, and Hendrick picked up the phone to call Lieutenant Commander Weldon.

This is Catharine Weldon, said the outgoing message, *I can't come to the phone right now, but if you leave your number and a brief message after the beep, I'll get back to you as soon as I can.*

Hendrick left his message. "Um, Miss Weldon, my name is Hendrick. You and I haven't been introduced. I worked for Gary, but I'm working for the government now. I was the guy who disposed of the … item in Windhoek that caused all those problems, and I need to speak with you about that." He left his number, hung up, and shook his head. *What a stupid, vague message*, he thought. *A beautiful woman like that will think I'm just another dope trying to get a date. She won't call back.*

He briefly considered leaving another message, but thought better of it, as he couldn't leave more specific information without creating a potential leak. Besides, calling twice would make him seem less like some random guy looking for a date and more like a *stalker*. He resolved to wait at least two days. If she was going to return the call, she'd probably do it by then.

She probably would have, too, if she wasn't doped up after arthroscopic surgery on her shoulder. And this time, she was under armed guard, and her cell phone under examination by the NSA.

<hr>

"How was the flight from Houston?" asked Admiral Simmons, as he shared a cup of coffee with Buck in his Washington office.

"Not too bad, sir," replied Buck listlessly. "I got some shuteye, and it really helped that we weren't bein' chased by little green men."

"You mean squarebeards?" said the admiral.

"Them, too," said Buck.

"But you don't sound happy."

Buck shrugged. "I feel bad. I escaped without a scratch, but I left both my shipmates in sick-bay."

The admiral offered a bit of reassurance. "A few days in a sling is nothing compared to the fate those squarebeards had in mind for you three."

Buck was about to say something, but stopped himself.

The admiral caught it. "Got something on your mind, Buck?"

"Just that—and this is just a feelin' I've got—I don't think the squarebeards give a crap if I live or die. Nor Callow."

"What did the doctors say about Callow's condition?" asked the admiral.

"Callow's got what one of the docs described as a bad case o' whiplash. They got him strapped in so's he can't turn his head much. But they say he'll be good as new in a couple weeks, maybe less."

The admiral shrugged. "So, if the squarebeards weren't after you or Callow, whom do you suppose they were gunning for?"

Buck sat up with renewed interest in the conversation. "Well, sir, the only one left is the lieutenant commander."

"Why would they want *her*?" asked the admiral, as though he hadn't considered it before.

"Well, admiral, she really kicked their ass in that little U-boat. You shoulda seen her. Born for command. Absolutely—" Buck stopped himself.

"Absolutely *ruthless*? Is that what you were going to say?"

"It all depends, admiral. Is that *good* for her?"

"You bet," said the admiral with a wry smile.

"Then *ruthless* it is," said Buck. "She never took her eye off the ball. Not for a split second. And her little makeshift band of misfits ended up destroying a flying saucer using only weapons at hand—weird-ass crap we happened to find on a research sub. In *my* book, sir, that's distinguished service. If it weren't super secret, I'd recommend it be taught at the naval academy."

"Duly noted," said the admiral. "Any other reason they might want her in particular?"

Buck shrugged. "I suppose they might regard hurting her as a way to get at the Kid from Canarsie. I'm more than a little worried those bastards'll try to murder her in the hospital."

"Since you left her, I've put a 24/7 armed guard on the room she's sharing with Callow. A total of six marines on three shifts."

Buck smiled. "Does my heart good to hear it, sir."

"But you're still worried," declared the admiral.

"Yes, sir," admitted Buck.

"So am I," said the admiral. "Any suspects?"

Buck gave it a little thought, then shook his head. "I don't know enough. Haven't seen enough."

"What about Queen Inanna?"

"You mean to ask: *Is this just a catfight over our ambassador?*" Buck shook his head dubiously. "I don't buy it."

"I don't either," agreed the admiral, "but *I* haven't seen the three of them in a room together. *You* have. What did you think?"

"Honestly, Inanna seemed more irritated hearing that Weldon fired a lethal weapon at one of the creeps than anything having to do with the professor. She seemed to think it was beneath a woman to perform an act so distasteful. And she even bit the professor's butt for *allowing* a woman to be put in a situation where she'd need to do somethin' like that."

"An old-fashioned girl, eh?" asked the admiral. "Well, I guess that's understandable, since she was born more than six thousand years ago. Did Inanna show any great affection for the professor?"

Buck shook his head. "My impression? She's nuts about him, but *way* too proud to let anybody see it, especially since the professor's stiff-armed her so far."

"You think she'll give up on him?"

"I expect so," said Buck. "She's just too proud to continue indefinitely. The thought of a public rejection by a mere mortal would be too much for her to risk."

"Well, that's all well and good," sighed the admiral, "but the real question right now is: *Who told those Anzû bastards that Catharine was on your shuttle?*"

"Could have been an infiltrator in *our* military, although I expect you carefully limited the number of people who knew she was goin' up that day."

"As far as we could manage, only six people knew: You, Callow, the ambassador, Catharine herself, me, and the Commander in Chief. Even the guys in Houston didn't know. In fact, they didn't even know a female was going up."

"So," said Buck, "that would leave the possibility of a turncoat among the Anunnaki."

The admiral nodded. "I think they've got a mole in their midst, and not one of ours. One who's sold out to Anzû."

"Doesn't that give the Anunnaki and us a common enemy?"

The admiral smiled cagily and changed the subject. "How long are you planning on staying in the navy?" he asked.

Buck shrugged. "Tryin' to get rid o' me?"

"No such thing, Buck. Just wanted to know what your plans are … if you've got plans."

"I guess I plan on staying indefinitely."

"I know the feeling," said the admiral. "Once it's under your skin, it's sort of who you are. Nothing else feels quite right, does it?"

"No, sir," said Buck, regarding the admiral awry. "Where you goin' with this, admiral?"

"Ever think you should be passing along the knowledge you've picked up in your years of flying?"

"Haven't given it much thought, to tell the truth."

The admiral began hesitantly. "I'd like to make a proposal, which I'd like you to seriously consider."

"Okay."

"Space Force has finally managed to incorporate cutting-edge technology into a fighter," said the admiral.

"Don't we have enough fighters in the *navy*?"

"Not of the kind that fight in space. Besides, this is a saucer."

"You mean Space Force is not gonna rely on a modified F-35 forever?"

"Nope," said the admiral. "I'd like you to familiarize yourself with the, uh, saucer, learn how to fly it, and write the book on how to *fight* it."

Buck was getting excited about the project. "You mean, how to fight it in *space*?"

"Where else?" said the admiral with a grin.

"I could see doin' that," said Buck, warming to the idea. "You know who'd also be *great* at that?"

The admiral knew whom Buck had in mind. "Why don't you tell me?"

"Gary," said Buck. "Gary Sullivan. That guy could fight a toolshed if they could get one to fly." He shook his head. "But nobody knows where he is."

The admiral folded his arms and leaned in confidentially. "*I* know where he is. And he owes me a favor."

"What kind of favor?" asked Buck.

"He got himself in a smuggling scrape in Casablanca. I got him out of it."

"Where's he livin'?" asked Buck.

"Little watering hole outside Windhoek, Namibia, called Omitara."

"Y'know, admiral," said Buck hesitantly, "Sullivan left the service because he was unhappy with it."

"Was it the food?"

Buck smirked. "Nah. Heaven knows, nobody stays in the service on account of the food. And nobody leaves 'cause of it, either." He grew solemn. "I don't know if you remember, sir, but he was squadron leader and lost a couple of pilots in action over the Bering Strait."

"I remember the incident," said the admiral. "It was that time when the Russian overflights got out of hand. A sneak attack on our F-35s, as I recall."

"Yes, sir," said Buck. "I'm impressed by the admiral's total recall of the incident, especially since it ended up being inconsequential in the scheme of things."

The admiral frowned. "Nothing's inconsequential if it results in the death of my men." He scratched his head. "But Sullivan didn't quit the service until six months later."

"It took a while to really wear him down, admiral. He told me he couldn't sleep for days at a time and had problems with his concentration, which, as you know, is deadly in a fighter pilot."

The admiral nodded grimly. "Well, it certainly hasn't kept him from flying."

"No, sir. Gary *loves* flying. It's what he's been taught to do. It's *aerial combat* he hates."

"We'll see," said the admiral. "We're not sending him up to fight, but to learn and teach. Help him along, if you can."

LATE MORNING ALONE in the Quonset hut, Hendrick looked through his wallet for the slip of paper given him by Agent Duffy with the number of the admiral's encrypted phone. He dialed the number and tucked the paper away.

"Simmons," said the man's voice.

"Good morning, admiral. This is Hendrick. Your number was given to me by Agent Duffy, and I was wondering if you could help me with some information that could be important in my … geological work."

"*Hendrick*," said the admiral as though searching for context. "Oh, yes, now I remember. Duffy told me to expect your call. What can I do for you?"

"Well ... when those two people came to London from Namibia recently, um, I understand they may have brought with them a jamming device that was in a case made of marble or soapstone. It would have come from, uh, very far away." He paused for a response.

"I know which faraway place you mean," said the admiral.

"Very well," said Hendrick. "Did they leave such a device with you or your people?"

Duffy had suggested that Hendrick's question might touch on this subject, so the admiral expected it. But the answer was the same either way. "They neither brought such a device with them nor suggested that one existed. I'm afraid I can't help you."

Hendrick shook his head. "Well, sir. They are believed to have had such a device when they landed at Heathrow Airport. Do you have any information that they handed it off to anyone?"

While the admiral would ordinarily have ended the conversation at this point, he detected an urgency in Hendrick's voice that made him loath to give up. Was it possible that Catharine and the professor's debriefing was deficient? Try though he might, he couldn't remember whom he'd assigned to do the debriefing. Is it possible they weren't debriefed at all? He began to sweat under the collar, because that would have been a rookie mistake on his part.

"I must tell you, Hendrick, that I have no such knowledge, nor any reason to suspect that they handed off such a device to anyone, but I'd like to help you if I can." He thought of Miriam Azeri and Professor Iskender. "Let me make some calls and I'll get back to you, either myself or through Duffy."

"Thank you, sir," said Hendrick. "It could make all the difference."

"Goodbye for now," said the admiral.

DAVID ATE AT the pyramidion commissary, where he'd been making an effort over the past few days to learn something of the food he was eating.

Most Anunnaki kept clear of him, but there was a small group of young males who actually sought out his company. They wanted to know the same thing *human* men wanted to know: *What is it like to be pursued by the Queen of Heaven?* He'd been tempted to try to answer that question and explain the complications it was causing in his own life, but these fellows were far too young to understand. At their age, he recalled, there was no saying *no* to the invitation of *any* beautiful, unattached woman—but to say *no* to the Queen of Heaven? The very suggestion would have been incomprehensible.

As he left the commissary, he bowed to the chef and thanked her, receiving a smile in return. He went out into the hallway, rounded the corner to his room, and stopped for a moment to study the irregular American flag mounted on his door. Doctor Zia was right; there was an extra white stripe at the bottom representing the fourteenth of America's thirteen original colonies.

As David was about to put his hand on the doorknob, he got the distinct feeling something was amiss, something well beyond the extra stripe on the flag. His nose was tickled by the scent of ... incense, which seemed to be rising from the small opening at the base of the door.

Could this be the wrong room? Ridiculous question. Who else's door would be emblazoned with an American flag? As he braced himself and slowly opened the door, he was hit by the overpowering scent of incense and exotic perfume. Remaining outside, he stuck his head in.

Inanna, in a maroon sari that flattered her perfect figure, lounged across the full-length couch. Shiduri was at her feet, anointing them with oil. On three tables, incense sticks had been lit and emitted a smoky aroma.

Inanna noticed David and smiled lazily.

"Join me. Come," said the Queen of Heaven. Though she tried to make the words 'join' and 'come' sound as innocent as possible, the setting she'd created belied any innocent interpretation, and all David could think of was the prospect of joining with her and coming in the most carnal sense.

David bowed to Inanna and took a seat in an upholstered chair several feet away.

Inanna pouted and feigned feeling slighted. "I have called you to my bed several times, David, yet you have only sent your regrets. Should I be insulted?"

David shook his head. "Not in the least, Your Majesty. You are a surpassing beauty, renowned throughout Earth. Your image and your various names have been regarded as international symbols of beauty and desire for thousands of years. And I share the world's appreciation of you." She seemed pleased with his words, but unsatisfied. He added, "And perhaps I flatter myself to feel a kinship with Your Majesty."

"So, why do you not accept the offer of my charms?"

"On Earth, madam—and I refer to Earth not to hold it out as ideal in any sense, but because it's the sole source of the customs by which I was reared—a man may not accept such charms proffered by any but his own woman. To possess *you*, Majesty, is so far beyond my stars that I cannot conceive of anything good, save momentary pleasure, coming from our conjoinment."

"I have made kings of my lovers," she said proudly, "and given birth to kings."

David nodded. "'Uneasy lies the head that wears the crown,' wrote our great Bard. I have no desire—and less competence—to rule over other men. And there is yet another reason, madam. I feel that you and I are … joined in family."

"Does any of this mean that you don't *wish* to make love with me?" she asked.

Though he didn't wish to shake his head, he did so nonetheless. "You are the most irresistible woman. I desire you beyond reason."

Inanna smiled with satisfaction and said, "Shiduri, leave us now."

David sat up and objected. "If Shiduri leaves, madam, I shall leave, too."

Inanna's eyebrow rose slowly. "You want her … to watch?"

"Of course not," he replied, blushing.

"Do you want her to join us? Shiduri," she said, "disrobe for the ambassador."

He stood up. "No, no, no!" He regarded Inanna with consternation. "Has Your Majesty not heard anything I've said? I cannot do this."

"Sit, David," she said, and he did. "You say you're forbidden to enjoy the sexual favors of any woman but your own."

David nodded.

"When you refer to your own woman, you refer to Weldon, is this not correct?"

"Correct," he said.

"But I have seen this butcher Weldon. She wears no ring to indicate her betrothal. Is she betrothed to you?"

He hated to admit it. "No, madam."

"Have you purchased her from her father?"

"What? *No!*"

Inanna looked confused. "Then, by what means are you betrothed?"

"By means of a mutual *promise*, Majesty."

"Between you and her father?"

David was exasperated. "It has nothing to *do* with her father. It's a promise between two lovers, Majesty."

Overhearing this, Shiduri gasped and sighed, clasping her hands over her heart. David momentarily pitied Shiduri. *Another hopeless romantic.*

"Shiduri!" said Inanna sternly, and turned to David. "And what if you and I *are* of the same family? What of that? You know I am known as Beloved of Anu, our king who died recently. He was my great-grandfather. Do you think he admired me chastely from afar? Hah! He was my *lover*! And I have seduced both his sons, Enki and Enlil, for what little they have given me. Does that make me somehow *unclean* to you?"

David knew he needed to negotiate this minefield carefully, for Inanna was truly incensed. "Not in the least, Majesty. I understand that these are the customs of your kind. It is the custom of *my* kind to avoid coupling with anyone closer in kinship than a second cousin. It's not a matter of uncleanliness, but a difference in custom."

Inanna seemed a bit mollified. "You and I are not closer than second cousins," she declared.

"But you and I *are* related, are we not?"

She granted a small concession. "I was distantly related to Joseph, who was my lover. And you are descended from him, but not from me. I'll leave it to you to decide how your earthly strictures apply to such a harmless situation."

"In any event," said David, "Hebrew traditions would not condemn your couplings of so long ago, as the laws were not handed down to mankind until Yahweh appeared to the Israelites at Mount Sinai."

"Yahweh?" exclaimed Inanna incredulously. "You mean my cousin Marduk!"

David was taken aback. "What are you saying?"

Inanna clammed up, embarrassed. "I'm sorry, David. I misspoke. I have been instructed not to speak of earthly religious beliefs, but I have knowledge of the history of Joseph's people, the ones who call themselves Hebrew. That word *Hebrew* is really *Nippuru*, which denominates a denizen of Nippur, the Sumerian city from which your ancestor Abraham came before moving to the Sinai Desert. Nippur was Enki's control center when last the Anunnaki lived on Earth, in what you call ancient times."

David was shocked to learn these things. "Isn't Marduk Enki's firstborn son?"

"He *was*," said Inanna. "Marduk is dead. He died on Earth around the same time as your Alexander the Great. Marduk wished to help civilize your kind by laying down a *few* laws, laws that were absolute and simple to remember." Her face reddened. "Oh, David, you can never mention what I said about Yahweh. Please. I *beg* of you. Promise me that you will never mention it, especially to Enki."

"I promise," said David. Suddenly fatigued, he looked longingly at Elijah's mantle, still neatly folded next to his laptop. It was so inviting that it overrode the room's inebriating scent of forbidden sex.

"I will go now," said Inanna. "We will continue discussion of our relationship in the near future."

While Shiduri efficiently doused and gathered up the incense sticks, waterbowl, and towels, Inanna kissed David on the cheek. As she withdrew, he couldn't help but gaze into her eyes and tenderly stroke her face, much as he would a beloved relative's. It wasn't until later that he realized that doing so would probably make her perceive it as a softening in his resistance to sexual congress with her. He bowed as Inanna left his room with a pretty wave.

But her protectiveness of his religious beliefs (mixed, perhaps, with her fear of Enki) once again showed her authentic goodheartedness. And made him want her even more. She seemed to have no idea that, although he found her brazenness distasteful, her vulnerability was simply irresistible.

CHAPTER 14

For the second time in a month, Catharine lay in a hospital bed with the movement of her left arm and shoulder mechanically restricted. This time, however, she was in Houston, protected by armed Marine guards day and night, and she'd had surgery, which still hurt like a bastard.

"Are they gonna bring in a display, so I can see what's happening, too?" asked Lieutenant Callow, who was sharing Catharine's room and guards.

Catharine felt bad for him. Although he'd managed to avoid surgery (thanks to her stopping him from flopping all over the cockpit during the dogfight), he was in a contraption that kept his head and neck immobilized.

"It's not a TV show, Callow. It's a dossier, and they're printing out a copy for me right now."

Callow moaned in pain. "Let me know if there's anything good in it, 'kay?"

"I'll read you all the dirty parts, don't worry," she quipped.

He tried to turn, which had no effect except to make him gasp in pain. "No," he grunted out, "I mean anything interesting."

"Keep your shirt on, Callow. Let me make some sense of it first. I promise I'll tell you anything interesting when I've done."

A hospital attendant carrying a thin manila folder walked up to the two marines stationed outside the room, one of whom stepped forward to examine the file before accepting it.

The marine leafed through the file, eyeballed both sides of every paper inside, ran his fingers up and down all edges, and dismissed the attendant. He turned around, walked into the room, and handed the file to Catharine. "You got enough light there to read, lieutenant commander?"

She assured him there was enough.

"Would you like my corporal to help you flip the pages?" he asked. "I ask because you seem to have only one good paw at the moment."

Catharine glanced through the door and noticed that the corporal was a woman. Though it was a tempting offer, having someone turn pages for her would be awkward, and she didn't want anyone else getting a good look at the file.

"No, thank you," said Catharine, "but if you could get the orderly to bring me one of those desks on wheels to place over my torso, I'd be much obliged."

"Sure thing, ma'am," he said, and left the room.

In a minute, she put the file on the wheeled desk and began to review it one page at a time, carefully placing each reviewed page face down in a small stack to her left.

"Why are you talkin' to yourself?" asked Callow.

"Oh, sorry," she said. "I didn't realize."

In a few minutes, she finished reviewing the file and called out. "Sergeant."

The sergeant came in. "Yes, ma'am?"

She handed him the file. "I need you to call Admiral Simmons on my behalf and ask him to confirm three things: first, that the photograph in this file is correct; second, that the ambassador has received a copy; and third, that Lieutenant Callow here is cleared for all information in the file." The sergeant accepted the file and left.

Callow, being careful not to move more than necessary, said, "What the *hell*, lieutenant commander? I'm in the damned Space Force and I was on the orbital detail *with* you."

"Callow, I'm going to share this information with you as soon as the admiral says it's okay. But before I do, I'm going to ask those two fine marines—to whom I cheerfully entrust my life—to step outside and close the door."

Callow was thoughtfully silent a moment, and said, "*That* kinda secret, huh?"

"You'll see," she replied.

The sergeant entered and handed Catharine the file. "Ma'am, I spoke with the admiral personally. The photograph is correct, the file was originally *delivered* to the ambassador, who has retained a copy, and Lieutenant Callow is cleared for all information in the file."

"Smartly done, sergeant," said Catharine. "Thank you." The sergeant nodded respectfully, and she reciprocated (a bit feebly), adding, "Please close the door securely on your way out, if you would."

"Yes, ma'am."

Once the door was closed, Callow said, "What's with the salute?"

"I guess," she shrugged, "when you have a direct line to the President's close military advisor, you're perceived as having clout."

"Guess so," said Callow. "Now, spill. What's in the file?"

She opened the file on the wheeled table and began leafing through the pages again. "This is the Anunnaki report on that swatch of the squarebeard cloth that I grabbed during the action on Great Slave Lake."

"What's it say?" asked Callow.

"Shut up and I'll tell you," she said. "Talk and I'll stop. Is that clear?"

"Yah," he said.

"Sorry," she said. "I'm exhausted and in a lot of pain." She flipped over a page. "The cloth was a plant-based textile."

"Which plant?"

"You're not shutting up," she said. "Maybe I'll just stop."

"You can't!" he said.

"I can, and I will. You ready to shut up now? I'll open the floor to questions when I'm done."

He sat quietly and bit his lip.

"The textile is made primarily from a cotton-like plant formerly used in textiles on Planet Nibiru. Its local name, translated from the Akkadian is *An's Feather*. The plant has no Greek name, as Greek has never been spoken on Nibiru."

She read silently for a moment, then spoke. "The stuff on the cloth that looked like black bile was in fact the sap of a Nibirune tree. Translated from the Akkadian, its local name is *stonewood*, after the wood's extraordinary hardness, resembling Australian ironwood in function and durability. The Council Table that we saw the other day is sixteen thousand years old; it's made of carefully preserved Nibirune stonewood."

Callow mumbled something like, "What the hell?"

"Wait, it gets worse." She turned over another paper. "The fecal material was *not* only animal-based feces, but contained a substance resembling vegetation-based compost. What we guessed was blood was only partially blood; it was also xylem and phloem, which is the stuff that travels up and down the root system of a plant. A portion of the reddish stuff was blood: *Human* blood, in fact."

"Those sick bastards," said Callow. "They drink human blood?"

"Nope," she said with a sigh. "According to the report, a squarebeard is a neomorphic (shape-shifted) form of an organism predominantly based upon an earlier life form. Here's a full-color photograph of the basic organism in its paleomorphic (original) form."

Catharine picked up the glossy color photo in her right hand, stared at it a moment, then extended it far enough toward Callow for him to see it.

He laughed. "That's a picture of a tree in the admiral's backyard, lieutenant commander."

"Look again," she said.

"Yeah?" he said. "What am I looking for?"

"What color is the sky in the photo?" she asked.

"Looks like a storm's brewin'," he said. "I guess I'd call it maroon."

She took the photo back. "That's evidently the color of the sky on the surface of Nibiru. This is a photo of a living stonewood tree."

Callow spent a moment in silent disbelief. At last, he said, "You mean, the squarebeards are … *plants*?"

Catharine resumed her recitation. "Partly. If you want to see an example of the *animal* component of a squarebeard, just look in the nearest mirror."

Callow grimaced with revulsion. "A squarebeard is a cross between a human and … a tree?" He shook his head, which hurt to do, and said, "That's disgusting—and unnatural."

She shrugged. "Strong words from someone who's half alien and half great ape."

Callow was befuddled. "So, what does this mean? Somebody genetically combined a tree and a human being into a squarebeard?"

Catharine nodded. "First, Enki combined one of his kind with a great ape to create humankind. Then Anzû combined humankind with a tree to create a squarebeard. That second seems pointless, but I'm sure Anzû had something in mind."

"But why would Anzû do that?"

"Says here that certain Nibirune plants have long been believed to have telepathic powers."

"How the hell would anyone know that? What do plants have to think about, anyway?"

"Well, for one thing, they evidently think about the survival of their species. Even on Earth, certain plants seem capable of signaling danger to others, even when all known methods of communication have been blocked."

"So, squarebeards are telepathic?"

"Seems so, at least on some level."

"Guess that would explain why we've never seen them talk to one another," said Callow.

"Plants are also largely emotionless," she added, reading from the file. "So that's why they could beat Lorraine mercilessly. They have no pity, at least for anything outside their own plant species."

"So they can be mindlessly cruel to people," remarked Callow.

"Says here that, at least on Nibiru and possibly on Earth, plants have no care for a single organism of their kind, but only for the survival of their species as a whole."

"So each squarebeard will sacrifice itself without a second thought," said Callow. "The perfect soldier."

"There's speculation in the file that they're incapable of unaided reproduction and have no sex organs. Also, without additional samples, the Anunnaki say they can't be sure, but the squarebeards appear to be clones of only a few distinct strains." She took her eyes off the file. "I suppose that would explain why some of them look exactly like others."

"Why did Anzû need to add human genes to a tree?" asked Callow, who added, "And why do all my questions sound insane?"

"Because it's a new abomination," said Catharine. "Just what we needed, right? The Anunnaki say that Anzû surely added an animal to the genetic mix to make the squarebeards ambulatory—meaning so they can walk around. *And why choose humans?* For their superior problem-solving skills."

"Smart, emotionless, telepathic plants with no scruples and no individual drive to survive," said Callow. "The perfect slaves."

"Not perfect," said Catharine. "I've noticed that, without an individual need to survive, they show a lack of initiative and quick reaction. And they lack the sense of individual jeopardy that makes for a superior warrior." She closed the file and tossed it on the wheeled table. "Give me a Buck Buchanan any day. He can take out a whole squadron of these bastards."

"But not a *group* … or a *wing*," intoned Callow.

"Meaning?" said Catharine.

"Meaning … even mind-numbed robots can win … if they outnumber us badly enough."

IN HER ROOM at the Grosvenor, Miriam made herself up in preparation for her second date with Shawn McCauley. She was pleased to see she still didn't require much makeup, just enough to add a bit of definition. The march of time had gone easy on her.

At their first meeting the other day at the buffet, Shawn had seemed eager to please and a good conversationalist, but he seemed subject to a vagueness or ... insecurity she found a little disquieting. He'd be holding forth about some aspect of his job or some little memory about growing up with David when suddenly he'd lose his train of thought and gaze out the window with a puzzled expression. It wasn't as though he was unaware of his lapses, either. To the contrary, his full awareness of them left him profoundly befuddled and embarrassed.

She decided to ignore Shawn's lapses as a temporary result of his weeks of confinement aboard an alien spaceship. After all, it isn't as though one can be expected to go *unchanged* through such adversity. And he was so endearingly apologetic whenever he suffered one of his lapses that she wrote the whole matter off as a temporary disability, nothing of lasting concern.

She took the elevator to street level, where Shawn awaited her in an old-style London cab at the carriage entrance. He got out to open her door, which made her smile, then closed it and stepped around to the other side, where he energetically got back in.

"Seven Park Place, please," he said to the driver. Turning to Miriam, he asked, "Have you been there before?"

"No," she replied, "but I've heard wonderful things about it. How about you?"

"Not yet," he said, "and I'm looking forward to sharing the experience with *you*. It came highly recommended. Tell me, how is Doctor Iskender?"

"Daniel's been asked by his old faculty at Addis Ababa to give a few lectures in his field of expertise, so he'll be leaving London late tomorrow. He's promised to return in a few weeks."

"Oh," said Shawn, sounding a little disappointed. "I was beginning to really enjoy the old fellow's company."

"Isn't he a wonder?"

"In a sense, he seems to live in two places," said Shawn. "One of them is happy and relaxed. That's how he lives in *your* world, I think. But he also occupies this alternate world of language, where he's consumed by the complexity and subtlety of it all. Interesting fellow."

In a few minutes, the cab pulled up by the restaurant and they got out. As Shawn paid the fare and the cab sped off, Miriam's phone rang. The screen read: *Admiral.*

"Hello?" she said.

"Good evening, Miriam," said the admiral. "Can you talk for a minute?"

"Well," she said, "Shawn and I just arrived at Seven Park for supper." Sure, it felt a bit like bragging, but she'd gone without such pleasures far too long.

"McCauley?" asked the admiral.

"Yes."

"When's your reservation for?"

She turned to Shawn and relayed the question. "When is the reservation?" Before he could reply, she pointed to the mouthpiece and whispered, "It's the admiral."

"Oh!" said Shawn and glanced at the time on his phone. "It's in ten minutes. I'll tell the maître d' we're here. Give the admiral my best regards."

"Ten minutes," she said to the admiral, "but please make it quick."

"I'll take much less time than that," said the admiral. "Do you remember when David and Catharine first came to London just before you and I met, whether either of them had a handheld device that looked like it was contained in a soapstone or marble housing?"

Miriam was baffled. She searched her memory and came up blank, then began to wonder why something like that would be so important that the admiral would call her weeks later to ask about it.

"No, admiral," she said. "I have no recollection of anything fitting that description. Of course, I wasn't with them very long. And their London hotel room had been broken into. Perhaps it was stolen. Is it important?"

"Well, probably not," said the admiral. "Is it possible Doctor Iskender may have seen it when you were elsewhere?"

"Now that you mention it, Daniel and David were alone at a pub for a while. Oh, but I expect Daniel would have mentioned to me anything he deemed important, and he never said a word."

"Is he in London now?" asked the admiral.

"He is, but he'll be gone tomorrow. He's heading for Addis Ababa tomorrow to start a round of lectures at the university."

"Do you have his mobile phone number?" asked the admiral. "I doubt there was anything that fit the description I gave you, and, even if there was, it's probably not very important, but a friend of mine is looking for it."

"Of course," said Miriam, and read out Iskender's number for the admiral.

"Thanks a lot," said the admiral. "Now, you have a wonderful time with Shawn. He's a great fellow and he's had a rough time of late. Incidentally, do you notice any … vagueness in his thought patterns?"

"Vagueness?" asked Miriam. "Well, he seems to momentarily become lost in thought occasionally. More than I would expect for a man of his relative youth, but it doesn't seem to interfere with his enjoyment of conversation. Why do you ask?"

"Just that I've been getting reports about some of the other people who were held by the Anunnaki, and they seem to be suffering unexpected lapses in speech or memory. They seem otherwise unaffected by their experience, though. Just keep an eye out for it. I imagine it's of no real consequence."

"I will, sir," she replied. "Anything else?"

"Just one thing, and it's the most important. Don't leave Seven Park until you've had the toffee apple dessert. In fact, tell them you'll want that for dessert as soon as the waiter comes over."

"Toffee apple," she said cheerily. "Got it. Ta-ta!"

"Ta-ta!" said the admiral with a laugh.

THE ADMIRAL REACHED Iskender in his room at the Grosvenor.

"Yes, admiral," said Daniel, "it's a pleasure to hear from you. Do you need me to translate something? Because, I'm afraid I'll be unavailable for a couple of weeks after today."

"No, Daniel," said the admiral. "One of my friends has sent me on a wild-goose chase, but it's bugging me, and I have to track it down."

"How can I help?" asked Daniel.

"When Catharine and the professor first got to London, before all that business with the spacecraft and the soldiers and all, did either of them have a small handheld device that looked like it was contained in a soapstone or marble case?"

Daniel was quiet for a moment, because he remembered seeing Catharine holding something of that description, but couldn't remember when or where.

"Daniel?" asked the admiral, "are you there? Damned connection—"

"I'm here, admiral," said Daniel. "I *do* remember seeing such a thing, but I can't remember … no, wait … *Yes*, I remember now. When we were at the safe-deposit box and all the items from the box had been spread about the table for examination, Catharine went through her purse … you know, as women will do when searching for some personal item or other … and for just a second she drew out something generally fitting that description. Now, for all I know, it may have been a makeup case or some such mundane thing, so I wouldn't make too much of my momentary observation, but it wasn't encased in the usual tortoise-shell plastic. The case resembled well-polished and unusual composite stone, perhaps marble, such as I had never seen. I remember remarking to myself that it must have been a keepsake of hers, because it looked like something—please pardon my ignorance of the military life—that someone in the armed services could definitely not afford to buy out of her own pay. Almost on the order of a solid-gold pistol or some such thing."

Now it was the admiral's turn to be silent.

"Admiral?" said Daniel.

"Did she remove it from her purse?" asked the admiral.

"Not that I saw, no."

"So, she probably took it with her when you all left?"

"I would assume so," said Daniel. "Look, admiral, I don't wish to tell tales out of school on someone as dedicated and courageous as Catharine, so please presume, if you would, that it was *not* what your friend is looking for. I certainly couldn't identify it with any certainty—"

"Don't worry, Daniel," said the admiral. "I have no doubt that, if it's something of importance, Catharine will own up to it as soon as I speak with her. I myself can attest to her loyalty and unbounded courage. It may have been—probably *was*—something entirely different from what my friend is looking for. If I ask Catharine or anyone else about it, I'll keep your name out of it, if at all possible."

"I would much appreciate it, admiral. Miriam would be quite cross with me if she suspected that I was pointing an accusatory finger at her friend."

"Not at all, Daniel. You needn't concern yourself. Enjoy your lectures. Will you have the same mobile phone with you in Ethiopia?"

"Yes, I will. Call me if you need me."

"Thanks, Daniel. Goodbye."

They hung up.

The admiral sat back in his favorite chair.

People are forgetting things they would ordinarily remember. *I forgot to have Catharine and David debriefed after the excitement in Westminster. Catharine forgot to tell me about this … thing. If David knew about it, he also neglected to tell me about it.* Shawn and the others who'd been held captive were also having memory lapses.

These lapses are related, and they're intentional on the part of ... someone.

But *whom*?

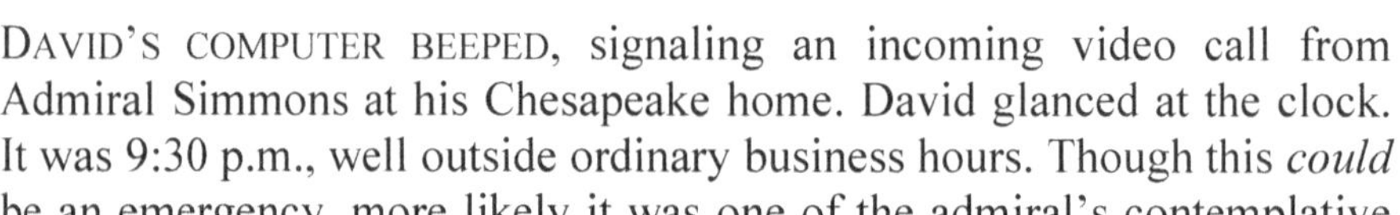

DAVID'S COMPUTER BEEPED, signaling an incoming video call from Admiral Simmons at his Chesapeake home. David glanced at the clock. It was 9:30 p.m., well outside ordinary business hours. Though this *could* be an emergency, more likely it was one of the admiral's contemplative after-hours calls, in which he liked to discuss strategy.

"Schubert here," said David. "Good evening, admiral. How are you?"

"Fine, fine," came the reply. "I think it's about time for a direct call between the President and Lord Enki."

"About what?" asked David. "I ask only because I'll *be* asked."

"A few things," said the admiral. "For one thing, Space Force is ready to begin flight tests on their new flying saucer, the SF-5."

"No kidding?" said David. "I always *thought* they were taking their sweet time developing their own craft. But why is this something the President would like to talk to Enki about?"

"The President doesn't yet know whether that's what he wants. I'm brainstorming with you before I discuss it with him."

"I see," said David. "Well, it would be prudent to tell Enki when and where we'll be flying, at least so he doesn't think we're the squarebeards and blow us out of the sky."

"That's part of it," said the admiral.

"And also," said David, "if we're testing weapons, we'll need him to cut his disabling ray, so our equipment will work."

"True. What do you think his reaction will be?"

David shrugged. "I don't know. I suppose he'd have confidence that he could control things if it turned out to be some sort of sneak attack, so he probably wouldn't object on principle. He'd want to know how many craft, the nature of the weapons, and the like. Also, I suppose he'd have to be concerned with the collateral signal he'd be sending the other nations of the world by making a special exception for the good ol' U.S. of A."

"You think Enki would cooperate?"

"Probably," said David.

"Why would he cooperate?" asked the admiral.

"I think that with Anzû in the picture, the Anunnaki would like a strong, dependable ally, especially one equipped with space fighters. While, from Enki's viewpoint, it would unavoidably bring certain risks—enough so that he might have opposed it as recently as a few weeks ago—he'd probably be less resistant now."

The admiral grunted. "The enemy of my enemy is my friend?"

"Something like that," said David. "What other topics are you considering for a summit?"

"Some of the people who remained in Anunnaki custody for a few weeks are having memory lapses … lapses in conversation. Stuff like that. By and large, they're much too young for such symptoms. I'd like to know what the Anunnaki did to them and how to undo it … or at least mitigate it."

"Pardon the personal note, admiral, but—"

"Yes, it includes Shawn. He's okay, but I spoke with Miriam—you know, they're dating—"

"Okay!" said David. "That's great! She's terrific, too."

The admiral smiled. "Yes, she certainly seems to be. Shawn's having … lapses, incompletely recalled memories, and so on. Nothing too upsetting, but I think, as a humanitarian matter, we ought to get to the bottom of it."

"Makes sense, although I have no idea what reception we'll get, since they obviously did it for a reason."

"Doesn't hurt to ask," said the admiral. "They may not even know the extent of it. It'll give them something they *ought* to do for us, and we can judge their overall intentions based on the quality of their cooperation."

"Both your suggestions make sense," said David, "but I'm not hearing anything compelling, you know, that really requires a summit."

The admiral nodded and tossed out his idea. "I think we should ask them if they intend to take over our planet."

"Whew!" said David, followed by a soft whistle. "That's a biggie. Why would he answer?"

"Do you mean: 'Why would he answer *truthfully*?'"

"Not really," said David. "Enki has a strong propensity to tell the truth, probably as an ethical matter, but also as a matter of pride. I think he'd regard it as lowering himself to give someone a false or misleading answer. And, let's face it, he's holding all the cards. He doesn't *need* to lie, or hold back. As you yourself have observed numerous times, if he wanted us dead, we'd be dead." David found that he'd persuaded himself of the answer. "If he has truly foul intentions, which I doubt, he'll just decline to answer."

"Is the question important enough for a summit?"

David nodded emphatically. "Oh, sure. But what do we do if he says, 'I'm going to clean house; kiss your ass goodbye'?"

"Or, as you say, if he declines to answer."

"Yeah. What then?"

"He must know he'd be declaring an asymmetric war with Earth," replied the admiral.

David rubbed his eyes. "Such a war—at this point, anyway—would give new meaning to the word *asymmetric*. It'd be Fredericksburg all over again," he said, referring to the one-sided slaughter of Union troops trying to cross the Rappahannock River under withering artillery fire.

"And Enki's sitting up there on Marye's Heights," said the admiral, referring to the high ground occupied by Confederate artillery during the battle.

"But remember, admiral, without Enki, the Flood would have been the end of our species. He doesn't want us destroyed."

"True," said the admiral. After a moment's silence, he said. "There's something else I need to talk with you about," said the admiral, "but it's too sensitive to discuss on this medium. When are you coming down?"

"Well, I think they expect me to stay a few weeks before taking a break from the embassage," David speculated, "but they can't very well object to my going to Washington to speak with the President. They know that *we* know they listen in on such conversations as they can."

David strained to think of what matter was so sensitive that it couldn't be discussed by the same means as they were discussing an upcoming summit meeting. "Can you give me a clue as to the topic?"

"Not tonight." The admiral's energy was flagging, and he was obviously ready to end the call. "Plenty to think about," he said. "I'll let you know what the President thinks."

"Thanks," said David and they hung up.

David scratched his head. *Something else to talk to me about? Something more confidential than a plan to demand a statement of Enki's intentions?* A troubling thought.

David shook it off and looked at Elijah's mantle, which he'd taken to leaving folded on his bed. He'd learned that, ordinarily, the mantle provided him some comfort and seemed (selectively, at least) to prevent Inanna from intruding into his dreams.

Occasionally, though, the mantle seemed to generate enigmatic dreams of its own, most of which David would forget shortly after waking, but a few of which would linger. Lately, he'd had a recurring dream in which he was lying on his bed staring at the moon, thinking how beautiful and precious it is. But when he awoke, his stomach was churning and full of dread.

CHAPTER 15

"I'LL NEED YOU to arrange a summit meeting between the President and Lord Enki," said the admiral calling a few days later, "but before you do, you're going to have to come down from your cushy little perch to meet with the President and me. That probably seems like a sacrifice to you, but I can offer you an inducement. Catharine has left the hospital in Houston; she's flying into D.C. early for the meeting, which *she'll* be attending, too. For some unfathomable reason, she wants to see you first. Uncle Sam has booked you two a suite at the Willard."

Nothing could have pleased David more. "How's Catharine's shoulder coming along?"

"Pretty well," said the admiral, "but you can ask her yourself quite soon. I've got a shuttle going up there to fetch you in a couple of hours."

"That gives me so little time to pack! Just kidding, since I brought almost nothing. However, I'll have to inform my hostess."

"Inanna? Well, no need to mention Catharine," said the admiral.

"I have no intention of doing so," said David. "Thanks, admiral."

"By the way, we're currently considering a one-on-one summit between the President and Lord Enki."

"Okay," said David, "but Enki might feel compelled to bring along the Council of Twelve, or such members as he can muster."

"Well, we'd prefer the meeting to be one-on-one but, just between us, we're prepared to negotiate on that issue. Only thing is: If he has multiple participants, we reserve the right to bring as many."

"I'll let him know, if he insists that the Council be permitted to attend," said David.

"Okay, David," said the admiral. "Remember, your trip is basically a four-day midwinter vacation in beautiful downtown Washington, D.C., such as it is. After that, it's right back to the grind. See you in a few days."

"I look forward to it, sir."

Click.

David called Shiduri and asked whether Her Majesty could see him briefly to pay his respects before his impending departure.

Shiduri excused herself to speak with Queen Inanna, but quickly came back on the line. "Her Majesty Inanna, Beloved of Anu, will receive you in the throne room in one hour."

"Thank you, Shiduri."

While selecting the things he intended to bring with him to Earth, he paused before packing Elijah's mantle. Although he had no intention of *wearing* it on this trip—or sleeping in it (as had become his custom on the pyramidion)—he decided to bring it anyway. Over the past few weeks, he'd become loath to part with it. Although he half-believed that was because of the mantle's value to posterity (or perhaps its monetary value), the truth was, he just wanted it near him all the time. And why not? After all, it weighed only a few pounds, and it *was* his, wasn't it?

⟶ ∘ 〰 ∘ ⟵

SHIDURI LED DAVID into the corridor outside Queen Inanna's throne room. He noticed with immediate relief that there was no detectable scent of incense or overwhelming perfume. So, Inanna hadn't used the past hour to prepare another attempted seduction.

As they rounded the turn into the throne room proper, he saw Inanna pottering about an intricate architect's model of a sprawling complex dominated by columnated structures in ancient Egyptian style. Preoccupied with the model, she failed to notice Shiduri leading David in.

Shiduri stopped some distance short of Inanna and whispered quietly to David. "She's like this all the time now, preoccupied with her little toys. I shall announce your arrival."

Shiduri turned toward Inanna and made a formal announcement. "Inanna, Queen of Heaven, Beloved of Anu, I bring unto your presence David Schubert, Ambassador of the United States of America."

Inanna took another moment before turning around and, when she did, she glanced at David absently for less than a second before returning her attention to the model. As protocol forbade David to speak until spoken to, he dutifully waited. Inanna picked up and examined one of the little pieces in the model, a figure of a walking woman holding a golden, sword-length ankh in her hand. He began to feel that Inanna was deliberately snubbing him, which he could understand (and would not have minded) if only he weren't expecting the imminent arrival of a shuttlecraft that would bring him down to Earth.

"Come, David," she said at last. "See my plans for the new Temple of Inanna."

He stepped forward and admired the workmanship of the model and the large number of stone buildings the complex would contain. "Where is this complex to be built, Your Majesty?"

Inanna turned her smooth, innocent face toward him. Though it was made up to look like Nefertiti's solemn, defiant countenance, ironically there was a youthfulness about Inanna's eyes that was utterly lacking in Nefertiti's, and it nearly broke his heart. She held her fingers up to her lips as though imploring him to keep her secret. "It will be built at Baalbek," she said conspiratorially and, in that moment, David's chest swelled with affection for this beauty who wished so earnestly to share with him the design of her temple, as though it were an imaginary cottage in the woods for them to share.

She pointed to the largest structure, which was apparently intended to be the size and shape of the Roman Temple of Jupiter that formerly occupied the site. "The roof of *my* temple will have a superior architectural support system that the Romans could not have dreamt of, so there will be no need to crowd the interior with so many internal columns."

She effortlessly lifted the roof of the model temple and showed him the layout of the chambers inside, including a luxurious one set aside for lovemaking. It immediately occurred to David that, whatever use she and he might make of the room together, it would eventually be rededicated to her ancient ritual of copulating with such kings as she might favor.

She replaced the roof and turned to him with a serious expression. "Shiduri tells me you will be away for a week or so."

He bowed respectfully. "It cannot be avoided Your Majesty. I need to speak to our President about issues that may soon be discussed with Lord Enki and possibly other members of the Council of Twelve."

"Politics," she said dismissively. "I have no interest in it. Tell me, will you be seeing … Weldon?"

"I expect I *will* be seeing Lieutenant Commander Weldon, Majesty," he said.

"*Seeing* her?" said Inanna with disgust. "You mean filling her up like a vessel."

David found her remark coarse. He pointed to the model of Inanna's temple. "On that score, what demands can Your Majesty justly make upon me, when Your Majesty plans a hall of stone to be dedicated to her legendary bouts of sex?"

"I would not do that if you would have me," she said with a pout.

"I'd be yours for your whole life."

And, like the fool that every man is for a beautiful woman, he believed her and regretted his own peevishness. But even if she were being truthful, her time of sexual continence on his account would be brief. *How long can a man live, after all?* Long before David was born, his kind had been fated for the dust. And when he died, she'd be right back at her epic fornications.

But what difference would it make *what* she does when he's dead? He remembered a paraphrase from the Bard: *No man knows aught of what he leaves.* And here was David, contemplating a future with Inanna that he himself would never let come to pass. *So, why am I torturing myself?*

Why? Because he still wanted some … connection with her. He took some comfort from the relative maturity of his feelings for her, and persuaded himself that his desire was not sexual, but rather of a higher order. He wanted her to remain with him indefinitely. He knew that, to have any hope of that, in the morass of his affections he must transform her affectively into a sister, and, what's more, a *younger* sister, someone needing his protection, who would eventually be married off to a suitable mate outside the family.

The image of his deceased wife flashed through his mind and, as usual, she was rolling her eyes at him.

⸻ ⟶∘⟨⟩∘⟵ ⸻

A FEW HOURS later, the modified F-35 landed at Joint Base Andrews outside Washington, where David had been told he'd be met by an official limo. Approaching the parking lot on foot, he saw a tall young man in a U.S. Navy uniform holding a handwritten sign saying *Canarsie.*

"Is Canarsie your destination or your passenger?" asked David.

"Passenger, sir," said the driver with a smile. "I recognize you from TV. May I take your bags?"

David handed the driver his laptop and a small bag.

The driver looked at him, puzzled. "Are you waiting for the rest of your luggage?"

"Nope," said David, "that's it."

"Right this way, sir," said the driver. He led David to a black, modestly stretched limo with American flag decals on the front doors and deeply tinted windows throughout. It looked heavy, as though it had been reinforced against possible attack.

The driver opened the right-side passenger door to admit David, and took his few bags around to the trunk.

As David stepped in and closed the door, he was surprised to find someone seated next to him. He looked up at his fellow passenger's face.

It was Catharine, wearing a big smile. She was in uniform, her left arm in a sling.

David didn't even sit foursquare on the seat before kissing her passionately. "I missed you so, *so* much," he whispered, surprised at his own ardency. He felt comically affectionate, like a dog whose mistress has returned home after an especially long day.

"Don't touch my left arm," she cautioned. Near tears, she added, "I missed you *so, so* much, too." She arched an eyebrow. "Well … have you been enlisted as Inanna's boy-toy?"

"Of course not," he said. "No Trevors here."

"No?" she said, feigning suspicion.

"Not a bit of it," he said as he sat back, "though it wasn't for her lack of trying."

"Oh?" she said.

He looked at her indignantly. "Look. I can't control what she does. I love *you*, fer chrissakes. When will you stop doubting that?"

"Never," she said. "You'll have to remind me every day, many *times* a day." She kissed him.

The driver, who'd quietly assumed his seat, pulled his door shut with a thump and turned to them with an expression of indulgent impatience. Evidently, the partition had been wide open and he'd heard every word.

"I love a good soap opera as much as the next guy," said the driver, "but I *do* need to know where we're going."

David was surprised to hear the driver's voice, and he realized he'd lost any sense of where he was. He looked at the driver, wide-eyed.

"Where *to*, Mister Ambassador?" the driver asked. "I've been instructed to take you to the Willard Hotel, but I need to know if there's been a change in itinerary."

"Oh, sorry," said David. "The Willard Hotel, please."

"Yes, sir," said the driver, who acknowledged Catharine with a respectful nod before closing the partition.

As they pulled out of the lot, David said to Catharine, "It's *I* who should be suspicious, y'know. Look at you. You're so beautiful, and you go jetting around with all these derring-do types. What assurance do *I* have—?"

She closed his mouth with a long, passionate kiss. "*There's* your assurance."

He smiled at her, then feigned indignation. "I feel the need for greater assurance."

She chuckled with quiet reserve. "You'll have to wait till we check in."

In a few minutes, the limo turned onto H Street Northwest heading toward the Willard. All traffic was being rerouted off H Street.

"Typical Washington nonsense," said David. "Some dignitary comes into town, so all traffic is detoured."

The limo pulled up to the barricade marked *FBI*, and there was a brief conversation between their driver and an FBI agent. David peered through the windshield, where he saw that, two blocks up where the Willard was located, several FBI cars with lights flashing were parked athwart traffic.

The barricade parted and the limo inched through alone. Once clear of the barricade and all FBI personnel, it picked up speed, and the barricade was closed behind them.

In front of the Willard, the FBI cars quickly parted for the limo.

Catharine, whose movement was restricted by her wound, asked, "What do you see?"

David turned to her anxiously. "It looks like all this security is for … *us*."

The limo drove onto a downramp marking the entrance to the hotel's underground parking lot, and inched toward a middle-aged man in a suit standing between two stanchions.

"Is that—?" David stopped himself.

Catharine said, "It's Agent Duffy, right?"

He turned to her, amazed. "Yeah, how'd you know? Are we under arrest?"

"Worse," she said. "We're under close guard, courtesy of Admiral Simmons. Ever since the squarebeards took a shot at my shuttle, he's been convinced they've got a vendetta against me personally. Evidently, they're trying to make a point about what happens to people who kick their asses."

"Do they even know what you look like?" asked David skeptically.

The corners of her mouth turned down. "The going theory is that, once one of them has seen you, they *all* know what you look like. Might as well be wearing a target. The admiral believes *you're* a high-value target, too, and describes our suite at the Willard as a *two-fer* target for them."

"Me?" said David. "Why would they give a crap about *me*?"

She shrugged. "You're a famous symbol of opposition to the aliens."

"*Different* aliens, though," pleaded David.

Her eyes wide, Catharine said, "Evidently, they don't care."

Agent Duffy opened David's door. "Good evening, ambassador," he said.

David stepped out and shook his hand. "Good evening, Agent Duffy. Quite the reception you've assembled for us."

"Yeah, well. Ever since I didn't bake you a cake that time in London, I've been lookin' for a way to make up for it." He pressed the back of his hand against David's chest urging him to take a step back.

Two stony-faced, heavily armed agents of the Department of Homeland Security assisted Catharine out of the car and closely flanked her in smart, military fashion, their eyes darting around the garage. Duffy nodded to them, and they escorted Catharine to the entrance door, which was opened by yet another agent.

"Come on, professor," said Duffy. "I'll walk with you."

Duffy turned to an agent that David vaguely remembered from the flight to DC when he first met Catharine. "Smitty," said Duffy, "guard the rear, wouldja?"

"Sure thing," replied Smitty, who took out his sidearm.

"Right this way," said Duffy, taking David by the arm. "We're all takin' the service elevator."

A worn but roomy service elevator awaited them with Catharine and her double escort already aboard.

"Step in, sir," said Duffy.

David stepped in far enough to ensure that Duffy and Smitty could fit comfortably behind him. Smitty pressed the button, the door closed, and the elevator rose.

David spoke quietly. "Do we really need all this security?"

Duffy nodded and whispered. "You tell me. Space Force says the bastards tracked her flight all the way to Andrews."

David nodded contemplatively, wondering how they were going to enjoy two romantic days together without being able to leave the hotel for so much as a good meal. He'd planned on taking Catharine for a shopping spree and spoiling her with the best of everything. But that wouldn't be possible now. He glanced worriedly at her, and she winked back at him, which made him feel as though everything might just turn out okay.

The whole party left the elevator. Arriving at the suite, Duffy opened the door and ushered everyone into a roomy vestibule with its own half-bath, two foldup cots, and no windows.

Duffy said, "I'll be sleeping downstairs. This is the common area, where my two agents will be staying."

"What?" said David. "They're *staying* with us?"

Duffy laughed. "Not exactly. They're confined to this room and its bathroom. You two have the rest of the suite to yourselves."

"When did I sign up for an armed guard?" said David.

"You didn't," said Duffy and pointed to Catharine. "*She* did." He quickly added, "Well, she wasn't asked exactly, but it's all part of being in the Service."

Catharine nodded to David apologetically.

Duffy patted David on the back. "Go and take a look at the suite. I think you'll like it. You've got room service and all the TV and movie channels."

David noticed that the agents carried automatic rifles, and were strapped with two sidearms apiece. He pulled Duffy aside. "I want a gun."

Duffy shook his head. "You're liable to hurt somebody."

"Look at this place," said David. "It's an armed camp. I'm not going to be the only schmuck who can't do anything if we're attacked. I want a *gun*."

Duffy's attitude softened. "You need a suit so you can meet with the President, right?"

David couldn't figure out what that had to do with anything.

Duffy said quietly. "We've got two suits comin' up here in a couple hours based on measurements taken when you were in Paris. There'll also be some shirts, shoes, and a box of accouterments. In the box will be a Glock just like the lieutenant commander's, with some ammunition. Promise me you won't use it unless you have no choice. And, if you get caught?" he smirked. "You found it on the floor."

"Promise."

THOUGH THE VESTIBULE was pretty far down the hall, the presence of the agents in the suite was a little off-putting.

It took David and Catharine a little while to get comfortable. At first, they chatted amiably, with him sitting at the foot of the bed and her sitting upright on a straight-backed upholstered chair.

"Is it more comfortable for you to sit up straight?" he asked.

"Not really," she said. "The key is keeping my back and shoulders straight, but it works just as well if I'm lying down."

"Are you on pain meds?"

She shook her head. "Not the hard stuff. I stopped it when I left the hospital. I figured I might have to react quickly if a … situation arose."

"Would you like to get out of your wet uniform?" he asked.

She looked down curiously at herself. "My uniform's not wet."

"Then, would you like to get out of your *dry* uniform?"

She smiled. "I'd like that very much, thank you. But I'll need help."

"That's what I'm here for," he said with a wink.

"Okay, but you'll have to be careful of my shoulder."

He helped her out of her jacket, removed her holster (which was touch-and-go in the Pain Department), and placed the Glock and its extra clip carefully on the nightstand by her side of the bed. The rest was pretty straightforward, and he helped her put on a nightgown, then lay her out straight on the bed with a minimum of discomfort.

Their lovemaking was calm and deliberate, but she seemed to enjoy it as much as he did, which he found difficult to believe, as he couldn't imagine anyone enjoying *anything* as much as he did making love to her. After their second bout, David lay next to her and she fell asleep. While he wanted very much to cradle her head under his arm, that would have been less than optimal for her shoulder.

He heard a distant knock that seemed to be coming from the direction of the vestibule. He grabbed a hotel robe, and crept up to the door separating the vestibule from the rest of the suite. He put his ear up against the door and listened for a full minute to be certain there was nothing sinister happening outside. Hearing nothing but the closing of the hallway door and some calm conversation between the two agents, he opened the door a crack and the agents looked up at him.

"Is that my suit and stuff?" he asked.

"Yes, sir," said one of the agents. "Would you like to take the boxes in now?"

"Yes, please," he replied, and they handed him so many clothing and shoe boxes that he had to put some down on his side of the door and reach out for more. All in all, there were eight boxes. "Thanks," he said to the agents and closed the door between them.

He carried the boxes to the bedroom where Catharine lay sound asleep, hung up the suits and shirts in the closet, and placed the two shoeboxes on the closet floor. Before going back to bed, he reached into one of the shoeboxes and found a Glock that closely resembled Catharine's, but no ammunition. Rifling through the other shoebox, he found the two matching clips. He set the gun and both clips on the nightstand next to his side of the bed.

Although he'd seen Catharine insert clips into her Glock and disengage the safety often enough to imitate her, he would have really liked her assurance that he was doing it right. Seeing her so soundly asleep, however, he decided it wasn't worth waking her up for.

EVER SINCE DAVID stopped eating animal-based food at Inanna's insistence, he'd begun waking up at six-thirty every morning, this morning included. He looked over at Catharine, who was still sleeping soundly, and decided not to awaken her. Instead, he put on sweatclothes and leaned back on the headboard.

There was noise coming from the foyer. He figured the agents had been feeling a bit creaky after sleeping on cots all night, and that the noise was probably just the natural byproduct of a coffee or breakfast delivery. But maybe not. He got up to investigate, and closed the bedroom door to avoid disturbing Catharine.

He brought his phone, the Glock, and both clips into one of the bathrooms in the hallway outside the bedroom.

He phoned Agent Duffy.

"Hello?" said a sleepy-sounding Duffy.

"Sorry to disturb, Agent Duffy, but do the agents in the foyer have some kind of shift change or coffee delivery at six-thirty in the morning?"

"Shit," he said. "No. I'll be right up."

"No, that's not n—" began David, but he stopped talking as soon as he realized Duffy had hung up. He placed a towel over the Glock to dampen the sound of magazine insertion, and chambered a round. He stuck his head out into the hallway leading to the foyer. The commotion out in the foyer was continuing, and had grown too loud to be a mere shift change or coffee delivery.

Suddenly, there was a heavy thud against the foyer wall as though something … or someone … had struck it with force. David had just resolved to awaken Catharine when he saw the knob on the foyer door turning slowly and surreptitiously. That meant the bad guys were coming.

David could only imagine what must have befallen the agents stationed in the foyer that would have allowed a bad guy to creep into the suite, but he repressed the worst of the horrors running through his overheated brain and waited attentively with his gun poised.

He resolved to shoot anyone who wasn't an FBI agent, and without giving them a chance to shoot him first or, worst of all, proceed into the bedroom.

The creep must have left open the doors to both the foyer and the hallway, because David could plainly hear the elevator door swish open. It was almost immediately followed by Duffy's voice saying, "Hey!"

So there must be at least *two* creeps, David concluded, and one of them is still out in the hallway. How many more there were, he couldn't be sure while holed up in a hallway bathroom.

A pistol shot rang out by the elevator. At first, David expected the report to cause the creep in the hallway to retreat, but was quickly disabused of that notion. The opposite result was more likely, he realized; the creep would advance. First of all, if the gunshot was Duffy's, it meant that the creep out in the hallway had been hit, and that the path of retreat for the creep inside the *suite* was now blocked. Second, if the creep in the suite was a squarebeard, he'd value the mission more than his own life, so he'd be emboldened to accelerate the matter at hand, which David had no doubt was the murder of Catharine Weldon.

Sure enough, the creep advanced and had nearly passed the bathroom door on his way to Catharine when David shouted, "Hey, shithead!"

The creep turned his head but, before he could complete the turn, he took two rounds to the head from David's Glock. From the opposite side of the creep's bullet-riddled head sprayed a reddish-brown fluid that spattered on the wall and immediately began dripping down in rivulets that were both like and unlike blood. Whatever the inhuman creep was, he collapsed to the floor in a heap.

"Oh, shit!" shouted Duffy through the foyer doorway. "You okay in there?"

"All clear in here, Duffy," shouted David, his voice reverberating off the bathroom tiles. "Don't trip on the body in the hallway."

A split second later, Catharine appeared at the bathroom door holding her Glock in her good hand. "Who trusted *you* with a gun?" she asked David, bringing her weapon down to her side.

"I ... found it on the floor," he offered sheepishly as Duffy ran in.

Duffy said, "Both of you go into the bedroom. I'll be in the foyer until my guys get up here." He looked down at the dead creep and up at the Glock in David's hand. "Holy crap! Waddya know?" he said. "Gimme that damned thing before anybody shows up here."

David handed the Glock to Duffy and said, "There's an extra magazine on the nightstand."

"I'll get it," said Duffy as he went for the clip.

David shrugged. "What are you going to tell the police? That Catharine shot him? Catharine's pistol hasn't even been fired."

Duffy grabbed the extra clip and returned to the hallway. "Ain't gonna be no investigation or cops. This is a national security matter and *we're* the cops. The only ones who can call for an investigation of this is Congress and they won't even know it happened, so there's nothin' to investigate."

"What safe house will you take us to now?" asked David.

"The big white one across the street," said Duffy, apparently referring to the White House. "I *told* Admiral Simmons it would be a mistake to put you two up in a hotel, and I was right, obviously."

"But they'll see you move us into the White House," protested David.

"What makes you think that?" asked Duffy.

David shook his head in disbelief. "It's across the *street*!"

"We'll take a circuitous route," said Duffy. "They'll never know."

"Will we be safe there?" asked Catharine. Her voice, which was uncharacteristically vulnerable, wrenched the hearts of both David and Duffy.

Duffy put his hand on her shoulder. "Lieutenant commander," he assured her, "it would take *division* strength for them to gain entry to the White House. That's not gonna happen. Rest easy. Besides, you probably won't be there long. The admiral will be sure to move up your meeting and get you two on your way." And with that, Duffy was off to the foyer, where his men were already gathering.

"But get us on our way to … *where*?" said Catharine as though Duffy were still present. She looked down at the dead squarebeard and something occurred to her. "Hold on a second." She reached into the pocket of her nightgown, pulled out a folding knife, and chose a short, sharp blade. "Keep Duffy out of here for a minute." She put the knife to the bottom of the dead creep's sweatshirt and cut it all the way up to his collar bone.

"Are you crazy?" asked David. "What if there's an investigation?"

"The navy owes me this much. Besides, you *hoid* Duffy," she said in her best Brooklyn accent. "'Ain't gonna be no investigation.'"

Catharine grabbed the opposing sides of the sliced-open sweatshirt and tore them asunder. She'd barely got a glance at the creep's chest when she recoiled and ran off to the commode to be rid of last night's supper.

The sweatshirt had remained wide open for only a second before flopping closed, but David had seen what was beneath it. The chest had been covered, not with skin, but rather a thin, skin-colored tree bark. That was repulsive enough. But to make things worse, swarming beneath the skin were independently moving bumps resembling worms, perhaps some sort of surviving parasite. Whatever they were, they suggested the tips of human fingers … trying to get out.

David's stomach wasn't as sensitive as Catharine's but, all the same, if he still had the Glock in his hand, he would have pumped this abomination full of lead. Two clips' worth.

WHEN DUFFY SAID that David and Catharine would be taking a circuitous route to the White House, he was understating matters. Since leaving the Willard, they'd been driven to a hangar in Langley, exchanged their limo for an old-model Volvo, which was driven out of the hangar area via a five-mile-long underground tunnel. From the tunnel's mouth, they'd been driven to Philadelphia, where they'd pulled into a multilevel garage and been transferred to an old (but serviceable) Buick. From there, they'd gone to Baltimore and waited in an underground tunnel for two hours, where they'd been transferred to an unfamiliar limo. Only then had they returned to Washington and entered the White House by means of a secret tunnel that seemed to start somewhere around Chevy Chase.

Duffy cheerfully stayed with them the whole way. During their seemingly pointless odyssey, he told them that the two agents that had been stationed in their foyer at the Willard were beat up pretty badly, but both were expected to recover fully in a few weeks' time. He also apologized in advance for the painted cinder-block basement quarters they'd be relegated to at the White House. ("Not exactly the Lincoln bedroom," he said.) He assured them, however, that they'd have privacy, and all their food would be supplied by the White House chef, who'd expressed keen interest in the challenge of preparing interesting plant-based meals for David.

It was a couple of hours before suppertime when they were at last led to their basement quarters at the White House by a U.S. Marine officer, who evidently held them both in awe. While their quarters consisted of adjoining cinder-block rooms painted federal blue, each about twenty by twenty, the rooms were indeed off in a private area, and the beds and bedding were first rate.

Catharine, who'd borne up pretty well through their meandering travels, began to flag at last, and David encouraged her to get some sleep before supper. She lay on her bed and drifted off almost immediately. He gazed at her, his heart full of sympathy.

It seemed to him that Catharine might be chilly, so he went to his room, opened the bag he'd brought with him from Inanna's pyramidion, and removed Elijah's mantle. Returning to Catharine's room, he spread the mantle over her wounded shoulder in the hope that it might have some talismanic healing power. He kissed her on the forehead and fell asleep in a chair by her bed.

CHAPTER 16

WHEN ADMIRAL SIMMONS came down to Catharine's room to invite her and David to a late supper, they were both asleep, so he knocked gently on the open door and waited for them to stir.

"You two have had quite a day," said the admiral. "I let you sleep for a couple of hours, but I'd like to talk to you both, if I may."

Catharine sat up. "Yes, sir," she said, rubbing her eyes and sitting up on the edge of the bed. Noticing that Elijah's mantle had been draped over her shoulder, she smiled at David, folded it neatly as she could with a hurt shoulder, and placed it on the pillow.

"Evening, admiral," said David groggily from his upholstered chair. "What can we do for you?"

The admiral took a seat in the only unoccupied chair, which was a twin of David's, and said, "Well, it's kind of a sensitive subject."

"Shoot," said Catharine.

"Catharine," said the admiral gingerly, "do you recall who debriefed you after you two were chased by the aliens all around Africa and Europe?"

Catharine riffled through her memory. "Admiral, you and I discussed at length what happened to us, but I don't recall a formal debriefing."

The admiral nodded and turned to David. "And you, David, were you debriefed?"

David shook his head. "Not in a formal way, if that's what you mean."

"Well, David," granted the admiral, "you weren't part of the intelligence apparatus at that time, so that's understandable. But, Catharine, didn't *you* find that odd?"

She shook her head. "I didn't at the time. It's not like we'd directly engaged the enemy or been taken captive. Why do you ask?"

The admiral nodded. "You know whose responsibility it was to see that you were fully debriefed?"

David shrugged, but Catharine gave the admiral a knowing look.

"Yours?" she said.

"Yep," said the admiral. "It was my responsibility. But I forgot. For the first time in my fifty years in the navy, I forgot. Or, more precisely, it never even *occurred* to me."

"Did we … neglect to tell you something at that time, sir?" asked David.

"Well," said the admiral, "I went back and checked my notes of your adventure and noticed a gaping omission that I completely missed at the time."

"What about?" asked David.

"When you recounted your experience, you reported that you'd come ashore from the boomer at the Port of Beira in Mozambique on southern Africa's *eastern* coast. The next thing you reported was that you managed to get Gary Sullivan to fly you to Heathrow from Omitara, which is right by Windhoek in *western* Africa."

Catharine and David listened attentively but said nothing. The admiral was obviously hoping to hear something.

"So?" asked David.

"So … how'd you get across Africa?" asked the admiral.

"We got a lift," said David.

"No," said the admiral, shaking his head. "A lift is what you get when a friend drives you home from a poker game. This was *fifteen hundred miles*. Were you given a lift … in a *car*?"

"Yes," said David, "it was a car … a flying car."

The admiral regarded David awry. "*Whose* flying car?"

"Doctor Zia's," replied David.

"Who's Doctor Zia?"

"He's Ziusudra," said David. "I think I mentioned him to you. He's the Sumerian version of Noah of the Bible. He's more than thirteen thousand years old." He scratched his head. "I never told you that he took us across Africa in his flying car?"

The admiral's jaw dropped comically. "No," he said, "I'm pretty sure I'd remember that."

"Zia didn't actually *drive*," said David. "The car was driven by a late-model artificial person named Enkidu, based on the *original* Enkidu, who was Gilgamesh's best friend."

"Gilgamesh," said the admiral, indulgently suspending his disbelief, "from thousands of years ago?"

"Yes, sir," said David. "There's been only one Gilgamesh of note."

The admiral calmly nodded, as though he'd been talking to a well-meaning but mentally unstable person who was rambling on incoherently. "Catharine," he said, "is that how you remember your trip across Africa?"

She nodded. "Pretty much. There was more, though. I remember that Enkidu stopped the car in mid-air once. We were a few feet above the treetops at the time. A bird flew by."

"A bird," echoed the admiral indulgently. *What could be more natural than a bird flying past a car that had stopped in mid-flight over the African plain?* His incredulity began to get the better of him. "Was it a *talking* bird?"

Catharine glanced at David, as though the admiral might be losing his marbles.

"No, sir," said Catharine. "I don't know why we didn't mention it. Maybe we expected you to be incredulous, as you are. I suppose it just seemed a lot to tell that was ... off the main point of the narrative."

The admiral was obviously exasperated. "So let me get this straight.

A thirteen-thousand-year-old man who saved humanity from the Great Flood has his robot take you across Africa in a flying car, and neither of you thought it important enough to *mention* this to me?" His face reddened.

David could see an explosion coming. "Admiral," he said, "permit me to explain, if I may. Doctor Zia had introduced himself to me while we were still in Paris."

"In *Paris*?" said the admiral. "*I* was in Paris. You never mentioned him."

"He came highly recommended by the hotelier. Doctor Zia and I shared a light breakfast before I headed over to the clothier's. He didn't tell me much of anything about himself at that time, but he seemed to suggest that we might be seeing each other again. We didn't see him again until the last (and only) morning we were in Beira. I'd had one of those awful dreams invaded by Inanna. When I awoke, Doctor Zia was pounding on our hotel room door. He told us that Inanna had located us, and that we could escape only by accompanying him in his car. We went with him—admittedly, on retelling that seems to have been overly trusting—but we didn't see a better alternative. We believed that Inanna's people would be arriving at our hotel to capture us in a matter of minutes."

The admiral made a concession. "I suppose we should be grateful to Zia. If Inanna's people had gotten you before he reached you, you'd be Inanna's consort instead of a visiting U.S. ambassador."

David was lost in thought a moment at that prospect—until Catharine jealously smacked him on the shoulder. He frowned at her and rubbed his shoulder. "When we got into Zia's car," said David, "he introduced us to his driver Enkidu who drove us out of town a few miles before the car … left the ground and flew at treetop level nearly all the way to Windhoek. It was Catharine who realized that, since we were being dogged, it would be imprudent for us to travel by public means from Windhoek Airport, so she asked Zia to drop us off at Gary's place in Omitara."

This seemed to mollify the admiral a bit.

"What did Zia tell you about himself?" asked the admiral.

David continued the tale. "Zia told us that he was Ziusudra and that, thousands of years ago, he'd been advised by Enki of the impending Great Flood. He told us he still works for Enki, that Inanna doesn't like him much, and that the feeling is mutual, which I can confirm from my own knowledge at this point. When he showed up at our hotel room in Beira, we were grateful for his help. As you'll recall, we knew absolutely nothing about Inanna, so we seized *any* means of escape. He treated us well."

The admiral asked, "Did he *give* you anything?"

"Yes," said David. "Zia gave us two things, one intentionally and the other unintentionally—at least in part. What he gave us *intentionally* was a little handheld jamming device that he said would jam Inanna's search frequency, but for no longer than twenty-four hours of total operation. As his car had its own jammer and was already jamming Inanna's signal, we didn't turn our jammer on until just before we walked into Gary's place. The other thing Zia gave us was a small piece of luggage to help us disguise ourselves as tourists, because we'd left in such haste we'd had to abandon all the new clothes you'd kindly forwarded to us, and never expected to see them again. When we were about to leave Omitara in Gary's plane, his assistant—" He searched for the name, but it wasn't coming to him, so he looked to Catharine "—Rodriguez, maybe?"

"Gonçalves," Catharine suggested.

"Yes, *Gonçalves*," said David. "He put our things up on a couple of sensing devices."

"What kind?" asked the admiral.

David strained to recall. "Well, let's see. There was an ordinary weight scale, but also something that sensed radio frequencies. Oh, and a Geiger counter."

"Geez," said the admiral. "What the devil is Sullivan smuggling out of that little hellhole?"

Catharine said, "Please don't jump to conclusions about Lieutenant Sullivan, admiral. He probably uses that stuff to ensure that he *doesn't* inadvertently smuggle anything really dangerous."

"That's a generous interpretation," said the admiral. "Please continue, David."

"Well," said David, "Gonçalves checked the jammer first, and it was jamming a single frequency, but it wasn't emitting radiation or anything else that was dangerous. Next he applied the same tests to the small bag lent to us by Doctor Zia. Turned out, there was a surprise in there."

"What kind of surprise?" asked the admiral.

"Sewn into one of the seams was a transmitter that was actively transmitting our location on the same frequency being jammed by the jammer."

"Zia was not as innocuous as he seemed, then?" said the admiral.

"Well," said David, "that's what I first suspected, but then I realized Zia didn't know the bug was there. It had been planted by Inanna's agents. Zia wasn't bugging us; Inanna was bugging *him*. *We* just happened to end up with the hot potato."

"Hmm, no honor among thieves," mused the admiral.

David regarded that as a bit hypercritical. "Anyway, as it turned out, the transmitter's attempts to give away our position were being overwhelmed by the jammer, which was also in operation. Unlike the jammer, the transmitter had no *off* switch. In order to ensure that the transmitter didn't give away our position, Gary arranged our flight path out of Omitara to take us directly over the slag pit where the transmitter was going to be destroyed. That way, we'd be continuously jamming it until the moment it stopped transmitting."

"Destroyed by dynamite, right?" asked the admiral. The story was beginning to mesh with all that Duffy had told him. "Do you remember the name of the man who threw the transmitter into the pit?"

David and Catharine exchanged a glance, but they both came up empty.

"Could his name have been Hendrick?" proposed the admiral.

Catharine didn't recall the name, but David did. "I think that *was* his name. How did you know?"

The admiral took out his phone and dialed a number. "Holly? Could you have the gentleman escorted down to the lieutenant commander's quarters in Sub-Basement *D*?" He listened for a few seconds, and said, "That's fine. I'll be here." He broke the connection.

The admiral turned back to David. "The destruction of the transmitter battery caused an explosion that was near-nuclear in force. Correct?"

"Yes," said David. "It damned near knocked us out of the sky."

"Okay," said the admiral, "now I want you to think very hard about my next question."

David and Catharine nodded nervously.

"Where is the jamming device now?"

David waited for Catharine to answer.

"Well," Catharine said, "unless it's been moved, it's in Miriam's safe-deposit box in Westminster. I squirreled it there."

The admiral was once again nearing the boiling point. "You left the equivalent of an unguarded atomic bomb in a city of millions?"

"At the time, sir, I was mainly concerned with stopping the Anunnaki from taking it. Besides, I couldn't know whether the battery in the jammer was as powerful as the one in the transmitter. We *still* don't know that."

"It could be *more* powerful!" said the admiral. "Did you think of that?"

"I thought it wouldn't be a problem as long as London wasn't being bombed, as it hasn't been since the end of the Second World War."

The admiral was exasperated. "Why didn't you tell me about it before now?"

Catharine was gobsmacked. "I—I—don't know, sir."

"I'll tell you why," said the admiral forbearingly. "For the same reason I forgot to have you debriefed, which is probably similar to the reason Shawn McCauley's unable to speak more than a few cogent sentences at a time. Somebody *wanted* us to forget. I don't know what kind of magic the Anunnaki are using to cause us to repress certain memories, but it's one of the things we'll have to explore at the coming summit."

"I've felt it, too," said David, as if in a trance. "The memory of Doctor Zia and the jamming device has returned to me occasionally as it normally would, but somehow I couldn't mentally attach an *action* to it. It was like: I remembered it, but didn't think there was anything I should *do* about it."

"As though it were trivial," said the admiral with a nod.

The sound of two sets of footsteps approached the room. The marine entered first. "As you wished, admiral, I've brought Mister Hendrick to you."

"Thank you, marine. Show him in, and return to your duties."

"Yes, sir," said the marine, who turned smartly about and invited Hendrick into the cubicle.

As soon as Catharine saw Hendrick's face, she lunged for her sidearm, only to recall that she'd been required to check it at the desk.

"What's wrong?" asked the admiral.

"The last time I saw this fellow," said Catharine, "he was aiming a loaded AK-47 at me." She rubbed her twinging shoulder.

Hendrick laughed. "That was at the *El Paso* and I was working for your friend Gary, ma'am. You may recall that I didn't know who you were, and you had flipped off the safety on your pistol."

David instinctively reached his hand out and patted Catharine's. His heart went out to her. She'd already suffered through one attempt on her life today.

"Don't worry, Catharine," said the admiral, "he's unarmed, I guarantee it. And he's on our side."

Hendrick smiled sympathetically at Catharine. "I'm a geologist by trade, ma'am."

"Then why were you carrying an automatic weapon for Gary?" she demanded.

"Because the local mine had closed and I was out of work. I have a wife and child to feed." He smiled with chagrin. "I had no choice."

The admiral said, "Hendrick here is the only geologist in the world to have held the transmitter in his hand and gotten a good look at it."

Catharine said darkly, "And I'm the only lieutenant commander who got a good look at it, and David's the only ambassador. Big deal."

The admiral seemed irritated. "Lieutenant commander, you will get with the program right now or be excluded from it."

Catharine shook off her sulk and relaxed. "Yes, sir. Sorry, sir."

The admiral turned to Hendrick. "The good news is that we've located the jammer."

"Sir?" said Hendrick.

"The other device with the soapstone handle."

Hendrick nodded sagely. "So it *was* a jammer. That makes sense. They're like a matched set. Where is it, sir?"

"Evidently, it's in England," said the admiral, "and I know the person who has it. I'll make sure she has a marine escort when she goes to pick it up, although I don't know how I'll persuade her to bring it here."

Catharine said, "Admiral, if you invite her to the White House, she'll come. It's a once-in-a-lifetime for most people."

The admiral smiled. "I suppose you're right."

"Maybe you should invite her to bring Shawn to … you know … see how he's doing."

"Another good idea," said the admiral. "I'll invite them both."

"What's so important about the jammer, sir?" asked David.

"Hendrick?" said the admiral.

Hendrick sighed. "To date, we've been unable to identify any mineral or combination of minerals that will block the Anunnaki rays disabling America's nuclear arsenal. At this moment, the arsenal is useless, even against other countries on Earth. I speculated that the housing of the two devices may have been fashioned of a Nibirune mineral that *blocks* rays that would otherwise have emanated from the electronic devices, so it may serve as an insulator against Anunnaki blocking rays more generally." He shrugged.

"Assuming you recover the device," said David, "how are you going to remove the handle to test the mineral without damaging the battery and triggering a cataclysmic explosion like the one in the slag pit in Namibia?"

"That's an excellent question," said Hendrick. "Once we've developed the technique that seems most promising, I am prepared to take that risk myself."

David shook his head. "I salute your commitment, Hendrick, but that could leave us with one fewer dedicated geologists and *no specimen*."

Hendrick shrugged. "I don't know where else to get this mineral."

David smirked. "Well, it has a name."

"What is it?"

"*Nibirode*," said David. "It's mined in the caves of Nibiru. And it's used to cover every wall in the private precinct of every pyramidion I've yet seen, but I can't imagine how I could obtain a sample."

"Besides," said the admiral, "if you took a chip, that's espionage, which is a violation of ambassadorial privilege. You could be shot for that. And that would leave us having to replace you with an ambassador who's *not* worshiped by Queen Inanna."

Catharine, who'd remained contemplative for the past few minutes, cheered up. "I think Hendrick's onto something," she said.

When Catharine didn't continue her thought, the admiral said, "We're all ears."

"When I went up to Enki's orbiting pyramidion with Buck and Callow," said Catharine, "we were in the public quarters, where there were ordinary painted walls like you'd see in an office. Callow wanted to take a selfie with Inanna in the *private* quarters. But Enki's instructions were that *no* photos be taken in the private quarters."

David nodded. "Because the backdrop of any selfies taken in the private quarters would be the very mineral Hendrick wants to analyze. So, of *course* they'd want to conceal it."

"Hidden in plain view," said the admiral contemplatively. He turned to Hendrick. "First, let's see if we can figure out how to test the mineral on the jammer without blowing anybody to kingdom come. If not, we'll go to Plan *B*."

"What's Plan *B*?" asked David.

"Damned if I know," said the admiral. "Let's get some grub."

AS IT TURNED out, the President was traveling and couldn't move up the meeting, so he left it at the original hour. For two days, David and Catharine were inseparable. They enjoyed terrific "grub," as the admiral had called it, delivered to their humble quarters by White House staff, and spent most of their time making love.

On the morning of the third day, which was the day of the appointment, they cleaned up and dressed properly. David donned a dark blue suit and new shoes.

Catharine wouldn't think of going in anything other than her skirted dress blues, which was a little tricky, as she'd have to remove the elastic bandage holding her left arm in place and inch her arm through the jacket's armhole. With David's help, she accomplished it with a minimum of discomfort.

When that was done, Catharine smiled intimately at David, and beckoned him with a crooked finger toward an elegant wooden box that sat atop her bureau.

"You want to see it?" she asked.

He had no idea what she meant until she opened the box and took out a brand-new Navy Cross.

David's heart welled up with pride.

"Impressed?" she asked, although the answer had to be obvious.

"Prouder than words can say," he said.

She used one hand to fidget with the pin on the reverse side. "The admiral said I could wear it, but only in the confines of the White House." She equivocated. "Oh, but I don't think—"

"Let's do it," David said, and affixed it to the place she indicated on her jacket.

He put out his elbow to escort her upstairs and beamed at her.

"*Now* who's eye candy?" he asked.

ADMIRAL SIMMONS WAS having coffee with the President in the Oval Office, the President having spent the past three days firming up his position in several Midwest battleground states.

"So, Bob," said the President, "what's the agenda going to be if we have a real summit?"

"Basically what we talked about over the phone. First, warm Enki up to the prospect of our conducting war games with the new Space Force fighter—"

"Which reminds me," said the President, "how's Buck doing with the new space fighter?"

"He loves the design, except for the laser cannon. Seems he prefers to tear things apart with explosive munitions."

"Well, we've all got to get used to new technology," said the President. "How about Gary Sullivan? Has he agreed to come back?"

"He's a little balky about it. He's got a good thing going. He flies super high-end artworks and precious metals in quantity."

The President raised an eyebrow. "Dirty?"

"More like *no questions asked*, he tells me. No armaments, no drugs, no currency, no human trafficking. Just about everything else is fair game."

"How'd you get his attention?" asked the President.

"Morocco owed us a favor. I asked them to board Sullivan's plane at the Casablanca airport, which they did. The plane was clean, but in the past Casablanca's been known to plant contraband. Before they did a search, Sullivan called me, and we called a halt to the whole process."

"So, the whole thing was a put-up job. Sounds like an offer he couldn't refuse," said the President. "Is that any way to run a navy?"

"Gary was grateful, so I hit him up for a couple of favors, one of which was for him to help Buck develop dogfight doctrine for the space fighter. Buck's great at making it up as he goes along, but Gary's more methodical, and a better teacher."

"Sounds like a good team."

Holly's voice came through the intercom.

"Mister President, Lieutenant Commander Weldon and Ambassador Schubert are here."

"Show them in," said the President.

The door swung open and Catharine entered first. The President popped to his feet and stepped forward to greet her with his hand extended.

The admiral shook his head at the deviation from protocol. But, what could you do? That's what happens when you choose a looker for an adjutant. Just for the sake of informality, he stood, as well.

"Catharine, how are you?" asked the President. "How's your south paw?"

"A little tender, Mister President, but I've had worse," she said. "The surgeons say I'll be pain-free in two weeks."

"That's what they always say," said the President with a smirk. "They *lie*," he added in a stage whisper.

"Like dogs," she said with a smile, shaking his hand.

"David," said the President, "how's it been, fending off the goddess of love?"

"Well, sir," said David, shaking the President's hand and glancing at Catharine, "you stepped right on that sore spot, didn't you?"

"It's my specialty," said the President, "it's why I'm beloved by *less* than half the country."

"It's been manageable so far," said David. "Turns out Inanna and I are relatives, so that's a helpful little turnoff for me."

"*She* doesn't mind that you're related?" asked the President.

David laughed. "Not in the least. You should read their history, sir. They're as inbred as can be. If they hadn't bred with humans, by now they'd all look alike."

After the small talk, which the President seemed to enjoy as a welcome diversion, it was clear that he'd already been brought fully up to speed by Admiral Simmons, who was first to address the hoped-for summit.

"David," said the admiral, "the President has changed his mind about a lot of things related to the summit. First, he'd like you to arrange for a *full* treaty summit, the subjects being the numerous cooperation arrangements that are customary between countries on Earth: mutual non-aggression, air and sea navigation, mutual defense, commerce, tariffs, civil rights, and so on. As for personnel, the President envisions a summit between heads of state, with such ambassadors, general officers, and other personnel as either side wishes. It should take place somewhere in the center of the country at a mutually acceptable air base, maybe Sioux Falls, and exclude the press, except to the extent desired by

Queen Inanna."

"Wow!" said David. "This is completely new. I'll see what I can do. Meanwhile, Mister President, the admiral and I discussed another issue, namely humanitarian cooperation for those whose minds have been affected by apparent manipulation."

The President nodded. "An excellent idea, but there's no reason to wait for the summit on that issue. It is, as you say, humanitarian, so we should begin discussing it with them immediately. Also, our military people have already begun discussing with theirs our need to test the new Space Force fighter, and the Anunnaki seem cooperative, although they've suggested a restricted radius for the operation. That situation is still fluid. The reason I want to proceed with a broad subject matter is that it will make everyone feel that peace is breaking out. Time permitting, I'll propose a private walk in the woods, where I'll start a conversation about our primary concern, which is what the hell they're doing here."

David smiled contemplatively.

"What do you think, Mister Ambassador?" asked the President.

"I think I now know why only one of us is President, Mister President."

Holly's voice came onto the intercom again. "Mister President: Ms. Azeri and Shawn McCauley are here. Shall I dismiss their marine escort?"

"Yes, Holly," said the President, "with my sincere gratitude."

"Sir," said Holly, "Mister Hendrick is also waiting. Shall I send them all in together?"

"Perfect," said the President.

The three entered. Shawn had met the President before, but they were all awestruck to be admitted to this hallowed office. Catharine hugged Miriam gingerly, mindful of her shoulder.

The President spoke. "I'd like to welcome you three to the White House. You've come here by diverse routes, but we've finally got you all together in one place. Ms. Azeri, have you brought the item with you?"

Miriam opened her purse and drew out the jamming device given to David and Catharine by Doctor Zia. She proffered it to the President, who politely declined and pointed to Hendrick.

"Here's the fellow who has a use for it," said the President. "His name is Hendrick; he's a geologist from Namibia who's kindly helping out the USA."

The admiral asked Catharine, "Is that the item you squirreled away in

Miriam's safe-deposit box?"

Catharine took a good look at it. "That's it, sir."

Miriam carefully handed it to Hendrick, whose eyes lit up at the sight of it. He accepted it from her and ran his index finger lovingly over the handle before putting it in his pocket.

"Thank you," Hendrick said to Miriam, and turned to the President and admiral. "And thank you gentlemen for uncovering this valuable artifact. I expect it will help our project enormously."

"Shawn," said the President, "how have things been for you since you were returned to us?"

Shawn smiled sheepishly and took a moment to gather his thoughts. "Things have gone well for me, Mister President. For one thing, I've met Miriam, who's quickly showing herself to be the love of my life."

This was greeted with *awws*, especially by Catharine.

"Did you finally get to escort her to the hotel buffet?" asked the President.

Shawn seemed about to answer, but stopped for no apparent reason. He knitted his brow and seemed momentarily lost to the world.

Miriam answered for him. "He sure did, Mister President, and I ate everything in sight!"

The company laughed, but David could see that Shawn was just not the same.

Lieutenant Gary Sullivan (retired) arrived at Nellis Air Force Base in Nevada carrying nothing but a duffel bag. Not that he thought the bag held enough clothing for his whole stay; it didn't. In this instance, underpacking was a protest against the Navy's expectation that he'd be staying for several months. Which he would be.

It was complicated.

The seaman who met him at the plane in an open-topped Jeep was friendly. An African-American kid from Mississippi named Thurston. He was one of those recruits who were highly professional and sensitive to an officer's moods, so it was impossible to pick a fight with him no matter how hard you tried. Gary pouted quietly for the whole ride to the commanding officer.

"Would you like me to wait, sir?" asked Thurston as his passenger got out.

Gary was tempted to hoist his duffel bag back into the Jeep and say,

Take me back to the plane. But he didn't. "Depends, Thurston. How far away are my quarters?"

"You're working on the Space Force project, sir?"

Gary sighed. "I suppose I am."

"SF officers' quarters are about a half-mile from here, so, with the lieutenant's permission, I think it best I wait."

Gary smiled at the kid. There was something idealistic about him that Gary naturally liked. "Permission granted," he said, and looked toward the CO's door. "Shouldn't be long."

The kid smiled, put the Jeep in park, and turned off the engine.

Inside, the CO's door was open and the CO was chatting on the phone and gazing out the window.

"Sorry, lieutenant," said the adjutant at the desk, a petty officer, third class. "He'll be off in just a minute."

Gary nodded. *Hurry up and wait. Just like when I left.*

The CO slammed the phone down, came out of his office and beamed at Gary. "Lieutenant Sullivan?"

Gary rose. The CO (who was a good deal younger than Gary) grabbed his hand and shook it vigorously, although not so tightly that he seemed to be trying to prove something. "I've heard a lot about you, lieutenant, and so has everybody on the project. I just want you to know how proud everybody at Nellis is to have you on our side. Thanks for coming."

"Well, thank you, lieutenant commander," said Gary. "Mind if I ask how you heard of me?"

"Admiral Simmons told me a few weeks ago he was trying to persuade you to help us out. That was him on the phone when you came in."

"So, then, you know all about me?" asked Gary.

The CO leaned in and spoke softly. "I know that, when a couple of your squadron members got sneak-attacked, you personally knocked the three MiGs out of the sky. Do I need to know more than that?"

Gary said, "Well, would you like to know what I was doing when the admiral asked me to return for this duty?"

The CO regarded him curiously. "If you'd care to tell me."

Gary leaned in confidentially. "Smuggling," he whispered.

The CO laughed quietly. "No shit?"

Gary smiled broadly.

"You're not gonna do that here, right?" asked the CO.

Gary shook his head.

"Good," said the CO and turned to his adjutant. "Dody, do you have the papers ready for this officer to sign?"

"Right here, sir," said the adjutant, holding up a clipboard full of papers.

The CO said loudly, "Ask this gentleman for his signature on all of them right quick, and don't waste his time. Believe me, it ain't healthy."

The adjutant rose and came around to the other side of the desk. He handed Gary a ballpoint pen and said, "Here you are, sir."

Gary signed at each place the adjutant pointed to.

"That's it. Thank you, sir," said the adjutant. "Will the lieutenant need a ride to the commissioned officers' living quarters?"

"Well, Seaman Thurston said he'd be waiting for me outside," he replied.

The CO shook Gary's hand. "Welcome aboard," he said.

"Thank *you*, sir," replied Gary and walked outside, feeling a damn sight better than when he landed.

The Jeep was still there and Thurston was sitting in the front seat, but some guy was slumped all over the back seat like a drunkard, with a newspaper over his face.

Thurston looked up at Gary and shrugged, as if to say, *I tried to keep him out, but I was outranked.*

The drunk's shoulder insignia was largely concealed by the newspaper, but enough was peeking out to give away his rank, which was the same as Gary's. It could only be one guy.

Gary hurled his duffel bag onto the guy, who let go an *oof* and fell off the seat.

"Oh, I'm sorry," said Gary unctuously, "I didn't see ya there." He held his breath, because, if it was anybody unexpected, he'd be spending his first three days in the brig.

The newspapers parted, and Buck Buchanan looked up at him darkly.

Gary breathed a sigh of relief. "You're not really drinkin', are ya?"

"Not at the moment," said Buck. "I was lying in wait."

Gary nodded. "Smooth," he said.

Buck gave him a shoulder noogie.

"Ow!" said Gary. "I just re-met you, Buck, and already I remember how much I don't like you."

"Feeling's mutual, of course," said Buck. "Hey, Thurston, take us to Hangar 32-B."

"I'm supposed to be taking the lieutenant to his quarters, sir," said the driver.

"It'll be just a few minutes, kid," said Buck. "Do like I said, please."

Thurston turned and looked at Gary. "Is the *other* lieutenant on board with this change of itinerary?"

Gary tried not to smile, but he did anyway. "Yeah, Thurston, I'm on board, and thank you for your courtesy." Gary looked at Buck and rolled his eyes. "This better be good," he said.

"Thurston," said Buck, "when we get there, please wait outside."

"Whatever," said Thurston, sounding disappointed.

"Sorry, dude," said Buck. "Ya gotta have clearance to come inside."

Their destination was no airplane-storage unit. Hangar 32-B was the biggest, busiest shop Gary had ever seen, filled with the sound of a familiar symphony. There were steel cutters, drill presses, electric screwdrivers and bolt drivers, ratchets, hammers, and people shouting at the top of their lungs across the shop floor.

Gary looked at the units that all these mechanics were working on. In three of the four corners of the hangar stood the fuselage of a standardized spacecraft under construction. Each was a flying saucer some forty feet in diameter, elevated eight feet above the floor. As they lacked any visible means of propulsion, Gary assumed they hadn't been installed yet. There was also no bubble, no transparent canopy over a cockpit. Nor was there a visible cockpit.

Buck walked Gary over to the fourth corner, which was quiet by comparison, although the din from the remainder of the shop was still quite audible. There stood a saucer that, from its condition and the absence of any mechanics working on it, appeared to be complete. Descending from a point near the hub of the disk was a staircase leading to the floor at roughly a forty-five-degree angle. This saucer, like the others, stood eight feet off the floor, and was held steady by a unitary scaffold that held it securely from all angles.

Buck had already noisily climbed the staircase into the saucer. "C'mon," he said, beckoning Gary excitedly.

Hesitantly, Gary climbed the staircase and entered the saucer, where he saw Buck had plopped himself into one of two seats before an exceptionally simple, albeit unlit, control panel with unlit video screens everywhere. The cockpit smelled like a new Cadillac. It was elegantly padded and rich-looking. No expense had been spared. Gary wondered what an early aviator would think upon viewing a craft so … comfortable.

Buck threw a switch and the saucer began to vibrate, but not like a machine; more like it was alive. "Okay," he said. "Now for the *pièce de résistance*." He flipped open a cover that had concealed a small plunger with a red cap." He turned to Gary. "Push it down," he said with a wide grin.

Gary shook his head. "Now, what good could come of that?" he asked. "There's no clearance around this craft. If this plunger turns on an engine, it's gonna blow a hole in somethin' or start a fire. I don't see any means of egress so this craft can get out of the hangar, either." He put his hands on his hips. "Are you *nuts*?"

Buck's big smile showed the space between his two front teeth. "Push the plunger, man."

Gary sighed. "Okay, Buck, but I want you to understand something. If I get court-martialed or billed for the damage, I'm gonna take it out o' your hide, and then I'm gonna kill ya. Deal?" He looked Buck straight in the eye.

"Deal," said Buck. "None of that's gonna happen, man. I've done it myself."

Gary put his palm over the plunger and depressed it all the way. Virtually immediately, the craft jumped four feet straight up … and stopped cold.

Before Gary could react, Buck howled with laughter and bounded down the metal stairs, his steps banging and rattling the staircase. "C'mon out!" he shouted.

"I can't leave the cockpit of a craft that's *operating*, you idiot!" shouted Gary, red-faced. "Didn't you ever own a frickin' *car*?"

"It's not *operating*, man," said Buck. "It's like the emergency brake is *on*. It's not gonna move, I swear it. Just come down here."

Gary threw his hands up in resignation and said, "Next time, I'm gonna demand to be shown around by a responsible adult." He quietly descended the staircase. When he reached the base of the stairs, Buck twirled him one hundred eighty degrees.

"What do you see?" asked Buck.

Gary looked beneath the craft and turned back to Buck with a confused look on his face. "Nothing."

"Exactly," said Buck, patting Gary's shoulder. "*Nothing*. What happened when the ship rose off its scaffolding? *Nothing*. So … what's holding it up?"

Gary smiled. "Nothing."

Buck nodded his head vigorously. "Can you frickin' *believe* it? Watch this." He ran under the craft and did a couple of jumping jacks.

Gary looked at Buck suspiciously. "Are you *sure* you're not in any danger under there, and making a bunch of stupid assumptions?"

"It's not gonna fall," said Buck, "because it doesn't know the Earth is tuggin' it down. It doesn't care. It isn't suspended above the ground. It's just … where it is."

Gary started to laugh giddily. "But wait, what if I pull the plunger back up?"

Eyes wide, Buck said, "Let's find out!" He ran past Gary and back up the stairs.

Gary followed him up nervously. When he reached the top of the stairs and stepped into the saucer, Buck tugged him over to the controls and pointed to the depressed plunger. "Pull it up."

"Have you done this before, you screwball?" demanded Gary.

"Cross my heart."

Buck hesitantly reached for the plunger and pulled it up. For a second, nothing happened. Then the craft slowly settled precisely the same distance it had risen and came to rest on the scaffold, which rattled slightly under its renewed burden.

"Waddya think?" asked Buck.

Gary covered his face with his hands and laughed. "I think this is a frickin' flying saucer." He turned to Buck. "When are we takin' it up?"

"In a few days," said Buck, slapping Gary lightly on the shoulder. He looked back at the controls, and grew serious. And then repeated himself as though he could barely believe what he was saying:

"In a few days."

CHAPTER 17

"WHAT'S THE ALL-FIRED hurry?" asked the cryologist over Hendrick's headphones.

"Well, George," said Hendrick into his headset, "for one thing, it's damned cold in this freezer and I'd rather not stay in here longer than I have to. For another, we've had this device in the fish tank at various temps for three weeks now and we're no closer to getting the stone casing off the jammer." The *fish tank* was a temperature-resistant, clear plexiglass case about the size and shape of a residential fish tank. "Zero progress over a period of twenty-one days doesn't scale up well. Let's see: extending that curve over one hundred twenty days, we'll still have … right, *no progress*. You see how the math works?"

"Geez, Hendrick," said the cryologist, "sarcasm doesn't help. We don't want to make a big hole in the New Mexico desert, right?"

Hendrick had half a mind to rip his gloves off and give the cryologist the finger, but if he did that at these temps, he could lose the finger to frostbite. And it would hardly help with *esprit de corps*. "Look, the principle is simple. We have two substances in direct contact with each other: the stone and the metal device. They naturally release heat at different rates. If we get the tank down to a low enough temperature, the different contraction rates of the two substances will break the bond between them."

The cryologist objected. "Or … the battery housing will crack and we'll both go up in a ball of flame. And that's to say nothing of this lab that it took half my career to design."

"No one has adequately explained to me," said Hendrick, "how extremely *low* temperatures can cause internal pressures anywhere approaching the heat generated by a dynamite explosion at point-blank range. We can safely make it a lot colder in this fish tank. At *some* temperature above absolute zero, the stone *has* to come off."

Hendrick peered through the safety glass into the fish tank. Its internal thermometer stood at one hundred eighty-eight degrees (Kelvin), roughly equivalent to one hundred twenty degrees below zero (Fahrenheit). The jammer had been subjected to the same temperature for three solid days with no visible separation between the metal device and its soapstone housing.

Hendrick asked, "When was the last time we put it under the microscope to check for separation?"

"Yesterday about this time," said George. "Do you want to look at it again?"

"Not really," said Hendrick. "What I want is to drive the temperature down further."

"Look, Hendrick," said George, "I'm just a cryologist. Maybe we need to get a physicist in here. But in theory, if the two pieces are linked together *not* by glue but by, say, interlocking parts and slots, it's possible that lowering the temp further could actually *increase* the pressure between the stone and the metal. *Enough to cause a breach of the battery?* I don't know. It depends on what's holding them together and the composition of the stone, both of which we're still only guessing at."

"No. We *do* know something about the composition of the stone now," said Hendrick.

"Not *enough*," said the cryologist. "Sure, we've identified a few rare earths and their isotopes, and some exotic salts, but the tiny chips we took from different points on the stone are not the same, meaning that the stone is *not* uniform throughout. All we really know is that there's a lot we *need* to know that we just don't. Come out here. I want to show you something."

Hendrick put his headset down, stepped out of the freezer, and immediately removed his earmuffs and gloves. He'd noticed that icy ears and hands were the first things to benefit from normal room temperature. He took off his jacket, hung it on a peg, and stepped up onto the little dais that held both the cryology control center and the cryologist. It was a little crowded with Hendrick up there, too.

"What are you showing me?" asked Hendrick.

"Look at the plots on this screen," said the cryologist. "The horizontal X-axis is a simple timeline. The Y-axis is temperature. The shaded area between the two plotted curves represents the range in which we believe we're likely to *avoid* a catastrophic outcome. The plots are based on the best datasets and assumptions we could come up with, given our limited knowledge of the contraction properties of the metal device, the stone housing, and whatever's holding them together." He pointed to the lower ranges of the plot. "You can see that below the fish tank's present temperature, the colder we make the tank, the greater the likelihood of a catastrophic breach in the battery housing over time. Stated inversely, as we approach zero degrees Kelvin (the theoretical point at which certain types of motion virtually cease), the window of relative safety vanishes. And you and I are probably toast."

Hendrick pointed to three points on the screen that the cryologist had marked in blue. "What are these?"

George sighed, took hold of the computer's mouse, and moved the cursor to the highest blue point. "The highest (warmest) blue point represents my best estimate of a point of near-complete safety. We reached that temp a week ago. Several days of exposure showed no change." He began moving the cursor down from the blue point he was describing. "The *intermediate* blue point, further down the vertical axis"—he brought the cursor over the new point, while assiduously avoiding touching either mouse button—"is where we are now. We've held it at this blue point for three days. I think we'd be criticized on grounds of impatience if we were to abandon it before at least another three days have passed."

The cryologist removed his hand from the mouse and sat back in his chair.

An idea occurred to Hendrick. "What happens if we lower the temp to—" He grabbed the mouse.

"Don't touch the mouse!" said the cryologist with alarm.

Hendrick recoiled and withdrew his hand. "You think I'll mess up your plot points? You should save your work, man. It'll calm you down."

"No, it's not that," said the cryologist. "It's that this screen isn't a dead plot. It's what's *controlling* the temperature in the fish tank."

Hendrick's eyebrows shot up.

The cryologist smiled apologetically. "That's why I never bring anybody back here. A little kid monkeying around for two minutes could destroy months of work."

"That sounds like a flawed workflow," said Hendrick with a frown. "Do you shut down the system every night?"

"Nope," said the cryologist, pointing to a physical key inserted in the console, from which hung an elastic lanyard. "When I remove the key, it disables the whole control center. Everything stays 'as is' until I come back."

Hendrick nodded. "Anyway," he said, pointing to the screen with his finger. "What's this lowest blue point?"

"That's the point that seems to represent the lowest temp we can go to without excessive risk," said the cryologist. He hastened to add, "As I said, I wouldn't even *consider* going there for another three days, because I don't think we've given the present temp enough time to do its work."

Hendrick shrugged. "So, we're going to waste at least another three days at this temp before we drop to the lowest blue point?"

"The time's not wasted if we get separation. But actually," said the cryologist, "I've rethought what we have to do if the current temp doesn't work, and you're not going to like my solution. Y'see, I won't try that temp at this facility. We're too close to a heavily populated military installation. Makes no sense to put so many people at risk."

"But where would we need to move the tank to try this temp?" asked Hendrick.

George sighed, and said hesitantly, "We'd have to erect a makeshift version of this facility out in the desert. And I mean *way* out in the desert. And the fish tank would need to be under observation *via* closed circuit, and governed by remote control. There's no way I'd risk my life—or yours—at such hazardous temperatures."

"How long would this new facility take to build?"

The cryologist shrugged. "Couple of months, I would guess."

Hendrick shrugged. "Well, that's a few more months' pay for me," said Hendrick with a smile, concealing his disappointment.

"And for me," said the cryologist. "I'm hungry. How about you?"

"Starved," said Hendrick. "Did you bring any food, George?"

"*Nada,*" said the cryologist. "I'm sick of the local canteen. I think I'll take out from the sandwich shop in town. It's only a half hour from here and I'd travel a lot further than that for some decent food." He rose, stepped down from the dais, and grabbed his parka from the coat pegs. "Want to come with me?"

"I'd rather keep an eye on the tank," said Hendrick. "Can you grab me a chicken salad sandwich and a bottle of water?"

"Sure thing," said George, searching the parka's pockets for his wallet. "Got the wallet. Now, let's see." He opened the billfold. "Okay, I've got cash. I'll put it on your tab." He smiled at Hendrick. "Toss me the console key, mate."

Hendrick pulled the key out of the console and tossed it to the cryologist. "Don't want to be blamed for losing all your hard work," he said.

George caught the key and walked out.

Once the door slammed shut, Hendrick came down off the dais, put his earmuffs and gloves back on, reentered the freezer, and sat down where he'd have the best view of the fish tank.

The compressors hissed angrily at him, signifying that they'd already kicked into high gear in compliance with the mouse click he'd secretly made the moment the cryologist's back was turned and before the safety key was removed.

⁂

BUCK AND GARY had studied the SF-5's engineering and flight manual thoroughly. Even though the craft was Space Force's first saucer, it had the designation "5" because it had gone through four major incremental versions before being deemed ready for production. (If Space Force ever developed an out-of-atmosphere bomber, it would have an SB-*X* designation.)

Then, Buck and Gary had copied the table of contents from an old F-35 aerial combat manual in the hope they could use it as a template for the SF-5s.

"The problem with this saucer flight manual," said Gary, "is that it really just covers engineering. As for teachin' anybody how to operate the damned thing, it's no more helpful than a Subaru repair manual would be for teachin' ya how to drive."

"Agreed," said Buck, tossing his copy of the saucer's manual onto the desk. "We've got our work cut out for us, 'cause we're gonna have to start with inserting the ignition key. These kids can't fight a craft they can't fly."

"Damned straight," said Gary. "That bein' the case, I suggest you and I take one of these babies up together. Like, right now. What's the status of our permission to fly them in-atmosphere?"

"I don't know at this moment," said Buck, picking up his phone, "but I know somebody in the State Department who oughta know." He dialed a number.

"David," said Buck with a smile in his voice, "how you doin', y'old dog? Where'd I reach ya?" Buck's smile dissipated. "The Midwestern United States? That's as specific as you can get?" He listened for a minute. "Of course I'll respect it." Buck cheered up. "Hey, Gary's here." *Pause.* "Yeah, Gary Sullivan. Well, you can say 'hey' to 'im yourself if I put you on speaker. Waddya think?" *Pause.* "Nobody else here, David. I'd *tell* ya." *Pause.* "Okay, hold on." He pressed *Speaker* and put the phone down on the desk.

"Sorry, Buck," said David from the phone's tiny speaker, "but I've remained on Earth longer than I told the Queen I would, and she might be ticked off to find out where I am. Hey, Gary!"

"Hey, Mister Ambassador," said Gary. "We have an acronym for that in the service; it's called AWOL. It sounds like maybe I should skip the niceties, so I'll just say it's good to hear your voice again."

"Yours, too. What can I do for you two air pirates?"

"Well," said Gary, "we're tryin' to write the book on this new craft. You're briefed in on that, right?"

"Sure thing."

"Well, it's kind o' hard to write a book tellin' these young people how to fly these things until we've clocked a few hundred hours in them ourselves. Now, I know we can't fly 'em in space yet, but there's a lot we can learn by flyin' 'em in-atmosphere. Are we cleared for that? I mean, your purple people-eaters ain't gonna shoot at us, are they?"

There was a long silence.

Gary said, "I'm sorry if we're pushin' ya hard on this, Dave—"

"No, not at all," said David. "It's an excellent question. The national doctrine of the United States is that we can fly military craft in our own airspace wherever and whenever we want, *ad inferos et ad coelum*, which means anywhere from hell to heaven. The immediate problem, which I'll try to overcome right away, is to get informal Anunnaki cooperation without formally *asking* for it."

"You mean, like, the USA shouldn't have to *ask* them for rights it already has as a sovereign nation?" asked Gary.

"Exactly that. And if you were a different pair of flying monkeys, I could tell you to just go ahead and fly in-atmosphere. On the other hand, I don't have enough friends to start losin' 'em through laziness. Let me talk to Enki's son, who's in charge of the military side of their expedition. I'll get back to you ASAP. Meantime: When's the earliest you'd like to fly 'em?"

"Soon as possible, chief," said Gary. "Frankly, I'm sick o' lookin' at Buck's ugly mug in this garish hangar and thought it might be more tolerable in the soft light of a cockpit." Buck guffawed loudly in the background.

"I'm pretty sure you're not gonna be allowed to carry laser cannon for now," said David. "They may be afraid you'll attack them even though they're way up in orbit."

"Well, I checked our trusty saucer manual," said Gary, "and the saucers are equipped for rapid swapouts between the F-35's twenty-five-millimeter cannon and laser cannon, depending on whether a particular saucer is bein' used in atmosphere or in space."

David gave it a bit of thought. "You think you could get them equipped with the F-35 cannon for the time being? I mean, especially since you're not leaving the atmosphere yet?"

"We're pretty much stalled here until we can get up in the air with *some* kind of aerial combat weapons, chief. We'll appreciate *any* leeway you can get us."

"You called the right dude, guys. Back to you soon."

Click.

<hr>

"THAT'S RIGHT, ADMIRAL," said David on the phone a few minutes later. "By terrestrial law, the Anunnaki have no right to interfere with our aviation within our borders, but as a practical matter our new saucers are equipped with laser cannon that could—if our guys were to lose their minds—reach the orbiting pyramidions. And since the pulse travels at the speed of light, the Anunnaki wouldn't have much, if any, notice. Of course, the Anunnaki might have some sort of automated defensive shields, but they haven't discussed them with us, and they may not be inclined to do so at this point."

"Do our guys need to use their laser weapons to practice in-atmosphere?" asked the admiral.

"Eventually, admiral, but not right now. For now, Buck and Gary just want to learn how to fly and fight the thing well enough to postulate how it can be used for in-atmosphere combat. Our saucers can replace the laser cannon with F-35 cannon for the time being. F-35 cannon can't reach the Anunnaki in orbit, but they'll give our guys at least some hands-on aerial combat experience."

"Can we tell the Anunnaki that our saucers won't carry laser weapons, and that the craft won't leave the atmosphere for the time being?" asked the admiral.

"I expect so, sir," said David, "though I expect *our* guys won't be happy about it."

"I'm not worried about our guys being happy at the moment," said the admiral. "We can straighten all this out at the summit at Ellsworth or Sioux Falls which is in, *what*, six weeks? Meantime, our guys'll pick up some in-atmosphere aviation and combat skills, and bring the young guys along. They can build on their learning later, but it'll have to be enough for now. Assure Enki that we'll fly only in-atmosphere and leave our laser weapons on the ground. Tell him we'll certify the number of saucers we have aloft at any given time. We'll also have to give him a radius from base that we won't exceed, say … four hundred miles."

"*Four hundred miles*, admiral?" said David incredulously. "These are hypersonic craft. At four thousand miles an hour, they're gonna chew up that radius in no time."

"Well, how far is it from Nellis AFB to the summit at Ellsworth or Sioux Falls?"

"About a thousand miles, sir."

"I don't want Enki worried about our making a possible sneak attack on their landing party. Tell them we won't fly more than six hundred miles from base. See what Enki says." The admiral chortled. "Sorry, kid, but *everything's* a negotiation."

"I'm aware, sir. It's my job. Let me see what I can do."

⟶ ⟶○◜◈◗○◁ ⟵

HENDRICK LOOKED UP from the fish tank to the old-fashioned clock on the wall and realized he'd been alone in the freezer for nearly an hour. When he returned his gaze to the jamming device, he couldn't believe his eyes.

The layer of stone had simply … fallen off, and now rested beside the electronic device. His sneaky mouse click at the cryology console had paid off without a resulting breach of the battery. At least yet. Although he wanted to jump up exultantly, he thought better of it; he needed to stick to the script he'd concocted in his mind, which required him to remain in the freezer and shower George with credit for his extraordinary patience. It wasn't the greatest script ever written, but it was pretty foolproof … at least he *thought* it would be.

Sitting immobile for another half-hour, Hendrick nervously watched the exposed battery, fully realizing that a breach might yet occur, and that he'd be blown apart in the first few milliseconds of the event. He wondered whether he would be conscious of the catastrophe or his brain would be too slow to register that his little well-meaning deception had come to a violent end.

Noise suddenly came through his headset from the console's microphone. George had re-entered the facility.

"You didn't tell me if you wanted mayo," George shouted through the freezer door, "so I got it without, but I grabbed a few Hellman's packets in case I was wrong."

When Hendrick didn't answer him off-mic, George grabbed the console headset and put it on. "D'ja hear me?" he asked.

"George, I have to hand it to you," said Hendrick. "Just like you expected, slow and steady won the race. About an hour after you left, the stone housing just ... fell off."

George stopped removing his outer clothing, dropped the sandwich bag on the counter, and yanked open the freezer door.

Hendrick turned around with a big smile. "You did it!" he said.

With an expression of disbelief, George leaned over Hendrick and peered into the fishtank. Sure as hell, the stone housing had just fallen off.

Hendrick advised him, "You should probably turn off the compressors now, just to make sure we don't cause an unnecessary battery breach."

"Why didn't you—?" began George, but he silenced himself when he realized that Hendrick would have been *unable* to turn off the compressors without the key. He reached into his pocket, drew out the lanyard with the key attached, and left the freezer.

Hendrick turned his chair to watch George through the glass partition. If Hendrick had thought this through correctly, the acting required of him would be minimal.

George walked over to the console and inserted the key. When he went to move the mouse, his eyes flashed as he saw the fishtank temperature at a dangerously low level. Evidently, he'd inadvertently dragged the cursor to the coldest blue point before leaving. He raised the cursor to the "safe" blue dot and the compressors shut down, allowing the temperature in the fishtank to slowly rise.

It occurred to George fleetingly that it *might* have been physically possible for Hendrick to move the cursor before removing the key. But the likelihood that Hendrick could move the cursor accurately in that split second was extremely low, and would have been inconsistent with Hendrick's character (though he *had* seemed impatient). But couldn't Hendrick see that the fishtank's internal thermometer showed a marked drop in temperature? George quickly wrote off that possibility as sheer paranoia. After all, why would Hendrick glance at the internal thermometer when he believed the temperature had been locked steady from the console?

Hendrick watched such thoughts parade through the cryologist's mind, persuading himself that he could actually track their progress. He continued to watch as more complex, defensive thoughts blossomed on

George's face. Hendrick rose, exited the freezer, and removed his earmuffs and gloves.

It was quite likely, thought George, that his mistake would have ended in catastrophe (and regardless how good the serendipitous result, it *had been* a mistake and it had been *his*). But no one need ever learn that he'd mindlessly clicked on the dangerous blue dot. After all, it wasn't as though this had been a scientific study that needed to be replicable or predictive. It wasn't as though the world was about to be flooded with these Nibirune devices and some technician would need to rely on George's results in removing their stone housing. This little project had been a one-off, he persuaded himself.

George glanced over at Hendrick and realized that, in all likelihood, Hendrick himself was unaware of the mistake as, by all appearances, Hendrick had sat bundled up in the freezer the whole time he'd been off on his sandwich run. That being the case, there was certainly no reason to point out his mistake to Hendrick. In fact, if he didn't tell Hendrick, the mistake would be like a tree that fell in the forest with no one around to hear—a matter of no consequence whatever. It might as well never have happened.

Wasn't it Feynman who'd postulated an infinite number of universes, in one or another of which every possible outcome would come to pass? That would mean that in many of those universes, this cryology facility (and its neighboring facilities) had gone up in a huge explosion. But not in *this* universe. And, thank heaven, it was this universe—and this *alone*—in which George had to live. He looked up and was surprised to see Hendrick patiently awaiting his attention.

Hendrick stood before him looking thoughtful for a moment, and said, "I *love* mayo. How many packets did you bring?"

"Four, I think," said George absentmindedly. "They're in the bag."

Hendrick opened the bag and fished out his bottle of water, sandwich, and the four mayo packets. "You're not joining me?"

"Now that the battery's exposed," said George nervously. "I think we've got to ensure that there's no hazard. I mean, we've been going on the theory that the stone was shielding some sort of emission, right?"

Hendrick paused. He'd been so preoccupied with the stone housing, he'd given little thought to the electronics or the battery. He sighed. If this were a perfect world, he'd down his lunch, then put the stone in a plastic sandwich bag and head over to the second facility set up right here on the base to test various composites for their ability to block Anunnaki rays.

"I guess you're right," said Hendrick. "Well, I saw a Geiger counter next door."

"I'll go and get it," said George. "Be right back."

True to his word, George marched back in with a Geiger counter and entered the freezer. He held the baton up to the device. "Ambient radioactivity."

"Check it on all sides," said Hendrick from the console.

George moved the baton all around the assembly, then turned it over and waved the baton over the device again. "Negative from every angle," he said. It occurred to George that it had been foolish for him to touch it unnecessarily. He could have used tongs … or at least some oven mitts, which were plentiful in the cryology storeroom.

Hendrick, for his part, was relieved that no radiation was being released, as it tended to confirm his expectation that the battery explosion back in Namibia was not nuclear, so that he hadn't been exposed to radiation. He put down the plastic knife and took a bite of his sandwich before realizing something else. "Is there someplace on the base where we can test it for radio emissions? It's a jammer, after all. And this is an air base. What if the device is jamming frequencies used for aviation or air-traffic control?"

"Yeah," said George, "but the gizmo is *off*. I'm a lot less worried about that." George snapped his fingers. "We'll bring it over to the radio shack. They have all that equipment." He looked longingly at the sandwich bag. "But let's eat first."

After lunch, George accompanied Hendrick to the radio shack. The tech on duty escorted them to an array of emissions testers that closely resembled Gonçalves's array half a world away in Omitara. Hendrick handed him the electronic portion of the jammer, while the stone housing remained firmly in his pocket.

"Well," said the tech, "as long as this thing is *off*, there's nothing unsafe coming off it. So, you can have it here on the base, if you want. It won't interfere with either aviation or air-traffic control. When it's off, it emits no particles; that's for sure. It does emit a weird kind of electromagnetic field that I'm unfamiliar with, but its effects don't extend beyond six inches or so from the device. So long as you keep it away from your head, it's cool. Do you want me to check for emissions when it's *on*?"

"No, thanks," replied Hendrick. "It's not our main interest right now. Can you point us to the geology testing facility?"

"Sure," said the tech, walking them to a window and pointing across an airstrip to what looked like a small hangar with an oxidized copper roof. "You see that hut?" he asked.

"I see it," said Hendrick. "Can I cross the runway to get to it?"

"Sure," said the tech. "Nothing due to land here for the foreseeable future."

Hendrick shook the tech's hand and walked out with the two parts of the jammer in separate plastic bags in his pocket. Outside the hut, Hendrick and George shook hands and parted ways, George returning to his cryology lab with a spring in his step.

Hendrick smiled inside at how well his ruse had worked.

⟶⟩०ⅭⰅⰅⅮ०⟨⟵

"My name's Hendrick," he said, introducing himself to the chief researcher.

"I was told to expect you sometime in the next month or so," said the researcher. "I'm hoping your early arrival means you've got good news. I'm Meaves, by the way."

"Pleasure to meet you," said Hendrick. "My early arrival at least means I've got something interesting for you to *test*. Whether it will turn out to have any effect at all, we don't know. That's for you to say. You've been testing different compounds here for some months, I take it?"

Meaves sighed. "That's correct, but with little to show for it."

"Have any of the compounds you've tested shown promise?"

"We've had extremely modest results with basalt."

"A particular type?" asked Hendrick.

"Well, this sample came from the South Pacific. As you know, all basalt is volcanic—"

"Of course," said Hendrick, "which itself is interesting."

"Why interesting?"

"Because I expect that the sample of rock I've brought today is volcanic in origin, as well. It comes from a place … with a lot of volcanoes."

"From where?" asked Meaves.

"I can't answer that, sorry," said Hendrick. "It's classified. Just out of curiosity, what percentage of the incoming rays was blocked by the basalt you tested?"

"Two one-thousandths of one percent," said Meaves. "Doesn't sound like much, but it's the only thing that's moved the dial at all, so it's given us at least some hope and direction."

"How about your twin installation at Cornell?"

"They've struck out with everything, and we've told them that we're proceeding with basalt varieties, so they should back off those."

Hendrick reached into his pocket and removed the bag containing the stone. "I've been instructed to perform this test with only *you* present. I don't want to be dramatic about it, but this is so secret that any leak of the test or its result would be a disaster for American security and would result in court martial of the leaker … followed by summary execution."

The blood drained from Meaves' face. "Give me two minutes. I'll ward my assistant away from the best equipment we've got."

In a couple of minutes, Meaves brought Hendrick into a room full of equipment and closed the door behind him.

Hendrick pointed to a large, boxy-looking device that resembled something he'd seen years before. "What's that?" he asked.

"It's a 3-D printer," said Meaves.

"How new?"

"It was last upgraded two weeks ago with brand new software. Thing is an absolute monster. It's like something out of a sci-fi movie. You put one thing in, and as many as three copies of it come out. Usually, you can't tell the difference between the original and the copies."

"What have you copied with it lately?" asked Hendrick.

"Most recently, a Glock pistol. It was amazing. When the copy came out, we injected a fresh clip into the magazine. As you know, the machining tolerances in that whole assembly are incredibly demanding, yet the gun fired flawlessly and was accurate and tough enough to use for an hour-long target practice."

Hendrick nodded. "Impressive."

"Of course, for that exercise the copier had access to authentic Polymer-2. This model copier can use just about any material, as long as it's not radioactive. If you can get the right materials, it'll make a copy as good as the original."

"Where's the device you've been using to test various compositions for their blocking characteristics?" asked Hendrick.

"It's right here," said Meaves, removing a dust cover closely resembling a bedsheet.

The device looked like a makeshift wooden crate with a sensor sticking up in the center under a mechanical stage used to hold the specimen still. "Not sexy, but it gets the job done."

Hendrick reached into his pocket and pulled out the bag containing the Nibirode. Before handing it to Meaves, he said, "I'm not sure this experiment is going to work. But, from a national security standpoint, this is the most valuable object on this planet right now. It is *absolutely* irreplaceable. Nothing can be allowed to happen to it. Do you understand?"

Meaves gulped. "I understand," he said solemnly, and accepted the stone. He placed it carefully on the mechanical stage, and used a pair of micrometer dials to ensure that the specimen was positioned directly above the aperture, and that the aperture was directly above the sensor. He turned off the room lights and switched on the device, which hummed. Precisely five seconds later, he switched it off, turned on the room lights, and peered down at the device's monochromatic screen to see the readout.

His eyes opened as wide as saucers. "Holy *shit*!"

Hendrick's heart began pumping so hard he could feel it throbbing in his ears. "What's the number?" he croaked.

Meaves blinked his eyes three times to clear his vision and ensure his reading wasn't the result of a momentary blur. "Forty-one-point-seven percent." He looked up at Hendrick. "Meaning, this small chip, covering maybe twenty degrees of arc over the sensor, is blocking almost forty-two percent of the Anunnaki's blocking ray. What the hell *is* it?"

Hendrick collapsed with relief into a chair, sighed audibly, and rubbed his whole face with his palms. The guarded phone calls with strangers, the time spent, the repetitive activity, and the risk of sudden death had all proved worth it. "I'm sorry," he said to Meaves, "what did you ask me?"

"I asked what the specimen is made of."

Hendrick slowly bobbed his head up and down. "That's precisely what you and I are going to find out. Now, if you'll excuse me, there's someone I have to call. By the way, do you have plans for the next few days?"

Meaves shook his head.

"Good," said Hendrick. "Don't make any. Navy brass will be coming here. By the way, when that 3-D copier scans something, is it totally non-destructive to the original?"

Meaves thought for a moment. "As far as I know. It should be. I know this much: It does many scans of the original, not just one, and from shifting locations. It uses visible light, X-rays, and ultrasound. I suppose there are substances that might be slightly changed by ultrasound, but I doubt visible light or X-rays could be expected to change anything."

"Can you tell it to skip the ultrasound?" asked Hendrick.

"I can, when the object is being scanned, but I can't guarantee it'll be able to make a copy from the scan until an ultrasound is done, as well. Why do you ask? Aren't the chemists going to pulverize your specimen, anyway?"

"Not the whole thing, and besides, I need a record of the precise appearance and measurements before they put their mitts on it."

CHAPTER 18

DAVID LIES ASLEEP in a large bed that rocks under him in the moonlight like a small boat on the water. A chilly salt breeze blows over him. The bed's rocking grows more pronounced, and there's a tiny splash next to his head.

He opens his eyes. Just over the side of the bed, the water is at nearly the same level as his pillow. Alarmed that his room must have flooded, he lifts his head, peers into the distance, and gets the shock of his life, for his bed is indeed afloat in a moonlit ocean with no land in sight.

The bright, full moon occupies the whole of the cloudless sky, and seems to be waxing, filling him with fear that it's coming down to crush him. Fearing suffocation, he becomes aware of his own breath quickening with alarm.

There's something wrong with the moon.

David awakened to a soft musical alarm in his room in Inanna's pyramidion. With fear churning in his stomach, he felt this dream would soon recur. Whatever problem underlay it remained unresolved.

His room was filled with earthlight. He leaned up on his elbows to look at his bedding and saw that he'd worn Elijah's mantle to bed. Though it had protected him against dream-incursions by Inanna, it evidently wouldn't protect him against bad dreams generally. It even occurred to him that his dream of the moon may have been brought on by the mantle itself or by its mysterious driving force.

Events of the past ten days came flooding back into his mind: the failed attempt on Catharine's life, his healing sojourn with her in the basement of the White House, their meeting in the Oval Office with the President and the admiral, Ningishzidda's acquiescence to the location of the upcoming summit and the list of issues to be addressed (as well as the terms under which the new Space Force wing would be permitted to practice aerial combat), and his scouting trip with Catharine to the air force base in South Dakota in advance of the upcoming summit.

With mixed feelings, he also recalled Inanna's treatment of him upon his return to her pyramidion the day before yesterday. She'd seemed completely uninterested in the summit, and only mildly interested in *him*. Her indifference had only made him care for her more deeply, and he wondered whether she knew it would or she'd truly lost interest in him. The only thing she'd shown real interest in was ensuring she'd be photographed at the summit in the most flattering light. Her concern was quite a contrast with Enki's, who'd insisted he not be seen by the press or photographed at all.

With the return of his wakeful mind, David began to think his anxiety was just displaced excitement. *With only four days left before the Anunnaki landing, who in my position would not be anxious?* And it put his mind at ease to know Catharine would be there at the summit when he arrived by shuttle tomorrow morning and that she'd remain onsite for the whole affair, albeit not always by his side.

He curled up in the mantle and prayed he'd have no more dreams that night.

⟶◦⬳◦⟵

THE TWO PRACTICE half-squadrons headed by Buck and Gary landed at dark after four hours of flight instruction.

Helmet in hand, Buck trod down the ramp from his saucer and walked over to Gary, who met him on the tarmac.

"So, waddya think?" asked Buck.

"Well," said Gary, "how many days have we been taking these guys up?"

"It's been a little over three weeks. Why?"

Gary sighed. "I don't know. The pilots in my half-squadron just seem kind of … lacking in initiative."

"Yeah," said Buck. "I noticed that in mine, too. If you give them an order, they follow it. If not, they fly the craft like it's a commercial airliner with babies on board. Which is especially nuts, since these things are unbelievably maneuverable."

"The young pilots don't even perk up during gunnery practice," said Gary. "It gets 'em a *little* more adventurous, but not much." He smiled. "Remember *us* during flight training? They had to extract us from the cockpit like a bad tooth. We *loved* to fly."

"Yes, we did," said Buck, remembering fondly. "You think maybe these new craft just make it too easy? Or maybe the young ones are just doin' it to qualify as airline pilots?"

Gary shook his head. "Nah. You know what I really think it is?"

"What?"

"They're learning how to dogfight when there's such a small likelihood they'll be called on to engage in one in real life. They know that, if somebody wants to take one of us out, they'll probably do it with a SAM."

"Yeah," said Buck, "but dogfighting's not the kind of skill you can pick up on the job. Once you get into a fight, it's too late to learn."

"Let's give 'em a couple of days fightin' off you and me," said Gary. "We'll take 'em on one by one, and use the laser pointers to score hits. If a newbie loses, he (or she) flies straight home with his tail between his legs. If you or I lose, we buy four pitchers of beer for the winner."

"Are we gonna remove the cannons?"

"No way!" said Gary. "That would change the weight distribution of the whole craft. Just switch the cannons off. We'll mount laser pointers on 'em. I'll let the ground crew know right now what they've gotta do. It'll take 'em a while, and we want this equipment ready to go first thing in the morning."

"Cool!" said Buck, as he started walking away.

"Where *you* goin'?" demanded Gary.

"Officers' quarters, to brush up on doctrine," shouted Buck. "No way one of these little bastards is gonna take *me* down!"

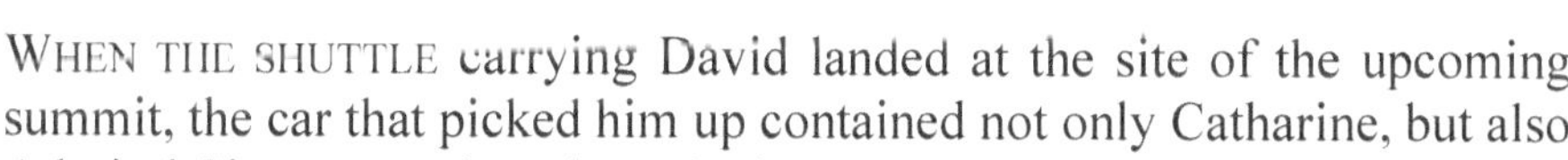

WHEN THE SHUTTLE carrying David landed at the site of the upcoming summit, the car that picked him up contained not only Catharine, but also Admiral Simmons. Though Catharine's arm was finally out of the sling, her expression was unusually apprehensive.

Out of respect for the admiral's rank, David shook *his* hand first. Although he beamed at Catharine, for the sake of appearances, he refrained from kissing her. The three chatted as they were driven to their quarters.

"So, David," asked the admiral, "is Inanna all ready for her closeup?"

"I don't know if she is now, sir, but she *will* be before she touches down, I can assure you."

"Vanity thy name is woman," said the admiral.

Catharine pursed her lips. "According to the Bard, it's '*frailty* thy name is woman,' and neither is true."

The admiral cowered comically. "Sorry."

David laughed. "Perhaps it would be more accurate to say, 'Vanity thy name is *Inanna*.'"

The admiral laughed. "That's why you're in the diplomatic corps, and they stuck me in the navy."

"Speaking of being in the diplomatic corps," said David, "is it permissible for an ambassador to carry a sidearm?"

The admiral shrugged. "I have no problem with it. I suppose the important question is whether you've also got Enki's approval."

"Done," said David. "I discussed it with Ningishzidda last night."

"What are you carrying?" asked Catharine.

"Same as you," said David.

"A Glock?" she said. "I don't see a bulge in your jacket."

David lifted his right pant leg to reveal an ankle holster.

Catharine clucked. "You know, you have to *practice* with a holster like that. It's awkward, and slows you down."

"I'll never be a quick-draw artist," said David. "It's a last resort." He turned to the admiral. "Have we heard anything from our Ethiopian friend?"

The admiral put his index finger to his mouth. "Let's talk about it at my quarters at the intelligence center. We're heading there first. Catharine's staying there, too. David, you'll be staying at State Department quarters."

"Ah," said David, "you've shunted me aside."

"Yes," said the admiral, "nobody of importance will be staying at the State Department with you … except the President and Secretary of State."

David's eyebrows shot up.

The admiral turned to him seriously. "You'd better advise the Secret Service about that sidearm as soon as you get there. You don't want them discovering it on their own. You'll spend the summit in the brig."

The car pulled up to intelligence quarters. Although it looked unassuming from the outside, the inside had gotten a fresh coat of paint, and one of the larger rooms had been outfitted like a first-class banquet hall. The admiral told the driver to wait while David and Catharine accompanied him to his quarters.

As soon as they were all inside the admiral's suite, he closed the door and looked around nervously. "I've had the CIA go over this room about a half-dozen times," he said. "They assure me it's clean as a whistle, but I never feel secure about it." He motioned his guests to sit by the fire.

"Brandy?"

"No, thank you, sir," came both replies.

The admiral poured himself one and sat across from them. "David, you asked me about our Ethiopian friend. Turns out he's the best investment we've made in years. Not only did he detach the housing from the gizmo," said the admiral, whose eyes darted around the room, "but it had, *uh*, the desired effect, and he developed a system to scale it up using a 3-D copier. It's already in mass production … and it's costing a fortune. Oh," he said, reaching into the pocket of his jacket, "he wanted me to show you this." The admiral handed David the jammer lent to them by Doctor Zia.

David looked closely at it. It seemed unchanged. He looked skeptically at the admiral and handed it back.

"This part," said the admiral, pointing to the stone housing, "is new. It's undistinguishable from the old one because it's precisely the same; not just in appearance but in composition, and in chemical, absorptive, and reflective properties. The original had to be sacrificed to analysis, but now we can make as many as we need, in any shape and size."

David smiled darkly at the admiral and Catharine. He said very softly, "We're back in business."

"We're on our way there," said the admiral. "Incidentally, I assume you've still never discussed the jammer with anyone outside our U.S. circle. Correct?"

David looked to Catharine. "That's right." Catharine nodded in agreement.

"Including Zia?" asked the admiral.

David tried to recall the inaugural visit paid to him by Zia, and all the conversations they'd had during their desperate attempt to notify Catharine that a nuclear bomb would soon explode. David nodded. "Including Zia."

"In that case," said the admiral, "our posture is that neither of you remembers receiving it from him. If he asks about it or seeks its return, he'll have to describe it to you thoroughly, and you'll try to remember what you did with it. At that point, we can make an executive decision whether to give it to him or not. We're pretty confident that the gizmo's housing bore no markings we've failed to copy, but there's no upside in giving him an opportunity to test it for authenticity."

Catharine said, "I don't think anyone will seek its return, except possibly Zia personally. My gut tells me he wasn't supposed to lend it to us in the first place, and he could be in the doghouse if he's found out."

"If your gut is right," says the admiral, "even if he gets it back, he'll just hold onto it and not tell anyone he lent it to you, in which case it won't be subjected to analysis."

David added, "And, without extensive analysis, he'd have no reason to believe it's been changed in any way or subjected to analysis by us."

Catharine said, "It's the perfect crime that'll never be detected."

The admiral shrugged. "And if it's examined, our engineers and physicists say there's nothing in there to tip them off. Let's hope they're right. Why don't you two check into your rooms and come back here? I'll reintroduce you to somebody you might remember."

DAVID TOLD THE driver to take him to the State Department center and await his return. State Department personnel weren't scheduled to arrive till tomorrow, but the Secret Service was already there in force.

David struck up a conversation with the officer on duty at the entrance desk and disclosed that he had a Glock in an ankle holster. The officer asked him to turn over both for examination. David put the Glock on the counter, then unstrapped the holster that held an extra couple of magazines and laid it next to the pistol.

The officer stripped the weapon efficiently and examined it closely. "Nice," he said. "This is new, isn't it?"

"Brand new," said David. "We ran into some bad people in D.C., so I thought it appropriate to prepare."

The officer looked at him strangely. "Are you the Kid from Kenosha?"

"Canarsie," said David with a smile. "Yep. That's me."

"Okay, Professor Schubert, I'm going to ask you to leave this with me for a couple of hours while we do a thorough background check."

David protested mildly. "I've already been subjected to one."

The Secret Service officer shook his head. "Not a *Secret Service* check. Remember, you're asking to carry this thing around the President of the United States. We're, uh … even more thorough."

"I'll *bet* you are," said David. "Can you point me to my room?"

"Sure thing."

In a few minutes, David had left his things in his room and was in the car on his way to Catharine's suite, where she awaited him just inside. She opened the door and let him in.

He closed the door behind him and held her close, ever mindful of her convalescent shoulder. He kissed her and she kissed him back, but he could sense a … sadness in her.

"Bored with me already?" he asked, half-joking.

She avoided his gaze. "Believe it or not, David, my mood has nothing to do with you."

He hesitated to speak, or even move. At this point in his life, he was sure he couldn't live without her. Since she apparently expected him to open the conversation, he asked, "Care to talk about it?"

He lifted an upholstered chair and put it down next to another one. He sat in one and patted the seat of the other. "C'mon," he said. "Sit down. Let's talk."

By this point, his heart was in his mouth. He'd never really been dumped before and wondered if this was how it began. He was suddenly sorry for every time he'd lost interest in a woman, or 'let her down easy,' or failed to return her phone calls. If this was what it felt like to be on the receiving end of that kind of treatment, well … it sucked.

Catharine sat down uneasily, as though dreading her turn to talk. "Lately," she began slowly, "I've been facing … death a lot."

In David's mind, the next thing she'd say would be: "*… so, I want to see who else is out there for me.*" But, much to his relief, that's not what she said.

"And," she continued, "I suddenly feel like I don't have a lot of time left."

"What makes you feel that way?" he asked, then had a follow-up thought. "Are you still on pain medication?"

She scoffed. "No, David. I haven't become a junkie. I just can't help but feel like there's this whole army looking to bump me off, and eventually, they'll succeed."

This put him in a strange spot. If she'd been a housewife with misgivings about her future, he might have played the big, strong man, and maybe that would have worked. But she was a lieutenant commander in the U.S. Navy—and a recent combat veteran. She'd recently been chased thirty thousand miles by faceless aliens, and escaped so *many* horrors: a hydrogen bomb blast, an attack by a hostile flying saucer, a near-sinking of a submarine, and an attempted assassination in a hotel room in Washington. That would be a bit much for anyone.

And he couldn't help but think that her despondency was exacerbated by the repulsiveness of the creatures seeking to destroy her, who seemed to be comprised at least in part of subcutaneous worms that survived for a time after their host's death. It made his own skin crawl just to think of it.

He knelt beside her, looked into her eyes, and spoke from the heart.

"If anyone is going to get to you, Catharine, he's going to have to get through me first. I know I'm not a one-man army, so maybe that doesn't seem like much of a guarantee to you, but know this: If you're not alive to be with me, I have no desire to live. And I haven't the *least* intention of dying any time soon. So let's both keep our eyes open and let's keep *us* together. We can do that." As her tears welled up, he rose before her and held her face awkwardly to his chest.

She sobbed a few times, and copious tears tumbled down her cheeks. After a couple of minutes, she pulled his face down to hers and kissed him on the mouth.

And, little by little, her ragged breathing became regular, and the air seemed to clear.

THE ADMIRAL HAD shown David and Catharine around all points of interest on the base, but left the Communications Center for last. His reason for making the comms center the big finale was a mystery to both of them.

The admiral gave them both a big smile before opening the doors to the comms center. Inside, it seemed a hundred people were talking into headsets at once. On second glance, it was only a couple of dozen. Still, they were greeted by quite a din.

At the center of the commotion was a woman whose back was turned to them: a muscular young woman with brown hair and broad shoulders. When the admiral tapped her on the shoulder, she turned around, and proved to be quite pretty in a rugged way. She was made up to bring out the contours of her face, especially her high, strong cheekbones.

David didn't recognize the woman at all.

But Catharine looked at her awry, as though she'd seen her somewhere before but there'd been a drastic change in her face.

The woman smiled at Catharine and her voice seemed to do the trick. "Hello, lieutenant commander."

Catharine seemed to recognize the voice and her face lit up. "Lorraine?"

"Yes," said Lorraine. "It's me!"

"Omigod!" squealed Catharine. "I barely recognized you! All the swelling has gone down and you're so … pretty! When last I saw you,

you were all bruised and puffy." She leaned forward and touched Lorraine's arm. "Call me Catharine."

"I needed ten stitches here," said Lorraine, pointing to her chin. "Can you see the scar?"

Catharine leaned forward. "Geez, I can't see a thing there. Where'd you have it done? Hollywood?"

The admiral cleared his throat and chimed in. "Lieutenant commander, I'll have you know we take care of our *own*."

Catharine pointed to Lorraine. "She's navy?" Without awaiting an answer, she turned to Lorraine. "You're *navy*?"

"Not exactly," said Lorraine. "I'm on the Space Force intel payroll." She leaned into Catharine confidentially. "I'm really with the agency."

"That would explain why you're queen of all trades, wouldn't it?"

Lorraine laughed. "I guess it would explain most of my skills, except midwifery."

"Where'd you pick *that* up?"

"Tribe. We're all taught survival skills, and that's one of 'em."

"Which tribe?" asked Catharine.

"The real name would be unfamiliar to you. But we're one of the remaining Huron tribes."

"Canadian?" asked Catharine.

Lorraine equivocated. "Actually, my people were there long before there was a Canada. My ancestors were among those who greeted Samuel de Champlain in 1613. We intermarried with the French. Hence, the name *Lorraine*, which has been in our family since that time. Unfortunately, many of my people succumbed to diseases brought by the French and, when we were in a severely weakened condition, many of our tribe were massacred by the Algonquin. Those who remained fought alongside the French in the French and Indian War. We were forced to give up our land several times and resettled in Oklahoma."

"That's quite a history lesson," said the admiral. "I wish the navy could make up for the gross mistreatment of your people. In any event, we're lucky to have you."

Lorraine blushed.

Catharine said to the admiral, "You have no idea. This woman can do just about anything." She leaned into Lorraine. "You know the squarebeards, like the ones who beat you, have tried repeatedly to kill me?"

Quick as lightning, Lorraine drew (seemingly from nowhere) a long, sharp combat knife and twirled it around. "I wouldn't worry about it if I were you," she said with a smile.

Catharine laughed, which was a relief to David, and said, "I'll be sure to point them out to you."

"No need," said Lorraine. "I know all too well what they look like."

CHAPTER 19

AT SUNRISE TWO days later, Enki's pyramidion slowly descended from orbit through the dusty haze above the airstrip at Ellsworth Air Force Base near Rapid City, South Dakota. At Anunnaki request, the base had been cleared of U.S. aircraft, save for a couple of MedEvac choppers and two heavily armored Super Hueys. The main body of aircraft had been flown to the South Dakota Air National Guard base at Sioux Falls and lined up in single file on the runways.

David stood before Ellsworth's principal meeting hall, wearing a suitable navy suit and a tasteful necktie of red, white, and blue. He watched as the pyramidion halted its descent a few hundred feet above the tarmac and prepared to release Lord Enki's shuttlecraft.

This will be an eventful day, thought David. (He had no idea *how* eventful.) He couldn't help but wonder how these negotiations and resultant treaties would be addressed in history books yet to be written. But this would be the day the Bible came to life, at least in part. While he expected that the summit would eventually be taken for granted, much like the surrender of the Confederacy at Appomattox, the San Francisco Earthquake, and the first moon landing, for at least a time it would be afforded the dignity it deserved. As for the future? Well, *no man knows aught of what he leaves*.

He found it ineffably disappointing that, for most people, even the theophanies at Mount Sinai and the Sermon on the Mount, for all their eternal significance, had nearly faded from living memory, the former melding into an old movie directed by Cecil B. DeMille, and the latter coalescing into a hazy, idealized drawing of a kind man with long brown hair and a beatific smile. While there remained those who clung to the true spirit of such events, their numbers had sadly dwindled. Such was the memory of the species of mortals known as humankind.

THE BASE OF Enki's pyramidion split open, and a shuttlecraft carefully descended through the opening and described a large circle around the airfield before coming to rest a few feet away from David, who waited on the airstrip. The shuttle's hatch opened, and David bowed at the waist in good ambassadorial style.

Enki grandly emerged in full Sumerian garb, his skin modestly covered except that his pleated *shendyt* failed to cover his muscular legs below the knee. For some reason (perhaps the *shendyt's* pleats), it occurred to David that the garment was probably a distant ancestor to the skirts worn by Scottish warriors since days of yore, called *kilts* in their recent form. Even in the hazy sunshine, Enki's countenance shone like no other.

"Good morning, my lord," said David.

"Good morning," said Enki, squinting in the hazy sunlight. "I forgot how oppressive can be the light of your ... pardon me, *our* sun, especially when it's near the horizon."

"We have brought along numerous pairs of sunglasses. Would your lordship like us to fetch a pair in your size?"

Enki shook his head. "I don't plan on staying outdoors." He beckoned to someone still in the shuttlecraft. "I hope I haven't offended you by bringing an old friend."

Doctor Zia stepped out of the shuttlecraft wearing the lightweight version of his customary blue suit. Like Enki, he squinted in the sunlight, wearing a sun-driven scowl until his eyes lighted on David. Zia bowed to Enki and stepped toward David with an extended hand. David shook it.

Enki shaded his eyes with his hand. "David, do you suppose we could go inside? Inanna will be arriving in a half-hour, and I'm eager to avoid the photographers who'll soon gather with bated breath around Her Majesty."

"Good point, my lord," said David, leading them into the assembly building. "Welcome to the United States of America, the State of South Dakota, and Ellsworth Air Force Base. The building we're entering will be used as our principal meeting hall. My lord, may I ask how many of the Council of Twelve will be gracing our assembly today?"

Enki nodded thoughtfully. "Inanna, who will be arriving shortly, plus five more who'll come to ratify (or object to) the agreements that have been reached, so there will eventually be seven in all. In addition, His Majesty Enlil will be participating remotely. The unavoidable delay in transmission and receipt will exceed two minutes, so His Majesty's participation will be limited to a short greeting at the opening of the day and a brief farewell at the end."

"Naturally, my lord," said David. "You are aware that, by agreement, the open sessions will be recorded audiovisually?"

"Certainly," said Enki as they walked to the Anunnaki caucus room.

"I assume that your lordship has decided not to bring the venerable Council table?"

"I decided to leave it aboard the pyramidion," said Enki. "It's heavy and extremely bulky. To be quite honest, I can barely stand the sight of it now, knowing that our great enemy has fashioned his abominable army of drones from trees of the kind used to build the table."

David nodded. "I've had the misfortune of seeing one such enemy close up," he said.

Enki's eyebrows shot up. "I hope you were not injured."

"No, my lord," said David. "I got the jump on him. He's quite dead, although having seen his chest after he died, I suppose I can make no such assurance with certainty."

"What do you mean?" asked Enki.

"It looked as though there were *things* under his skin that were still moving."

Enki was repulsed. "Has the corpse been analyzed?"

"Absolutely, my lord," said David. "The test results and ... um, remains ... were delivered according to Ningishzidda's instructions."

"Thank you," said Enki. He scowled with disgust. "Things moving under the skin of a dead adversary? Are you certain?"

"I'm certain they were moving, my lord. Whether they were alive or not, I can't say."

"It makes me wish to order the burning of the Council table."

Zia shook his head and leaned confidentially toward his master.

But before Zia could say a word, Enki scowled. "No, *of course* I won't give such an order. There would be hell to pay from the rest of the Council."

Reaching the Anunnaki caucus room, David opened the door and extended his arm in invitation to Enki and Zia to enter without him. "By agreement, the President and the admiral will arrive in one hour. If your lordship requires any food or attention of *any* kind, please do not hesitate to call me. I'm number eleven on the directory."

"You have roast beef?" asked Enki.

David smiled. "We do indeed my lord, just as you like it. We also have Beef Wellington, which you may care to try."

"But made without pork, correct?"

"Correct. That was strictly forbidden by Ningishzidda. Also no dairy, so your lordship can enjoy it without scruple."

"Good," said Enki. "Pigs are filthy animals. Unfit to eat."

David smiled to himself. *The Anunnaki don't eat pork; Hebrews don't eat pork. Anunnaki don't eat meat and dairy together, and neither do Hebrews. Either Anunnaki and Hebrews got their dietary strictures from the same Creator, or we Hebrews got ours from the Anunnaki.* He bowed again, and left the building.

⟶ ◦⟨⟨⟩⟩◦ ⟵

A LITTLE MORE than a half-hour later, David greeted Queen Inanna as she stepped out of her shuttlecraft onto the tarmac near a hangar whose use had been converted for the day from helicopter repair to glamour photography.

"Your Majesty is stunning as always," David said, and meant it. He offered her his arm, which she accepted with a comely smile. He escorted her into the studio, staunchly refusing to betray any of the awkwardness he felt because of the difference in their relative stature. Not only was she Queen of Heaven, but she was also a full head taller.

The hangar had proven much larger than necessary for Inanna's purposes, so David had had it set up to make as dramatic a statement as possible, keeping its interior entirely dark except for the brightly lit studio area at its center.

As David swung open the side door to the hangar, the sweep at its base emitted a brushing sound against the floor, and there arose a barely perceptible scent of machine lubricant. Though Her Majesty was hardly accustomed to such odors, she gave it no notice, so delighted was she to see a full fashion studio inside, complete with multiple backdrops, numerous clothing racks, private dressing quarters, innumerable lights of many colors, fans (for photos of windblown hair and gowns), and a photographer with three assistants, equipped with every conceivable type of filter.

"Oh, David," she said, "thank you. You've thought of everything!"

"Madam, it was you who thought of everything. All I did was bring it together for you, which was my privilege."

She glanced about the hangar and twirled for him. "What do you think of my traveling outfit?"

"You grace every item of clothing you wear," he said. "You look … *magnificent.*"

Looking inordinately pleased with his response, she leaned into him, nearly gloating. "Thank you, but you'd better attend to your Weldon now. She's standing in a dark corner behind you." Inanna lightly touched his cheek and blithely walked away in the direction of the photographer's studio.

David could have kicked himself for offering up such extravagant flattery, which Inanna had obviously solicited just so Catharine would overhear it. He braced himself to turn toward Catharine, but she beat him to it, walking up behind him, saying, "If you tell *me* I look *magnificent*, I'll box your ears."

David turned to Catharine. Without saying a word, he took her in his arms and kissed her full on the mouth, going so far as to sweep her off her feet, which seemed to have the desired effect. When the kiss ended, she straightened her uniform, evidently gratified but flustered by the experience.

"Are you sure that was wise?" she asked. "Her Majesty will be most cross."

A photographer's bulb crashed to the floor off in the studio area. "I'm not turning to look," said David, "and don't you, either." He locked eyes with Catharine. "Her Majesty *does* look magnificent," he said quietly, "but in my eyes she can't hold a candle to you. And, as far as how she feels about that kiss: It shows how I really feel about you. I don't care if she doesn't like it. In any event, it serves her right for pulling a dirty trick to drive a wedge between you and me."

Though Catharine clearly frowned upon David's kiss being used as a demonstration directed toward another woman, his explanation seemed to put things aright for the time being. They left the hangar together, then parted ways to their individual duties, she to staff the admiral's temporary office during his absence, and he to the negotiations taking place between heads of state in the main conference room.

Enki and the President had already agreed on a non-aggression pact containing, among other things, Anunnaki agreement to forbear from disabling American arms in a manner impairing the exercise of America's right of self-defense against other terrestrial powers.

Agreement had also been reached on terms under which the Anunnaki could land their craft on Earth without violating the national sovereignty of a terrestrial power. David was concerned that, in this agreement, the USA could be deemed to have arrogated to itself authority to act on behalf of all terrestrial nations, so he insisted that it contain the USA's disclaimer of authority to bind any terrestrial power other than itself. If things progressed as he hoped they would, other earthly powers would sign on later.

Earlier, when David went to show Inanna her photo studio, the parties had just begun negotiating terms of a pact governing air and sea navigation, as well as most-favored-nation status on a range of commercial and tariff activities. Upon David's return to the session, he was greatly pleased with the progress that had been made, and especially proud of the credit freely conferred upon him by both the President and Lord Enki for his diligent preparatory work.

THE NEVADA BASE commander vetoed Gary and Buck's proposal to disengage the fledgling squadron's cannons for today's practice dogfights. As a consequence, the ground crew had been required to jerry-rig a toggle switch on each craft's console that would allow the pilot to disengage or re-engage the cannon on the flip of a switch. The necessary wiring and testing on ten saucers had taken all night and all morning.

As a consequence, it was nearly mid-afternoon by the time the squadron got off the ground, leaving only a few hours of daylight. Once in the air, Gary made a general announcement to the whole squadron. "Our heading will be three degrees off due north, but we'll remain in formation until further notice. In about fifteen minutes, on my command Lieutenant Buchanan will break formation and head out into the wild blue yonder. Five minutes later, on my command, the most senior trainee, namely, Ransom, will break formation and promptly get his ass kicked by Lieutenant Buchanan, after which the defeated flyer will return to base alone with his tail between his legs. At that point, Lieutenant Buchanan will take over as squadron leader and, on his command, *I* will break formation and prepare to kick the ass of the next-most-senior flyer, and so on, until you babies are all sittin' at home nursin' your fragile egos. Questions?"

There was a brief silence on the radio. "Sir?" said Hutton, who was the least-senior pilot and a bit of a wise-ass.

"Yeah, Hutton, make it quick."

"Sir, what happens when both instructors are on their way back to base and there's nobody left for me to shoot down?"

"Secure that shit, Hutton," said Gary before getting off-mic and laughing aloud. *That's the spirit we've been looking for*, he thought. He pressed the mic button. "But, just in case one of you losers gets lucky, the winner gets four pitchers of beer tonight, courtesy of the dope who let you win. Now if you'd be so kind, please shut up for a few minutes."

A private call came in from Buck. "Gary, let's not forget this is a summit day over at Ellsworth, so we better not exceed our radius limit. They could deem it a sneak attack."

"Can't guarantee we won't exceed the radius during simulated combat, Buck, but there's no way we'll overfly the summit. Our heading is a good twenty degrees north of Ellsworth."

AS IT TURNED out, David's preparatory work had been so thorough and evenhanded that only a single day was needed for the summit. By the end of the day's negotiations, which covered all significant treaties and working arrangements, agreement had been reached with surprisingly little in the way of unanticipated requests for assurance. Several members of the Council had descended from orbit to the principal meeting room, met privately with Enki at length and voted their approval right down the line, with little discussion and no dissent. By late afternoon, nearly all attending members of the Council of Twelve had returned to orbit. Many State Department personnel had also left, leaving Ellison Air Force Base very much the dry, dusty, and depopulated airstrip it was just before negotiations began.

In the nearly vacant main meeting hall, in a spirit of bonhomie Enki regaled the President, the admiral, and David with stories of ancient Nibiru, while Doctor Zia listened quietly, having no doubt heard such tales before. Evidently, for many Sars, Nibiru had been quite a violent planet on which intractable north-south wars of succession had dragged on with incalculable loss of life.

Enki said, "David, did you know that Anzû is not the first to meld an intelligent animal with a Nibirune plant?"

David was surprised. "No, my lord. Who did it before Anzû?"

"There were several, but their drones always suffered from the same infirmities. For one thing, although drones are fearless and unfettered by ethics, as you've observed they lack initiative and personal commitment. And they lack the ability to procreate. There are additional circumstances that make it difficult to establish an army of such drones."

"Which other circumstances?" asked David.

"Well," Enki began, "only very few individual humans are capable of serving as progenitor for a strain of drones, and the process of identifying a suitable progenitor is difficult and time-consuming."

"For what reasons?"

"For reasons not well understood," admitted Enki. "One of the sciences we've been unable to fully grasp, because of its wondrous complexity, is biochemistry. The Anunnaki understand only a small part of it. Although scoundrels like Anzû spend much of their time studying it, even their understanding is not so advanced as you might imagine.

"Another weakness of an army of drones arises out of the limits of their telepathic abilities. As you've deduced, because a drone shares its knowledge telepathically, its death does not necessarily result in a complete loss of information, as it may have passed on its knowledge before dying. But a drone can pass knowledge only to another drone, or upstream directly to its strain's progenitor. So that's one limitation. In addition, a progenitor (unlike a drone) remains an unadulterated animal."

"Does no information pass telepathically from the progenitor to the drone?"

Enki shook his head. "All that's imparted by the progenitor to the drone telepathically is *intention*, or what might be called *orders*. That's their sole command mechanism."

David could see that the admiral was following the discussion with great interest, and so continued his questions. "But does information pass upstream telepathically from the progenitor to an ultimate leader, such as Anzû?"

"Not reliably. Few pure animals (even progenitors) are reliable telepathic transmitters of information, regardless how carefully they're selected. So, the ultimate leader, as you call him, will always maintain an electronic audiovisual link with each progenitor."

"And does a progenitor receive orders from the ultimate leader?"

"Yes but, again, only by electronic means, much as an American officer might receive orders from a superior officer by radio."

Another thought occurred to David. "What happens when the progenitor's *intention* dissolves, say, by his dying?"

"Then the drones of his strain lose all sense of purpose as well, and they wander about like idiots. That's the end of the strain's usefulness and, at least according to our most current learning, there's no way of transferring their allegiance. As you know, Anunnaki have never relied on drones, nor on mind control. We have always valued humans as rational beings."

"Speaking of mind control over humans, Lord Enki," said David, "we have a sensitive matter to discuss with you."

Enki nodded inquisitively as Doctor Zia shifted nervously in his chair.

"During Queen Inanna's landing at Baalbek," said David, "several earthlings were released, having been held because, as Her Majesty said, they had witnessed events that they should not have seen. Although they were released, at least in some cases those former captives have had serious problems in remembering things and organizing their thoughts."

Enki nodded grimly. "As you know it is our preference to avoid killing any intelligent being, if at all possible, so I presume such people had witnessed events pertaining to our affairs, and so a measure of selective memorial suppression was evidently applied."

"How long does such a measure take to wear off?"

"Well, the hope is that memory of the forbidden event will *never* return, but all other—even peripheral—memories should return within about one Earth year."

"Is there anything you can do to accelerate the recovery?" asked David, thinking primarily of Shawn.

"If you swear to keep this secret among those in this room, I'll answer."

"We will, my lord," said the President.

Enki regarded the admiral and David patiently.

"I swear," they said at the same time.

Enki held up the palm of his right hand. "With my hand I can often accelerate recovery, but before I undertake to do so, I need to learn what events were witnessed. If an event was truly momentous, then, for security reasons, I will not do so. If the event was trivial, or with the passage of time has *become* trivial, I will be pleased to do so upon your request."

The admiral spoke. "We have one particular person working for our State Department whom we would urge you to heal."

"Send all the information you have concerning what the person may have seen to Ningishzidda," replied Enki, "and he will investigate and report to me. It should take only a few days. For any inconvenience or discomfort suffered by this person in the meantime, I can only apologize." He sighed. "The memorial suppression technique is a bit ham-handed, and so frowned upon. I'm a bit surprised to hear that it was used at all."

"There are a couple of other people who seem to have been subjected to selective memorial suppression," said the admiral, "and they have found themselves struggling to recall events whose disclosure ought not to present a problem to the Anunnaki."

David's glance darted toward Doctor Zia, whose faced showed signs of alarm.

"Do I know such people?" asked Enki.

Zia quickly rose and bowed to Enki. "Pardon me, my lord, but I took the liberty of applying a tiny amount of memorial suppression to David before he became ambassador, as well as to his companion Weldon."

Enki scowled at him. "Why?" he demanded.

Zia sighed and knelt before his master. "I had—against advice—interfered in Her Majesty's attempt to abduct David and Weldon for her own private purposes. When I learned that they had been located by Her Majesty, I had Enkidu transport them across Africa in my vehicle, but I wished to cover my tracks to avoid the inevitable confrontation with Her Majesty. I sincerely regret having done so, and beg your lordship's forgiveness."

Enki shook his head gravely. "You are like the sorcerer's apprentice, Ziusudra, unequipped to handle such powerful techniques." He sighed. "I will nevertheless forgive you, but only if David and Weldon forgive you first, which I will not impel them to do." He turned to David. "Is Weldon here?"

The admiral said, "I can have her here in a few minutes."

"Please do so," said Enki and shook his head in disappointment.

Five minutes later, Catharine appeared at the door to the principal conference room, evidently surprised to see Doctor Zia on his knees before Enki. She acknowledged the President, bowed to Lord Enki, and said to the admiral, "Permission to enter, sir?"

The admiral nodded gravely. "If you swear to keep secret all that you see or hear in this place, permission granted."

Catharine nodded. "I swear."

"Welcome aboard," said the admiral drily.

Catharine entered hesitantly as the admiral explained the situation to her. When he concluded, he said: "The question for you and David is whether you're prepared to forgive Doctor Zia's transgression against you in using selective memorial suppression."

She looked to David who nodded his approval.

"I forgive you, Doctor Zia," she said.

Enki gracefully placed his massive hand below Zia's chin and said, "Rise, Ziusudra. You are forgiven."

Zia rose with tears in his eyes and humbly drew back a few steps. He cleared his throat and said, "I profoundly regret arrogating such power to myself, my lord."

Enki beckoned David and Catharine to stand before him. "Please kneel," he said, and they did. Enki applied the palm of one great hand to each of their foreheads and said, "Close your eyes."

David momentarily felt a strong electrical charge at the top of his head, and that was all.

"Rise now," said Enki. "And recover."

The President looked to the admiral in awe, and shrugged. "Some things may be forever beyond our understanding."

Enki turned to the President and said, "Spoken like a great man of old."

The admiral spoke shyly. "Is it possible such memorial suppression might have 'rubbed off' on someone else?" he asked.

"Not possible," said Enki. "The process is neurophysiological, and purely internal."

The admiral nodded sadly to hear it confirmed that the cause of his failure to have Catharine and David debriefed was his own natural forgetfulness, perhaps due to age.

⎯⎯⎯⎯⎯⎯◇∘⊂⫘⊃∘◇⎯⎯⎯⎯⎯

THE SQUADRON HAD been cruising at the top of the atmosphere for several minutes when Gary switched on their private frequency. "Okay, Buck, time to head off. Remember, your job is to make Ransom work harder, not humiliate 'im. Make him come back determined to improve."

"Roger," said Buck. "Peelin' off now. I may come back with some branches stickin' out. Let 'em know I'm gone, and gimme a five-minute head start."

"Happy hunting," said Gary, and set one of his scopes to give him a high-resolution image of the treetops a couple of hundred miles ahead, well north of the Canadian border, where he expected Buck to hide from radar.

Gary checked his other instruments and was a little surprised to see that his squadron was approaching the border between Montana and North Dakota, which meant they'd already exceeded permissible radius. *Damn these restrictions!* He really didn't want to give the order to reverse course, but he was considering whether to do just that when his scope picked up several reflective glints from the treetops where he expected Buck to hide.

None of the glints could have been Buck. First, there was no way

Buck could have reached that spot in the few seconds since he'd split off. Second, there were multiple glints, while there was only one Buck.

Gary's heart began to race, and his stomach filled with dread.

"Prob'ly nothin'," he said to himself.

But he didn't believe it.

CHAPTER 20

"WHAT THE HELL is glinting down there?" Gary asked himself aloud.

The scopes of his new craft didn't feed him mere snapshots; rather, they enhanced the photos with artifacts providing data that would be unavailable from a snapshot. To Gary, the glints looked too regular in shape and color to be anything but computer enhancements. As the panoply of enhancements was still unfamiliar to him, he brought the online manual up to one of his screens and searched for *Enhancement Symbology*, below which was a sub-entry called *Identifying Low-Altitude Phenomena*. He clicked on that and found several entries, and the boldfaced word: *Examples*.

One example was labeled *Migratory Birds*. He clicked on it and got an eight-second GIF of a flock of birds taken from a near-space vantage point by an earlier prototype of the SF-5. The migratory birds didn't resemble the glints on the scope, so he called up an eight-second GIF of metallic chaff being ejected by a fighter at low altitude. It so happened that similar chaff was carried by every craft in his squadron. *Nope.* Chaff wasn't what was down there now.

He scrolled through GIFs of several more low-altitude phenomena, but none resembled the glints he was now seeing—except for the last, which the manual identified as a squadron of SF-5s, the same saucers his squadron was flying.

Now his heart really got pumping. He did an onscreen side-by-side comparison of the GIF and his live feed, and concluded that he was currently looking down at a squadron of flying saucers on their way from Canada's Northwest Territories to … Ellsworth Air Force Base, the site of the summit between Enki and the President. Gary's stomach turned as he realized that many military aircraft had likely been moved off the Ellsworth base in preparation for the summit.

He called Buck first. "Abort, Buck. Abort the games. We've got a real-world shitstorm comin' our way. This is not a drill. Rejoin the squadron at once. Over."

Buck's voice came in weakly from some distance away. "Aw, Gary, I had a great—"

Gary interrupted him. "Your squarebeards are gonna try to kill the President, Buck. Shut up and get back up here *with speed*, RTFN. Over."

"I'm there," said Buck, his voice a little shaky with surprise at Gary's uncharacteristically rough handling. "Gimme two minutes. Over."

Gary spoke on the whole-squadron channel. "All pilots, listen up and be quiet. The practice exercise is hereby aborted immediately. Repeat, *aborted*. We appear to be stumbling into a real goddam air battle. This is not a drill. Stand by for further orders, and maintain radio silence, 'cause I got a coupla really important calls to make right now. Over."

He let up on the mic button and inhaled and exhaled shakily, his heartbeat thrumming in his ears. He found Ellsworth's encrypted frequency and switched on the mic again. "Calling Ellsworth Air Force Base, this is a military emergency. Repeat, a military emergency. Please acknowledge at once. Over."

A female voice crackled on. "This is Ellsworth Air Force Base acknowledging emergency transmission. Please identify yourself. Over."

"This is U.S. Navy Lieutenant Gary Sullivan, squadron leader of a fledgling group of SF-5s. I'm in the stratosphere right now, eyeballing what appears to be a squadron of potentially hostile spacecraft at low altitude, heading due south, out of Canada and straight for your base. Over."

"Hold on, please," said the woman excitedly. There was a delay, during which the base's radio room was undoubtedly racing desperately to verify his assertion. The woman's voice came back on. "Our radar is not seeing what you're seeing, lieutenant. This is Lorraine, by the way. Over."

"Copy that, Lorraine," said Gary. "They may be flyin' under your radar, at treetop altitude. Over."

Lorraine evidently needed assurance that the call was real. "Please identify the base that your squadron is flying out of. Over."

"Nellis Air Force Base, Nevada. Over."

"You said this is Gary Sullivan?" she asked.

"Yes. Over."

"Lieutenant, can you please name for me the co-leader of your squadron? Over."

"Buck Buchanan," said Gary. "Over."

"Check. He and I have seen some action together. Can you put his voice on a sec? Just so's I can be absolutely sure? Over."

"Hold on." Gary patched in Buck. "Buck, your buddy Lorraine is workin' the radio at Ellsworth. She wants to hear your squeaky voice."

Buck's voice came on. "You mean Lorraine the Midwifing Submariner? Is that you, kid?"

"It's me, Buck," said Lorraine. "Please identify the wound you suffered during that action. Over."

"A wicked shiner was all. Over."

"Shit!" said Lorraine, turning to her fellow radiomen without letting her thumb off the mic. "This call is real. Everybody be quiet! *Now*, goddamit!" The level of crosstalk dropped on her end.

"Listen, Lorraine," said Gary. "You've gotta get everything that can fly off your tarmac and in the air right away, or this is gonna be another Pearl Harbor. Over."

"*Everything off my tarmac?*" she scoffed. "Here's what I've got on my tarmac: a total of four choppers. And two of *those* are MedEvacs. Over."

"What?" said Gary.

"Everything with fixed wings has been moved to Sioux Falls. I think all *they've* got in the air is two F-35s. Over."

"Well, advise Sioux Falls at once to get everything into the air and come to your defense. Over."

There was a moment's silence.

Lorraine's voice came back on. "Done." There were a few more seconds' silence before she spoke again. "Man, this better be the real deal or we're *all* screwed. Over."

"We're screwed either way up here, Lorraine. What more can you put in the air?" asked Gary. "Over."

Lorraine sighed. "Nothing. Can you help us? Over."

Can you help us? is exactly what Gary was dreading to hear. He could feel his testicles curl up in search of safety. "Lorraine, we've only got two experienced pilots up here. The rest are novices on this craft. I'm gonna have to send them home. Nobody up here has any missiles. All we've got is cannon. Over."

"Lieutenant," said Lorraine sternly, "you've got to get your squadron between those incoming bogeys and this base. You *know* who's here. Over."

"Yeah, I know," said Gary reluctantly. "Over."

Buck piped in. "Lorraine, you got a direct line to the Anunnaki general? Over."

"Yep. Over."

"Well, tell him to call in his fighters right away," said Buck. "Over."

"I'll get clearance to bring them in," said Lorraine. "Meantime, lieutenant, we need fighters *right now* between those bogeys and this base. Please get down there and make some wreckage. Over."

Gary sighed. "Two of us will, Lorraine, but the wreckage will probably be *ours*. Meantime, without authorization from the Commander in Chief, we can't attack those bastards—hell, we can't even approach Ellsworth. Get us clearance, please. Meanwhile, I'll address my squadron. Over."

Before switching to the squadron channel, Gary said to Buck. "We can't bring these kids into this fight, Buck. It's a frickin' suicide run."

"They won't go home, Gary," Buck said matter-of-factly. "They'll follow us in. They're U.S. Navy pilots, fer chrissakes."

Gary shook his head. "Any way ya look at it, this is gonna be tricky. To those F-35s and the Anunnaki fighters, we're gonna look a lot like the bandits."

As DAVID STOOD up after being healed by Enki's touch, vivid memories of his trip across Africa with Zia and Catharine began to return. But one glance at Catharine's astonished expression showed that the effect on her had been far more pronounced. Suppressed memories must have been flooding her conscious mind, because she seemed *dazed*.

The President was speaking when a call came into David's mobile phone. The admiral frowned at David, as all phones were supposed to be silenced while in the presence of the President or Lord Enki.

David himself was quite irritated by the call, as he'd indeed silenced the ringer for all callers except the President, the State Department, Catharine (all of whom were present), and ... Lorraine. He stepped away from the others and took the phone out of his pocket. The readout said Lorraine was the caller.

David accepted the call, cupped his hand over his mouth and the mouthpiece, and spoke in hushed tones. "Yes, Lorraine?" he said impatiently.

"Ambassador," she said, "we just heard from Gary Sullivan and Buck Buchanan leading a practice squadron of SF-5s. Gary just spotted some low-flying bogeys they said look to be enemy saucers headed our way out of Canada."

Alarms went off in David's head, but still he muttered. "Hold on, Lorraine. The admiral's here. I'll get him and ask you to start over."

David pressed the Mute button and did a quick assessment of whether to speak openly before the President, and especially Enki. As Enki might interpret any attempt at secrecy in such a situation as underhandedness, David made the conscious decision to speak aloud.

"Admiral," he said, "it's Lorraine in the radio room. She says Gary and Buck have spotted incoming bandits."

The admiral, clearly alarmed, glanced at the President, who nodded his approval.

"Put her on the squawk box," said the admiral.

David cranked up the phone's volume, lay the phone on the table, and pressed the Mute button again. "Lorraine, you're speaking to the President, Lord Enki, Admiral Simmons, Lieutenant Commander Weldon, and me. Start over, please."

Lorraine took a moment to assay her audience and then plodded ahead. "We just heard from Lieutenants Sullivan and Buchanan leading a practice squadron of U.S. Space Force SF-5s flying out of Nellis Air Force Base, Nevada. Gary spotted some low-flying bogeys that look to be unidentified saucers headed our way out of Canada. As per the admiral's standing orders, I've told Sioux Falls to get everything they've got off the ground and send their fighters this way. I've also called Ningishzidda and invited him to bring his fighters, so long as Lord Enki approves."

Without hesitation Enki said, "I approve."

The admiral clenched his teeth, because he expected he already knew the answer to his next question. "What U.S. assets are in the air now?"

"Sioux Falls has two F-35s aloft," said Lorraine, "but they're running low on fuel, and both are heading back to Sioux Falls to refuel. That leaves us with … *nothing* up there at the moment, sir. I've advised Lieutenants Sullivan and Buchanan, however, to intercede until friendly forces have arrived to fight alongside them, so long as the admiral approves. Sullivan told me that he and Buchanan will try to intercept, but that they expect to be badly outnumbered. Also, they have no missiles; they were up there for dogfight practice. Sullivan said he has no choice but to send the novice members of the practice squadron back to Nevada, sir, as they lack experience on the SF-5."

"Well," said the admiral reluctantly, "I'll have to go with his judgment on that score. Worst case, Lorraine, what kind of damage can be inflicted on this base?"

"All we've got on the base is four choppers, some tarmac, some buildings, and this radio tower."

"Thank you, Lorraine," said the admiral.

David jumped into the conversation before it could be disconnected. "Admiral, if I may?"

The admiral extended his arm, inviting David to talk.

"Lorraine, this is David. Did Gary or Buck say anything about any missiles headed our way?"

"No," replied Lorraine. "No mention. Our radar is spinning non-stop, however. Permit me to check with them." There was a silence. "No, sir. We've got several radar systems pumping, with one devoted exclusively to checking for incoming missiles. The sky is clear of missiles in this hemisphere."

"Thanks," said David. "No one else here seems to have any more questions. We'll call you back when we've got something to say. If there's anything interesting going on, call me back." He hung up and turned to the admiral. "Assuming they're Anzû's forces, admiral, they're not heading here to knock out a few choppers and chew up the runway. They've got eyes in the sky, and they know we don't have much here to wreck."

The admiral nodded. "Think they're playing *King of the Hill*?"

"No, sir. If they were interested in knocking the President and Lord Enki off the hill, they would have sent a missile, whether nuclear or fuel-air. I think the game they're playing is more like *Capture the Flag.*"

Enki's expression was dark, and his eyes shone. "What are the games you're speaking of?" he asked.

The President explained to Enki. "In *King of the Hill*, each player tries to knock the king off the hill in order to take his place. In *Capture the Flag*, the flag represents the king, and each side attempts to capture it."

Enki asked David, "So, you think they will try to capture the President and me?"

David nodded.

The admiral said, "Out of an abundance of caution, I think we'd better proceed on that assumption. It's time to alert the base's security forces."

⌐◦◦◦◦⌐

GARY ADDRESSED THE squadron.

"Ladies and gentlemen," he began, "there's a squadron of bandits about to descend on Ellsworth Air Force Base, where the summit is under way between the President and Lord Enki. The bandits appear to be small saucers about our size, but I expect they're far more technologically advanced, and I'm pretty certain they have laser cannon. Our twenty-five-millimeter cannon is no match for their laser cannon unless we catch them at unawares. Lieutenant Buchanan and I will try to knock them off their game until the cavalry arrives. Meanwhile, as none of you is certified on the SF-5, I'm ordering the rest of you to return to base directly without delay."

"Sir," said Ransom, "may I remind you that neither you nor Lieutenant Buchanan is certified on this craft? Over."

Gary wasn't sure how to answer that, because it was true.

"And, as senior student," continued Ransom, "I feel it's my obligation to point out that the mechanics who installed these switches inadvertently disabled the Retreat switches at the same time. In fact, mine seems to have been removed entirely. Over."

Gary rolled his eyes. "Ransom, what are you *talking* about? Over."

The second most senior student pilot was a woman named Muñoz with a South American accent that was hard to pin down. She said, "It's true, sir. I can't find the Retreat switch anywhere. They also appear to have removed the Run-Home-Like-a-Little-Weenie pull-bar. Yeah, I can't find it anywhere. And those nerds even ripped out that page of the manual. Over."

"Mine, too!" Hutton chimed in, a bit cheeky for the most junior flyer. "I can't believe it. Those grease monkeys musta had a party in here last night. I just looked in the glove compartment. There's no manual in there, just a coupla empty beer cans. Over."

Buck came on. "Straighten up, Hutton. There's no glove compartment in this craft."

"They took out your *glove compartment*?" asked Hutton incredulously. "Well, at least I've still got the *compartment*. And they left the tire-pressure gauge, 'cept it's got some black gummy stuff all over it. And … what's this? Oh, *gross*! A bunch o' Little Debbie wrappers."

Exasperated, Buck came back on. "Squadron Leader, please pick up on my private channel."

Gary switched to Buck's channel. "Yah?"

"I told you they wouldn't go back. They're just gonna give you shit till you relent."

"Ya think?" asked Gary sarcastically. "So, what should I do? Threaten 'em with courts-martial?"

"These kids are ready to lay down their lives for you. You think they're gonna run from a *court-martial*? If what you're trying to do is cement them *against* you, then threatening court-martial is just the ticket."

"So … what should I do?" asked Gary.

"Give 'em a battle plan, give 'em orders, and bring 'em *with* us."

"We could lose some of 'em," said Gary.

"We could lose *us*, Gary," said Buck. "But if you bring them with us, you'll forge the survivors into one kick-ass squadron. Besides, we don't have time for discussion. We should be engaged with the enemy already."

THE ADMIRAL EXPLAINED to the President and Lord Enki the scope of infantry protection around the base. "Our perimeter is protected by the Twenty-Eighth Security Forces Squadron," he said. "If we're attacked, the plan is to stand our ground unless our perimeter becomes endangered, then pull back to a smaller preplanned perimeter that can be readily protected until help arrives." He picked up a land phone.

"Admiral Simmons here," he said. "Give me the chief master sergeant."

The master sergeant came onto the phone and the admiral brought him up to speed.

The chief master sergeant must have flicked a switch while they were talking, because distant air-raid sirens began sounding in every direction.

"Right now," said the admiral, "our guys are up there trying to make sure you don't have to deal with strafing, but it's no sure thing. I'd get those choppers out of sight, if you can do so without taking them airborne. I've seen how airborne choppers get nailed by fighters, and it ain't pretty." There was a silence. The admiral scowled. "You want us to get to the *safe room*?" he asked incredulously. "Don't you think that's a little premature?"

The admiral, who'd been leaning down while speaking on the phone, looked up at the President and Lord Enki, and sighed. "Well," he said into the phone, "I guess there's no problem with our starting to move. Yes, yes. Okay." The admiral hung up and turned to those present. "We'd better start moving toward the safe room."

"What about Queen Inanna?" asked David. "Is she still on the base?"

"Catharine," said the President, "if she's still here, please escort her to the safe room. If you find her gone, come to the safe room as quick as you can. David, you come with us."

David's stomach turned as he watched Catharine run off.

⟶∘⟳∘⟵

"OKAY, LADIES AND gentlemen," said Gary into the squadron channel, "you've worn me out. But first, let me check. Does any of you have the brains to return to base on my order?"

There followed ten seconds of silence.

"Okay," continued Gary, "here's the deal. Our object is to get the enemy aircraft to turn away from Ellsworth and do battle with us. I'm not sure how many of them there are, but if I'm reading this scope right, they have about twice our number. That means we can't expect to win a standup fight. So we've gotta be sneaky. We're going to put on all the stealth measures we've got and drop to their altitude twenty miles behind them, put the pedal to the metal, overtake them, and attack from the rear. To get their numbers down, every one of you needs to tear up at least one bandit before they know what hit 'em. That means we need to engage in coordinated fire, so await my signal. Choose your target carefully to spread out our fire evenly, and commence firing five seconds after my signal. If, after my signal, you hear one of your fellow pilots fire prematurely or if you're fired upon, begin firing immediately, after which you may fire at will. If you have the luxury of choice, draw them north, away from Ellison. We're hoping by that time we'll have some help. A slew of F-35s is coming to our aid from the Sioux City base and, if we're lucky, we'll have some Anunnaki help, too. When they get here in force, it's gonna be time for us to get outta Dodge, because we look too much like the bandits and I don't want any friendly-fire incidents. So listen closely for my order to return to base. And if you disobey *that*, I'll throw you in the brig so fast, it'll make your frickin' head spin. Any questions? Over."

"Sir, Ransom here. Can we be sure the Anunnaki fighters are on our side? Over."

"We sure can," said Gary. "They've got plenty o' skin in this game. I'm sure they don't want to lose Lord Enki. Any questions about Little Debbie wrappers, Hutton? Over."

"No, sir," said Hutton, "I've got one stuck to the sole of my boot, but I don't expect to be dancin' in this craft for the time being. So I should be okay. Thanks for caring. Over."

"Make sure you *stay* okay, wiseass. And that goes for the rest of you. No dead heroes today. Anyone else?"

Silence.

"Okay," said Gary, "now let's all find our converter switches and turn our cannon back on."

"Gee, good catch, boss," said Ransom. "Whew!"

Gary chuckled. "I'm *prayin'* that your jokin', kid. Now, follow my lead, and maintain radio silence until we're engaged. Once the shooting begins, radio silence is lifted. In the unlikely event you're forced down, wait an hour before triggering your homing beacon unless you're in physically bad shape, in which case, pound that baby as soon as you can. Good luck, and good hunting. Out."

Chapter 21

Gary's squadron had been lucky so far, achieving a position barely a mile behind the bandits with no sign of being detected. The SF-5's scopes and guidance system were sensitive enough to keep them barely above the treetops. In the case of a few tall trees, Gary's heart had leapt into his mouth, so near had he come to collision. But in each instance, the guidance system had anticipated the problem and avoided it. He assumed the rest of the squadron had experienced the same thing.

Once the scopes provided a visual of the bandits, though they bore no insignia, it was eminently clear who they were. The enemy squadron was arrayed in two ranks, suggesting that it could be broken up badly by firing on the rear rank and then continuing to blast the front rank without interruption.

Gary checked his scopes and found that, at current airspeed, the bandits were only a couple of minutes from Ellsworth Air Force Base. So, they were already over the USA. He briefly considered breaking radio silence to remind his squadron to keep their eyes open for the possibility of being attacked from their rear, but decided against it; this setup was almost too good to be true, and he wasn't going to risk the element of surprise for an unnecessary admonition. These were great pilots with great equipment. He picked up his own (and thus the squadron's) air speed.

As soon as his squadron came into cannon range of the bandits, he pressed the button that commenced the automated countdown signal. Gary took aim at the dead-center bandit and counted down. *Five, four, three, two, one.* He pressed the trigger button. After such a long silence, the noise from the cannon was positively deafening, and his heart pumped hard. He held the button down until a withering barrage had destroyed his target.

His scope allowed him to follow the tracers from the rest of the squadron to their targets, and his chest swelled with pride when he realized they were spacing their fire precisely as instructed, so that no two pilots were bunching up fire on a single target while letting another bandit escape unscathed.

Time was telescoped to the point that Gary found himself unable to estimate how long it took for the bandits to start smoking and dropping out of formation. While it seemed like thirty seconds, it was probably closer to ten. At least four bandits exploded while still in formation, throwing smoke and shrapnel all over. He hoped liked hell that none of it would hit his team.

As Gary flew through the smoke thrown off by his own destroyed target, he could see at least three bandits in the front rank peel upwards. He spoke into the mic.

"Good shooting, folks. Be aware, some of the front rank are going up. I assume they're doin' a loop to get behind us. Watch your scopes. If you see them anywhere behind you, veer off course and head north for the heavens. You'll need room to maneuver to escape those laser cannon. Whatever you do, make sure it's what they *don't* expect. They're none too bright—"

His transmission was interrupted by an incoming transmission. "Calling squadron leader of those SF-5s. This is Lieutenant Arthur Conrad, leader of an incoming squadron of U.S. Air Force F-35s out of Ellison. Please acknowledge at once. Over."

Gary hit the button. "This is Lieutenant Gary Sullivan, leader of the squadron of SF-5s presently engaged with a squadron of bandits just north of Ellsworth. Receipt acknowledged. Over."

"Did you say you're the famous Gary Sullivan? Over."

"Well, I didn't *say* that, but I guess I am. Over."

"Shoulda known. Well, congratulations, sir. Your little flying saucers chewed up that bandit squadron pretty good. I think you got half of 'em, but you're gonna have to break off and leave the cleanup to us. You guys look too much like the bandits, and we've got a full loadout of air-to-air missiles that we need to be able to use. Don't want any mistakes. Over."

"Roger that," said Gary. "Give us thirty seconds and we'll be clear. Wait, can you see if any of my guys are down in the woods? Over."

There was a momentary pause. "We're seeing some splotches of smoke down in the trees, but we can't tell from here whether it's from theirs or ours. Don't worry. If there are any good guys down there, we'll find 'em and bring 'em back to ya. Please clear the area at once. Over."

Gary switched to the squadron channel. "SF-5 squadron, peel off at once and re-assume formation behind me. We gotta get out of town right now. There's a squadron of F-35s gonna do cleanup. And they're all missiled up. Everybody disengage and scoot. Over."

Buck's voice came on sounding excited. "Buchanan here. I've got a bandit on my tail. So far, I've outmaneuvered him, but I sure could use a little help. I'm above and behind you, Gary. Over."

Hutton broke in. "Never mind, Lieutenant Sullivan. I've got Buck's bandit in my sights. Over."

Gary looked at his scope just in time to see Hutton blow the bandit out of the sky. The signal from Buck was steady, so he'd escaped serious damage.

A second later, Hutton came on. "Dammit! I just bumped some shrapnel from the dead bandit and I'm gettin' a serious shimmy. Over."

"Clear the area if you can, and get down to the ground ASAP, Hutton," said Gary. "I'll come and get you. Over."

One of the great features of the SF-5 was that, once it shed its horizontal speed, it could do a reliable vertical landing, as long as the airframe was relatively undamaged.

"Buck," said Gary, "you're now squadron leader. Get the rest of these characters out of here. Return to base. Over."

"You sure, boss?" asked Buck. "Over."

"Piece o' cake, Buck. I'm watchin' Hutton do a vertical landing right now. I'll land, strip the intel off his craft, take the keycards, and bring him back safe. Now do a countoff and get the squadron clear of hostilities. Over."

Buck came onto the squadron channel, announced he was now leader, and read out the altitude and coordinates of the re-formation point. In a minute, he reported that all hands were accounted for, and Gary breathed a big sigh of relief.

Gary circled his craft around Hutton's landing site and was relieved to see that Hutton's craft had received only slight damage. It was a little scorched and dented, but there was no sign of fire.

While the Air Force F-35s' dogfights raged above, Gary landed his craft a stone's throw from Hutton's and exited the saucer.

As soon as he got out, the clean smell of old, undisturbed forest was overwhelming. He walked over to Hutton's craft and stood in front of the video cam, waving his arms.

Hutton obviously saw him, because he popped open the lower hatch and bounded down the stairs carrying two laptops, a box of manuals, and a set of keycards. He pressed a button on the keycard chain that withdrew the stairs up into the belly of the craft and securely closed the seal.

As Hutton approached, there was something dragging along on the bottom of his boot.

"What's this?" Gary said, stooping. He tugged whatever it was off Hutton's boot, stood up with it in his hand, and scratched his head in befuddlement. It was a Little Debbie wrapper.

⟶∘◐⟋⟍◑∘⟵

THE HEADS OF state had just begun their walk to the safe room when they heard numerous explosions in the northern sky. It sounded like there was a major air battle over the next town.

"Keep moving toward the safe room," the admiral shouted back as he ran out the door and into the open to see what was happening.

Seconds later, the ground fire began on the perimeter of the air base. One glance at the sky explained the timing. The bandits had been thwarted by U.S. forces, and news of their defeat had instantly been transmitted to enemy infantry who had somehow managed to infiltrate the base.

This was incredible; a foreign infantry attack on U.S. territory within the contiguous forty-eight states. He struggled to recall from history the most recent such occasion, and the nearest he could figure was Pancho Villa's brief, shallow incursion into U.S. territory during the Mexican Border War in 1916. The admiral prayed that the base's security forces had had sufficient notice to fend off the attack.

He reentered the building complex and looked down the long hallway leading toward the safe room. Still in the hallway, the heads of state and Doctor Zia had been joined by four Secret Service agents and an Air Force Security sergeant. Schubert was nowhere to be seen.

As the admiral caught up with them, he overheard the sergeant: "Our security forces are presently under assault at the northeast corner of the base from alien forces carrying both conventional firearms and handheld laser weapons. As you gentlemen probably know, you are now located in the base's southwest quadrant. Up till now, we've spotted no enemy artillery. While *our* security forces have such weapons, the present plan is to hold them in reserve until we can determine the depth and scope of enemy forces on the ground. Meanwhile, appropriate weapons have been distributed to our troops, together with appropriate defensive clothing and eye protection. We have also notified Strategic Air Command and requested backup forces and full-scale aerial defense."

The sergeant turned and, spotting the admiral, saluted smartly.

The admiral frowned skeptically. "Good afternoon, sergeant. Did I just hear you say that we have nothing in the air to provide us with information about the depth and scope of enemy forces?"

The sergeant was chagrined. "Well, sir, as you can see," he said pointing toward the northern sky, which was not visible from indoors, "our available fighters have been tied up in an air battle—"

"That's *over*," said the admiral, poking the sergeant's chest for emphasis. "We've won that. Now, call your superiors and get some eyes up there to give us a global view of the situation. Don't neglect to consult the satellites. The small arms fire in the northeast quadrant could be nothing more than a diversion—"

The admiral was rudely interrupted by the sound of heavy artillery followed by a deafening explosion nearby. A huge segment of cinder-block wall back the way they'd come had been blown out by an explosive shell, exposing the hallway to the outside elements.

⸺⟡⸺

THOUGH DAVID TRIED to retrace his steps to the chopper hangar where he'd set up Inanna's glamour studio, he soon lost his bearings and found himself desperately searching for Catharine without a plan.

David was the only person as far as the eye could see who was dressed in anything but an airman's battle uniform. Although Catharine's navy dress blues would have been easy to distinguish under ideal conditions, the dust thrown up by combat in the northeast quadrant had begun to waft all over the base, making it hard to distinguish uniforms. Worse, the sun was now entirely hidden behind clouds, and had begun its inevitable descent to the horizon.

A strong gust blew across the base from the west and momentarily dissipated the dust cloud. In that split second, David spotted the chopper hangar and raced toward it.

All the hangar doors were sealed shut, as they'd been when he was here this morning. He ran around the side to the heavy metal swing door he'd passed through earlier with Inanna, but that was shut, too. He removed one of his fancy loafers and banged on the door with the heel, but it failed to make much noise.

To David's amazement, a security forces soldier opened the door from inside. Seeing David's civilian dress, the soldier saluted, no doubt on the cautious assumption that anybody on the base wearing civilian clothes today was likely a bigwig. Behind the soldier, inside the hangar sat the base's four choppers, and there was no remaining sign of a photographer's studio.

David put his loafer back on. "I'm Ambassador Schubert—"

"I recognize you," said the soldier.

"I'm looking for Lieutenant Commander Weldon, who came here a short time ago looking for Inanna."

There was a blank expression on the soldier's face. "Weldon? What does he look like?"

At the moment, David was more interested in results than decorum. "*She's* a gorgeous blonde naval officer in dress blues."

The soldier's eyes lit up. "Oh! Why didn't you say so? She was here about ten minutes ago. Asked about a queen. I told her I'd been here for two hours and there hadn't been any queen here in all that time. She wanted to know more, so I brought over my buddy Simon who's been here all day. Hold on." The soldier turned and shouted to someone inside the hangar. "Simon!" When he got no answer, he shouted louder. "*Simon!* Somebody's here lookin' for that blonde." Someone shouted a lengthy response, though David couldn't make it out from where he stood. The soldier turned back to him. "Simon says she asked about Inanna. Is Inanna the queen?"

David nodded. "Yes. And?"

"Simon told her Inanna had left for her shuttle about two hours before," said the soldier. "She asked Simon which direction Inanna's shuttle was in, and he pointed to the northeast quadrant." The soldier stepped out the door, propped it open behind him with his hand, and gazed toward the northeast quadrant. His face fell. "Geez," he said, "I hope she didn't wander off in that direction. Looks like a real mess over there."

"Thanks," said David, and privately thanked the Lord that, besides Enki, no members of the Council of Twelve were still on the base.

He turned around just in time to see one wall of the building housing the main meeting hall hit by a heavy artillery round. The wall collapsed immediately, although its base remained almost unbroken. Sections of falling cinderblock had raised a dust so fine and plentiful that it looked as though the world's largest bag of concrete had dropped and burst open.

As best David could mentally reconstruct, the destroyed wall had formed one side of the hallway that the President, Lord Enki, and Doctor Zia needed to traverse to reach the safe room. As he ran toward the site of the explosion, he frantically tried to recall whether Catharine had heard the admiral say they'd be moving to the safe room. Because if she'd despaired of finding Inanna on the base, she'd surely have headed there, in which case they'd be heading for the same destination. He prayed that was true.

David ran down the wrecked hallway, wending his way around the larger pieces of wrecked masonry and hopping over the smaller ones, all while attempting to fan his way through the dusty smoke that choked him.

He reached the place where he'd left the heads of state. Finding neither a living person nor bloody remains, he continued in the direction they'd been walking.

From behind came the sound of marching troops rapidly approaching. He stepped up his pace. At the end of the hallway he reached a windowless metal door. Peering up through the dust as well as he could, he spotted numerous closed-circuit cameras aimed directly at him. He wondered if this was the entrance to the safe room and whether they could see him from inside.

At first, he seemed to have reached a dead end, but then realized that on his left was a hallway leading into a modest-sized assembly room where the ceiling lights were still on. He was about to take that path when he found himself seized by two strong hands and dragged backwards through the heavy metal door, which had evidently been opened and now shut behind him.

He found himself in a large, reinforced vestibule leading to another reinforced doorway much like the first. Glancing up, he saw a high-definition video screen trained on the adjacent assembly room, which was still vacant.

The strong hands that had seized him twirled him around. They evidently belonged to a Secret Serviceman. Although from the man's decisive and energetic movements he seemed young, his actual age was impossible to tell, as his hair and face were dusted with white powder.

"Ready to enter the safe room, sir?" asked the man.

"Depends," said David. "Who's in there?"

"You *know* who's in there," said the man cautiously.

"No, I don't, but can you tell me: Is Lieutenant Commander Weldon in there?" When the man looked confused, David added, "Pretty blonde? Navy uniform?"

The man shook his head. "Nobody fitting that description in there."

"Then I'm staying out here," said David resolutely.

The Secret Serviceman evidently had not expected David's response. "The safe room's just a reinforced room with a million video screens, sir. That's all it is."

David shook his head sternly.

"Well," said the Secret Serviceman, "I don't have orders to drag you inside, Mister Ambassador, but I'll need you to wait here to see if I can get you clearance to ... wander around out here." He shot David a skeptical look. "If they ask me what you intend to do out here—besides getting captured or killed—what should I tell them?"

"Tell the admiral there's precious cargo out here that I'm unwilling to part with."

The man regarded him dubiously.

"Just *tell* him," said David peremptorily. "He'll understand."

The man opened the inner door and shut it behind him.

While David awaited his return, he watched the video screen. The soldiers whose approach he'd heard earlier filed into the adjacent assembly room and formed into ranks. David's hackles were raised; they were squarebearded drones, their faces so similar to one another that they must have been of the same strain. There were about forty in all, and they seemed to wait expectantly for someone else to enter.

The Secret Serviceman emerged from the safe room and closed its door behind him. Allowing a bit of exasperation into his voice, he said, "The admiral says you're a free man and he understands your motivation. He wanted me to add a bit of advice for you, though. He said you should remember you're an ambassador representing the United States, and as such are forbidden to engage in combat. Do you have a further message for the admiral?"

Although David didn't wish to seem disrespectful, his eyes remained pinned to the video screen. In the video image, a squarebearded officer entered and stood facing his soldiers with his back to the camera. He was manhandling a prisoner who was considerably smaller than he, and David's ire rose as he realized the prisoner was Catharine, her dust-covered navy jacket missing buttons and flapping open while she was cruelly shaken by the officer. Still, she stood proudly, though the stress was visible on her face, streaked as it was with dust and tears.

The alien officer, whose back remained to the camera, seemed to be holding something up to his mouth. A microphone, probably. That meant the bastard could talk. And that meant he wasn't a drone, but rather what Enki had called a progenitor, and therefore a human being incapable of communicating with his superior telepathically.

David tried to look at the Secret Serviceman, but he simply could not peel his eyes off the riveting events taking place on the video screen.

The enemy officer finally turned around and showed the camera his face, which was exactly the same as all the soldiers arrayed before him. And he *was* talking into a microphone on his headset.

At last, David turned to the Secret Serviceman. "Please pass this message along to the admiral: As an ambassador may not engage in combat, *I quit*." He pointed to the outer door he'd been dragged through. "Now, open that door, please, and let me out."

"*Jeez*," muttered the exasperated Secret Serviceman, but did as he was told.

David stepped out of the anteroom, and shivered to hear the door shut firmly behind him. *No going back now.* He reached down to his ankle holster and pulled out the Glock, made sure there was a full magazine, chambered a round, and removed the safety.

David was about to do the most brazenly insane thing he'd ever done—right up there with pulling a handgun on General Shulgi.

He stepped around the corner and found that the officer was actually closer to him than expected. There would be no long walk to the officer in front of a platoon of drones with automatic weapons and no hearts. He just had to step out of the shadows and blow the officer's head off.

"Tell me where they are, or I'll kill you right now," said the progenitor, shaking Catharine again.

David's heart pounded and he felt vaguely nauseated, but he said a quick prayer in the vernacular, and was as ready as he'd ever be. He marched out into the open and, before anyone could react, placed the Glock's muzzle to the base of the officer's head and pulled the trigger.

The results were spectacularly gory. The top of the officer's head flew off toward the ceiling and blood gushed everywhere, spattering him and Catharine who, though amazed at this turn of events, had the presence of mind to jerk away from the officer's dying grip.

The drones, who'd reacted tensely to David's entrance, now cast their eyes aside and aimlessly broke ranks. A few dropped their weapons, and several sat down in place. So, Enki's observations of the problems with drone armies were correct. *Kill the progenitor, kill the strain.*

Later on, David would have a vague recollection of Catharine gratefully hugging him and calling his name, and a platoon of Air Force Security Service troops marching into the room, but the thing he'd remember most clearly was his sudden realization that the pilot light in the progenitor's headset remained lit.

In the midst of the smoke and carnage that filled the room, David knelt before the vanquished progenitor and tore the headset from its bloody remains. Hands covered in gore, David separated the earpiece from the camera and wiped the camera clean. He held the earpiece to his ear and looked into the camera, which he held a foot from his face. Twisting his features into the harshest war face he could summon, he glowered at the red dot behind the lens.

"Can you hear me, Anzû?" he growled.

Yessss, came a serpentine voice—not through the earpiece, but seemingly from the center of David's brain. Though David had already become inured to the tumult swirling about him, he was now completely transfixed. The voice spoke again. *I can hear you, David of the line of Joseph, of the line of Adapa. You choose to remain faithful to Enki, do you? Although he fashioned humankind, did you know that he also tricked your ancient ancestor Adapa into declining Anu's gift of immortality for your whole species?*

David realized that there was no need for him to speak aloud; somehow Anzû had established a telepathic link to him. He needed simply to *think* his message and Anzû would hear. He continued to gaze nonetheless into the hypnotic red dot.

What Anzû had said about the famous Sumerian tale of Adapa differed from Azeri's reporting of it.

What I have read, replied David, *is that Anu summoned Adapa to Planet Nibiru, ostensibly to ask Adapa's reason for breaking the wing of the South Wind. But Enki had forewarned Adapa that he'd been summoned only to be poisoned with the food and drink of the gods, which would surely kill him. When Adapa appeared before Anu, he followed Enki's advice and declined all food and drink. And so Adapa lived on.*

David could sense Anzû's chesty laugh.

But, lived on for how long, David? replied Anzû. *For the blink of an eye? Yesss*, he hissed, *that is the tale as Enki told it to the Sumerians, and as they dutifully recorded it on their tablets, but it's untrue. In fact, that tale is the most profound lie ever perpetrated on humankind.*

David found himself impelled by curiosity. *How is it untrue?*

Stop being a credulous child, hissed Anzû. *You, as a mortal man, know well how fragile are the lives of your kind. You can be killed by eating the wrong mushroom, or tripping over a rock. Do you really believe that, if Anu wished to kill Adapa, he would have had need to transport him to Nibiru and feed him the food of the gods? Don't be a fool. To achieve something as commonplace as Adapa's death, Anu would have barely needed to flick his little finger.*

David tried to resist Anzû's words, which, he reminded himself, were those of a deceiver.

So, David asked Anzû silently, *what would have happened if Adapa had consumed the food of the gods?* To his consternation, he could sense that Anzû was deeply self-satisfied to have prompted David to pose this question.

You have been blinded, gloated Anzû, *but now you begin to see. The food of the gods confers not death but immortality, and not only upon the Anunnaki themselves but upon humankind, which is itself half Anunnaki, after all. Enki did no less than to rob you of your birthright.*

Still, David's mind rebelled, and he replied, *If Anu wished to confer immortality on mankind, why would Enki have frustrated his intention?*

That is truly the question you must ask yourself, David. The smug voice was almost kindly now. *But let me first counterpose another question to you. Would Enki have done so if Anu's grant of immortality would merely have transformed humankind from the Anunnakis' slaves into their brothers?*

David replied, *I don't know; probably not.*

Anzû then answered his own question with a wave of emphasis that flooded David's mind. *Enki stopped Adapa from attaining immortality because he knew that, if men became immortal, mankind would soon transcend the Anunnaki. Enki had fashioned you, you see, and he knew you better than you knew yourselves. In the space of a single Sar—even without the near-perfect retention of knowledge afforded by immortali- ty—you have attained the lion's share of Anunnaki knowledge. In another few Sars your knowledge will greatly exceed theirs, and you will forever be greater than they. If your kind had been made immortal in the time of Adapa, you would already have gained the upper hand.*

David fought the idea, which struck him as both improbable and somehow evil.

Do you require further proof? demanded Anzû incredulously. *You have met the Dagon—those whom the Anunnaki call the frog people. Why do you suppose the Dagon have come to Earth?*

David replied, *To keep an eye on the Anunnaki, whom they fear.*

No! came Anzû's exasperated reply, which felt like a shout of disap- proval in David's mind. *If the Dagon wished to keep an eye on the Anunnaki, they would have gone to Nibiru, not Earth. Don't you see?*

I do not, replied David.

The Dagon fear YOU! replied Anzû. *They fear humankind!* Appar- ently as a concession to David's bewilderment, Anzû toned down his exasperation. *Will you at least think on this?*

Despite David's palpable fatigue, he mustered enough energy to impart what he originally intended. *I cannot help but think on it*, replied David. *But, as you say, I am a mere mortal, and so know little or nothing about immortality. What I am intimately familiar with is death. You have attempted to capture or kill this woman for months. If you do not leave her alone from now on, then the next time you see my face—and you will see it at least once more—I swear that on that day you will meet death face to face. I do not share the scruple that persuaded Enki to spare your life.*

It took no more than a moment for Anzû to reply bitterly. *I know that you share no such scruple. Enki knows it, too. So do the Dagon. Your kind is to be feared. I will consider your demand. Only think on this, too: What could you achieve with immortality?*

CHAPTER 22

DAVID FOUND HIMSELF in bed. He opened his eyes on Catharine's smiling face. She was fully clothed, sitting upright on an adjacent bunk.

"Hello, beautiful," he said drowsily.

"Hello, my hero!" she said and stroked his hair.

My hero? he wondered, and recent events flooded back on him. From the remove of a day, or however long it had been, his actions didn't strike him as heroic. *Reckless?* Yes. *Cowardly* perhaps, some might find it, to creep up behind a villain and blow his head off. But he shoved those thoughts aside. He'd done well. His beloved was safe. Sometimes that has to be enough.

"Where am I?" he asked.

"Bethesda," she replied. "You're in a naval hospital, recovering from … well, recovering."

"From?"

"Nothing life-threatening," she said. "How much do you remember?"

"I remember killing that bastard and—" He found himself reluctant to continue, since the rest had taken place only in his mind. Well … in his and Anzû's.

"After you killed that *thing*, you knelt in front of the body, took his headset apart and stared at it for a while. You seemed to be asleep with your eyes wide open. Nobody could get your attention. After a couple of minutes, you collapsed, so they picked you up and put you on intravenous."

He looked up and saw he was still on intravenous. "Why?"

She shrugged. "They did a brain scan."

"Did they find it missing?"

She laughed. "No, everything was normal."

"Just normal?" he asked, feigning disappointment.

"Well, they found a lot of brain activity in a place where people don't have much."

David nodded sagely. "Poughkeepsie?"

She smiled. "No, in the Gore-Tex cortex, or something. I don't remember. Ask the doctors. It's where they see more activity in people with dream disturbances and …" Her voice trailed off.

"And … *what*?"

"Psychic phenomena," she said. "Stuff like that. Maybe you're headed for the Discovery Channel. Or the History Channel."

"Or the English Channel?" he suggested.

"Definitely," and with that her mood changed. "What happened? What private place did you go to in your mind?"

"Let's talk about that later," he said. "How did things turn out at the base?"

She nodded. "All's right with the world."

He breathed a sigh of relief. "How about you? Did that bastard hurt you?"

She shook her head. "Not really. He threatened to kill me. And he did tug on my left shoulder a few times, which hurt like the dickens, but mostly because of my earlier injury."

"How does it feel now?" he asked sympathetically.

"Now it feels pretty good," she said, working her shoulder. "The docs did some scans and said it's gonna be just fine."

"What did the security services do with all the drones?"

"They blindfolded them, put plugs in their ears, and threw them in the lockup for the time being. The security people said that, even though the drones have gone stupid, the bad guys may be able to see through their eyes and hear through their ears."

David shook his head. "I think the only person the drones could send information to is the guy I shot."

"Hey, how did you know all this?" asked Catharine. "How did you know that killing that one guy would disable all the drones?"

"Enki said so," replied David. "I trust that his lordship is well?"

She nodded.

"And the President and the admiral?"

She nodded again. "The admiral gave me a message for you."

"Oh?"

"He said he failed to receive your last message," she said, regarding him askew. "What does that mean?"

He chuckled. "It means I'm still an ambassador."

"I don't get it," she said.

"The admiral had reminded me that an ambassador does not engage in combat. When I realized I could end the standoff with one bullet, I quit my post."

"Awww," she said. "You quit your post for *me*?"

"I've done a lot more than that for you, lady," he said, "if you think about it." Something else occurred to him. "That reminds me. When Enki took that memory suppressor off, you looked like you were having some trouble with the memories that came back."

She grew serious, and nodded. "Between us, something obvious came back to me that I'd never realized before."

"What's that?"

She leaned in confidentially. "You remember how my laptop disappeared?"

"Yeah," he said, "it was stolen by the two flying cigars that flanked the admiral's plane over the Atlantic."

"Right," said Catharine. "Now, do you remember when we first saw the squarebeards?"

He nodded. "At the Paris clothiers."

"Well, those squarebeards had my laptop, right?"

"Yeah, so what?" asked David.

"How'd they get it?"

David scratched his head. "I suppose they were operating those two flying cigars that flanked the admiral's plane."

Catharine continued. "After we saw the squarebeards with my laptop, we were immediately followed by aliens in a similar-looking cigar, right? And they had that ray gun thing, and we escaped in the minisub?"

"Yeah." He wasn't sure what she was getting at.

"That would suggest," said Catharine, "that the squarebeards were also operating the cigars that followed us while we were on the ground, that caused that police chopper to fall on the guy who was helping us."

He nodded. "Ibrahim, may he rest in peace. Stands to reason."

"But I seem to remember learning that the flying cigar that followed us on the ground in Paris was operated by the Anunnaki."

He nodded.

"So, the cigar that stole my laptop was also Anunnaki, right?"

He felt uneasy replying. "Yeah," he said tentatively.

"So now," said Catharine and asked again, "how'd the squarebeards get my laptop?"

"Well," he said, finally seeing what she was getting at, "it's not the only possibility, but it could have been given to them by an Anunnaki in league with Anzû."

"Right, and we've already come to suspect that there's a turncoat."

"Did you raise this with the old man?" asked David.

She shook her head. "I just realized it yesterday and wanted to discuss it with you first."

"Better raise it with him super-confidentially," said David. "Top Secret. We have to make sure not to tip off the traitor, if there is one."

She said, "I will. And, on a happier note, Enki has decided that it would be a good idea to show humans what Nibiru looks like. He said that King Enlil has a virtual reality recording of a lengthy flyover. Turns out, Enlil is not actually on Nibiru, but in a craft that's much closer."

"So I deduced," said David.

She cocked her head. "How'd you deduce that?"

"Well, we know from the Dagon that the Anunnaki can't transmit electromagnetic waves at a speed exceeding that of light. Since the delay in Enlil's signal to Earth was only about two and a half minutes, it means he's much closer to Earth than Nibiru is. Enlil is, maybe, a hundred thirty million miles from Earth. Perhaps half again the distance from Earth to the sun."

"Oh," she said. "Well, Enlil has the virtual-reality program on his spaceship, and guess who the President is going to recommend to put on the VR helmets?"

"Gary and Buck?"

"No, you and me!" said Catharine. "As soon as you're feeling better."

"I'd imagine a flyover like that would be very informative, don't you think?"

Her mood turned dark. "David, do you think Anzû will be sending more assassins my way?"

He cupped her hand in his. "I don't think so, unless he's cornered. But look on the bright side. When I was looking into that camera, I told him if he didn't leave you alone, I'd kill him."

"You were communicating with him telepathically?"

He beckoned her to come close enough to whisper in her ear. "I suppose," he said, and kissed her gently. "And I think I came in loud and clear."

THE END

Thank you for reading *Maker from the Lost Planet*. If you enjoyed the book, please consider leaving a review on your favorite retailer. Reviews greatly help authors both with reaching new readers and improving our stories. I would love to read your thoughts.

Here's a special preview of the third and final book in this thrilling trilogy, *Destroyer from the Lost Planet*.

DESTROYER FROM THE LOST PLANET
CHAPTER 1

WHEN THE PROGENITOR roughly seized Catharine by the arm, David crept up behind him and blew his head off; simple as that. Though David had had no qualms about his actions at the time, he was troubled by them now.

He tossed and turned in his bed, unable to sleep, and it struck him as ironic that he was feeling low now mainly because he hadn't felt low *then*. He still didn't feel guilty for what he'd done, but rather for not having felt guilty at the time. He remarked to himself (not for the first time) that the mind is a tricky place.

It's always been difficult, Enki had said, for the power-mad to identify someone suitable to serve as a progenitor for a strain of drones. *Why?* David wondered. *What special qualities are necessary for a suitable progenitor?* David doubted that such qualities included a propensity for leadership or particularly high intelligence.

No, what a progenitor needed was the ability *telepathically* to receive imagery from his drones and *telepathically* to send them his commands. As the progenitor's neurophysiology would provide the basis for his drones', it stood to reason that the progenitor himself would require such psychic capabilities. And such activity was probably the *only* innate characteristic needed to become a progenitor. Everything else could probably be taught.

Unsurprisingly, the neurologists had recently confirmed that David's brain showed activity associated with psychic phenomena. Did that mean that David himself would be a suitable candidate for progenitor?

His mind wandered. He thought back on shooting the progenitor, and wondered who his victim had been earlier in life. A carpenter? A pawnbroker? A law professor? Had he received the gift of long life? If so, from Anzû? *How long would the progenitor have lived if I hadn't shot him?*

It troubled David that he'd become increasingly preoccupied by his own mortality, but what he found most troubling was that it had apparently been Anzû's principal intention, during their brief discussion, to instill that very preoccupation in his mind. And he resented the feeling that he was, in a sense, running a program implanted by Anzû.

Finding his room too warm, David folded Elijah's mantle, placed it on the nightstand, and kicked his other blankets to the floor.

Drifting off, once more he was confronted by his dream of the falling moon. But this time he was not alone … and neither was the moon.

David lies asleep in a large bed that rocks under him. A chilly salt breeze blows over his face. His eyes still closed, he caresses the hand of his sleeping bedmate. Inanna was so beautiful, so warm, so feminine all night that he feels nothing but gratitude for her persistent advances, and regret for his earlier rebuffs.

The bed's rocking grows more pronounced, and there's a tiny splash next to his head. He opens his eyes to find the bed floating on a moonlit ocean with no land in sight.

The cloudless night sky is lit by two celestial lights: the moon, and a planet enveloped in a smoky, maroon-tinged atmosphere. The two celestial bodies appear almost to touch each other, and seem so close to the Earth that David imagines he can feel their combined pull.

His breathing and his heartbeat accelerate. He sits up, preparing to rouse his bedmate but, looking upon her, he hesitates—so beautiful is she in the white moonlight and the maroon glow of its strange companion. Despite the immediate peril, he's loath to disturb her. Instead, he's tempted ... so tempted ... to touch her.

But reaching over to rouse her, he's horrified by the decrepitude of his own hand, mere bones partly covered by desiccated scraps of blackened skin, the segments of each digit strung to the others with ligaments no more substantial than worn rubber bands. His arm, similarly skeletal, is covered by wasted skin like the weathered hide of an abandoned carcass, covered with the brown and black splotches of age and death. To his horror, it occurs to him that, just as his limb is rotten, his face must be a veritable death's head.

Were he to rouse Inanna now, surely she would recoil from him in disgust. He thinks better of it and withdraws his hand.

How could he have gotten so old so quickly? For the first time, he wonders when *this dismaying scene is taking place. Searching for an answer, his gaze returns to the sky.*

The moon and the strange planet have each moved a few degrees of arc, but at different rates, the faster-moving planet now partially hidden behind the moon. As David watches the majestic movement of the spheres, suddenly the moon shivers, as from an impact with the planet behind it. A stress fracture appears on the moon's face near its northern pole, where a huge chasm forms and begins ripping its way toward the southern pole, so that the moon must soon crack in half. And he realizes that he's seeing events that will (or may) take place four hundred years hence.

The moon splits and begins to crumble. A large chunk breaks away from the main body and begins to rotate slowly, exposing a part of the moon's core to the sun's light for the first time in what must be billions of years. A haze of pulverized lunar soil develops around the main fissure.

David's heart aches to witness the end of all things.

Though until now his nautical bed has remained upright and afloat, the sea has begun to heave and roll in response to the moon's disintegration. The bed pitches and yaws, and David realizes that it cannot long remain atop the peaks of the mounting waves threatening to engulf it.

Searching desperately for some means to assure Inanna's safety, he overcomes his self-disgust just long enough to reach out with his necrotic arm and draw her further into the fragile safety of their little vessel.

But the sleeping Inanna rolls off and disappears soundlessly under the waves. Gone forever. Dead.

He's failed her.

His vision goes black and his mind is jarred by Anzû's sibilant, disembodied voice.

So ... you dwell upon this catastrophe? asks Anzû.

I wish to save Inanna, David replies.

Simply a pipedream, hisses Anzû. *The celestial collision you imagine won't happen for four hundred years, and you can't live more than another sixty of those. How can you hope to save her—or anyone else—from this event, when you will have been dead more than three hundred years?*

The voice fades, leaving a sickness in the pit of David's stomach.

⸺⸺⸺◦◦⸻◦◦⸺⸺⸺

THE NEXT MORNING, David received a message from Houston that a

Space Force colonel was on his way up to Inanna's pyramidion to debrief him.

At the appointed hour, there was a knock at the door and David opened it to find an efficient-looking colonel in uniform, sporting salt-and-pepper sideburns. David offered him an upholstered seat and took a cater-corner seat for himself.

"I'm Doctor Jensen Young," said the colonel as he sat down. "You look familiar."

"Do I?"

"Aren't you … the King of Connecticut?"

"No, I'm not," said David. "In fact, I don't think Connecticut is a kingdom. Unless you count the king from *A Connecticut Yankee in King Arthur's Court*. But, even if you do, I think Arthur was the King of *England*."

"Where are *you* from?"

"I'm just a kid from Canarsie, which is located in Brooklyn, New York."

Doctor Young snapped his fingers. "That's it, the Kid from Canarsie."

David was in no mood to be patronized. "Let's cut the baloney, colonel. You knew who I was before you came up here. How many ambassadors to the Anunnaki are there, after all? In fact, I'd bet you have a dossier about me in your briefcase and you were reading it until you came aboard."

The colonel gave him a confessional smile and posed a question no doubt prompted by David's bloodshot eyes and slightly slumped posture. "How have you been sleeping?"

"I thought you came here to do a military debriefing," said David skeptically.

"I did," said the colonel, eying David warily. "But I'm also a psychiatrist."

"Is that why you're asking about the quality of my sleep?"

The colonel shrugged.

David said sullenly, "Suppose I don't want a psychiatrist."

The colonel shrugged again. "Look, professor. You've been in an incident in which you shot and killed someone. It's part of my job to see if you need some time off and a little talk therapy. Sometimes, someone who's been through a violent incident needs to be removed from the situation for a while to ensure they're … stable and not overstressed."

"And that's why you're asking about my sleep?"

The colonel shot him a sympathetic smile. "Just making conversation," he said. He arched his eyebrows. "So?"

"So ... *what*?"

"So ... how have you been sleeping?"

David sighed. "I've slept better, I suppose."

"Something troubling you?"

David could feel his inner troll gaining strength. "Well, except for the Earth being invaded by two separate sets of aliens, at least one of which would like to see me and my lover dead ... nothing, really." He adjusted his seat. "How've *you* been sleeping?"

The colonel smiled patronizingly. "*I'll* ask the questions."

David shrugged and smiled pointedly. "Just making conversation," he echoed. David's insistence on controlling the interview had begun to irk his visitor, who opened his eyes wide and blew out a breath. This made it a perfect time for badgering. "So," David observed wryly, "*you're* not sleeping well either, I see."

"I'm sleeping *fine*," said the colonel as he opened his briefcase and pulled out a file devoted to David.

"I see I was right about the dossier, too," David observed.

The colonel conceded the point with an exasperated nod. "Let's talk about how you feel about the ... incident the other day."

David let himself feel his dismay. "I feel kind of crappy about it."

"Crappy? In what sense?"

The question was a bit too open-ended for David to take it seriously. "In a *crappy* sense, I guess." The colonel waited for him to continue. "You know, that wasn't the first time I'd shot one of those *things*."

The colonel cocked his head, obviously not following what David had said. "Do you feel like you might have done the wrong thing?"

David shook his head. "No. The choice was clear both times. To be honest, I think those freaks are less than human, anyway."

"Those *freaks*?" asked the colonel.

David cocked his head skeptically. "How much do you know about these ... incidents?"

"Not as much as I would like. Who are *those freaks*?"

"The squarebeards," said David, and waited for the colonel's reaction.

"*Squarebeards*," echoed the colonel quietly. Clearly, he had no idea what David was talking about.

"*Whoa!*" said David. "What's your security clearance?"

"Top secret," said the colonel. "Why?"

"Then you're not cleared for this intelligence." When the colonel sat up with surprise, David added, "And why do you think I'd need 'time off and some talk therapy'?"

"Well," replied the colonel, "you're a *peacemaker*, not combat-trained, so we naturally expected that your own violent action might be particularly ... traumatic for you."

"Who's *we*?" asked David.

"Me ... and the person who sent me."

"Who sent you?"

The colonel checked the cover of the dossier. "Navy Admiral Simmons. Do you know him?"

David nodded. "I know him well. Would you mind if I call him before we begin?"

"Not at all. Perhaps his endorsement will put your mind at ease."

David called the admiral, who picked up on the second ring. "Good morning, admiral. Dave Schubert. You sent me a Space Force head-shrinker?"

"What?" said the admiral. "Oh, yes. Since I neglected to have you debriefed after your ... trip with Catharine, I just wanted to make sure you didn't again escape the insufferable boredom of being debriefed."

As the colonel was within earshot, David tried to speak circumspectly. "The colonel doesn't seem familiar with what happened after the summit."

"Not surprised," said the admiral. "The agency has deliberately suppressed knowledge of the whole incident."

"Nothing's gotten out about it?"

"There have been a couple of rumors," said the admiral, "but they were quickly squelched."

"Does the colonel have a 'need to know'?"

"Ah," said the admiral. "I see where you're going with this. Hand him the phone."

David extended the phone to the colonel. "The admiral would like to speak with you."

The colonel gave David a skeptical glance and put the phone up to his ear. After a few turns of *yes, admiral, I see*, he handed the phone back to David.

"Listen, David," said the admiral. "He doesn't need to know what happened on the ground. This isn't a military debrief. We've already got everything on video. I sent him up there for medical purposes only. I told him you'd had to shoot someone. That's all he needs to know. So, just avoid the specifics, but do me a favor and make him feel like he didn't waste the trip."

"Okay, admiral," said David, "and thanks." He hung up.

The colonel reached into his briefcase for a blood-pressure cuff. "Roll up your sleeve, please," he said dispassionately. He applied the cuff to David's upper arm and pumped it up. "Hmm," he said, "your blood pressure's quite good. That's a good sign. Are you on medication?"

David shook his head. "Whole-food, plant-based diet," he said.

The colonel's eyebrows shot up. "That explains it. Tell me, where do you get your protein?"

"It's really not an issue," said David, "but mostly from beans and other legumes."

"Take B-12?"

David nodded. "Every day."

"Good for you," said the colonel as he put the blood-pressure cuff away. "Now … have you had trouble sleeping?"

David pondered how to respond. He considered saying: *I've been having a repeating nightmare about the end of the world, which begins with a collision between the moon and a strange planet that comes around every few thousand years. In my dream, I feel like a failure because I'm unable to save the Queen of Heaven from drowning; I've been dead for four hundred years, you see. Also, I suspect that an evil alien planning to conquer the world with his army of plant-based monsters is trying to bribe me with an offer of immortality.* But that might start a whole conversation. So instead, he said, "Not really."

"No?" asked the colonel with eyebrows raised.

"Well," said David reluctantly, "sometimes it takes me a long time to drift off. I keep remembering what it felt like to pull the trigger."

The colonel nodded sagely. "That's to be expected. Pretty normal, really."

"That's reassuring," said David, pleased to have faked a normal-sounding reply on such short notice.

"You want me to give you something to help you drift off?" asked the colonel.

David equivocated.

The colonel said, "Totally non-addictive, I promise."

"Do you have it with you?"

"I expect so," said the colonel, reaching into his briefcase. "I was told not to expect this ship to have a normal pharmacy." He pulled out a translucent pill box. "Yes, I have some." He handed David the pill box. "Just don't take more than one a day, and only take them when you're sure you want to sleep." He snapped his briefcase shut and headed for the door. Before leaving, he turned and said, "The admiral told me that, if you were to tell me all that happened, I'd be unable to cure your nightmares, but you'd give me plenty of my own." He looked at his feet and shuffled a moment. "So … thanks for not giving me nightmares. But I really *do* know what I'm doing. If it gets to the point where you can't handle it alone any longer, promise you'll call me." He handed David an old-fashioned business card.

"I promise," said David, accepting the card and seeing the doctor out.

David realized he was *already* approaching the point where he couldn't handle things alone and needed to talk with someone. Since the problem was *not* all in his head, however, he realized that professional help wouldn't suffice. He needed someone who understood his predicament. But no one knew the substance of his telepathic conversation with Anzû. Not even Catharine.

He tossed the pillbox in the trash, grabbed the phone, and called the admiral, who answered on the first ring.

"Yes, David," said the admiral, "did you forget something?"

"I've had a couple of conversations you need to know about, but we can't talk about them on this line."

"From the tone of your voice, it sounds pressing," said the admiral. "I'm at my home for the next couple of days. Tell you what: I'll send up a shuttle for you tomorrow morning to bring you down here. And I'll try to get our mutual friend to come over, too."

"You and I will need to talk alone for a while."

"Okay, then I'll ask her to come a couple of hours later."

David breathed a sigh of relief. "Sounds great, admiral."

"See you then," said the admiral.

After a moment's silence, David said somberly, "Thank you, sir."

The admiral picked up the cue right away and, after a brief silence, replied, "It's what I'm here for."

Can't wait to see what happens next? Get your copy of *Destroyer from the Lost Planet* here.

https://books2read.com/u/bPN6wx

ABOUT THE AUTHOR

Neal Roberts and his wife live happily on Long Island, New York. They have two grown children and a handful of grandchildren. Neal is a practicing attorney and adjunct law professor, and spends as much time as possible researching his next novel while enhancing his lawyer's pallor. When he's not writing contemporary sci-fi novels or practicing law, he can generally be found teaching in the field of intellectual property law. Connect with Neal at his website (authornealroberts.com) or on Facebook (Facebook.com/authornealroberts) and join his mailing list (bitly.com/FreeHistorical) to know when upcoming books release and to grab your free short.

ALSO BY NEAL ROBERTS

In the Den of the English Lion

A Second Daniel, In the Den of the English Lion, Book 1 (Historical Mystery): London 1558. An orphan from a far-off land is renamed "Noah Ames," and given every advantage the English Crown can bestow.

London 1592. Now an experienced barrister, Noah witnesses what appears to be a botched robbery outside the Rose Theater, a crime he soon suspects to be part of a plot against Queen Elizabeth herself. Steadfast in his loyalty to the Queen, Noah must use every bit of his knowledge and skill to lure her most disloyal subject onto the only battlefield where Noah has the advantage … a court of law – though in doing so he risks public exposure of his darkest secret, a secret so shocking that its revelation could cost him everything: the love of the only woman who can offer him happiness, his livelihood … even his life.

The Impress of Heaven, In the Den of the English Lion, Book 2 (Historical Mystery): LONDON 1600. When the Earl of Essex is removed from command and placed under arrest for reaching a forbidden truce with the Irish rebels, Serjeant Noah Ames reluctantly accepts a commission to investigate the earl's fitness for command, and the two are pitted against each other once again. Meanwhile, Noah's beautiful daughter, Lady Jessica, has sought to remarry into the nobility, but events have thus far frustrated her plans. One day, Noah attends a briefing where the Queen's new commander displays maps of English military positions in Ireland. Noah's suspicions are aroused when he sees that one map is missing a watermark appearing on all the others. When he informs his young barrister friend Jonathan of his concern, he inadvertently sets in motion events that throw Jonathan and Lady Jessica together on a journey across England into ever greater peril.

A Dragon in the Ashes, In the Den of the English Lion, Book 3 (Historical Mystery): LONDON 1600. When an attempt is made on Queen

Elizabeth's life, Serjeant Noah Ames races to her rescue, then sets out to identify the culprit among a band of foreigners who've newly arrived from the Continent to join with the seditious Lord Essex. In the course of his investigation, Noah uncloaks an unmitigated reign of evil that has resulted in the murders of kings, queens, and religious minorities ... and which now threatens Noah's life for reasons no one would ever suspect. Will Noah pay the ultimate price for forgetting that the past is never past?

All the Men as Mad as He, In the Den of the English Lion, Book 4 (Historical Mystery): LONDON 1600. Though Queen Elizabeth has ordered the Earl of Essex's release from confinement, she's thwarted his return to social and military grace by barring him from court for an indefinite term. Unsatisfied with this humiliation, the Queen considers whether to cut off his sole remaining income, as well. Noah Ames strongly advises against it on grounds that the Queen will thereby lose any remaining influence over Essex's conduct and also place him in desperate financial straits. When several seemingly unrelated men are found murdered, Noah begins to suspect that such murders reveal Essex's treasonous intention to return to court in bloody defiance of the Queen's order.

Shakespeare's Treason, In the Den of the English Lion, Book 5 (Historical Mystery): LONDON 1600. The Earls of Essex and Southampton, imprisoned in the Tower of London pending their trial for high treason, incriminate Noah Ames's dear friend Sir Henry Neville. When the one man whose testimony can save Sir Henry suddenly vanishes, Noah must solve the mystery of his abduction and bring him back in time to save Sir Henry from a traitor's death.

From Heaven to Earth They Came

Goddess from the Lost Planet, From Heaven to Earth They Came, Book 1

Maker from the Lost Planet, From Heaven to Earth They Came, Book 2

Destroyer from the Lost Planet, From Heaven to Earth They Came, Book 3

www.ingramcontent.com/pod-product-compliance
Lightning Source LLC
Chambersburg PA
CBHW021145310726
48971CB00002B/490